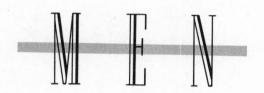

MEN

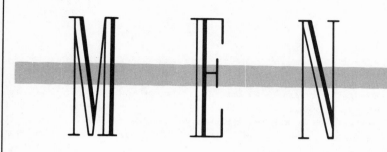

MARGARET

DIEHL

SOHO

Published in the United States of America by
Soho Press, Inc.
One Union Square
New York, NY 10003

Library of Congress Cataloging-in-Publication Data

Diehl, Margaret 1955-
Men: a novel / Margaret Diehl.
p. cm.
ISBN 0-939149-14-1
I. Title
PS3554.I343M4 1988
813′ .54—dc 19   88-9691
CIP
Design and composition by The Sarabande Press.

Manufactured in the United States of America
FIRST EDITION

to Charles and Kate

PART

II

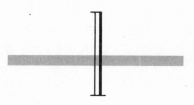

ex with Teo did not involve any major activity. His hands on my body were half asleep or introspective, and I thought frequently of other men. There were stretches of sheer affection for the pale, lazy body on top of me—or more likely beneath me—peaceful times when the rhythm of sex lulled us both, carrying us far away from the heat of orgasm. Sometimes then Teo would start talking about the future in the fantastical way he had, I would chime in, and before I knew quite what was happening, we'd be lying side by side, chaste as twins, and Teo would be drinking from the spare bottle he kept under the bed.

I didn't mind, or not much. I knew there was nothing more to expect from him and he was my choice among all the men I'd met at school. We were friends; Teo was a very good friend, lazy as he was. He was loyal, and he never went home when you didn't want him to. I loved being friends with a man. At that point I would have chosen friendship over passion, if I could only have one (if I were given a choice). I used to argue about this with my roommate Janey. She thought you could always have friendships with women, and it was true that Janey was a very good friend. But it wasn't the same.

Having sex with Teo, however disappointing, made us close in a way I couldn't be with her. I felt intimate. I felt like our thoughts intersected. Not our opinions or emotions necessarily, but our random thought, our memories. They seemed to rise out of me on wings, like insects, and land in his curly hair. And vice versa.

Teo asked me to go to New York with him when school was out. His parents had moved to California but the apartment hadn't been sold yet. His father thought property values would go up after Reagan beat Carter that fall.

My grandmother had no objection (Had I expected her to? She was more subtle than that.) and even gave me some money although I'd expected to have to get a job. "You've earned the summer off," she said.

The apartment, in a doorman building on the Upper East Side, was decorated completely in gray: gray leather furniture, gray carpet, gray walls, glass and metal tables, gray velvet drapes. There was no ornamentation except for a set of Japanese prints on the wall. I went over to look at them and Teo said, "She had to get those during the beef price crisis a while ago."

"What do you mean?"

"Well, she wanted to stop eating meat but didn't want to admit it was because of the money, since we are, after all, rich. So she got into this thing about how fish and vegetables are so much better for you. Look at the Japanese, they live so much longer or something. She went totally Jap for a while to lend credence to the whole thing. My father wouldn't let her take too many liberties with his décor, but he allowed these. . . . They're understated, after all, and out of the light."

The kitchen was barren of food, but perfectly appointed with enough Sabatier knives to outfit the Manson family. Teo's parents' room had a king-size bed and a king-size television, photographs of Teo as a boy, and some rather strange collages made out of buttons. "My mother's sister," said Teo, noting my interest in the button art. "She lives in a very genteel loony bin in Baltimore. I think she mostly drinks, but she also makes these and sends us one every Christmas."

"Poor woman."

"She's happier than my mother. Which isn't, you know, saying much. I visited her there once. Lots of green lawns and gentle ladies. I took her a bottle of white crème de menthe. She put it under her pillow and talked about the sorrow of life, dreams, lost love — it was very poetic. I found out later it was mostly paraphrase of Tennessee Williams."

Teo's room was painted rosy pink and was cluttered with records and clothes. Over his bed hung a huge photograph of his old girlfriend Laura. He took it down and put up one of Ella Fitzgerald since he didn't, he said, have one of me.

The bathroom was my favorite. The tub was extra long and surrounded with a wide, tiled shelf for soaps and shampoos. Walls, floor, and bath were leafy green, the ceiling was white and the oversize towels lavender. The mirror was framed in lights. The faucets were antique brass, and there was a cushioned wicker chair next to a wicker cabinet of beauty supplies and old issues of *Vogue*.

"I take it your father didn't design this room?"

"Nope. He's got his own bathroom off their bedroom."

"I didn't notice it."

"You're not supposed to. It's a fifth the size of this one, set up solely for the shower, shave, and shit. He manages all three in about five minutes."

"So you share this with your mother?"

"Yep."

"Do you use her shampoo?"

"She uses mine."

Teo ordered groceries from Gristede's and I made a dinner of lamb chops, mushrooms cooked in garlic and cream, and wild rice. He opened one of his father's bottles of Margaux and we ate in the living room, next to the open window. Teo liked to look at the action on the streets: abusive cabdrivers, old ladies scooping up poodle shit, young couples jaywalking. It was not an exciting part of town, but I didn't notice. I was getting used to the odor of the City as it drifted inside, and wondering if its oddly energizing effect was a psychological response to Manhattan or whether it was simply the sea, which I knew surrounded us, though its smell was undetectable. I felt at sea, like I was crossing the Atlantic. The roar of traffic could easily be the crash of waves on the beach and the horns and screams and the blare of radios was not unlike the noise of sea gulls, sea monsters. Teo was clearly excited. He ate rapidly and drank his wine in great swallows, though he made sure to swill it around in his mouth appreciatively first. When he was done, he watched me impatiently, then made me stand by the window with him and lean out alarmingly.

"It's all yours, baby," he said, waving his drunken arms, and I stared down twelve floors, at the great divided expanse of Park Avenue.

Many afternoons we lay in bed from two until six or seven, watching rectangles of light on the wall deepen, then fade, listening to the traffic surge, apartment doors slam, and Teo beside me talked on and on.

He told me about childhood rainy days, shut in his room with a transistor radio while his mother went shopping. He spoke about his dog, Martha, whom he used to walk in Central Park, and about an old man there who liked to pat his ass. Teo would allow this only after the old man patted Martha's ass first and told her how beautiful she was.

He talked about how to make the perfect dog: the color of an Irish setter, the paws of a Doberman, the tail of a collie, and the musculature of a Saint Bernard. We'll name it Patrick, I said, and Patrick kept us ghostly company after that. Teo would ask him where he'd roamed to, what sorry sights he had seen, and in the corner I often glimpsed the questioning tilt of a reddish jaw. Teo imagined Patrick checking the world war zones every night, and bringing abandoned babies to American hospitals. He told Patrick they'd only be abandoned again, by the bureaucrats, but Patrick didn't listen. He was a single-minded dog. Finally Teo's warnings sank in, and he brought the babies to us. We don't want 'em, said Teo. Let's throw 'em in the closet. He waved his hand in time with a breeze that gently shut the closet door.

We drank more beer. Did you ever skateboard through a red light? Shoplift? See your mother naked in her bath, oozing blood? No.

When you were little, were you afraid of grown-up shoes left lying on the floor, high windows, eating in the dark? Yes.

Did you ever have maids? No, Grandmother would never have servants, we did our own work.

Maids were the best. They let you do whatever you wanted, and as a reward you stole them cigarettes and scotch. Maids went home on the bus and sometimes when you threw big, wet gobs of toilet paper out the apartment windows at buses, you were afraid maybe that was the bus your maid took.

Teo's voice was as warm as his flesh, which seemed to have soaked up centuries of bed. I would listen to him; then I would lay my head on his chest, and his tropic rumble would lull me to sleep. When I woke up in the evening dazed, he would kindly take me out to dinner.

He had grown up in Manhattan, the only child of wealthy parents, and attended an exclusive private high school it took him five years to graduate from. "My girlfriend was a year behind me," he said in explanation. He had a tight circle of friends and during his senior year, while his parents were back and forth from California, where his father had been transferred, he took them out every night, spending on jazz and bourbon the money his mother gave him for emergencies. He described the music, the clubs, the after-hours bars they glided home from at dawn. In school he and his buddies would nurse hangovers with flasks of whiskey and write each other's papers, each concentrating on the subject he or she knew best.

Teo wrote everything for their class in urban culture, which was a rather vague attempt by the headmaster to make superior New Yorkers out of them. He interviewed old jazz musicians and organized his paper improvisationally; for his girlfriend's paper he made a collage from the advertisements of gallery shows. His friend Slade wrote the lab reports, and Teo's girlfriend Laura did all the math homework, making creative mistakes. As a result, Teo had had a vision of what could be done through cooperation, and individual effort had not seemed interesting since. In fact, he found it sinister. Anything that made him lonely was sinister. His little band had been a minority in high school, degenerates when that was no longer fashionable. They stuck together and dismissed everyone else as Morlocks—the carnivorous, industrial apes of H. G. Wells's *The Time Machine.*

"We were Eloi, destined for sacrifice, enjoying a brief, sybaritic youth before the end. I was so happy, Stella. I had my woman, I had my friends. I loved Laura. I'll never love a woman like that again. And Slade, my right-hand man."

Slade was living with Laura in Cambridge now, but Teo said he didn't mind. Or rather, he minded that he lost Laura, but not that Slade took her. "It was her decision, anyway. I always knew she'd break up with me. It happened the day after she got accepted to Radcliffe. She told me I wasn't a serious person. I was tissue."

"As in toilet tissue?"

"No, the tissue that comes in gift boxes—pretty, flimsy. Slade was leather. She was silk."

"She sounds like a real bitch. But I like your slang. Tell me more."

"Drinkers were priests or vampires. Priests were generous with their booze, offering the sacrament to everybody; vampires would steal your last drop. I was a priest . . ."

"And Laura was a vampire?"

"No, she wasn't much of a drinker. She was the court taster. I was the court jester. Slade was king and Jules was the magician—he has these long, cold hands and devil's eyes. For a while I was Dauphin. Right-to-lifers were the righteous of any persuasion, people who say, 'I got a right!'"

"Especially when it interfered with your pleasures?"

"Well, shurr . . . Slade was Texas, I was Louisiana, Laura was New York, and Jules was Southern California. He's there now. When I call him up and ask him what it's like, he says I wouldn't understand. What does that mean—I'm stupid?"

I well understood his nostalgia, though it seemed sillier than mine. Its very silliness made it easier for me to participate in. He was only talking about high school—and an unreal one at that, where the students went to after-hours joints and rode home in limousines.

Janey had set me up with Teo in my sophomore year. He was blind date number four. Janey had said, "He's really cute. Sort of big and soft, and he'll take you wherever you want to go for dinner." I was skeptical. Of the last three dates she had set up, the first told me up front that I couldn't kiss him unless I loved him, the second was married, and the third was very nice and intelligent and smelled awful. But I accepted the date with Teo, made a reservation at the Blue Strawberry in Portsmouth, and opened a bottle of red wine to let it breathe.

Teo opened a second bottle of wine and we missed our reservation. He promised to take me somewhere else later, and he played me his tapes of Ella Fitzgerald singing Duke Ellington.

Take love easy, easy, easy.
Never let your feelings show.

Make it breezy, breezy, breezy
Easy come and easy go.

"I love Ella," he said. "She's so sweet and dignified. Isn't she? I wish she was my mother."

"Teo." I was surprised not at his choice but that he would say so.

"If she were my mother, I'd buy her a big house in Connecticut."

"She probably already has a big house."

"I know. She has everything."

She sang, "I love Paris in the springtime / I love Paris in the fall." I drank more champagne than I was used to and Teo entertained me with an installment of his life story. When I determined that he had passed out for good, I crept into Janey's room.

"I like him," I said, sitting on the edge of her bed. She was reading *Tristram Shandy* and eating marshmallows.

"I knew you would. Somehow I knew he was just your type."

The morning after our first date we skipped classes and took a critical tour of campus. Teo had a hangover and his hands trembled as he drank the beer he bought as soon as we left the apartment. He sloshed Tuborg all down his shirt front and tried to sneer at the neat couples we saw picking their way across the stream to the math building. But his face was too sweet to hold a sneer; he merely looked demented. When I laughed at him, he laughed too, gloriously careless. Because of the drink, I suppose, his big body radiated heat, and walking with his arm around me in the New Hampshire cold was like cozying up to a radiator.

We spent the rest of the day wandering, holding hands and drinking beer. Teo's voice was eager and his face flushed as he told stories about New York, drinking, losing his virginity in the ladies' room of the Art Theater in Greenwich Village.

When it got dark, he took me out for an expensive dinner and ordered French champagne. I had to drive his Datsun home, since he could barely handle it sober, and he told me it was mine to use whenever I wanted. We carried the rest of his Ella tapes in from the car and as I danced, alone — Teo wouldn't budge from the couch — I felt happier than I had in years. There was something very soothing about this big, handsome, blue-eyed boy with his taffy-colored curls and his turquoise cashmere scarf. He lounged among the cushions, drinking brandy and telling me, every twenty minutes or so, how wonderful I was, how he hadn't thought there was anyone like me in Durham.

When we went to bed, there was no change in his friendly, almost brotherly demeanor. He kept talking as he took his clothes off, and when he kissed me there was a flavor of childhood make-out parties. He did, as a lover, what someone had taught him to do, and I liked it well enough. The best part was that he was just drunk enough to have trouble coming, giving me time—for the first time—to figure out how to do it in the unfavorable position of intercourse. It was all a matter of concentration, though the plumpness of his groin and belly helped.

We began seeing each other every day. There was never any question about it. Teo missed me fiercely when we were apart and he hated his roommate, so our apartment was where he spent most of his time. I was glad. I was so fond of him. When I woke up in the morning and saw his big head on the pillow, I felt an immediate urge to cook him breakfast. I never did. He refused to eat before noon. Instead he'd take me to a coffee shop and while I ate eggs and bacon and toast and juice, he'd happily watch, still wearing his camel-hair overcoat and scarf, drinking cup after cup of black coffee. Then he'd drive me to my first class while I instructed him in the use of gears.

Teo was intelligent and took a polite interest in his studies. He went to all of his classes once a week and offered a friendly greeting to his professors whenever he ran across them. The rest of the time he liked to lie in my bed drinking beer. Sometimes he'd ask me to read aloud his textbooks and he appeared to listen, although there wasn't much point. He'd flunk out this semester, or next. He couldn't concentrate. He explained to me that his brain was being destroyed by alcohol. I didn't believe him, but understood that he was killing off his college days. I was sorry for that, though it didn't seem terribly important. He talked, always, of more exciting places than school. He had been to Europe and South America, and though he was vague on the details, the names of the cities were glamorous enough. He intended to someday have a farmhouse in the wine country of France or perhaps

Italy, and invite all his friends to live there with their lovers. Or maybe he would buy a townhouse in the West Village, decorate it in black and white, hire barefoot Indian servants, and build a glassed-in garden where Ella would sing and Joe Pass play guitar, where musicians would stop in, after their gigs, for an early morning jam session. All this was when his parents died, and he was rich. Or when he got rich some other way; he had nothing against his parents.

Teo and I did not have much of a social life. He refused to go to the few parties I was invited to, and the only person I would allow in our beery bedroom was Janey. She'd sit for an hour or two, complaining about Aaron, who was practically living at the math building. Aaron wasn't horny anymore. He didn't bathe. She had asked her favorite professor to have an affair with her and he'd refused. She wanted to know what was wrong with her that a man could prefer a computer or a wife?

Teo and I weren't much help. We lay side by side, listening, sheets up to our chins. There were cracker crumbs, pencils, and orange rinds strewn around our bodies. I told her to try another professor, an older one. Teo suggested she stalk the math building naked and see if anyone noticed. We both agreed she was too good for Aaron. But we closed her out in the end. She would leave and we would return to our simple delights: drinking, listening to Ella, and occasionally fucking.

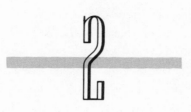

T eo and I did not live synchronous lives in New York. He never
got up before two or three and even then was sluggish, sitting
around in his underwear reading whichever newspapers and
magazines had come in the mail. At first I waited for him. I
prowled the apartment for five or six hours, making long lists
of what I wanted to do and looking in on him where he lay, flushed, his
face trembling in sleep. I learned to use his parents' Mellier coffeepot
and sipped coffee as muddy as the bottom of the Elder River while I
read through his mother's collection of mostly never-opened cookbooks. When he awoke, I babied him, bringing hot croissants and
cold strawberry juice—he had given up coffee, saying it was bad for
his nerves—and I smiled reproachfully when he tilted the vodka in.

I didn't want us to drink so much in New York. In New York there
were things to do. For Teo the return to the city meant a switch from
beer to his father's vast collection of high-priced booze. He liked
making exotic drinks with crushed ice and several liquors, and he
would follow me around, his bare feet soundless on the silvery gray
carpet, holding out a big goblet of strangely colored goo for me to
taste. I was cautious. I still didn't quite understand how one drink
could get you as drunk as a six-pack.

After a while I couldn't stand it, and I went out in the mornings. I
learned the city by walking it, from Soho to 110th Street, from the
Hudson to the East River. There were long stretches where the
sidewalks on Sunday mornings were half deserted and I could imag-

ine I was living in almost any decade of the twentieth century. On weekdays, as I pushed through the throngs and crossed in front of taxis straining like leashed hounds, I kept these glimpses of an emptier city fixed in my mind as an antidote to panic.

I had never seen such crowds. The heat made everything worse, of course. Walking among strangers, I was with people I knew intimately by smell. I began to understand a dog's point of view. So much to sniff out. But I wasn't able to cope with the overload of information and would push my way anxiously into one of the big department stores where the icy, perfumed air hit me like a tranquilizing drug. The crowds were there too, but they weren't quite so human. Neither was I. I was invisible in those stores except for my shoes, which for some reason were always stared at. I bought a few things, skimpy tops and a ruffled skirt, some silk flowers for my hair and a five-dollar lipstick, but soon browsed only among what I knew I would never buy, and used the bathroom.

I went to all the famous museums. I went to Rockefeller Center and the Empire State Building. I went to the East Village. I ate lunch in every conceivable place, sampling pastrami, souvlaki, cannoli, knishes, gnocchi and sushi, Nathan's hotdogs and *mousseline de trois poissons avec un* watercress salad and half a bottle of Vouvray. I bought a postcard of Baryshnikov for Janey and one of H. G. Wells for Grandmother. I admired the architecture, the people, the clothing, and the bookstores. I got lonely and went home to my woken-up boy.

Teo would be ready by then with a list of choices for me. Restaurants and bars I had never heard of, musicians I had never heard of, movies that weren't to be taken seriously. Teo didn't like to sit still, unable to have a drink, for two hours. He absorbed most of his culture by reading reviews in *The New York Times*.

I'd choose arbitrarily. All the famous restaurants were obscure to me. But the names were French and I felt privileged as he called to make the reservation. This was some of what I had come to New York for, this casual way of going out to dinner to elegant and wonderful places. To Lutèce, to La Grenouille and Le Cirque, Teo charging it all. I hadn't known food could be so good. That extra level of art was a revelation to me — so this was what happened if you kept practicing, if you were a genius.

We showered together in his leafy green bathroom and dressed each other. Teo, big and clean, his pubic hair silky from its jojoba oil shampoo, conditioner, and blowdry. He wore yellow boxer shorts, white chinos, and a pastel cotton shirt with a silk scarf around his neck. He had scarfs in turquoise, scarlet, yellow, and purple, and he also wore his mother's muted prints with the designer's name in the corner. I wore my black dress or my red dress, lots of blue eye shadow, and my hair however Teo chose to arrange it. He made braids threaded with copper wire, pinched off with a red plastic clothespin. "I haven't had a doll since I was five," said Teo, "when Martha ate Nefertiti."

Wherever we went, we always ended up in a bar. Usually it was in the Village, though Gregory's and P. J. Clarke's were not neglected. The Riviera Café was a favorite of ours. There, sitting at an outside table, drinking carafe after carafe of white wine, we had all the entertainment we needed. Teo did most of the drinking, and I did most of the watching. So much male flesh parading by, most of it gay. So many beautiful women in low-cut summer dresses.

Teo talked obsessively. Not only about his friends but about acquaintances, teachers, a girl he had glimpsed on a subway once, barefoot, in an evening dress, her face hidden behind a veil of hair, dead drunk. "She was beautiful." I was interested, not in these characters, but in what he was looking for. A clue to something, a forgotten day that would illumine—what? What to do next? The way he talked reminded me of running my fingers over a smooth roll of Scotch tape, looking for the little rough edge to pry up. I couldn't quite figure out where his life had gotten stuck, if that was what had happened. The transition to college, obviously, was traumatic, but so much so? I suppose it might have been instructive that he never talked about his parents, but I wasn't much interested in those depths. My own childhood vista seemed uncomplicated to me: magical and melancholy, yet distinct in its outline. My parents had left me, so I searched for love. I would never be satisfied because my desire transcended the sexual, even though from them I had inherited a powerfully sexual nature. I had worked this out roughly and was content with it. The important thing was that my parents' influence didn't seem negative to me anymore. I felt strong enough to provide what my past demanded; I took it as a challenge. This optimism came largely as a result of my intimacy with Teo, which had dissolved the loneliness of college. I did not feel the same optimism in regard to him. Whatever influence was at work on him was decidedly negative. I hoped it wasn't his parents. It repelled me to think of those middle-aged people tampering with the soul of the sweet, yeasty-smelling boy across from me.

I tried to help. I listened, I was affectionate, and I finally couldn't stand it. His talk poured out in a dense wave of personality. I knew what he was going to say before he said it. Or rather, I didn't think of it ahead, I experienced constant déjà vu. When I thought that Teo, when he looked at me, usually saw two Stellas, as he had confided, one more shadowy than the other, and when I began to allow for this, moving uneasily in my chair as his face grew slacker and his eyes unfocused, squirming as if it were up to me to join the two images together—then I thought perhaps our concentration on each other was dangerous.

I asked Teo if he didn't know anyone in the City, if we weren't going to have a social life at all? Nobody stays in the City in the summer, he said, that's why I like it, it's so empty here. I said that I had to talk to someone besides him once in a while. He pondered that for a few nights, then offered his solution. We went to smaller, neighborhood bars and he made friends. He did it very easily. In the time it took me to go to the bathroom, he'd round up several. Young, preppie couples with their mouths gaping at his drunken heartiness, or disillusioned alcoholics so used to instant friendship they couldn't remember the other kind. I didn't like any of them. I especially didn't like the ones that were hard to get rid of, that regarded me as the annoying girlfriend of this charming, good-time boy. I got tired of people poking their cigarettes at me as if they were practicing for when they were steady enough to hold a gun. People enough older than me that they could simply say how young I was when it was too much trouble to intelligently disagree. Teo was protective. He insulted anyone who insulted me. Yet he liked all these new listeners; it was too late for me to say that I wanted, after all, to be alone with him.

After a while, I began going home by myself at midnight or one. I left Teo in the bar with his companions and his beer, cigarette ashes all over the table, making phone calls. He called Slade and Laura in Boston, Jules in Texas, his friend Oscar in East Hampton, and charged it to his parents' number. He could rarely remember the next day what he'd said, and even less what they'd said, so he'd call again, asking how they were. It must have been, for them, like talking to a brain-damaged man.

Alone in the apartment I took long baths, using Teo's mother's French bath oils and English bath brush. I washed off the smoke of the bar and the soot of the City, I shampooed my hair, then turned the shower on so it fell down like rain to where I lay on my back, eyes closed against the soap, breasts floating on the rising waters. I thought about my lovers. I had had seven. Tobias, whom I still loved for the memory of my infatuation; my biology teacher Mr. Cross; four boys in college; and Teo. Two with light hair, five with dark. Four blue-eyed, one green-eyed, two brown-eyed. None of them very tall. None short. None black or foreign. Just seven men to choose among when I lay alone with my hand between my legs, fantasizing. Often they were not enough. I imagined giants, approaching from every direction. Bronzed, monolithic, with a slow, rolling gait. Immense faces bending down, immense hands lifting me . . . phalluses as symbolically and architecturally magnificent as the ones Freud once dreamed of.

My sex life with Teo dwindled almost to nothing. On the first of many such nights, he kissed me passionately at the door, his hand groping under my nightgown, then spit out a stream of slurred and vulgar remarks as I guided him through the obstacles of the living room to bed. Undressed, he suddenly lost force. He muttered something, his head suspiciously still in the crook of my neck. I turned and mouthed down his body, willing the soft penis into life. It lolled against my lips. Teo had his head on the pillow now, his eyes wide open; I could see him blink up at the ceiling. I laid my cheek on his thigh.

"Come on, Sweetheart," I whispered, "stand up and talk to me." Teo's penis squinted from its folds like an old man from a curtained window.

"Forget it," he said. I slid up the bed again and lay beside him. "Really?"

"Really. Too much booze."

"Maybe you should stop drinking so much."

"I can't."

"Why not?"

"I don't want to."

"Then you don't mean you can't."

"I want to want to, but I can't want to. Not seriously." We lay for a long time in silence and I thought he had fallen asleep. "Drinking," he said, "is like living on a tropical island when you know you should move back to Pittsburgh. Like, maybe all your friends are there, and you know you'll live longer, but, you know, it's Pittsburgh." I put my arms around him. "Don't worry about me," he said.

"You'll get lonely, eventually, won't you?"

"It's curious—don't laugh. When I'm drunk I can hear people's voices in my head. My friends, yours. Sometimes my own voice split up into parts. Speaking one after the other, very intelligent, and I just listen . . . I'm in my brain then, living totally in my brain."

"I feel sorry for your penis."

"Women often do."

"This has happened before? Part of your charm?" I asked sarcastically.

"Because I'm drunk they knew it's not their fault, so they can forgive me. It's a medical problem. They get to be doctors, all women want to be doctors. Poultices, acupressure, assertiveness training . . ."

"Shit," I said.

"Go to sleep, I'll fuck you in the morning."

"You won't be up in the morning."

"I'll fuck you in the afternoon, I'll fuck you in the evening, I'll fuck you on the kitchen table . . ." But he didn't. The way he looked the next day, I didn't want him to.

When my mother left she was twenty-three. At seventeen she had lived away from home less than a year, at a boarding school in Pennsylvania from which she was expelled when my father was caught in her bed. He had come to tell her he had dropped out of the

University of Virginia after a fight with his father over his grades. She also had something to tell—that she was pregnant. They had barely begun to comfort each other when my mother's roommate, casually banished from the room, returned with the dorm mistress. My mother wrapped her arms more securely around my father's body and it took three girls to pry her loose.

My grandmother told me this when I once asked her if I could go to boarding school. She would not, she said, ever again sit in a head-mistress's office and listen to a child of hers referred to, however euphemistically, as an insane slut. Or as anything else, for that matter.

Grandmother had driven my parents back to her house in Elder River, New Hampshire, and taken them to the courthouse the next week to get married—a move that prompted my father's final sever-ance from his family. Seven months later I was born and they stayed on at my grandmother's house, my father selling cars, insurance, vacuum cleaners, and playing the saxophone, my mother doing as little as possible. I remember her standing in the kitchen, holding her hair on top of her head with both hands, her neck bent so the bone stuck out, her white arms angling around her face, my father getting up from his chair to kiss the protruding bone. I remember my father snapping his fingers to a Little Richard record while my mother stuffed newspaper in her ears. She hated music, any kind of music. The only time my father ever got mad at her was when she hid his saxophone in a snowbank. She was not repentant.

My grandmother says my mother should have been born deaf since she never listened to anything but compliments, and even those she preferred in the form of smiles, gifts, and caresses. It's true that my mother frequently didn't respond when she was spoken to. Even the simplest question would provoke only a stare: a milky, blue, ineffable stare, which seemed not so much a refusal as a preoccupation. Because I think her attention, once you had it, was very close.

If my grandmother was annoyed by her daughter's silence, and by her habit of lying on the couch all day, head flung back, bare feet dangling over the arm, cigarette ashes dripping on the rug, Grand-mother was more annoyed by her gaiety. Once every week or two, wearing a full skirt and white peasant blouse, my mother would dance, her feet stomping the floor my grandmother was trying to vacuum. She danced without music to a constantly changing rhythm. She excited me and I would skip around her, hopping and jumping and trying to catch the beat until I felt sick, or until I was restrained in my grandmother's severe embrace. My mother in her full skirt kept dancing. She was not graceful, she tended to stumble, and later would show my father her bruises, which he would kiss.

Her gaiety seemed to have a cause: a great event was about to occur. When she took my hands and swung me around like her skirt, my feet off the ground, my giggles high and helpless, I knew I had a part in this event — and that my grandmother didn't, which is why she warned so sharply that I would get dizzy, or fall down the stairs, or throw up, or have a fit. But before the great event, whatever it was, could take place, my mother would lose interest, suddenly registering my grandmother's complaints.

"Put her to bed then," my mother would say, dropping my hands and hurrying off to my father, who was sitting in his armchair with a book, pretending he didn't hear what was happening. Once my mother was draped over his lap though, he was willing to be the man of the family.

"We'll put the child to bed, Lally," he would say authoritatively, and it was so. They led me upstairs between them, my small, sticky hands in theirs, and whispered endearments to each other. They thought I didn't understand, and I didn't. But I hated being so small, with all that talk floating by above my head. That was my air they were using, even if I didn't fill it up yet.

My father was red-haired and blue-eyed, with a beak of a nose, firm lips, and a skin always turning color with emotion. He was eager, he was impatient, he was hurt. He was always responding. He irritated both my mother and my grandmother with his ardent presence, and with his willingness to do whatever the other one asked of him. The only time he stayed aloof was when they were fighting. My grandmother liked his helpfulness but not his sentiment, my mother his passion but not his tact. She would interfere in whatever household chore he had been asked to do; she would coax him upstairs or outside with a gleeful triumph. His glance at my grandmother as he deserted the task she had given him was romantic: see what your beautiful daughter does to me. She hated it. I would watch her frown after them and be afraid; I thought of myself as my parents' possession, which she might turn against in her anger.

I remember very clearly when I fell in love with my father and how long it lasted. I was four and we were alone in the house. He took advantage of this to play his sax as loud as he wanted to, the horn booming through the downstairs rooms. I was scared and climbed into his lap. He hoisted me higher and let me touch his lips as he played, my fingers wandering across the vibrating flesh.

I could feel his lungs inflate against his chest, the air forced up, the shaping of his mouth—and then the golden horn's response. He let me press down a key, and the music sank; I pressed another and it rose to a high squeak.

By the time my mother got home I was saturated with music, it was rolling through me so I could barely stand. I listened to my father talk to her, his horn now put away, and knew he was not using his real voice. His real voice was much bigger; it was an awesome outpouring of sound.

Whenever the women went out, after that, I would stay home, if I was given a choice. When they were safely gone, I followed my father upstairs where he kept his sax in a beat-up case in his bedroom closet. I watched with pleasure as he lifted the instrument out, fitted the strap around his neck, and hooked it on. Sometimes he'd sit on his bed and play, sometimes he'd sit in the kitchen. Wherever he was, I sat in his lap, my eyes fixed on his tongue as it licked and licked the wooden reed. I waited, shivering, for those first, booming notes.

When they came it was like a call to another universe, a male universe, where horns sounded and lions roared, where all the wild animals I knew vaguely from storybooks commingled, their golden voices raised in a feast of language—a language I thought my father understood in the same way I understood English. He was traveling there through the bright tube of his saxophone, his eyes screwed shut, his upper body shaking back and forth, and I had to follow as best I could, listening under the music for his laboring breath. I never quite got there, I never knew what it was all about, I was lost in the yellow roar.

Inevitably, one day he wanted to practice alone. He put me down off his lap. I climbed back up. He locked me in my room, and as I cried against the keyhole, he played louder; then he walked his horn downstairs, where I could barely hear it at all.

When my mother returned and found me sobbing, she gathered me up in her arms, rocked me, said never would she allow him to lock me up again; nobody should ever be locked up. She carried me into the bathroom and we bathed together in a tubful of steaming water. We washed our hair and our toes and our private places, and she soothed me.

After that I loved only my mother. I gathered flowers for her beautiful hair, I made her lemonade, and when she had backaches, I walked barefoot up and down her soft spine. I wondered when she would divorce my father. I knew he would leave someday. He was not at home in our house.

He did go, as I'd foreseen, but he took her with him, as I should have known he would. He could never bear to be away from her. I can almost forgive him this—not, as my grandmother thinks, because I was better off without them, but because the memory of that summer day is strangely magical, one I would not want to relinquish. Because at that moment, when my father left, I began to love him again. Not him specifically, the man with the saxophone, but him as part of the pair, my parents, who left home to seek adventure. I had often seen them walk out the garden gate, dressed up and laughing, going to Boston for dinner or a show, and had envied their pleasure, but never had adult life seemed so much like a fairy tale children are left out of. I lay quietly in bed that first night while Grandmother explained that she would never leave me, that I would always live here. I didn't cry. I was not quite six years old.

My grandmother was pleased that I so quickly accepted her as my parent. It wasn't hard to do. With my parents gone, the ground was cleared between us; I was not afraid, though I felt her power—it attracted me. I didn't tell her how I missed them. How it was a physical longing, drawing my heart out of my chest to hang in the air; how often I thought of my mother's laughter.

She had worn a yellow dress and high-heeled yellow sandals. Her pink toenail polish had been applied with a sloppy touch. "Come on," she said, "we'll be late, we'll be late."

"Late for what?" His hand was curled around her waist and he was looking back at the house.

"We'll be late," she repeated, shimmying away from him. She stepped carefully on the flagstones around which the grass grew long, but her head and shoulders and bare arms, and especially her laugh, surged ahead eagerly to the gate.

He followed her, holding his saxophone case in one hand. He wetted his lips with his tongue. "You're so slow," she said, glancing over her shoulder. "They'll see us."

"They won't see us — they'll never see us again," he replied, and their eyes met. She stopped and tilted her face up for a kiss. He obliged, his mouth going all around hers.

She pulled away. "Can we go now, please?"

"Of course, baby. We're going." He opened the gate for her, and she twirled through. He shut it with a click and she laughed excitedly. They had no baggage; perhaps it was already in the car. Or perhaps they took nothing but a summer suit, a yellow dress, a little money in their pockets, and the spray of purple lilac my mother twisted off its stem and pressed to her face as they turned and I lost sight of them.

I was sitting in the bushes to the side of the house, eating a banana. I had hollowed out a fort there where the dirt was cool and I could see the sky through a crisscross of tiny branches. After they left I sat still for a long time, not sure if it was real. They couldn't mean we'd never see them again — yet at the same time I knew they did mean it. My parents had always seemed out of place at my grandmother's house, visitors straining to leave, gazing at the distant hills, but having to wait through seasons and seasons for the enchantment to lift. Why had it lifted now, and where were they going? It didn't occur to me to follow them. (Later I thought I had missed my only great opportunity.) But instead I watched the wind blow the lilac branches against the gate; I felt an ant crawl up my leg; I listened to the car recede toward the highway.

Where had they gone? Where was it, that place described by their intense eagerness to get there, a place I was afraid I would never find?

One night I left Teo in the bar by himself and started walking
home. It was about ten thirty, the air was moist and warm,
sweet with the New York sweetness of half-dressed bodies,
garbage, and the open back doors of restaurants. The whole
city smelled like a kitchen, after a party, before the hostess
has cleaned up. Leftover cake and wine, wilting flowers. Third
Avenue in the Seventies, on a Saturday night. The men with fluffy
haircuts, the women in gold chains and high heels. So many men, so
many women. So many lives going on that I became a part of, however
minor, simply by threading my way through the crowd. Each life was
a possibility that excited me, yet I did not feel like one of them. One of
the crowd. One of the women. I felt like an animal gliding through
strong moonlight, at every instant differentiating between shadow
and danger. Full of a forever inarticulate, undiminished wonder.

I saw three men leaning against a brownstone. One was thin and
sharp-featured, one plump and sweating, but it was the third who
caught my eye. He was big, with a large face, a wide jaw, and an out-
thrust, bladelike nose. It was a massive face that seemed to float free
in his ocean of brick-colored curls. He was staring at me, as well.

He walked over, lifted a box of cigarettes out of his shirt pocket and
offered them. Balkan Sobranies. I took one. He struck a wooden match
on the fly of his jeans and lit my cigarette. I smiled at that, and he
smiled back, then made a gesture as if to catch his balls on fire,

grimaced, and threw the match away. He held his arm out and I took it.

"You've lost your friends," I said. They had vanished around the building without a word to him.

"That's all right. I know where to find them. You want a drink?"

"Okay."

"What's your name?"

"Stella."

"I'm Nathan. I hope you don't mind me asking you this — but would you have gone with either of my friends?"

"No."

"I didn't think so." We walked in silence for a minute. I loved the feel of his solid, hard-muscled arm beneath mine. It changed the whole scene; I felt deeply implicated in everything. "You looked at me the way women don't usually look at me," he said.

"They do now."

"No, I don't see it. They look bold at you, like they know what they want. Like they knew already before they ever saw you. I find it insulting."

"I know what you mean. That's why men's looks are usually insulting."

"But your look was different. You looked . . . surprised. Like maybe you were really seeing something."

"I was. I don't know what."

He smiled shyly and led me into a bar. We sat down at a tiny, black table in the corner. We were only a foot apart. I could see every pore of his skin and each reddish eyelash. His eyes were blue and small, with an inward, attracting force. His big hands and wrists covered most of the table, but didn't touch mine. I was feeling very peculiar. This was only a pickup, something I had never done before yet had assumed I someday would, something I attached no special importance to; and Nathan was not so good-looking or so charming as to overwhelm me. Still, I felt overwhelmed.

"I have to go get our drinks," he said. "Scotch okay?"

"Fine."

He got up and I watched him shoulder his way through the crowd. It was more than desire that connected us. It was like the feeling you have for your first best friend on the day you realize you're best friends. My body was shivery with tenderness and with deliberate innocence. When he returned with our drinks, I took the ribbon out of my hair and let it fall around me, princesslike. He leaned forward and ran a finger down my cheek. He smelled of resin and scotch. He began to talk to me.

Nathan was a carpenter. He told me about wood, about the peculiarities of each kind, its rarity, what it was good for. I listened, not bored but not interested in a conversational way. I liked his voice. Each phrase he spoke increased my tenderness; I felt like my senses were intertwining, penetrating each other.

When he paused, I replied and said the right things, though I barely knew what I was saying. I didn't have any need for words; I thought maybe I never would again. Only the need to look and be looked at, and to feel those looks like birds flying in, or music, or perfumes winding through the brain. Yet I knew what I was doing—flirting with a strange man with whom I would have sex later. I was aware of the risk of it, and I felt tough as well as dreamy.

Nathan began to ask me questions. I told him a lot about my life that Teo would not have recognized. It was as if, all along, I'd been leading a secret life that I needed Nathan to bring out. I talked easily—about little, forgotten events of the day, about dreams, about coincidences. He loved coincidences so I told him more; suddenly I could remember hundreds. All recent. "Coincidences gather when something is about to happen," he said, and we smiled at each other. Our desire became more insistent. He stroked my arm to the elbow and held my knees between his own. His thighs had a strong grip and I wanted to slide so much closer. The rim of the table cut into my belly as I pressed forward and he moved his hands up to my shoulders. "Let's get out of here," he said.

"Just a minute." I pushed my way back to the bathroom and looked in the mirror. I looked wild and excited but not as much as I felt. I bit my lips to make them red. There was the rasp of a match and the woman who'd been combing her hair was now smoking a joint.

She sucked in the smoke, held it briefly, then said, "What do you think, is my shirt unbuttoned too far?" The tops of her breasts were soft and plump and looked very nice against her purple silk blouse.

She was older than me, maybe twenty-five, and wore a lot of bronze makeup.

"In the seventeenth century in Europe, women wore dresses that showed their nipples," I said, "so surely in the twentieth you can show that much."

"Oh, yeah?" she said. "How come I never knew that?" She offered me the joint and I shook my head.

"Schools these days."

"Do you mean, like, prostitutes?"

"No, ladies. There are portraits of them." I remember how it had shocked me at first, looking at reproductions of them. I couldn't believe men hadn't ripped off their dresses and raped the countesses on the spot. So much for provocative dress and the male instincts. It's all in the eyes.

"Really?" She unbuttoned another button.

"Of course they didn't walk the streets of New York alone at night."

"Oh, I won't be alone by the time I leave." She smiled at herself in the mirror, teasing the hair she had just brushed down. "Are you alone?"

"No."

"Well, have fun."

Nathan was standing by the table when I got back. Another couple was already sitting there, waving their cigarettes at each other. "Watch for a girl in a purple shirt coming out of the bathroom," I said.

"I see her."

"She wanted to know how much more of her breasts to show."

"How much more does she have?"

"I forgot to tell her the Restoration ladies wore theirs pushed up with corsets. Is that more or less suggestive than having them jiggle wildly?"

"What are you talking about?" he asked, steering me through the dense flesh. I felt my own breasts brush against two or three male arms. Nobody noticed.

I said, " It makes me feel crazy that everyone in here is doing what we're doing."

"Why? Who cares what they do?"

"I don't care exactly. I mean, I don't object."

"You're nervous?"

"No . . ." What I felt was high, so high it was like being on a flying carpet, something intricate and Arabian, with threads of gold, yet seeing the streets of Manhattan below me and doubting it could be real. I smiled at Nathan and he hugged me. "You're right," I said, "it doesn't matter at all what they do."

We got into a taxi. As he kissed me, I lost the last of my doubts. This was not a thing to think about but to do, to do once and never again. The lake of desire that buoyed me up through my days of happiness and unhappiness, that supported every activity, every hope and trifling friendship, must now be acknowledged; I felt like a civilized mermaid going home for a visit, diving deep.

I don't remember Nathan's apartment except that it was in the basement and smelled like new wood. We were in bed immediately and I closed my eyes. Oh, this could be anyone, I thought, a man's hoarse breathing, his penis entering me in the dark—but was not anyone, was Nathan, strong, oaklike Nathan. So this was Nathan. What does Nathan have to do with me? I asked the question; I received the answer; but I couldn't tell you now what it was.

His chest gleamed with sweat. His oval and muscular belly thrust out, he labored, his cock pushed in and in. Then I was held tight, I felt the orgasm kick and tremble down his body; his cold feet curled around my ankles. He lifted his head and looked at me. "Just you wait a minute," he said. I smiled and he kissed my lips and my eyes. We waited, in silence, looking at each other until his penis got hard again. I didn't move. I felt like I was pulling the blood back down with my smile, down from his brain and his heart and his gut to engorge in my body.

Then we fucked slowly, Nathan propping himself up with one hand while the other traveled from nipples to clitoris. He was rough, pinching me with an abundance of lust I understood and forgave. I opened my legs wider. I was sweating with pleasure being born, pushing out through my skin: freed, it flowed like mercury, it was too much to hold in awareness, a multitude of sensation, a thousand devils—or angels. When I came I was silent, I was mute, writhing, I paid such deep attention; then I heard, from far off, Nathan coming, with a snort like a train.

It was going to be over. It was over. He got up and brought me a glass of water and a towel. He offered me strawberries. "Let's go to sleep," I said.

I woke up and slipped out of there before dawn. It must have been right after the bars closed. People drifted through the streets with swollen eyes, I heard the jangling of braceleted wrists as women's hands clutched at masculine arms, and the men staggered. I strode through, feeling mistress of them all.

When I got home I crawled into bed beside Teo. He opened one eye. "Where'd you go?"

"Home with a man."

"Have a nice time?"

"Yes."

"Good." He fell asleep again.

In the afternoon, when he got up, I had juice squeezed, the apartment clean, curtains drawn, and stores of food and liquor replenished. Teo sat down at the table naked and asked for an Alka-Seltzer ice-cream soda: Alka-Seltzer, water, and Häagen-Dazs vanilla ice cream. I made it for him, glancing over repeatedly to where he sat, bleary and slumped, breathing with a wheeze. I noticed he was getting fat. His belly lay in two big folds on his lap, and he had plump little breasts.

"Are you mad?" I asked finally as he drank his soda.

"Nnnaahhh . . . how could I be mad? This is no life for a young girl."

"Or a young boy," I said.

"Each to his own vice." He looked at me mournfully. "I'm a little jealous, maybe. But I don't blame you . . . it's not like we're in love. Are we?"

"No."

"I didn't think so. Too bad . . . sex just ain't what it used to be."

"I still like it."

"I noticed. I like getting drunk, and I'm impotent and disgusting, I know—"

"You're not disgusting. You're funny when you're drunk. I don't mind it. I just worry about you sometimes."

"Yeah."

"Is it just because you can't get it up occasionally that you're bored with sex?"

"It's so repetitive," he murmured.

"So's getting drunk!"

"But I don't remember it. So it's not really repetition. It's more like—the Eternal Now."

"Oh, God, I hope not. I hope it's not eternal."

Teo lit a cigarette and smiled at me through the smoke, my wise and corrupt baby. "Now is always eternal, don't you know anything?"

"Very little." I thought how easily I could do without all that kind of knowledge if I lived my nights like last night. On pure instinct, returning everything to its source in desire.

"Being drunk is like dreaming and knowing you're dreaming. So you can do anything, you can act on your impulses, but you're safe all the time. That's what it feels like. Until the pain starts." He drank the last of his soda and put a record on. Ella singing, "Always true to you, darlin', in my fashion."

I rolled my eyes at his selection and said, "It sounds like a dangerous way to feel." I had heard him in this drunken dream state talking to people as if they were projections of himself, as if he were God woozily fallen into the world. It made me angry at him but also fascinated me a little.

"No more dangerous than picking up men," he said.

"Oh, I don't know."

"You could get murdered."

"But I won't."

He shrugged. "Just don't bring anybody here."

"Of course not!"

"I don't mind, but the doormen are spies for my parents." Teo's parents called every Sunday. He was usually hungover and had to be dragged to the phone. He grunted at five-minute intervals, his mono-syllables unintelligible to me.

"Don't they get upset when you sound like that?" I once asked.

"It's standard," he replied. "You should hear my cousin Phil talk to Aunt Dot. He sounds like he's squeezing out a hard shit. Besides, my mother finds it reassuring. If I was too nice to her, she'd think I was gay."

I met Zeke on the subway. It was four in the afternoon, and I was thinking about sex, playing back my night with Nathan, wondering if Teo would be horny tonight, if I cared whether Teo was horny, and if I would ever, really, pick up a man like that again, when I noticed him. He was sitting across from me, arms and legs wide apart, like a spider, taking up two seats with his hard, stringy body. He was wearing shorts and I admired the black hair on his thighs; I saw it as a deliberate erotic display, as if his pubic hair were showing. I stared at it, and the stare became sex in itself: there was me, there was a pair of hairy thighs, and we had a unique relationship. I understood the need of that flesh to be looked upon, to be praised and desired during its few years on Earth, even in the subway, even by strangers, perhaps especially so. The darkness of the skin was an important factor in its beauty, I thought. It looked like skin that would naturally grow such curls, do it for love or ambition, as pretty women have beautiful children. I stared, and the muscles in his thighs twitched.

After a while I looked up at his face. He had a long, black mustache and black eyes, and when he caught my glance, he immediately got up and came to sit by me. "Hello?"

"Hi." I felt confused. He had seemed so anonymous across the subway car . . . this wasn't quite the same atmosphere as the East Seventies. But I could smell him now, he smelled like lemons and coffee and summer sweat, and like something else, something autumnal . . . I sniffed delicately.

"You would like to come with Zeke? You would like to spend the afternoon with me?"

"Where?"

"Anywhere. Where do you want to go?"

"Why should I go with you?"

"Because you are bored. Come on." He got up when the train

stopped. I didn't move. The deadening stares of the people around me were inhibiting, and I felt an agonizing indecision; how did I know I really wanted to? That he wouldn't repulse me ten minutes later? That he wouldn't rob me, or hurt me, kill me, that he wouldn't ruin the wonderful chance of my night with Nathan by proving that such sex can also be sordid and horrible?

"You must come," he said urgently. "Or you will not have a good day. You will not see me again. I will go."

That didn't seem quite fair. I got up and followed him.

"I'm not exactly bored," I said. We were in midtown and it was broiling hot. He put his arm loosely around me.

"Once upon a time—you remember that?"

"Remember what?"

"How fairy tales start—once upon a time?"

"Of course."

"Okay. Once upon a time, I lived in Greece. When I was a little boy. I came here at seven. I wanted to come here. I liked it then. But I think it is uglier and uglier." He paused. "When I see someone like you I always talk to her. Not just because you are a pretty girl, but you like me. If somebody likes me, I always like them." He gave me a sidelong glance to see how I was taking it. His eyes were dense with blackness, like bedrooms where the morning has been shut out for centuries.

"In Greece, you know," he said, "we have lots of myths about how people meet, sometimes with gods and goddesses. There are lots of stories and they are very true, don't you think?"

"Yes." Leda and the swan? Paris and Helen? Odysseus and Nausicaä? I couldn't see myself as any of those women, but what difference did that make? Let him use his whole country to seduce me, let him be foreign and mythical. All men are, I thought, or should be.

"In New York you have singles bars. I hate them," he said forcefully. "If a man and woman want each other, they don't need to go to a bar. They will meet anywhere. These people," he said in disgust, "they are afraid to talk to anyone they haven't met in the office or at a friend's, yet they go to bars and stand around like it's okay there. They are cows. Not just the women, the men are cows, too; they are more cows."

"You see yourself as a bull, do you?"

He laughed and tightened his arm around my shoulder. We were walking west on Forty-sixth street, where it starts to look dangerous, and I appreciated his firm grip that kept me so close we were overlapping. "No. Bulls are stupid and they are not good lovers. If I was an animal I would be . . . a wolf."

"Yes," I said.

"Not the wolf that ate Red Riding Hood's grandmamma," he said, snapping his jaws like a hungry beast. "No, wolves are very civilized, they have dignity. It is very good between the male and the female, in wolves."

"Why? What's it like?"

"Like it will be with us. You are coming to my apartment, you know that's where we're going?" I nodded. He patted me right above the breast. "I will show you how a wolf makes love, and I will not eat you up." He fingered his mustache and looked at me carefully. His eyes gleamed with a certain doubt; I guessed we must be close to his front door. "You like me?"

"So far."

He laughed and all the doubt left his eyes. He looked fierce, his Adam's apple jutting as he stopped and took a key out of his pocket. "We are here," he said. "You must tell me your name before we go inside."

"Stella."

"A good name for you," he said approvingly. "Like a star, with all that yellow hair."

Zeke's apartment had long, dusty, black curtains, not only at the windows, but cutting off each corner so the room was octagonal. There were red and black candles on the round tables, Mozart on the stereo, and cold beer. I sat on the floor while he opened the beer, and when he had handed me one, he sat down across the room from me. He smiled at me from beneath the wings of his mustache, I smiled back, and the music swelled between us.

I drank my beer very fast, soaring into a miraculous light-headedness. There was someone else inside me. Uncoiling like a snake, she stretched and stretched, until she touched every cell in my body. Then she/I slithered over to Zeke. It was good to stay close to the floor, breasts and thighs rubbing on the old wood. I felt like the curve of my hips was merely the visible part of a spiral that continued on infinitely, that when I moved them the motion traveled on that spiral to ever more remote locations.

Zeke reached out for me, his furry hand pulling my hair and pinching my neck. Not painfully, not painfully at all. I kissed him and he leaned back, letting my tongue stab in, tasting and feeling in its blind intrepitude. His fingers writhed under my shirt with a creepy intensity, drawing at my breasts, as if sex had to be coaxed out of a woman. I thought of boys who had lain their caresses on me gently, or massaged them in over every inch, like body lotion.

Zeke pulled my shirt off and I pulled off his. I rubbed my nose in his chest hair, which smelled like sandalwood, which led me into dry, autumn forests where the leaves crumbled underfoot, and women, or shewolves, waited through ominous afternoons for their mates. Men's chests always seem so vacant, even the thump of their hearts doesn't convince. Yet it's compelling, that vacancy, it appeals; if breasts ask to be lain upon, like pillows, a flat chest wants to be inscribed by the tongue.

The sound of Mozart from the stereo suddenly ceased. In the moment of silence, before we heard the noise of New York around us, we took off the rest of our clothes and were quickly fucking. I clamped my arms tightly across his sinewy back, and he held me even harder. Lust was suddenly simple—no more reveries, only the fastest and hardest fucking, the most energetic pinching and biting, the fiercest, sucking kisses. Excitement blazed through me, I took pleasure wherever I wanted it, I had orgasms without having to maneuver for position. Zeke glared down at me with his bedrooms-of-endless-night eyes, and I thought I preferred his look of rage which was not rage to Nathan's labor, Teo's smugness, or Tobias's amusement. When he came, his teeth clenched and ground together, like the gears of a spastic machine. Then he opened his mouth and smiled.

"So, do you still like me?"

"I like you a lot."

"I like you, too."

He made us coffee. We sat next to each other on the floor, naked, sipped, and didn't talk. That was just fine with me. I was thinking, in a leisurely way, about this new activity of mine and wondering why strangers seemed so much more exciting than boyfriends. I was impatient with the very idea of boyfriends. There seemed to be more maleness in Zeke, in every twitch of his long eyebrows, than in anyone I could imagine living with. I felt utterly sexual with him, in a different way than I had with Tobias. Then I had been sick with love for something beyond his body that I used his body to try to get to. Something beyond his mind, when I got to know his mind, something that maybe wasn't there, but was anyway a subtle and mocking thing. Now I felt I was acting on what I knew, and only that. It surprised me how well I knew it, how easy it was. Zeke put his arm around me and I bent my head down to his cock. It was half erect. I put my mouth on it and we had a conversation; its spasms of hardness, twitches, and sudden languor more interesting than the usual doglike devotion.

I began picking up men two or three times a week. I rarely felt embarrassment, and never distress. I wondered at the image of one-night stands — loneliness, desperation, or else callousness, brute lust. Conquest. Perhaps conquest, but only as a fringe benefit. There was no loneliness at all. Rather its opposite: union, surrounded by solitude in its most royal form.

After Zeke I became more aggressive and often made the first move myself. I can't remember the things I said; they would just rise to my lips while I concentrated, in delight, on the sensation, prickly, melting, and somehow aesthetic, that told me I had found someone suitable. I was very selective, though the criteria were unconscious. Perhaps I simply followed Zeke's advice and liked whoever liked me. I was never rejected, although often they were very surprised.

"I'll never believe this really happened to me," said a bemused architect, legs like pale trees, belly a rising planet. I had met him in a deli where he was buying bologna. "It's only for today, isn't it?"

"Yes," I replied. I had my cheek on his arm, I was smiling at the soft, fat flesh.

"I'm grateful." Why shouldn't he be? His girlfriend lived in Maine. "I'll treasure the memory."

My architect was a type I often chose. An ordinary man, with a boundless sweetness under the surface. A man who realized there was something unusual between us and called it fate—a man not in the habit of using that word. A man who could love a woman forever.

I also met the tough ones, sure of their charm. They took my affection in stride and made plans for our future together, the little smile on their lips telling me that future would be canceled whenever they chose. They were harder to handle, but more interesting. Where else but in the flesh would I have met Rudy, lean, sharp and wicked, who talked six hours straight about the fights he'd been in, each jab and gout of blood more vivid to me than Technicolor, yet still only words . . . perhaps not true, not even as true as a movie. Rudy fucked like a machine, again and again, until I could not believe he still felt anything. I pleaded with him to stop but he paid no attention. He finally let me go at dawn when his face, bruised-looking under the eyes, collapsed into boyhood. He told me I had class, real class.

Men like Rudy frightened me, although I was never sure there was anything to be afraid of. If I had known, I think, I wouldn't have liked it. But I couldn't tell. Rudy, when he was done with his violent stories, recited a long poem he had written, a street-language love song with echoes of Shakespearean melancholy and occasional asides to the universe. It didn't occur to him that this poem would ever end; when he felt inspired, he tacked on a few new verses. "I just wrote that part," he said. "Right now while I'm talking to you. Just made it up. You see? I'm a poet! Listen!"

A week later, Vince, a darker and more brooding soul, after talking to me for hours about the rights and privileges of men, when he was sure I had it straight, made me a 3 A.M. breakfast of scrambled eggs and biscuits. Then he washed the dishes and explained to me, in a convoluted way, that as long as men didn't have to do anything they didn't want to, they would do more than half of everything because they should. He knew that men had responsibilities, in the world and in the house, while at the same time they could not be compelled to honor those responsibilities. I replied, gently, that women also objected to compulsion. I do whatever I please, I said. I see you do, he replied, you come here with me. And you do whatever you please, I said, but if we were living together we'd have to compromise. No woman would ever live with me, he said, they don't understand me. I understand, I said, that's not the problem. There is no problem, said Vince, wiping the table, not in my life.

I almost liked best the walking home. It was usually early in the morning, the air soft and bright or soft and milky, and everywhere I saw people going to work. They walked more slowly than the nine o'clock crowd and more individually, coming and going in all directions, and crossing diagonally against the nearly empty streets. They carried lunches or toolboxes in their hands and greeted each other, voices ringing out as they never do later, when car noise rules the air.

If I was downtown I'd stop at the Pink Teacup on Bleecker, and eat eggs and grits with that peculiar hunger that's half fatigue, imagining I'd stay up all day, full of drowsy, lighthearted lovingness, imagining I'd never have to sleep again if I moved slowly enough. Then to make my way up Lexington or Madison, watching the grocery and news stores open one by one, to stop and buy pastry for tea, though I knew I'd be asleep at teatime, then, with sore thighs and a much-kissed mouth, I looked with delight and friendliness on all I passed.

Teo warned me a few more times of the danger of what I was doing, but did not try seriously to dissuade me. I took care of him as best I could, making fettucine al pesto, spaghetti carbonara, and spinach ravioli with fresh tomato sauce, keeping the apartment clean, and dreaming up new cures for hangovers. His favorite was a long, cool bath while I read to him from the biography of Dylan Thomas, then described in soothing tones and meticulous detail the meal we would have when he felt better. Teo only ate once a day now, in the evening, when his stomach was strong enough, but he craved food for several hours beforehand.

On the nights when I went out, I ate little, and I split the cash on hand with Teo. He went to the bars; I went roaming. I wore running shoes, pants, and slinky shirts. Teo bought me a purple satin one at Bloomingdale's that I particularly favored.

My face changed, those nights. My eyes grew larger, my mouth more sensitive—it had a thousand expressions—and my hair trailed behind me like perfume. It wasn't unusual to walk five miles. The exercise stirred up that snaky other; she uncoiled, flirting with the air. Then I would pause with a cigarette at the windows of bars, or on a stoop, laughing inside at my attitude of detached appraisal. That laughter was almost the best part—that certainty of youth and power and invisible forces on my side. I became adept at refusing the wrong men, instantly adopting an asexual glare, hunching my shoulders, and sticking my feet out. My new beauty would drop away. It was no problem—aggressive men are the most easily disgusted.

When I had found the one I wanted, and chosen him, and he understood that he was to take me home with him, the thrill of strangeness built up incredible desire in me. I could feel my blood glow through my skin. I walked in wild haste. My companion's surprise and my knowingness seemed to result in the same skewed reality; I was so attuned, I often walked ahead to the building he had not yet said was his.

Once through the door of his apartment, I felt a moment of fear, like that of an animal entering a cage. It was a sort of cage, for both of us: a place to be confined and exhibited. Later, the bars would bend easily to my touch, like the strings of a guitar. But in the beginning, sex was a difficulty; it takes work to accustom one body to another, to transfer an abstract or soulful desire for a man to a particular intimacy with his flesh. Who would not take the challenge, I thought, knowing how many do not. To undress or be undressed, to cling and kiss without love but with honesty, made me feel like Eve, alone with the only man on Earth, a stranger, without a past, as he was.

I was alone, admittedly. Whatever the men felt, I doubt they ever felt like Adam. My strangeness was incorporated into their own myths, if they had any. If I was Eve, I was also a spy, using sex for some more intense scrutiny of them. But that came a little later. When I first arrived, I was in thrall to my imagination, furious with a desire it seemed the body in bed with me would be unable to combat. This middle-aged fat man, that eighteen-year-old, this ponderous grade-school teacher with his ritual methods of quieting nervousness . . . how could they respond to what surely demanded someone brilliant in these matters? But they all did; we were partners.

As long as the fucking lasted, that is. Carl, a short, muscled, suspicious man, lamed in Vietnam, called me a witch. "Thank you," I said.

"It's not a compliment. You weakened me."

I raised an eyebrow. "How did I do that?"

"With your intensity. It isn't right. Not for a thing like this. Only if you loved me would it be right."

"Well, I don't love you. Sorry if you feel cheated." I smiled down at my young body sprawled out on his dark blue sheets. How could I have cheated him?

"You'd like to drain me, wouldn't you? With your female power?"

"Don't you have any male power? Are you helpless?" I asked petulantly. I had been having a good time; he was very strong, very well built.

"I don't like to have to use it for sex."

"What's it for then?" By now I thought he was a raving idiot, but there's a certain amount of tact necessary in these situations, so I asked politely.

"Survival."

I sighed. "Do you mind if I make myself something to eat?"

"Yes."

"I'll leave then." I was glad he had refused me.

"Give me a massage first. My leg hurts where it was wounded."

"No, thanks," I said, putting my jeans on.

"Do it!"

"Fuck you."

"You wouldn't say that to me if I wasn't lame."

"If you weren't lame, you'd still be lame. Good-bye."

"Didn't I give you a good fuck?"

"Sure. But your cologne stinks."

"It was very expensive. It smells nice. You just don't know anything—" I shut the door. He was the worst I had, but he understood something. He was wrong, though, to say I weakened him; I don't believe that at all.

More common was the reaction of Gordon, a blond advertising executive, who got out his calendar and, sitting nude on the side of the bed, figured out how many times in the next few weeks he could see me. Tuesday at one. Thursday night. Monday before work . . . I laughed and said I'd call him. He pinned me down, his knees on either side of my waist, and made me promise I'd call soon. "I used to do this to my sisters," he said, his hands clamping my upper arms to the bed. "But not this." He kissed me leisurely, then said, "You have no idea how much money I have to spend. I don't mean my salary, though it's a lot, but the budget I control—"

"Why are you telling me this?"

"I don't know. Not to impress you. I'm wondering why you have such an effect on me."

"It'll wear off after a while," I said.

"Maybe. I'm an experienced man though. You're different."

"Maybe your experience has just been repetition."

"You could be right. I don't look for a lot of variety. I never thought there was that much to find."

"You go to the wrong clubs."

"Is that it? Is the counterculture really full of women like you?"

"There is no counterculture anymore, Gordon, this is the nineteen eighties."

"What is it then?"

"Chaos. The random collision of souls. Just don't believe anything upfront, that's all."

"I'm a little confused."

"You should take some time off."

"That's what my secretary says."

"Take your secretary wherever she wants to go. I can't explain it to you."

"I think you're just being mysterious to tease me."

"That's part of it."

"You like to tease me?"

"You like to be teased."

When I did meet someone, like Clark, that I wouldn't have minded seeing again, his respect for the integrity of the one-night stand forced me to keep silent. Clark was a lawyer with a striking re-semblance to Anthony Perkins. I had picked him up in a popular East Side bar, or he had picked me up—it was hard to tell, our eyes met, and he slid off his stool at the same time I leaned forward, throwing a smile, blond hair, and breasts in his direction.

"Let's go, shall we?" he said, putting a ten on the bar. Oh, I'm ready for this, I thought, as he took my arm elegantly, then bent his head to whisper dirty compliments in my ear.

I stayed up all night with him. After he fucked me in every

conceivable position, with a gentle and absentminded smile, he prowled his huge, antique-filled apartment naked, his slender and sinuous body arousing a kind of romantic horniness, like a thirties movie. Clark explained to me that in the last five years all his once-great ambition had drained out of him like cheap dye out of cloth. He felt so colorless, so calm, he thought he might be devoid of personality, yet he treasured this state more than any of his showy accomplishments. He felt out of danger now. I understood this; I thought that someday I, too, might feel that way. All this intensity, this rush of sensation and obscure emotion—unpaid for emotion—was made to be given up, wasn't it? Even more than ambition, it was by its nature temporary? I admired his serenity, his gliding walk, his penis that did not mind that its owner had renounced success. Maybe someday Clark would be too poor to buy women drinks, but I didn't think he would need to. He had only to uncover himself, at least to me; he had only to touch me with his long, tapering fingers. I coaxed him to bed again and he remarked that it was our fifth time, we were no longer strangers. He said it sadly and I didn't reply.

In the morning he dressed me in one of his Italian suits, with a silk tie and a pale blue linen shirt. "Take them as a memento," he said. He escorted me downstairs for a taxi, paid the man ahead, twice what it would cost, and handed me, through the window, his copy of the *Times*.

hen fall came, Teo decided he wasn't going back to school. As soon as he said so, I knew I wasn't going either. He opened a bottle of champagne and we talked, amid increasingly helpless laughter, about how back in New Hampshire we would lead the lives to which we had become accustomed. He said he would buy a limo and chauffeur and we'd go to the Whistling Oyster in Ogunquit for lunch between classes, and on weekends he'd ride me around cruising for men while he drank bourbon and chatted with the chauffeur, a wise and cultivated man from Haiti with a working knowledge of Obeah, which we'd use to weed the native stock of the town . . .

He wrote to his parents, saying he was taking courses at the New School, thinking about a career, and working out at the gym a lot. I called Grandmother.

She wasn't upset; she wasn't even surprised. She said I could consider New York my senior year, and she'd support me. In my relief and gratitude, I told her I spent a lot of time at the Met, which was true, a lot of time browsing through bookstores — and I told her about my sexual adventures. She listened to this in silence, an even, unalarmed silence that sucked more details out of me than I had planned to give. Teo, recuperating from our celebration with a cold beer pressed to his forehead, shook his head in wonder at my honesty. "Was that really your grandmother?" he asked when I hung up.

"Of course. She's not like most grandmothers," I said haughtily, remembering her purchase of my diaphragm the summer before I met Tobias. Then she had said she didn't want to know when I was having sex, and I didn't tell her. But it was different now. I was an adult, and she herself was dating again. More important, I had to talk about it. I had to insist on what it meant to me, because it was so elusive and so strange.

"She's not like most *people*," said Teo. "I wasn't aware she understood you so well. It's uncanny." He pressed his beer can to one cheek and then the other. It was Miller Lite, Teo's morning beer. He had written to the company offering to be in a commercial, "When you want to ease into the day slowly, when even a Heinie is too rough . . ." but they hadn't answered.

"Why? You think I'm so mysterious?"

"Nahhh . . . but most people would see it as *Looking for Mr. Goodbar.*"

"I don't know 'most people.'"

"You know quite a few," he replied, snapping open his beer can and securing it to his mouth for an intensive drink. In the pause that followed he stared at me mildly, the dazed pulse at the back of his eyes in concert with his lips and throat.

"What do you mean?" I asked when I thought he could answer.

"These guys—what's their opinion?"

"How should I know? I never see them after they've had a chance to think about it."

"Poor guys. Probably don't know what hit 'em."

"It would just degenerate if I saw them again," I said.

"It'll degenerate anyway."

"Don't say that!" I wailed.

"Okay, it won't. What do I know? I'm just jealous because I can't fuck you anymore."

"I thought sex bored you these days."

"Well, I thought so, too. But you make such a good case for it. I thought drinking myself to death was fun but look at you! Mysterious affinities with strangers, passionate sex every night—"

"Not every night," I protested.

"—and you're blooming with health. No tics, no trembling, no nightmares. You sally forth like some medieval fool and come back unharmed, reeking of pleasure, pretty—"

"Honey," I said.

"Oh, don't bother comforting me. It won't work. But we did have some nice times, didn't we?"

"Yes," I said, though I wouldn't want them back. I remembered my conversation with Janey when I said that friendship was more important than passion. I was wrong. Nothing was more important than passion. Nothing even came close . . . I might never fall in love again, I thought, yet what did that matter, I was in love every night. Well, not every night, as I had said to Teo, much less than every night. The desire for a stranger built up more slowly now and I savored it longer, knowing I could satisfy it whenever, holding off— thinking in terms of rarity and timing, finding a man when I wanted him most, and not a moment before. Choosing a man with whom the bond was strongest and most fluid, a man like Clark or the fat architect, a sweet man, or a selfish man, an aesthete or a narcissist, but not an angry man. Angry men could be interesting but they were aloof, you had to figure them out by the sparks they threw off.

A West Indian of stunning beauty said to me one night, "You will remember me, girl. There's no one like me in New York City, not one person like me." I agreed. I pleased him by looking him over, inch by inch, holding his arm in my two hands, lifting his thigh, admiring the perfection of his skin, his musculature and his long bones. Each of his eyes was as large as both of mine, or almost; when he closed them his lips parted and I saw a gleam of white teeth. I poured Spanish wine into his cup and held it for him to drink.

I never knew ahead when I would look for a man. Sometimes the desire would gather all day, moody and restless, like unexplainable sorrow, and I would be assaulted at the same time by longing, and a feeling of the rightness of the world; I would stop in the middle of the sidewalk to gaze at a silhouette of buildings against the sky, jerk my eyes away, only to have them caught by a thin-bodied tree with twenty-seven yellow leaves dangling from its branches. Then the feeling would suddenly disappear, desire would go flat, I felt ordinary, which meant I felt lonely. I would go home to Teo and cook him a particularly nice dinner.

Teo drank a little less, for a while. It was an experiment, he said, now that he had nothing to look forward to but his own life, however he chose to live it. His mother had sent him a plane ticket to San Francisco and five hundred dollars, and said that would be it. I liked having him soberer; he enjoyed our dinners more. I learned to cook seafood. I made scallops with black bean sauce, and swordfish with broiled red peppers and green olive oil. We even had a sex life, although not what you'd call a romantic one. Teo would come in the bedroom while I was watching television and make me take my clothes off. He liked to masturbate while watching naked me watch the tube; he preferred that I didn't look at him. What was mostly on was the presidential campaign, and even now I can't look at Ronald Reagan without hearing Teo's hoarse voice: "Lift your ass higher. Higher, that's it, keep it there, don't move, oh, baby, what a pretty ass you've got . . . there must be something wrong with that man, don't you think? He's fucking insane."

After the election Teo went into a deep depression. He said the next war would be starting soon; he said this so often I began to think he was looking forward to it. His experiment with drinking less ceased, he drank more than ever and spent whole days and nights in bed, calling for water occasionally and spitting out streams of saliva in a bowl placed by his bedside for the purpose. He was trying to make his money last, so he never went out; he drank lying naked on the couch, listening to Janis Joplin and the Rolling Stones. His clothes didn't fit anymore but he said he went naked the better to incite the pity of God. Or me, I thought, as I waited upon him. I was afraid he would kill himself, and when I said so, he smiled. He told me that, when he was lying in bed with a hangover, he liked to imagine his own death, especially the autopsy and the burial. He didn't fantasize about his parents', or anybody's, grief. He skipped the funeral; he merely enjoyed the quietude of his body in death, its hollowing by expert hands, its slow and gentle rot.

I told him to snap out of it. I begged him to quit drinking. I called various alcohol treatment centers and they all said what I already knew, that he had to want to stop first. He didn't have much to say on

that subject, except that he probably would someday. Soon. Not yet
. . . after the New Year maybe. He thought his parents might send
him some more money for Christmas.

He did have his moments. Some nights he dressed up in an old red
silk dressing gown that had belonged to one of his uncles, and a pair
of black velvet slippers. While I drank with him, he discoursed on
the insights alcohol provided. In the drunken state, he said, he could
feel his connection with everyone in the world, he dwelt in the realm
of emotion. He didn't claim that this made him able to communicate
better, he knew that wasn't so, but he felt a sympathy for life and he
wanted to gather it all, past and future included, into his embrace; he
wanted to be with the world.

I reminded him of his hungover longings for death and he replied
yes, that was the other side of it. Didn't it seem worth it though? He
confided to me that alcohol was alive, it was truly a spirit, which is
why it was so powerful, but which also made it something you could
love. When it entered his veins, it was like a phone call from an old
friend, if you can imagine the voice in your ear continuing down and
spreading throughout your whole body.

It sounds like a parasite, I said. Yes, he agreed, but a beautiful
parasite, warm and lovely, one that you keep taking in. That's the joy
of it, you get to do it over and over.

On those happy drunken nights he would get himself to bed without
mishap and on the next day rise at noon and soak in the bath, telling
me cheerily that he might be able to, soon, look for a job.

I wanted to do that also. I was tired of doing nothing. I rarely went
out because I worried about Teo, and when I did go out, I felt more
and more embarrassed at that inevitable question, "What do you do?"
The trouble was I didn't want to do anything here. New York didn't
seem the right place to get a job. I didn't want to take the subway at
rush hour or pay a third of my income in taxes. Yet to go back to New
Hampshire was out of the question.

Teo solved the problem for me on Christmas day. I went out for a
long walk in the morning, since he was still in bed, and I enjoyed the
quiet streets so much I didn't come back until three. I found him on
the kitchen floor, passed out, the raw roast beef between his knees.
The walls and counters were sprayed with red, as if there'd been a

massacre. He'd been trying to make the borscht we were going to have as a first course, and he lifted the lid of the Cuisinart too soon. "I'm sorry," he said when he woke up. "I started on the champagne."

"You finished the champagne."

"I thought you'd like it if I made dinner for a change."

"Never mind."

"Here's your present." He handed me the ticket to San Francisco his parents had sent him. "I thought you might like getting out of here for a while."

Teo's friends Laura and Slade were in town for the holidays and I talked to them on the phone, explaining Teo's condition. Slade said not to worry, he'd take care of his old buddy. I also wrote a letter to his parents. I didn't know what they could do, but I thought they ought to do something. Teo escorted me to the airport in a cab and we kissed good-bye. "I'll let you know when I get that place in France," he said. "You can come visit."

"Okay. Take care of yourself."

He smiled. "The eternal optimist, aren't you?"

"Shit."

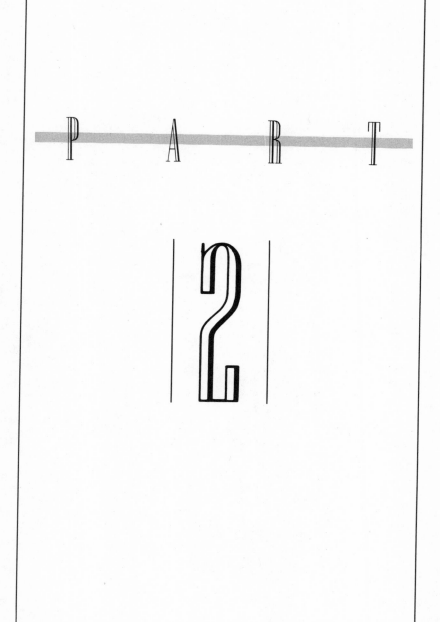

P A R T

2

My grandmother, Lally Porter, was fifty when my parents left. She was tall and angular, with a crown of white braids, and I thought her very old indeed. Her back didn't touch the chair when she sat at the dinner table, and she cut up her meat with such delicate incisions, her hands poised high above the plate she never seemed to look at. She wore scarlet lipstick, old tweed jackets, and ancient silk skirts that just brushed the tops of her black boots.

It wasn't hard for me to get along with her. The things she insisted on—table manners, courtesy, good grades at school—all came easily to me. When I was punished for sneaking out of bed at night, or putting the neighbor's kitten in the bathtub, it was never in anger but with a serene sense of justice. For the first offense I had to spend a night sleeping on the living-room floor, surrounded by the stooping, unfamiliar shapes of chairs and lamps; for the second, to sit shivering in cold bathwater while my grandmother wrapped the kitten in my towel and rocked it like a baby. The result was not to squelch my adventurousness but to make me consider more carefully. If I stole a cookie, what would she make me eat? If I smoked one of her cigarettes would she make me sleep in the fireplace, where, I was convinced, bats lived?

Whenever Grandmother punished me, she had an air of being my conspirator in a matter of great excitement and importance: the moral education of my soul. She used the word *soul* not in a religious sense but as a synonym for *character*—*character* itself not being quite mysterious enough for her. Although I didn't like being punished, of course, I felt attended to, and sometimes I thought I was being invisibly improved—invisible to me, that is; to her it would be as obvious as the difference between one of her flower arrangements and one of mine. She was like an artist who finally discovers the material that will take her imprint: she reared me with a constant, relieved benevolence.

Our Victorian house was set in the middle of a narrow strip of land between Crandall Road and Ogden. It was bordered on a third side by the Elder River, and on a fourth by a patchwork of fields and woods that stretched, it seemed to me, for miles. There was an apple orchard by the river, and many flowering trees. The front yard was vast and untended, full of dandelions and daisies in the summer, and you had to pick your way through long grass to the porch, where sat two stone dogs that my great-grandfather had brought back from England after the first war. Their purpose, I thought, was to warn people off, since nobody ever came in that way. They came, the few who did, around the back, through the garden gate, and into the kitchen with its wood stove and its gas stove, its old, upstanding sink, and its oak floors polished by our feet and many decades of spilled butter, olive oil, and bacon fat. There Agnes sat on her little low stool by the window.

Agnes was grandmother's contemporary, her old school friend. She was a short, gnomelike woman, dark-haired, cow-eyed, with weak ankles and unlucky toes. She cut holes in the corners of her black shoes to accommodate the spread of her feet, but no sooner was this done than her toes were stubbed, pricked by thorns, bee stung, or drenched in cold mud. I grew used to the sight of them swollen up in a tub of warm, salty water, or mummified in cotton. So it did not surprise me that Agnes stayed inside as much as possible. Her small, round face was often at the window, framed by the white curtain clutched under her chin, as she watched me playing in the garden. When I was very young I thought Agnes was our servant. As a teenager I speculated that she was my grandmother's lover. She was, in a sense, both of these, although she received no wages and as far as I know there was no sex between them. They were friends, but not equals.

As a young girl Agnes had admired my grandmother, had had a crush on her, and had never gotten over it. My grandmother did not allow her to get over it. I imagine her at fifteen unafraid of her power, not squeamish about using it, artful in the extreme. I imagine her simply keeping Agnes as a spider might keep a blue fly for its pretty color. Lally was the rich girl in the big house on the river. Her father was a judge, her grandfather a capitalist who employed lots of young girls like Agnes in his Massachusetts mills. Agnes's father was a farmer until 1931, when he killed himself. The family's few acres were lost, her mother and brothers found what work they could, and Agnes was taken in by my grandmother's family to finish high school and keep their proud only child company. She was never a servant, though in those days there were servants. She simply lived there, not budging when my grandmother went to Radcliffe, or when she married Bobby Porter. Agnes was there in 1938 when Lally came home for her mother's funeral, in 1940 when she came home for her father's, in 1943 when my grandfather went off to die in the Pacific and Lally moved home for good with my new born mother.

Probably, in the end, it was the house Agnes loved best. She had a fierce passion for it, surpassing even my grandmother's. She liked especially to prowl the third floor, which we didn't use. I would sneak up after her sometimes to watch her moving from room to room with a slowness that had nothing to do with her age, rubbing and polishing furniture, changing sheets and smoothing them until they lay as flat and crisp as the white envelopes in my great-great-grandfather's walnut desk. I remember the little black dustcloth she used with its hollow where her index finger fitted. She took such care for the intricate surfaces of things, a care she did not take downstairs. She had a fondness for these particular objects—guns, golf clubs, trophies—the male paraphernalia of a family whose men were all dead.

Judges, businessmen, husbands, gone with leather boots into the grave. Or simply gone. Agnes liked men and missed my father deeply.

If she was not on the third floor, she was in the kitchen. It was amazing how much she could do without getting up from her stool. She knitted, crocheted, mended, wrote shopping lists, and swept the floor with a long-handled broom. She talked to herself, and loosened her blouse, and tightened her bra strap and sighed. She fanned herself with the fly swatter. She listened to the radio and read gothic novels, telling me the plots in elaborate detail. For a while I thought everyone had illegitimate babies, or mad wives, and that most women were a good deal stupider than the ones I knew.

When I brought home my first-grade readers it was Agnes who was most interested. She would slowly open the book, its paper covers immediately crimping in her hands, peer at the few large-type sentences, look at the picture, and cackle. "What did those dummies do today?" she would ask.

"Tommy decided he wants to be a fireman, and Sally wants to be a nurse," I replied, full of delight at her dark face hovering over the glossy pages.

"Sticking needles and cleaning bedpans," she said scornfully. Then I would put the books away, leaving any homework to be done on the bus the next morning.

Several times a year, in the spring, summer, and early fall, Agnes made herbal medicines. Grandmother and I would go out on a Saturday morning, gather what she needed from the woods and garden—violets, camomile, rose hips, elder bark—and leave her alone for the rest of the weekend. She made ointment for burns and insect bites, salve for poison ivy, tea for colds and sore throats, serums for constipation, nightmares, and restlessness, and a sweet rose-scented cream that my grandmother rubbed on her neck every night. Later Tobias would ask me if she was a witch but I had regretfully to say no. No cows got sick, nor did the winds quiet when she spoke. More to the point, perhaps, she didn't believe in the Goddess but in the Virgin Mary. Grandmother teased her about this now and then, and Agnes would reply that a person has to believe in something, and Catholicism was as good as anything else. My grandmother did not agree; Catholicism was only as good as a very, very few things, none of which, she said, could be mentioned in front of a child.

Grandmother had her own opinion about what went on in the heavens. She'd become interested in outer space as a girl, listening to her aunts talk about seeing Haley's comet. She had read *A Princess of Mars* and the other novels in that series, and followed all the astronomic news avidly. It had been a custom of the house since my grandmother was a little girl to have games on Sunday evenings. Her father the judge, her mother the suffragette who received messages on her Ouija board supporting her political beliefs, would gather with friends and relatives in the library under an array of stuffed animal heads to play charades, or twenty questions. My grandmother kept up this tradition, although her game was a little different.

She would sit with a pad of ruled paper in her lap, her star chart spread out on the table before her. It was a beautiful map, blue as the night sky, with whorls of yellow and white galaxies. It was my task to pick out a star, which I did with my eyes closed, letting my finger dangle down to that distant blaze of light. Then we would name the star, taking turns each week. Agnes believed stars should have pretty names, like the heroines of novels: Annabelle, Georgiana, Stephanie. It was the only part of the game she enjoyed and we never complained about her choices. Grandmother and I were more eclectic. She, of course, had a vaster store of names than I: she named Atalanta, Odette, Quetzalcoatl and Maldorer. But she also named Robert C. Porter and Harry Soames (Harry was our mailman.) I named Chincoteague, Chocolate, Narnia, and Madelyn. Madelyn was my mother's name. Grandmother didn't like it anymore, she said; she'd done a better job when she named me Stella. Madelyn, I'm afraid, was a very unfortunate star system.

Grandmother would write the name at the top of the page and on the star chart with a reference number. Then we would decide the number of planets and which planet would be the lucky one: the one that had life, the favored child, named always after its star-mother. At this point Agnes and I would settle back in our chairs after a last glimpse out the window at our familiar Earth. Above us the bear and the elk stared from their glass eyes, no less out of place in this cozy room than they would be on Odette, planet of rushing winds and treacherous violet seas.

Agnes drank tea and I ate cookies while Grandmother began to talk. What effect would seven moons have on a small planet? What intelligence would develop in a species without foe? Could any creature adjust to perpetual planetquake? I remember the absorption in her voice as she put the planet together from her not inconsiderable knowledge of science and her much greater, I suspect, knowledge of science fiction. I understood little of her reasoning and less of her terms, yet gradually her creations became real to me, occupying their own distinct place in my cosmology. An atmosphere of continual lightning and thunder, tinted rosy red, or an arid landscape where it took a thousand years for a flower to grow—these were the pictures I grew up on, this was the unknown, as to some children it's India, or the North Pole. When Grandmother explained to me how many millions of stars there were in the universe—in this universe—it seemed to me logical that some must correspond to her imaginings, that at least one must be exactly as she said it was. So that, like Agnes, I was often bored, yet I continued to listen.

The evolution of life was always a fairly rapid thing. Only in Grandmother's dark moods was intelligence not achieved; a vision of eternal dinosaurs grazing eternal swamps, or many-jointed insects creating the perfect communist nightmare meant she'd been listening to the news again. But when she was good she gave us civilization and history.

Most of her societies I've forgotten, some I found again in college, studying the French Revolution, reading anthropology, reading fiction. Occasionally I remember whole paragraphs of her speech, it comes to me in her cultivated New England voice with its undertone of rustling leaves:

"The triad—or triangle—is probably the most stable of sexual arrangements. There is room for anger, there is room for solitude without depriving a partner of company, and there is no danger of the individuals believing they are one—unless of course they're Catholic."

"All cultures should make sure that childbearing is done out of necessity, not choice. The woman who deliberates too long on pregnancy often has the delusion that she has created the child, and whichever of the two is weakest will suffer."

"Plants and animals mutate so quickly that the cookbooks must be rewritten every year. The profession of chef is the most exalted and very few ever attain it."

Often we had a fire going, and Agnes would get up to poke it, her small, hunched figure in a fifteen-year-old dress, looking to me very much like a being from another world. She kept a handkerchief pinned to her ample bosom, wore tiny gold hoops in her ears, and a rubber band restrained an inch of her bristling dark hair. She was not impressed with my grandmother's imagination. Science she had an uneasy respect for, as long as the biological sciences were left out of it, and history and literature were all very well, but, as she said, "Nobody ever saw spacemen, and nobody ever will. Not green Martians nor eggplants that turn into cabbages."

"How do you know, Agnes? An ape turned into you."

"I'm descended from the Lady Eve and a good thing, too," she grumbled. "Somebody in this house."

"And I from Lilith," said Grandmother lightly. "And Stella from me—at least we're sure of that. Isn't it time for you to go to bed, Stella?"

"I don't know." I was staring at the orange heart of the fire, wondering if my parents had left the planet.

"Fairy tales," said Agnes. They were fairy tales—the only ones Grandmother told, and I treasure them now. But then I preferred her earthbound, although I never would have said so. She knew anyway; putting me to bed, she talked about what we'd do tomorrow, and the stars retreated to their proper places.

My favorite thing to do was to help Grandmother cook dinner. She was always merry and energetic when she cooked, as if there were a crowd of hungry soldiers on her porch instead of one listless middle-aged woman and one small girl. I, standing on a stool next to her, my face flushed by the heat of the stove, I was in my element. Food was something I understood. A handful of fresh thyme thrown into the soup threw up a cloud of scented steam for me to breathe, as I imagined Zeus and Hera breathing in the smoke of sacrificial fires. (Zeus and Hera lived on Gaea, which was a planet much like Earth.) Mushroom slices fell without a sound away from the knife, their white interiors cool and smooth as flesh. A chicken dismembered gave me an acute sense of my power as a human being, while bread rising or cream sauce thickening proved me ignorant, a novice among mysteries. Grandmother said that if a cook is careful she can't fail; the meat won't refuse to brown, or the cake batter to sweeten. But after care was taken, there was room for play. An egg could be tossed into soup, or two leftover soups could marry. The result might be a miracle, or simply a meal. I was intoxicated with the idea of breakfast, lunch, and dinner every day for the rest of my life.

A typical dinner of ours: borscht with sour cream, pork roast cooked in apple brandy and garlic, wild rice, and bitter chocolate pot de crème. It would take hours to prepare and I didn't think that unusual. Grandmother's cooking has been of more use to me than anything else I learned, but at the time it was simply a pleasure to wield the big knife or the cracked wooden spoon.

For weeks I would race home from school to peel the fruit that would marinate in red wine for dessert, or grate the almonds for a torte, or stud a leg of lamb with garlic. Then Grandmother would get bored with cooking; she would start reading in the afternoons, shutting herself up in her bedroom with a shawl around her shoulders. I would have to rejoin my friends, of which I had a great many, most of whom I didn't like.

Our property with its river, canoe, apple orchard, and flat meadows was the favorite playground of all the children under fourteen. The only way to get rid of them was for Grandmother to come to the door; they were all afraid of her. But when she was in the mood to stay in, she stayed in, and I never dreamed of telling her to go outside simply to scatter them.

I had no choice but to play their games and be bored, or keep to the woods, sneaking from tree to tree and laughing to myself when one of them was sent to find me. I had several good hiding places. The shrill, piping voice calling, "Stella! Where are you?" contrasted unfavorably with my noiseless foot upon a rock. I couldn't understand why other children liked to spend so much time together.

When I was nine or ten one of my schoolmates told me I ought to pray for my parents' return. I asked Grandmother how one went about this, and she told me to read the Bible. I suppose she thought this would discourage me, or at least distract me for awhile. I took the black book she gave me into my room and began at the beginning. I was fascinated. It had never occurred to me that the Earth had to be created, just as Grandmother's planets did. I was very grateful to God for doing it before I was born. "And the Earth was without form and void / and darkness was upon the face of the deep," I said to Grandmother.

"I know," she replied as she scooped out the bag of organs from a chicken. "Some people think it still is." She treated me to a short discourse on the idea that the material world is an illusion; soon I retreated back to my room with the Bible. I read on. I wasn't much interested in Adam and Eve, who seemed to have little personality, and I certainly didn't care about Cain, Abel, and the rest. So I started to skip around, and that way discovered the Twenty-third Psalm.

> The Lord is my shepherd,
> I shall not want
> He maketh me to lie down in green pastures,
> He leadeth me beside the still waters.

The Lord was very clear to me then — he was young and black-haired, and like Adam before the fall, he wore no clothes. He looked a little like the gardener who worked for Grandmother one summer, but didn't sweat so much.

I would repeat the first few lines over and over while lying in the field beside the apple orchard, hidden in long grass. The smell of the blossoms, the drone of bees, and the mild, blue sky all filled me with a vast well-being. I knew what it was — it was anticipation of the Lord, who was just about to appear in this grassy meadow. I would soon see him stride down the slope of the sky. He would come and lie very close to me.

What would happen then was thrillingly vague. Nothing so crude as the kisses I had seen my parents exchange, but like them. More like the kisses I gave my mother during which I always held back and felt my bones turn fluid with tenderness. Most like, perhaps, what I felt at dusk watching the pink light deepen over the fields, and the river's darkness intensify. I was content with the mystery. The joy trembling on my skin, poised for the moment when my black-haired naked deity appeared, was itself enough of a gift. I courted it with the words of the psalm, with the beauty of the spring meadow, or of pearl-gray branches in winter, loaded with pounds of snow. I courted it for years—all the years my parents didn't return.

The fall I was sixteen I met Tobias. It was a beautiful day and I was sitting in the graveyard, wondering why I'd never played hooky before. The town was so still, the graveyard especially so. Yellow leaves were scattered on the grass and the smooth, humped stones grazed like sheep under a cloudless sky. The graveyard was on my way to school and I'd turned my bike in on impulse.

I looked up from my book and there was Tobias, looking at me. He was of medium height, in his mid to late twenties, thin, dressed in blue jeans and a blue-jean jacket, with pale gold skin, dark gold, curly hair, and a short mouth that looked corseted into its voluptuous shape. "You're playing hooky," he said.

"Yes."

"I've never seen you here in the mornings."

"You come here?" Obviously.

"I walk through. I like graveyards in small towns. All the people stirring below. Wanting to get up and move back into their houses."

"They don't want to do that in city graveyards?"

"No, their houses have been torn down to build offices. They're afraid of the crime rate. Too many weirdos abroad at night." I said nothing. "Here," he continued, "I can imagine the old witches meeting for a gossip, bored with death, cheated of all the devil promised them—of course—and priding themselves on the soundness of their Puritan bones." Tobias was smiling, quite pleased with himself. I was attracted to him, so I believed in the judgment of that smile. He was charming, he was witty. "Are you here to visit a dear departed?" he asked.

"I don't know any dead people," I replied.

"Not the best company. Very shy."

"I have a lot of relatives in this cemetery, but I never met any of them. They were all dead before I was born."

"It's just as well. You probably wouldn't have liked them. I never liked any of my relations."

"Are they all dead?"

"No, but I never see them."

"Why not?"

"Because I don't like them. Have you ever come here at night?"

"I did on Halloween once, a few years ago."

"What were you doing?"

"Oh—me and some kids started to dig up Arnold Popper's grave. He didn't have a stone yet." That was the night I first drank beer.

"Did you find him?"

"Everybody chickened out." Nobody had wanted to actually dig. They wanted to hold hands in the moonlight, at a safe distance, and watch.

"Not you?"

"Well, I would have gone on but I didn't want to do it alone."

"I would have thought you were the type that likes to be alone. Am I wrong?"

"Not alone with Arnold Popper."

"How did the old boy pop off?"

"He got drunk and smashed up his car. His wife went around saying it was really the best thing since sooner or later he would have killed someone else."

"Wifely love."

"She was glad she wasn't with him. He really stank."

"Of booze?"

"No. He used to be a state champion swimmer and he was always walking by the river and falling in. He'd sink to the bottom before he crawled out and then he'd walk around with the mud all over him."

"Sounds like a charming man. So why were you digging him up? To give him a proper burial in the river? Or simply to annoy him?"

"Jody Michaux wanted to drag him out to the street, maybe to somebody's doorstep, as a Halloween prank. Ring the doorbell. But the rest of us just wanted to see him." I looked at Tobias suspiciously. He made me feel like one of them. That Halloween night, kissed by three different boys, I had felt gloriously popular, and at the same time utterly above it all. For a while I maintained that, shuttling from boyfriend to boyfriend, making fun of the ones left behind. But then I ran out of interested boys and lapsed into solitude again. I hadn't been kissed since February. "What are you doing here, in Elder River?" I asked in my best peremptory Grandmother voice.

"Writing a book."

"Really? What sort?"

"Poetry."

"Really? I love poetry." That sounded lame, so I added, "Rimbaud, Baudelaire . . ."

"You've got good taste. How did you discover them?"

"My grandmother taught me French using their poems."

"You must have an unusual grandmother. What's her name?"

"Lally Porter."

"Tell me about her."

I did so, and I told him about my parents and Agnes as well, and about school and how boring it was. He asked a lot of questions, more questions than he ever asked again, and I responded eagerly. I told him everything I could think of, and finally my name, Stella James. "What's yours?" I asked.

"Tobias Farquahr."

"Where do you come from?"

"Worcester, Mass."

"What's it like there?"

"Worcest place I've ever been."

"So you're going to stay here?"

"Until my money runs out. Then I guess I'll have to go back to teaching."

"Not high school?"

"No, I taught at U. Mass. Freshman English, where they're even stupider than they are in high school. Trying to teach them anything is like one of the punishments of Tantalus."

"That's too bad."

"They didn't like it much either." He looked at his watch. "I have to go."

"Where?" I asked, disappointed.

"Home to write." He bowed slightly and walked off. I watched him as he threaded his way through the tombstones, his body all in blue against the pale, chiseled gray, and I fell in love. It could have been just a moment's infatuation, but I clung to the moment until I fell all the way in. I was greedy for feeling in those days.

I saw him again the next day in the graveyard, not quite by chance. "Good afternoon," he said, coming up behind me and looking over my shoulder at the book I was reading. It was Rilke, *Duino Elegies*, translated by Leishman and Spender. "You don't read him in German?" he said.

"No. I don't see how anybody could learn German. Just look at the words."

"Like barbed wire, I agree. But the poems are so beautiful in translation, it makes you curious. 'Every angel is terrible. Still though, alas! / I invoke you, almost deadly birds of the soul / knowing what you are.'"

His voice soared as he quoted and it made me shiver. *Knowing what you are.* He was a stranger to me yet I knew him. I knew every inch of his visible flesh, I knew how his head tilted when he spoke poetry, and how the force of his attention came and went in his vivid eyes. I knew that my desire was a kind of hook in him, that he'd never be able to get completely away. I thought about this, sitting in silence, looking down at my open book.

"Have you ever cut your hair?" he asked.

"Not that I can remember." My hair was bright yellow and fell to my thighs. I was used to people admiring it. My own feelings alternated between pride and disdain. I grew hair better than anyone else clearly, but it was just hair.

"Don't. If it gets in your way, you can put it on top of your head."

"It doesn't get in my way. I usually braid it."

"That's good. That will keep your thoughts in order."

"My thoughts don't need order."

"Everything needs order. More and more and more of it."

I had no idea what he was talking about and said nothing. He gave me the same farewell bow he had yesterday. I felt panicky. How could this be all? It was my own fault for not saying something, for not entertaining him further than offering the picture of myself sitting with yellow hair on a gravestone, reading Rilke. It was clear that he was already thinking of something else.

"Good-bye," I said plaintively.

"Good-bye."

I was too embarrassed to go back to the graveyard. I went to the library instead, several evenings, sitting late in the violet dusk while everyone shut their books and went home. I kept an eye on the door but Tobias didn't show up. Of course, I thought, he has his own library.

I hung around town after school. I walked down each street slowly, pretending to look in the windows while I glanced out of the corners of my eyes. I learned a lot about what I could see out of the corners of my eyes, but I didn't see Tobias. I drank ice-cream sodas in Sandy's, where several of my classmates waited on tables. I enjoyed, as Grandmother might have done, the pleasure of ordering around the queen of the eleventh-grade study hall, with her proud, shiplike breasts. I wrote the story of my infatuation in a notebook entitled *Geometry*. I recorded my chills and tremors, the desire I could shoot like a billiard ball from cunt to throat to the tips of my fingers and toes. I had a new sense of my own body, strongly visual, as if I lived flanked by mirrors.

The outside was admirable, I knew, simply because it was so young. I was at an age where, while still waiting to grow up, I had reached one level of perfection. I was five-foot-six, slim, with long arms and a long neck, a narrow waist, and an ass I pretended to think too big, when such things were discussed in the girl's room at school, but which I was actually pleased with. But I was conscious of much more than the outside. I knew the sixteen silky layers of my skin, I knew my small, white fat cells and my red blood cells charged with perilous hormones; I knew my satisfied genes, sitting back now from the finished portrait for a proud look before its decay. I knew the cluster of eggs whose potential I was not yet interested in. Most of all I knew that my lust, though it flickered through all these parts and organs, was born in my brain. It was the attitude I took toward it all.

I believed in wildness and sexual anarchy, especially female sexual anarchy. This was a belief I had come to only recently; the night after I met Tobias, in fact. Swimming in the river after Agnes and Grandmother had gone to bed, I had taken off my white bikini and let it float downstream. Fish darted between my legs; the black reeds moved to and fro across my breasts, coldly touching. I thought about the men I had desired. Baudelaire. Jack Nicholson. Leroy from the Mobil station with his gap-toothed grin. Leroy had a taste for the bleached housewives from the southside apartments. He liked them in their thirties, overweight. Tobias. I had risen naked out of the water and twirled around and around on the bank, letting the wind dry me. Then I walked through the back door into the kitchen, drank a glass of milk, and climbed to bed: river nymph come out of the darkness to this part-Christian home, leaving my wet footprints on the stairs.

obias called and asked me to dinner. "I can't tonight," I said.
It was my turn to cook, Grandmother having gotten tired,
again, of the task.

"How about tomorrow?"

"Okay."

"What would you like to eat?"

"Anything."

"Well, it won't be much . . . I'll read you some of my poems."

"Great." He gave me directions, which I didn't need but listened to
anyway, then hung up. I made dinner in barely controlled excitement,
peeling and dicing turnips for a soup, beating eggs for a quiche.
Grandmother left the menu up to me when I cooked, and I always tried
to impress her. I didn't stop to think that dinner should also please
Agnes, who liked meat. Meat was too easy, I'd decided, too basic. A
quiche with spinach and scallions, that was elegance.

We ate in the dining room around a centerpiece of red maple
leaves. Grandmother sat at the head of the table, Agnes and I on
either side. I poured white wine for Grandmother, beer for Agnes, and
iced coffee for myself, then waited for Grandmother to begin.

She sat upright, lifting the silver spoon to her lips slowly. She
considered the taste, then inclined her head to me in approval. I ate,
waiting for the right moment to speak. I was still waiting when Agnes
said, "Who's your boyfriend?"

"What?"

"Boyfriend. On the phone. It was a boy." She hadn't answered the phone, but I had no doubt she could tell from the tone of my voice.

"It was a man," I said boldly. She laughed soundlessly, not displeased.

"Who was it?" asked my grandmother.

"His name is Tobias Farquahr. He's a poet. He asked me to dinner tomorrow night."

"How old is he?"

"I don't know. Twenty-five?"

"He'll be too much for you," said my grandmother.

"How do you know?"

"Unless he's stupid, a twenty-five-year-old man, especially a poet, will know just how to handle a girl like you," she said as she finished her soup and looked at me quietly.

"So what?" asked Agnes.

"He's not going to handle me," I said angrily. "You see everything as power. You always do. There are other ways —"

"Very few. We'll see. Writers are usually vain and selfish, egotistic, cruel to their wives." She listed these traits calmly, with an insufferable assurance.

"I'm not going to marry him!"

"Why not?" asked Agnes.

"Whether you do or not, you'll probably be sorry, although I certainly hope not. What does he look like?"

"He's the most beautiful man I've ever seen in my life."

"Your father —" Agnes began.

"I was afraid of that," Grandmother said. "Handsome men are the worst. They never forget themselves. I met Gore Vidal once. He came over to our table when I was lunching with Arvy Talbot. He spent the whole fifteen minutes ogling himself in the mirror."

Who cared, I thought, if Tobias was vain. So would I be, if I looked like him.

"Anyway, he invited me to dinner. Can I go?"

"Of course you can. That's entirely your business. If I warn you, it's because I could hardly do otherwise. You're entitled to the benefits of my experience." She looked at me benignly. "Scatter those benefits as you may." She spread her lean arms and I laughed. Her eyes were a cool and glittering gray, poised at a tilt in her triangular, peachy, crushed-velvet face. I cleared the soup bowls and served the quiche.

I had known I would be able to go. What grounds for refusal were there but sex, and Grandmother kept her distance from sex. It was something I'd have to learn on my own; she'd made that clear when she took me to be fitted for a diaphragm, several months earlier. I'd protested I didn't need one yet and she'd said she didn't want to worry about when I did need one. My summer body in shorts and a T-shirt had perhaps looked dangerous to her, or at least alarming. I remember her gaze flitting over me. Brown and long-limbed and gawky, I rode meekly home from the doctor's office with a square, white box on my lap.

At five the next afternoon I was riding my bicycle to Tobias's house, which was three miles out of town. It was almost dark and I kept to the center of the mostly untraveled road, more scared of the thick woods on either side than of cars. At the last stretch, when I could see the light, I leaned back on my bike, folded my arms, and glided down to the little ugly house. I knew the people who used to live there — Adelaide Cater, a relative of mine, with her lank, greenish-blond hair, wide hips, and nicotine-stained fingers. I used to see her dawdling in the supermarket, oblivious to her baby crying, as she read the labels on things she never bought. Adelaide had sold the house when Ronald Cater — known as Dogface — had left her for Mary Jordan. Adelaide took tiny Betsey to a two-room apartment in town and waited for her life to resume. A Mr. Newell from Newburyport owned the house now.

I put the kickstand down on my bike and walked up to the front door. I was nervous and didn't know how I'd be able to eat anything. Tobias opened the door before I knocked, looking down at me, the light framing him in the doorway. He was wearing jeans and a dark blue sweater, his hair bright, twisted gold against the blue. I wondered how it could be that what I desired so strongly and with such constant excitement was to him simply his body, taken for granted. No man could be vain enough to think himself as beautiful as I thought Tobias.

"Come in," he said.

The door opened directly into the living room. The powder-blue wall-to-wall carpet was covered with stacks of books, empty bottles, sweaters, empty cigarette packages, socks, and newspapers. There were two kitchen chairs in the room and he swept the books off the second one, motioning me to sit. He sat opposite me, drank from a bottle of beer and set it on the green coffee table, which, besides a standing lamp, was the only other piece of furniture in the room. "Well," he said, "so you came."

"Why not?"

"I can think of a few reasons." He didn't elaborate, and I didn't want him to. "Your cheeks are red. You look like a healthy Swiss maid."

"It's a good long ride here. Gets the blood moving."

"I should get a bike, I drive too much."

"You could walk," I said, feeling my youth as an advantage now. I was healthy.

"I do at night. But everything in this town closes at nine."

"I'd be scared walking through these woods at night. It's spooky."

"The woods can't hurt you if you don't let them. The spirits might tease and frighten, but if you're strong, they don't touch. Or you can command them, if you learn how."

"Do you know how?"

"No. I don't want to be a magician. It's enough for me to be safe, and all that requires is to admit that what you are afraid of is there, that your fear is valid, and to learn about the spirit world, especially its limits. Third, to have confidence, to assert your right to walk unmolested. Strength is always respected. Of course there are some people who will always be afraid, and rightly so, because they're weak. Their personality has no solidity to it, they're already ghosts."

"I think if I admitted that there really are spirits and things in the woods, I'd be more afraid. The only way I keep calm is to reassure myself that it's only imagination."

"To say it's only imagination is like saying, when you listen to music, you're only hearing it. The imagination is the organ with which we perceive spirits, it's our way into their world. But you're wrong to think disbelieving in them helps. It might if you really disbelieved. But you don't. You're not sure. And uncertainty can be defenselessness."

"What kinds of spirits do you think live in the woods?" I asked.

"Oh, there are all kinds. Dryads, trolls, ghosts, demons, even angels." He listed them nonchalantly. "Let me read you something." He got up and searched through the stack of books on the floor, then read me a poem by Yeats, "The Stolen Child."

"I've read that poem before," I said. "I like it. But poetry doesn't make you believe in anything."

"Of course it does. Let me read you something you've never heard." He got up again and went into the bedroom. I was still nervous. The whole conversation seemed exotic to me, but I wasn't sure that anything Tobias said wouldn't seem exotic to me.

He came back with a green folder and began to read me poems. They were mostly love poems—no fairies or angels in them as far as I could tell—rhythmic and sexy, the action obscure, fluid phrases running into each other with shifts of pronoun and place that left me confused. I tried to think of what to say but he kept reading, without pause for comment, until finally he put them down. I felt clumsy. "I like them," I said, "but I don't always understand what's going on."

"What don't you understand?"

"Well, in that last one, he's in bed with her, then she's gone, I think? And he's remembering her, or is it another woman? Or does she come back?"

"He's remembering her. Maybe it's another woman, too."

"Oh. It's really beautiful. I like your rhythms."

He looked at me for a moment with a smile, leaning his chair back against the wall. His eyes were so vividly blue above the blue of his sweater.

"But there aren't any spirits in them," I said.

"Don't you think sex is a kind of spirit? One who comes out of the woods to possess you?"

"What about when you're not near the woods?"

"But it's stronger there, isn't it?"

"I don't know." I wouldn't look at him. It was much too strong already.

"Come on," he said suddenly, jumping up. "Let's go in the kitchen and make dinner."

The kitchen had squishy green linoleum, an old refrigerator, a four-burner gas stove, yellow wallpaper, a table, a chair, and a stool.

"Soup," he said, taking a can of Campbell's Tomato out of the cupboard. "Grilled cheese sandwiches." He took the bread and cheese out of the refrigerator. I said nothing. He tossed me the can and an opener. "Open that, will you?"

I did so reluctantly as he sliced the cheese. The soup looked horrible, jellylike and orange-red, like napalm. I pushed it far away on the table. Tobias put a skillet on the flame and started to lay the sandwiches in it.

"Aren't you going to use butter?" I asked.

"This pan is seasoned. I don't need butter."

"Use some. I like it," I insisted. He looked annoyed but took a stick out and cut a sliver into the pan. The sandwiches sizzled and I thought they might turn out okay.

"How much milk do you like in your soup?" he asked.

I had never had canned soup but I said firmly, "A lot." The quivering mass melted slowly in the saucepan, turning pink when he added the milk. He stirred it with a teaspoon, then, when it was barely warm, poured it into two bowls. I put the sandwiches on plates.

We both ate quickly, like children in a school cafeteria, and didn't talk. Tobias made instant coffee and took off his sweater when he sat down again with his cup. He had no shirt on. I didn't know how to react. Was he just going to sit there calmly and perhaps in a few minutes take off his pants? I could take my shirt off. But it seemed a very odd way to go about the whole thing.

I sipped my coffee and pretended nothing was amiss. I could think of nothing to say and was afraid Tobias was bored with me. Food and nervousness had made me drowsy, and Tobias's chest had what was left of my attention. He was staring at the wall, drinking his coffee. Finally he looked at me.

"I have an Orgone Box in the back yard," he said. "Do you want to try it out?"

I was very proud of myself for knowing what an Orgone Box was.

Grandmother had the complete works of Wilhelm Reich, although I couldn't imagine her reading them. "Uh, sure. Won't it be cold, though?" I knew you were supposed to be naked.

"You don't feel the cold." He set his coffee cup down and went out the back door without another look at me. His sweater was still off and he had no shoes on. I followed him, after pausing to swallow the rest of my coffee. The taste of it was harsh in my throat as I stepped out into the darkness of the back porch. There was the sound of a small animal scurrying away from the garbage, and the sight of Tobias up ahead, a pale figure striding through the short grass. I was angry at his going ahead. I wished I had the pride to leave, but this infatuation was so strong, it utterly commanded me. Not even the sudden wind blowing through my T-shirt could chill me; there was no cold, he was right, there was no pain, only sensation, and my breasts craved sensation. I could have thrust them in a wasps' nest or a pool of molten lava and they would've found pleasure there.

I walked across the yard, stood next to him so our hips touched, and looked at the Orgone Box. It was made out of wood, the size of a large packing crate, with a panel door. "The inside is lined with aluminum," he said, "which focuses the orgone rays and directs them to our bodies. Reich discovered orgone energy in the thirties. He thought it enhanced the orgasmic potential in people, as well as curing many diseases."

"I know," I said. He smiled at me, his face foxy and pagan in the dim light, and rubbed his hipbone slowly against mine. I listened to the scratch our blue jeans made as they touched.

"We should go in one at a time," he said. I was of course disappointed. It seemed to me he was torturing me with this delay. I wanted to cry that I'd been waiting for years already, *for years*. The scent of his body was making me a little crazy, I forgot that six months ago I rarely thought about sex. "I'll go first," he said, his face intent on the orgone bath ahead. I don't think he had any idea how much I wanted him. Maybe he thought I'd be relaxed by the peculiar experience.

He took his pants off and dropped them on a bush. He wore no underpants. I glanced out of the corner of my eye, not wanting to seem too eager, but it was very dark and I couldn't really distinguish anything. Then he had the door open and was inside. I had a glimpse of him sitting cross-legged against a background of crinkly, silver foil, his body thin and riddled with a weird brilliance, like a genius in a garret. He told me to close the door and I obeyed.

I stood out there alone for a few minutes thinking about how horny I was. It went against everything I had read that a young, willing, attractive girl had to wait in the dark for a man to finish absorbing orgone energy before he would fuck her. It offended me. Yet I was also aroused by his games. It was exciting to feel desire another little while, knowing it was only going to be a little while.

I picked up Tobias's jeans from the bush where he had thrown them, pressed the crotch to my nose, and inhaled deeply. The smell was overwhelming. Denim and sweat and cock and the dirt of several weeks without a washing. I stuck my tongue through the open zipper until I felt the cold metal against my teeth. There was nothing in there, yet I could almost taste it. Stirring, responding to my tongue, uncoiling its greater thickness. I put the pants down. I was embarrassed to be alone with myself.

After another five minutes, Tobias came out. His body had an aura of silvery light, but I was beyond being able to trust my impressions. I looked directly at his penis this time, and saw the pale tube of it swing in its nest of hair as he stepped down. It was not very impressive. He put on his blue jeans and told me to undress.

I pulled my T-shirt off in one motion and arched my shoulders, then slowly unbuttoned my pants. He was standing a little to the side, and I couldn't tell if he was watching. I let my jeans fall to the ground and stepped out of my underpants. "Are you cold?" he asked.

"No."

"I was very warm inside. I felt like I was being breathed on. It's strange, I've never had quite that sensation before."

"You shone when you came out," I said.

"Yes, that always happens. Go on in now."

I went inside. He closed the door. I sat down on the foil floor and decided to try to feel this so-called orgone energy.

I sat very still, trying not to think of sex. After a while I noticed that my body seemed to be humming. Not only vibrating but actually humming—emitting sounds I couldn't quite hear. I felt like an engine in a spaceship. It occurred to me I could be moving and not even know it. Perhaps Tobias was really a magician and was sending me off to the stars to explore for him, as in C. S. Lewis's *The Magician's Nephew*.

I realized I was getting warm also, but it wasn't a very pleasant warmth. There was no one breathing on me. Of course not; he was probably back at the house, leaving me to be primed by the universe. I could feel the walls of my cunt like an empty elevator shooting up and down a dozen floors. Never finding the one floor where the people are waiting, pushing the button over and over. I began to laugh, thinking of it as revenge on Tobias, because I didn't think he'd want me laughing in gleeful dirty-mindedness in his Orgone Box. My sexual energy was fighting his army of orgones, I was flaunting my nakedness to the universe-trapping walls.

When he let me out again, my laughter deserted me. I was heavy and sore with desire. He was so beautiful, the sharpness of his cheekbones, the glint of his eyes, the glow of his skin and his red, curved lips. "How was it?" he asked.

"I felt like I was in a spaceship."

"That's all?"

"I felt a kind of tingling."

"Your body is flushed," he said. I stood still and let him look at me. He put his hand between my legs and gripped me hard. I felt embarrassed to be so wet, but in bliss at his touch. "What were you thinking about exactly?" he asked, coming closer so that his face was right up against mine, his eyes crazily radiant. His fingers slid inside.

"You."

"I know that. What about me?"

"Why should I tell you?" I asked faintly.

"Because I'm asking you too." He put his lips over mine briefly and I tasted the juice of his mouth, then he lifted them off again.

"I felt empty." He waited. "I thought about your cock." I used the word defiantly.

"What did you think about it?"

"That's all I'm going to say." He kissed me then, his tongue probing as deep as his fingers, and I wanted to fall forward without restraint, to impale myself on him forever. It was all I could do not to scream with the glory of it. Then he removed himself from me for a moment and took his pants off. Desolate, I knelt down and stroked his erect penis. It was large, silky, circumcised, and felt exactly like the ones described in *Fanny Hill*, a copy of which I had stolen from a bookstore in Boston. I held it against my cheek, then stood up and embraced him.

"Are you a virgin?" he asked, opening me with his hands and feeling me again.

"Yes."

"We should have done something with your virginity first. Virgins have great magical significance, you know. For Black Masses and fertility rites." His cock was poised at the entrance. The wind picked up and I shivered violently.

"Oh, shit," I said, "I have to put my diaphragm in."

"Don't worry, I've had a vasectomy."

"You did? Why?"

"For just such occasions," he said drily.

"You don't want kids?"

"No, I don't want kids." Then he pushed the head of his cock inside me and I gasped. He continued slowly working his way in while his lips distracted me from the pain and the wind blew harder. The taste of his mouth was exquisite. It felt as if the kissing and the fucking were happening in the same spot, the pain dissolving in that marriage. My back was cold now, naked to the November night, but I could've been lying in a snowbank for all I cared.

I stood for a long time, burning hot and freezing, held up by his gripping hands as his cock thudded into me. I felt so animal out there in the field, with the bare trees watching, as I strove to keep my balance and not lose that span of flesh. It was just the way I wanted it to be. In his bed would have been just the way I wanted it to be, too, or on the floor, or anywhere else he put me. How do people live their whole lives like this? I wondered. Within that question was the glee that I would find out.

When Tobias came I was disappointed, yet pleased at his cries. His pleasure was my achievement. I hadn't expected to come myself; I hadn't even thought about it. I just wanted the fucking to go on forever.

He stepped back from me and I shivered, feeling his semen leak onto my thighs. "We'd better go in, you'll catch cold," he said, and handed me my clothes. I clutched them to my chest and ran to the back porch. I wanted to be coddled and petted and especially kissed. I was already longing for another taste of his mouth.

He came after me and opened the kitchen door. "Did it hurt?" he asked as we stepped inside.

"Yes."

"Sorry. Well, now you've done it. How does it feel not to be a virgin anymore?" He had his jeans on and was clearing the table. I felt very naked.

"Fine. Okay. Can I take a bath?"

"Sure. The tub's not clean."

"I don't care. You want to take one with me?"

"No. I don't think so." He lit a cigarette. The acrid smoke drifted across the table at me as I looked at his lips, which spent so much of their time on ordinary activities. I wondered how long it would take me to get tired of kissing him, if he was mine. But I couldn't imagine such liberty.

I took my bath, simmering my sore flesh. I was still horny but not so wildly. Something had been quieted. I felt like a woman now and was amazed it had been so easy. I had actually satisfied a desire so intense I had thought it must pertain to something impossible.

I went over and over the memory, unwilling to let it lie for even a second. His slow working inside, his thrusts once he got comfortable, his narrow, quick tongue, his hands on my shoulderblades, his breathing, the stepped-up rhythm as he came. I separated each action, lingered over them, then ran them together again. When he first put his hand between my legs. His eyes so close to mine. The moan when he came. His breathing. . . . and so on.

Finally I got out of the tub and went back in the kitchen, wrapped in an old, stained towel. Tobias was sitting at the table, writing in a notebook. "What are you writing?" I asked.

"Just working on something. A poem I've had trouble finishing." He looked up at me from under heavy brows, the lines of concentration on his forehead aging him until I was afraid. Maybe he was thirty. I felt very girlish standing there in a wet towel. "You want to come sit on my lap?" I did and he gently took my towel off. He parted my legs and inspected what he had wrought. "Well, you look all right," he said.

"It doesn't hurt now."

"Did you bleed?"

"No."

"Girls don't anymore," he mused. "It's strange."

"I've been using Tampax for years."

"Did you bleed the first time you put one in?"

"Well, I was already bleeding."

"Oh. Right."

"But there wasn't any pain. I guess I just don't have a hymen."

"Perhaps they're disappearing as the species evolves, like tails. You have a bit of a tail," he said, feeling my ass. "Right here above the crack there's a bone that sticks out." He had turned me sideways and was exploring with enthusiasm.

"I know. I fall on it all the time and it really hurts." His finger was probing my anus. I suffered it for a minute but when he went deeper, flinched. "Don't do that."

"Why not? Don't you like it?"

"No."

"I like it. Just relax."

"Please don't." He stopped and leaned back, sighing. I pulled the towel around myself again.

"You should learn to like that."

"Why?"

"There's a lot of pleasure to be gotten there. Pleasure for you."

"Well, I'm not tired of the other way yet. Are you?"

He laughed. "No, I'm not tired of it." He bounced me on his knee. "Tell me what you do with your teenage boyfriends."

"No." He sighed again and bit my shoulder. "I have to go home now," I said.

"Let me read you something first." He read me the poem he had been working on and it was about me — "The yellow-haired girl in the graveyard / Reading" — so I forgave him his lack of romance and put my bike happily in the back of his car.

He kept his arm around me as he drove and I laid my head on his chest. When he stopped in front of the house I hesitated before opening the car door. "Shall I come over tomorrow?"

"If you want to."

"When?"

"Whenever you like."

"After school?"

"Fine."

"You won't be working?"

"It doesn't matter if I am. You can do your homework or read."

"Okay. Good-night."

"Good-night." He kissed me lightly with an undertone of amusement: Tobias found the fact that I was only sixteen not shameful or erotic, but merely funny. As if to say—someday you'll realize how far from serious sex is. I didn't care. I had begun.

he day was overcast, the fallen leaves purple and black, and the sky had that dull look of being cut into shape—a piece of felt glued between the spiky, moist branches. I rode quickly, trying to outpace my own nervousness. When I arrived and knocked, at first I didn't hear his shout to come in. I knocked again, and he shouted, "I said, 'Come in.'" He came out of the bedroom as I closed the front door. His eyes looked inward, and his face was pale. "Hello," he said, and paused.

"Am I interrupting you?"

"I'm working but come on in. You can hang around in here. I'll be finished in a while." I sat down and he gave me a quick smile. "You know, do whatever you want. Eat anything, drink anything. Read anything."

"Okay." He went back in the bedroom and closed the door. I put down my books and my jacket. It wasn't bad to be left alone. If he had kissed me first—

I walked around the room, looking at everything. There was more to see than last night. A hash pipe stood on the coffee table amid a litter of burnt matches; beside it were several open art books—Blake, Goya, Fragonard. In one of them I found a postcard of Michelangelo's *David* from someone named Peter. In another a small envelope of black pubic hair labeled *Mary*.

I smoked what was left of the hash and looked at the pictures. It was

Fragonard's *The Swing* that held me. There was such lightness and gaiety in it, yet it was so clearly a painting; no sense of the human model came through. Perversely, that made me the more wish to be her, with her fuzzy, vague curls. She was daydreaming; she'd been daydreaming for a hundred years, and she'd pared herself down to pink and blue, to a slipper flung in the air.

Abruptly, I put the book down. I felt that if Tobias came out now, I'd turn my face away. I wanted to go home, I wanted to be thirty already, lounging on red satin sheets. The dope, I thought, I shouldn't have smoked it. It made me shy. I got up restlessly and prowled the allowed rooms of the house, avoiding his door. I inspected a second, small bedroom, empty except for the lingering smell of baby, the bathroom with its harsh, blinking light, and the kitchen. On the counter were bottles of saki, crème de menthe, vodka, slivovitz, Southern Comfort, and red wine. On the shelf above the sink, ginger, camomile, curry powder, and vitamin E. In the cupboard, tomato soup, spaghetti, sardines.

In memory of Janis Joplin, I took a swig of Southern Comfort, and then another, licking the sweet syrup from the corners of my mouth. I composed a meal in my head: Bloody Marys à la Campbell's soup, spaghetti with a slivovitz-and-vitamin-E sauce. Not being hungry, I took another swig, then screwed the top on tightly, alarmed at the rush of blood to my cheeks.

The green linoleum floor seemed wavier than ever, the color of seasickness. I sat down at the table, looking out the window to the small, leaf-covered yard. The Orgone Box looked, from here, like nothing but a shed. This was my first taste of adulthood and here I was, in a house far more typical of the life of the town than the one I grew up in. I couldn't see how Tobias could bear to live alone. The dreary November sky crept right up to the window.

Furtively, I took off my blouse. Near enough to feel the chill through the glass, my pale chest, naked in the darkening kitchen, wobbled uncertainly. I remembered dressing in my closet at thirteen, so worried Grandmother or Agnes would see what was growing. It was so unlike the imperceptible lengthening of arm and leg, this outward try, without bone or sinew. As if all my unreasonable longing had taken shape, an infinitely girlish shape of pure expectancy. I knew that they were beautiful and the beauty wouldn't last. Unlike arm and leg they had nothing to lean on; the flesh would fall with its own weight and feed the next generation, or nobody.

But now they were beautiful. Tobias had not yet touched them. Perhaps he never would.

I hadn't heard him come in. His hands were on my shoulders, shocking them with heat. "Sorry to keep you waiting," he said.

"Oh . . ." I still looked out the window, where I could see his reflection, blurred and fiery against the backyard. I breathed in the acrid odor of his clothes, permeated with hashish and tobacco, and, underneath, the melodious, sweet scent of his body.

"Is there someone outside?"

"No."

"This is for me then?"

"I don't know." He ran his hands lightly down my sides and then up my back, kneading the muscles around my spinal cord. My skin shivered at his touch and my breasts pointed at the window. He reached one hand down and lifted me off the chair.

I was pressed against him as his hand snaked between my legs and insinuated under the damp cotton of my panties. One finger, then two. Our mouths touched, then his tongue was inside; then he broke off the kiss to bite my neck. I squirmed but he had me by the crotch so I leaned back, away from his teeth. He laughed while I bent back farther, laughing too, held up by his two hands sandwiching my ass. He let me go. "You want a stint in the Orgone Box?" he asked. "I think it turns you on."

"No." I didn't want to go out into that cold field again. Nor the hot foil room either. That virgin fuck, that was fine, but now it was different. Now he would love me.

"Okay." He pushed me ahead of him and I hobbled, my skirt swirling around my knees, my panties inched down my thighs by Tobias's quick fingers as I walked. They fell and I kicked them off, then stood, waiting, by the door to his bedroom. "It's too messy in there," he said. "Papers everywhere. Come here."

He was undressing himself, looking at me under his heavy brows and enjoying his effect on me. He was slow to pull back the tongue of his belt and free the pointed, metal prong. The belt sagged open, he slid it from the loops and dropped it carelessly to coil on the floor. His jeans had a buttoned fly which made no sound as it was undone. He took them off and was naked underneath. I went over to him, embarrassed to look directly, from any but the most intimate distance, at his penis.

I was fascinated by its crookedness, its bend to the left. Once he was inside me, I thought, no one could guess its direction, there was no geometry that could predict the line of our joining.

I stood, nuzzling the tip of it with my thighs. I thought to tease him but then he kissed me and put his hard, dry fingers on my ass. As his lips opened mine, and his hands sank in my flesh, I knew he was more than just a man. He had alloys of gold in his bones. He had secret contact with angels. He had a spark of Promethean fire.

We fucked on the living-room floor, Tobias displaying all his artistry of motion. I wondered how many men fucked like this, dipping in and out with the rhythm of oars in water, then twirling sideways like a screw, then plunging ahead—all of it calculated smoothly to excite, all of it paid great attention to by that smiling open-eyed face. I wondered if I would ever learn the female counterpart, the subtle roll and pull of my hips I was as yet too insecure to attempt.

Tobias's kisses were the most passionate part of it all. Over and over he explored behind my teeth and under my lips, met my tongue with enthusiasm, unabashedly licked and swallowed. In turn, I sucked on his mouth and thought I was sucking on his heart. Boys I had kissed before had not tasted so individual. Tobias had such a complicated flavor, like something that had aged for centuries.

"You're so tight," he said with a happy sigh.

When he had come, he went out of me, and into the kitchen. I watched through the open door as he heated up saki in an enamel pan. I was still full of desire but, like the day before, appeased by the thrill of experience. I was learning the ways of his body, soon I would know everything.

Tobias came back with two cups of the hot wine. "For the pain," he said.

"It didn't hurt this time," I said, "just a pleasant sort of ache."

"A pleasant ache? Well, perhaps—"

"What?"

"Perhaps someday pain will become pleasure." He looked at me over the rim of the brass cup: those curious, intent, electrical eyes.

"I doubt it. I'm not a masochist."

"Those words—*masochist, sadist*—they're political. There's no need to categorize people like that. They make sex a matter to be controlled—this is good, that is sick."

"Well, isn't it sick to want to be hurt?"

"Everyone wants to be hurt. Why do you read tragedy? You suffer with the hero but you feel an uplift at the end. He dies so you can reflect on the significance of his death. It's the same with sex. Pain is fascinating when it's not too much, when you're not in jail being beaten by thugs. Pain teaches you."

"I feel enough pain as it is."

"Then, how about inflicting some?"

"Okay, where do I start?" I asked sarcastically.

He smiled. "Where do you want to start?"

"On you somewhere."

"Go ahead." He watched me with his catlike grin. He had drunk all his saki and his lips were warm and pink. I should've punched him in the jaw. I thought of it, saw the bone break and the blood pour out, and I wanted to cry. I pinched his belly.

"You can do better than that."

"I don't want to," I said, sulking. "Hurting people doesn't turn me on."

"Women always say that. I wonder if it's true? They certainly hurt people. Maybe it gives them thrills of another, nonsexual sort. That's possible. I'll have to think about it."

"I don't know about other women," I said. "I'm sure I'd like to hurt somebody out of revenge, although maybe not physically."

"I'm not talking about revenge. Or jealousy. I'm talking about a pure, unmotivated—or un-personally-motivated—desire to inflict pain."

I said, "Since women always have a good motive for whatever pain they might want to inflict, it's going to be hard to carry out any experiments. But is that what you like? I haven't noticed you beating me up. Is that coming next?" I almost wished he would try it. I could take him.

"No. I don't have much of a taste for it myself. I prefer receiving it, in small doses, as a kind of stimulation."

I heard him say this; I can even remember how soft and defenseless, yet mocking, his naked body looked. But I immediately put it out of my mind. It didn't jibe with my image of a man who had secret contact with angels. I finished my saki and told him I was going to take a bath.

"You certainly are clean. You know, some people like to keep the scent of their lovers on them as long as possible."

"I can always come back for more," I replied, though I felt a keen grief at his words. He was right, I was going to wash off this second skin made of his hand prints and lip prints, of his sweat, breath, and semen. I didn't want to be clean. I wanted the rumble of the bathwater and the shut door and the numbing heat.

I took my bath and was lonely. The bathroom was small and the walls were crumbling and the high window was crusted with dirt. He would never love me. There was no possible way, no charm I could exhibit that would do more than please him. I could please him but I couldn't tempt him. I had no power, none at all.

I stayed in the water a long time, perversely washing off every trace of him. When I was done I smelled like the brown, liquid, peppermint-flavored soap he used. I knew that while I felt helpless in the grip of this infatuation, at the same time I was sustaining it. I was doing it, even if I couldn't stop. I decided, as I dried and dressed myself, that I would just have to do it better.

Tobias was reading aloud Blake's "The Sick Rose" when I went back in the living room. "Oh Rose, thou art sick, / The invisible worm / That flies in the night, / In the howling storm, / Has found out thy bed / Of crimson joy, / And his dark secret love / Does thy life destroy." He half closed his eyes and said, "There's such glee in that poem, don't you think?"

"I'm not sure. It depends how you read it. You read it with glee."

"It's like Milton's elaborate descriptions of Hell—he loves it. Scat himself couldn't do better."

"Scat?"

"One of his many names. Lucifer. The Prince of Darkness."

"Is that why you say scat to cats?"

"Possibly. Possibly. They would of course know the name, being familiars, and be afraid of it, as of their master."

I thought a minute. "I don't think Blake wrote with glee," I said. "Though perhaps he liked the worm."

"Of course he liked the worm. He loved the worm. The worm is the adventurer. The worm is the action. Poets thrive on destruction—it's all they can really get a handle on. To describe creation is much more difficult, and usually sounds self-serving. One misses the terror of it. Think of Shakespeare's sonnets—they always get boring when he starts in on his own powers. Smug. But we can all understand the worm and his cohorts. Listen."

He read to me for an hour in English, French, and Latin. I told him I didn't understand Latin, but he kept on, translating roughly as he went. From poems by Milton and Baudelaire, which easily demonstrated his thesis, he progressed to love lyrics—Yeats and Catullus—which also did so, almost. I was sitting with my legs tucked under me, falling asleep. I did like the poems; I only wished he would stop for a while.

There was no point where I could interrupt. Before he had finished a poem, he had picked up the next book and would recite the ending of the first from memory while finding the new one. His excitement impressed me, yet my attention wandered back to sex. As it had the day before, every moment of our fucking went through my head again and again, each time with a jolt of pleasure that showed no sign of fading. Tobias sat smiling, like a skinny, sexual Buddha, with his back curved over the books, his expressive face reading the poems as if they were lakes he was diving into, as if he could feel the words break against his skin. He had turned the lamp on and it lit up one half of him, showing me his golden complexion, the smooth muscles, and one dark nipple. I could make out the faint marks of my fingers on his stomach, and the remains of our sex in droplets between his thighs. I strove to fix all this in my mind instead of listening to him because I could always read the poems for myself.

Finally I said, "I have to go home. Grandmother expects me for dinner."

"Shall I give you a ride?"

"No, I can take my bike. It's not late."

"Okay." He watched me dress for a moment. "You won't be afraid of the dark?"

"No." I didn't know whether I would be or not, but I wanted to be alone, to think in the silence, to prepare myself. It might take a long time, I thought. I pulled on my boots and zipped them.

"Wait a minute." He got up and went into the other room. He came out with a black pen and a blank piece of paper, then sat down and drew a circle with another circle inside it, like a wheel, then a cross inside that. He lettered Greek words around the rim and inside the cross. "This will keep you safe." He folded it and put it in my shirt pocket.

"What is it?"

"The Sixth Pentacle of Jupiter. 'It serveth for protection against all earthly dangers.'"

"Oh. What do the Greek words mean?"

" 'Thou shalt never perish.'"

"Thanks," I said.

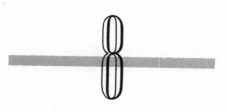

I went over to see Tobias every day. Grandmother didn't mind if I wasn't home for dinner anymore, she left me alone. She and Agnes ate fruit and cheese, crackers and sweets, nibbling like mice from hour to hour. It was odd climbing the stairs, all the house lights off except the lamp in Agnes's room. Still feeling Tobias between my thighs, I stopped in the doorway to say good-night to them, two old ladies in nightgowns framed against the black window, heads close together as they bit off pieces of candied ginger. I stood in my blue jeans and boots, seeming, even to myself, unnaturally young. Grandmother would smile at me and say, "Good evening, Stella."

"Hello, Grandmother. Agnes. Did you get enough to eat? Should I make some tea?" She inclined her head and I saw their teacups, or the fluted crystal glasses she used for liqueur, among the clutter on the bedside table. "Is there anything I can get you?" I was so helpful, it must have been annoying.

Agnes would look me up and down, and then make a remark like, "You don't look very well. Your eyes are all swollen up," or, "Your shirt is on inside out," or, "It's a good thing they don't wear miniskirts anymore, your legs are so thin." I never replied to these criticisms. I knew she was pleased with what was happening. She would peer at me with her monkey eyes and twist her fingers through her gray hair with abandon, like an inspired deaf queen. At her side

Grandmother in ancient silk watched me coolly. I did not want to know
what she was thinking. But there were simpler things between us
than the matter of Tobias, and when she picked a cigarette out of the
pack on the bedside table, I was always there with a match, leaning
forward so she wouldn't have to move, bending so close I could smell
the rose-scented neck cream she used. She always thanked me for my
courtesy with a smile—that smile of old age, which contains so much
a teenager can't quite understand. She wasn't even sixty, but she'd
been practicing for years.

School didn't exist for me that winter. The teachers' voices were like
birdsong, my classmates' very nearly so. I treasured my daylight
hours as hours of solitude, hours to contemplate the evening ahead.

I should have had a girlfriend. Someone who didn't like Tobias, or
like the sound of him, so I could defend him yet be secure that my
good friend didn't think him worthy of me. But I ignored the girls I
knew and by the time I got to Tobias's, my solitude was wearing thin; I
was lonely. I thought of my mother being danced around in my father's
arms. I remembered her pushing him away because she preferred to
look out the window, then her coming back and displacing the book on
his lap.

Tobias was always working when I arrived. I could've gone home
and not come until he was ready for me, but it was impossible to stay
away. I preferred to sit alone, inhaling the stale smoke of Turkish
cigarettes and punk, than to be aware, as I was all day, of the miles
between us, the long road through the woods. I would put my books
down quietly and sit on the floor, sit almost motionless, while my
nerves sang, reaching high, clear, indeed weird notes; I felt slightly
mad, as if I were waiting for a ghost.

When he came out of his room, he would sit down with a sigh very
close to me and light a cigarette. His thinness, the flatness of his
chest made my eyes swim with longing. I would take the butt from his
lips and smoke a little. He would smile at me in greeting and I would
think, I have him now.

Of course I didn't have him. What I had were long afternoons in his
living room where heavy black drapes I had liberated from Grand-

mother's attic shut out the winter, where the heat, turned wastefully high, rattled and hissed its way out, and the blue carpet was grainy with crushed match heads and cracker crumbs.

Tobias ate mountains of saltines spread with strawberry jam when he was stoned; otherwise he viewed the kitchen as a sort of chemistry lab and was interested in grotesque effects. An omelet he served me once was cooked in Gallo Hearty Burgundy. The resulting violet-brown stain on the eggs showed up their lacy quality; they looked like an antique collar horribly metamorphosing into flesh. He ate them cheerfully; I refused.

I had the poetry he read to me or played on his stereo: Allen Ginsberg reading Blake, Tennessee Williams reading Hart Crane. I had sessions in the Orgone Box where, naked and lonely, I admitted to myself that it might be years before I found real love, that if I had any character I would wait. But then, I thought, I had not been brought up to have character, but to have soul. Grandmother's New England was the New England of the Transcendentalists and Emily Dickinson; in fact we were distantly related to Dickinson and my grandmother read me her poems like family letters. "The Soul selects her own Society— / Then—shuts the Door— / To her divine Major-ity— / Obtrude no more—" Such a soul, being totally in the dark, takes a long time to learn.

I didn't have his bed. It was covered with manuscripts he didn't want to disturb. He had shown it to me once, so I could see the poetry stacked there and that it was not, anyway, big enough for two. It was an iron bed, very high off the ground, and narrow. He had bought it from a widow in South Boston for fifteen dollars. I questioned him further, being determined, and he admitted she had slept in it with her husband for thirty years. The weight of that silenced me: thirty years in bed.

He decided to give in to me and lifted the papers off. I was shy in that austere room, where there was nothing else but the manuscript. He led me to the bed where the wall lamps aimed harshly and spread me out on the cold sheets, and only pride kept me from saying that I would prefer, after all, to do it in the living room.

The bed was fine for fucking, but afterward Tobias fell asleep and began to nudge me off it. The crimson blanket wrapped tightly around him in the valley while I teetered on the ridge, glancing at the long way down to the floor. Tobias flung an arm out and I jumped before I could fall, wondering which it was, wife or husband, whom the bed had rejected for thirty years.

What I had was his conversation. From the time I arrived and he smoked his first cigarette, he quizzed me relentlessly on what I knew about this or that poet, idea, movement. At first I was embarrassed at my ignorance but soon realized that the questions were only a formality, he would have explained it all to me anyway. I nodded intelligently while he set forth the history of surrealism, or gnosticism, or pornography. I learned so much that, later, in college, everything was easy — so easy I thought I must be missing something. It occurred to me more than once that Tobias was just like my grandmother, but I didn't really believe it. I was so used to being lectured at.

The feeling of being in Tobias's house, anticipating sex, listening to him talk, drinking Southern Comfort from a teacup while the snow fell outside, tilted my sense of reality so that I was receptive as I would never be again. I believed in magic. From what he had told me, I had concluded that magic works by the operation of the will, and I thought my will second to nobody's. Every time I kissed him, every time I looked at him, I was bathing him in my love, I was radiating it from the walls of my cunt while his crooked penis pursued its crooked course. I still didn't have orgasms; I couldn't concentrate on myself that long. I took pleasure — a swoony, continual-first-thrust kind of pleasure, and my body acquired the habit of his weight, his odor and style. Yet more and more I devoted those moments to pure command, to sending out mental nets with which to entangle him.

My most intense sexual feelings came when we were not fucking, but were just about to. The anticipation was the event, or rather the savor of the event. Sitting in the green kitchen, as I sometimes did, listening to the raccoons on the porch and the trees in the wind, to the hum of the refrigerator and the whistle of the tea kettle, while Tobias wrote poetry in his room, I was content. What else would I have done if I hadn't waited with longing, if I hadn't believed my desire bound us together?

He had an adult life — those poems that would someday be published. I had my infatuation, my lust always ready to become love, or at least to make the promises of love—to swear fidelity, to give away the world. I believed I could win any contest of amorous feeling, that this rapture was a rare achievement, and whenever we talked, when the subject came up, I was always on the side of passion.

Tobias wasn't exactly against passion, but his admiration was of a different order than mine. After reading one of Yeats's poems written for Maud Gonne, he would burst into laughter. He seemed to revel in his knowledge of that love's sad history, yet he went back to the poems often, he was very fond of them. When my argument threatened to become more personal—though it was never so personal as a declaration—he would sit back, eyes narrowed and lips pursed, in an attitude of critical listening that made the words dribble out of my mouth half formed.

He said to me once, "When you calm down, in a few years—"

I interrupted before he could go any further: "What do you mean, 'calm down'? What makes you think I'll calm down? I won't. I'll never be as apathetic as you are."

"I'm not apathetic," he said calmly. "I'm drugged."

"It's the same thing."

"Not at all. I merely don't express my emotions. Sometimes I mean to."

I looked at him suspiciously. The hash pipe was resting between his curved red lips like an instrument whose music I was not allowed to hear. I didn't smoke with him; it depressed me. "What emotions do you have?" I said.

"Mostly, fear."

"Of me?"

"No, not of you. You want one concerning you?"

I didn't answer but gave him a look clearly indicating my lack of patience with his stupidity.

"I feel very fond of you when you're in the bathtub," he said slowly. "I want to come in and scrub you."

"But you don't."

"No. You go in there to get rid of me, don't you?"

I hesitated. "I don't know . . . Why, is that why you want to come in?"

He sighed. "Probably. I'd probably look through the keyhole if there was one. You know what I dreamed last night? I was on the back of an eagle, flying high above the mountains, it was night and I was naked, and then I fell off. All I could think of as I dropped to earth was why didn't I fuck the eagle while I had the chance."

He usually drove me home well before midnight. I was always sleepy so I didn't mind leaving, although the hour or two after sex was in some ways the pleasantest time we spent together. No more reading aloud, no more working, no more waiting. It was I who did most of the talking, telling him stories about Elder River. Whatever I couldn't remember I invented, always erring in favor of scandal and degeneracy. Madness, incest, murder, that was what we liked. He lit candles and lay on his back, smiling up at the ceiling, listening. When my stories gave out, he would lie there in the silence, his thin chest in its blue sweater breathing so shallowly. I watched him, the candles burning lower, until he leaped up and picked his car keys off the table.

Tobias drove slowly and carefully, with both hands on the wheel. He looked very much older than I; he was twenty-seven. I wanted to insinuate myself between the windshield and his face, but I sat quietly. In the car, while the car moved homeward, I understood briefly the value of discretion. I didn't bombard him with telepathic lust. I looked at the cold trees and the caked snow glinting on the patches of raggedy town, trailers, and mailboxes, then the Sunoco station, the Mini-Mart, and Union Street where the dogs always barked. What Grandmother called the new section, though it was older than I. We stopped at red lights and stop signs when the streets were empty, pausing for long moments of law-abidingness, Tobias's fingers tapping on the wheel.

We were almost equals during this ten-minute ride, and when the car pulled in my driveway and Tobias, after lifting my bike out, put his hands on my shoulders and kissed me good-night, we were equals. He bent down in his black coat, his lips pressed on mine, already cold, and I felt the weight of the house at my back and kissed him sweetly, bestowing on him my young, uncorrupted breath.

. . .

In March, Agnes discovered that she had breast cancer. The doctors operated swiftly and told her she had every chance to get well. They could see no more cancer in her. She didn't believe them, saying she'd never known a doctor to be right in her life. She told stories of young women given hysterectomies by mistake, of nerves cut during an operation that left a boy with a curved, clawlike hand, of faces sewn up into wolf-snarls, and mysterious diseases transmitted by a doctor's touch. A woman she used to know, she said, married to a doctor, suffered from rashes and chest pains and tingling pains in the feet and every time he came near her, her symptoms worsened until he died, when she finally got well. Grandmother didn't scoff at these tales; she said they were mostly true, just as doctors' everyday livesaving was. But Agnes had breast cancer, and neither of them knew any home remedies for that.

Agnes believed she would die in six months or a year. I think she didn't understand how one could not die after losing a breast. Breasts were vital organs, ones she never used in the ordinary way, but which had some necessary function she was not surprised doctors knew nothing of. Agnes's breasts were such a large part of her. They thrust out so far in front that when she was standing she could see nothing of her lower body. She had to buy dresses carefully to accommodate them and when she was naked, I'm sure she couldn't move without them lurching in response. When she was young, she must have been whistled at and teased; at fifty-seven they crept down her belly, no longer beautiful perhaps, but her own, and formidable.

She lay in bed, her face thinner than I had ever seen it, the dark fuzz around her mouth more noticeable than ever before. Her eyes were very bright and she had difficulty speaking at times. Just depression, said the doctor cheerfully, shock, all that. She's a strong girl, she'll get over it. She's in mourning, said Grandmother.

Ha Ha! In mourning, yes that's it. She's scared, said my grandmother. Well, yes, said the doctor.

I sat by Agnes's bedside and her small, plump hand reached out for mine. She had rarely touched me before. We were not affectionate with each other, I had always thought she didn't love me, but her comfort at my presence was obvious, and I was flattered. Often she was silent, lying not asleep but with her eyes closed in her hot, rosy-pink bedroom. Agnes slept in a single bed, under many pink and yellow blankets, with a mended old lace spread on top. Beside the bed was a table with a fringed lamp and a faded pink and silver chaise longue covered with magazines. The wallpaper was darker pink, flocked with baskets of flowers, the Chinese carpet blue and white, the white yellowed in places. When my grandmother was a girl, this was the guest room. It was smaller than the others on the second floor, only half the size of Grandmother's. The dark furniture was a set, which pleased Agnes but made it less beautiful to my eye. The windows, like those in my grandmother's room, looked over the orchard.

As the weeks passed, Agnes began to talk to me. The belief that death was near loosed images: rotting corpses, fire, worms, darkness, freezing cold. Everything but nothing, of that she couldn't conceive, although she seemed to have no hope of Heaven, nor did she mention sin or guilt. The place she imagined had no time or law that I could discover; it was a horror story, a haunted world where the dead walked through each other's bones.

I was impatient with this. My idea of death was glorious — "Yea, though I walk through the valley of the shadow of death / I will fear no evil." I thought her attitude gruesome. I understood that she was afraid, and I was sorry for her, but I didn't, after all, expect her to die. The doctor said she wouldn't, and, besides, I just didn't think she would. As she droned on about the possibility of the soul being trapped in the body, aware of every wriggle of the worms, I thought about reading her something from the Bible, something uplifting. "Blessed are the meek / for they shall inherit the earth"? "Thy two breasts are like two young roes . . . Oh, my beloved"?

I knew I could find words to comfort her. But I was greedy, they were my own. The Twenty-third Psalm, with its thread of joy, seemed to belong to a moment of my time earlier than I could remember.

Though I offered Agnes none of the joy of those words, she took it anyway. After listening to her nightmares for three months, I could no longer read the Bible without thinking of death. Too much — everything — had been stuffed beneath the skin of beautiful language, I didn't think it could contain it all. Agnes was sick; it was a time for calm rationality, for the family — what was left of it — to stick together.

I asked Grandmother why Agnes's brothers didn't visit her. She said they used to, but Agnes had gotten angry at their attempts to sponge off her—Grandmother—and told them she was no longer interested in their lost jobs, their divorces, their drinking problems. Since her illness they had called once but she was still angry at them and refused their sympathy. Grandmother was very glad of that; they were a vile lot, she said, whining about family but caring only for themselves. They had put their own mother in a state nursing home, though Grandmother had lent the eldest several thousand for home care. He had spent it, she believed, on a beatnik whore named Elvira.

My grandmother ran the house alone that spring. She didn't want any help from me. She cooked simple meals and filled the downstairs with flowers and violin music. Yet Agnes did not walk through the downstairs rooms, which were vibrant with music and bursts of color. She stayed in bed, hearing only a thin layer of sound and feebly admiring the blossoms that wilted in her hot room.

Of course I saw Tobias less often than before but made up for it with increased passion. I ground my body against his, learning moves even more spectacular than his own. I thought soon I'd have an orgasm. I knew I could do it if he touched me with his hands, but I didn't want that. I wanted our fucking to do it all, I wanted him to be supporting himself with his hands and looking down into my eyes when I came.

Tobias was interested in my stepped-up passion; it confirmed several theories of his. One had to do with the presence of death—I didn't want to hear about it—the other about the effect of the Orgone Box, which we still used from time to time. I asked him if he thought I should bring Agnes here, to be cured by it. Reich had claimed it worked on some cancers. "Of course," he said. "Would she be willing?"

"Probably not."

I asked her anyway. "No," she said.

"Why not?"

"No."

"It might work."

"I stink," she said. "Can't you smell it? Like garbage. Like old turkey soup." She looked up at me, her brown, bulging pupils reminding me of lumps of gristle, of jellied poultry fat, of leftovers in little white jars. I stared at her, stricken, and she laughed.

"You don't stink," I said.

"I do inside. I can smell it. There's rotten parts and there's pure parts. There's more rotten parts now. I don't want them. It would be like bringing the dead back."

"But Agnes—" I didn't know what to say.

"Tell me something." Her face was suddenly coy. She looked like one of those fairy babies, changelings, which are said to be born elderly.

"Yes?"

"What's it like when that writer-man puts his thing in you?"

I was stunned. "I don't think I can describe it. It's great."

"They always said we wouldn't like it. My mother said so. But I used to listen—your parents' bedroom was right next to mine, you know."

"So?" I asked unwillingly.

"Your mother used to squeak like a mouse. 'Eek!'" She made a sound I couldn't imagine my mother, or anyone else, ever making to express pleasure. "Your father would grunt, at the end, and she would tell him to be quiet. I used to listen."

"You shouldn't have."

"Why not?" Her doughy face with its little raisin eyes peered up at me. "They didn't have to live here if they didn't want to."

"Well, they didn't very long," I said, wondering if it had been Agnes, after all, who had driven them off. She saw what I was thinking.

"Oh, they didn't leave because of me. It was her. They wanted to be somewhere they could stay in bed all day and not have her looking at them funny at the dinner table."

"What about me?" I said.

"Oh, you were growing up. They didn't like that. Your mother wanted to always be eighteen. Your father was going to take you with them, but she talked him out of it."

"How do you know that?" I asked in shock.

"I heard them talking the night before." As I thought about it, I was less surprised. He always did what she wanted. "She said, 'I think she's going to take after Mamma.' She was afraid of that, you see. She thought Lally was a witch and you were her little spy."

"But Daddy wanted me to go?" I asked faintly. The whole conversation was very strange to me. I really couldn't remember them well at all. This didn't lessen their importance—rather increased it—but it did tend to make my emotions seem abstract, permanent things in my mind I could approach or keep my distance from.

"Oh, yes. He said, 'She's my daughter.' But he never could do anything with Madelyn."

She cackled again, her old-fairy face gleeful at my anger. "That's a man for you! That's a man for you! I'm glad I never got stuck with one. He'd be here now with his loose teeth and his hairy nostrils . . . Your mother was always wild. I thought you'd run away after them the way you mooned about."

"I was only five," I said.

"Nobody ever looked for them. That was probably a big surprise. They run all that way with nobody on their tail."

" 'Run all that way' where?"

"I don't know. I heard them arguing. She said Paris. He said Texas. She said Spain. He said California. She said New York. Who knows?"

"I could look for them now," I said, not meaning it. I felt a deep embarrassment at the thought of my gawky, sexual, sixteen-year-old body intruding on those lovers in their faraway life. I wanted to find them, but not as I was now. I would have to be much older.

"Don't waste your time," she said.

"Good-bye. Don't forget to call me. Okay?" They assured me they would not. Grandmother was taking Agnes to the hospital in Boston for another series of chemotherapy treatments. She'd already had two; the cancer, as she'd predicted, had come back. It was October. As I looked at her through the car window I knew she would die. Her face was dry and wrinkled, her body stick-thin and yellow, the flesh like wads of old cloth, decaying. I hadn't noticed it was so bad until just that moment.

"Good-bye," I said again as Grandmother started the car. She had her luggage in the back seat. She was planning to stay at a hotel near the hospital for the duration of the treatments, as she'd done before. She assumed I could take care of myself. I'd won my driver's license over the summer, and Agnes's car was left for me.

It was a snowy Tuesday morning and I was afraid. It had nothing to do with being alone. I had been alone before. But all of a sudden Agnes's illness seemed sinister, dangerous, not only to her but to me, as if her months in bed had acted as bait to lure death into our house. Mightn't he still linger here, witless, cold, confused by her prompt departure, fastening on me instead? My reason wasn't equal to this first death of my life, this coming death, this properly attended death. All the apparatus devised to deal with it seemed horrible to me. Better to expose her on a moonlit hillside in the snow. If it was me, that's what I'd do. I wouldn't go in the hospital. I wouldn't stay here. I couldn't stay here.

I got in Agnes's car and started it. I would go to Tobias's, although it was still morning and I never went until after school on weekdays. Surely he owed me something by now, some comfort. Even if I mentioned nothing—I wasn't sure he was the right person with whom to discuss death—he would distract me, he would be there.

Agnes's car was a dark blue Cadillac, old when she bought it five years ago, low and wide, gliding smoothly as a shark down the hill. I had to sit up straight and squint to feel safe in it, my eyes flickering, as I had been taught, from windshield to rear window and out the sides, scanning every intersection, driveway, and bush for creeping cars, bikes, dogs, children, suicides, falling trees, disabled helicopters. For the unexpected, Mr. Cobwallader, my driving instructor, had said. The unexpected.

I stopped short at the red light on Garden Street, the car idling speedily beneath me. I knew that was wrong but forgot what to do about it. It made me uneasy, and when the light changed I lifted my foot instantly from the brake. I realized just in time that there was a little white-haired lady still crossing in front of me. Her hair was like the cocoons of snow on the pine branches, lumpy and glistening, and she wore a faded violet overcoat with a toffee velvet collar. She smiled at me as she picked up one foot after another, her ankles trim and translucent under sheer stockings. Her big face nodded when she smiled, covered with wrinkles yet still fresh and pink. She trotted on. My hand trembled on the steering wheel.

I drove through town slowly until the houses gave way to trees, and I dared to go a little faster. I parked by the side of the road just before Tobias's house; his driveway was short and narrow and I wasn't sure I could pull up next to his Ford without scratching it or plowing into the snow.

It was just as well I had, because there was another car in the driveway, a black VW. I hesitated, scuffing my sneakers in the tamped-down snow by the mailbox, then walked slowly up the driveway, peering into the VW. Of course Tobias had friends, I had never doubted it. It would be someone his age who would think of me as a child, and Tobias, not having seen this friend for a while, would prefer to be alone with him. The car was full of McDonalds boxes and candy wrappers, and there was a black sweater on the back seat.

I decided not to bother Tobias but walked quickly to peer in the window. He never looked out, he ignored his surroundings as much as possible, and I figured he wouldn't see me.

In the living room was a green backpack, a corduroy jacket, two coffee cups, a bag of oranges, a Swiss Army knife, Tobias's books, but no people. I heard laughter coming from the bedroom, low coiling-together laughter. I was not pleased. I pressed my cold cheek to the windowpane, wondering what I would do if he had a woman in there. Did I have the right to be jealous? Or if she had known him longer, did that give her the right? Mary of the keepsake black pubic hair, I thought, who wears black sweaters and drives a black VW.

The laughter stopped and they came into the living room. They were naked, arms loosely around each other's waists. Tobias's friend was only a few years older than I, with curly, rusty-red hair, a face marred in a few places by acne, pale eyes, and a graceful, smooth body with a pinkish, sickle-shaped penis.

Tobias stopped walking and kissed the stranger on the mouth. I watched with a kind of fascination in place of all that I would feel later. My eyes slid over the red-haired boy who now seemed frail in Tobias's embrace. He was sickly, I decided, puny. I turned my eyes to my love, whose caresses were much more lingering and specific than they had ever been with me. So that's it, I thought as his hands moved with proprietary pleasure over his lover's buttocks. He likes that, he prefers that. They turned in a shuffling dance so that now Tobias's back was to me. I was left to contemplate his beauty from behind. Yes, it was beautiful but clearly had nothing to do with me. The rounded shoulders, the ridged spine, the narrow ass with its deep cleft—none of my business.

They broke the kiss. The boy said something to Tobias, patted his cheek, and went into the bathroom. Tobias turned to the window and saw me.

I didn't wait for his expression to move past surprise. I fled to the car and turned the key desperately. The car roared and I floored it, leaping past the icy trees and banked snow, around the curve, farther and farther away. I felt mostly a nakedness of which actual nakedness is a pale reflection; my breasts burned as if spat upon.

I drove through town and the bodies of men all accused me of stupidity: middle-aged men in earmuffs with red faces, bald men with stomachs like sacks of groceries, even the square, waxy, slit-eyed face of Clem Dugle peering out his squad-car window at me as I sped by, his fresh cup of coffee ensuring he would not pursue. They were all men who liked women, whom some woman had chosen to lie beside, with what pleasure I couldn't guess, but without this shame. I was longing to be made love to now by some boy who'd idolized me for years—the faithful suitor, who'd forgive my defection. I drove to school, searching my mind for such a one—ardent, forgotten.

It was lunchtime and the halls were crowded. I pushed my way through, sure that my face was tragic, but nobody looked twice. Since I met Tobias I had barely spoken to anyone at school. Now that they no longer played on my grandmother's property, my classmates cared very little if I ignored them.

Except Cathy Murgatroyd. I saw her at her locker, putting her books away. She had been my best friend in ninth grade and had tried to talk to me several times this year. I couldn't remember how I responded. I went up to her as she slammed her locker shut and asked her to have a cigarette with me outside.

"Oh, hello, Stella." She looked at me for a minute with her serious brown eyes.

"Come have a smoke with me," I repeated lamely.

"I didn't know you smoked."

"I do. Will you come?"

"I'm hungry. Oh, all right. What's the matter?" I walked ahead of her, urging her out the door. "What's wrong?" she asked.

"I don't know. I'm depressed," I replied sullenly. I couldn't come right out and say it.

"It's no wonder the way you isolate yourself. Loneliness can lead to a lot of mental problems. It can kill, you know, just like cigarette smoking." I remembered now our conversations of the last few months, Cathy's concern at my reclusiveness, my impatience with her breaking into my daydreams of Tobias.

She leaned over and took the cigarette out of my mouth before I could light it. "I saw some pictures in a book the other day," she said. Lungs. One of a smoker, one of a nonsmoker. The nonsmoker's lungs were so white and pure looking, like snow. The smoker's lungs were all black and shriveled up." I smiled; how her words made me crave a cigarette! But I didn't want to annoy her, so I nodded and opened the Cadillac door.

"Let's sit in here. It's warmer."

She went around and slid in beside me, her neat legs swinging like the parts of a well-made machine. "So you've got wheels. This is Agnes's car, isn't it? Or did she give it to you and buy a new one?"

"No, she's just letting me use it."

"You're lucky. Are you going to be able to use it every day?"

"No, just while she's in the hospital dying," I said.

"Oh! I'm sorry, I had no idea . . . It's the cancer?"

"Yes."

"Is it . . . is she? Are they sure? I mean . . ."

"I think so."

"Oh, poor Stella, no wonder you're upset. That's so sad. She's like one of your family, isn't she?"

"Kind of."

Her face had gone quite pale and her lips were parted. "So you're all alone?"

"Yes." I started, to my horror, to cry.

"Oh, Stella, come over to my house after school. You can have dinner with us and spend the night." Her hand was on my arm, her breath on my cheek. I could imagine her tucking me in bed with a kiss. I couldn't imagine telling her about Tobias. "Don't cry," she said tenderly, brushing my tears away.

I promised Cathy I'd meet her at her locker at three o'clock and we walked back inside as the bell rang. Once she had gone to her class, I slipped out the back door and into my trusty Cadillac, which zoomed me home to my lonely house where I could cry as much as I pleased.

Cathy—or someone—called at three thirty but I didn't answer. I turned out all the lights and lay in a hot bath in the dark. I thought of Tobias: by himself, with me, with his boyfriend. The jealousy worked in deeper. I was sure he'd been fantasizing about this boy all along, while pretending to enjoy sex with me. He'd taken me because I was easy, because I was young, because I had small tits. I lay in the bathtub crying all evening until I was drunk on tears, the waves of misery leaving me faint, yet wanting more, wanting to drown in it. I wanted to die that night, have a funeral, be buried, then come back to life quietly, in another country.

The next day Tobias called. "Stella. It's me. Peter's gone now. Would you like to come over and talk?"

"No."

"Are you sure?"

"Yes."

"Well, feel free to change your mind. I'm sorry." Whether he was sorry for what he'd done (unlikely), sorry that I'd seen (more likely), or sorry for my reaction (most likely), he didn't say. I hung up.

Peter. What a perfect name. Peter for penis, or *peteur* in French: one who farts, asshole. Assholes are so rudimentary, I thought, so lacking in detail and grace. How could he prefer them?

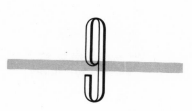

I was alone for a week. Each day began with the struggle to stay asleep. My dreams were all nightmares, yet I preferred them to waking, which I did only when my dreams sputtered out around noon and something like a large hand pushed me up into consciousness. Each day I looked in the mirror with a certain satisfaction. My face was the pinkish-gray color of chewed lamb, my eyes the same hue with pinpoints of blue at the centers. My hair tangled viciously.

Breakfast was tea and boiled eggs, which I also ate for lunch and for dinner. I ate while wandering from room to room, cup in hand, eyes flitting from object to familiar object. The things I liked in the house that week were: the grandfather clock in the dining room, the round, pink teapot with its knitted cosy, and the plum-colored carpeting on the stairs. As a child I used to sit halfway down those stairs, listening to the adult talk. The dusty carpet would prickle through my night-gown. Now I sat there with my chipped teacup of eggs and carefully ate, leaving the cup there when I was finished, on the bare wood beside the banister.

I left cups all over the house and soon had to move on to the good china. It was too delicate for my mood. I longed to crush it and watch my blood run into the egg the way the eggs' blood ran out in sixth grade when we dissected the twenty-four almost-hatched chicks.

When the eggs ran out on the third day, I ate canned white

asparagus, nibbling down the limp stems, and sardines, stopping after one bite to admire the halved bodies and messy insides. Then I made brownies — without an egg — which came out flat and tasteless. I was seized with a kind of glee at this failure and, crumbling the remains in a bowl, added a carton of soured milk to make a "pudding." This I left on the back porch for animals, although what I was imagining was not animals but wild children, children who'd lived undetected in the New Hampshire woods since their dissident ancestors had been banished from Puritan settlements.

Finally I must have fasted for a while. Draped on the stairs in an old nightgown, I read the first three volumes of Proust. I was very impressed with his ability to go on and on so it seemed I would never have to step back into my own life. Whole days vanished as I gradually allied myself with this jealous man. Coming out of one of these eight-hour sessions, I was dreamy and content: life was profound. And there were hundreds of thousands more of Proust's words to read.

On the last day I went up to the third floor, where my great-grandfather and his two brothers had spent their boyhood in the 1880s and 90s, and where two of them, the brothers, had spent their lives. One died at fifteen, the other at fifty, a bachelor. They had had a tutor who taught them their lessons up here, on the scarred schoolboy desks pushed into the corners of the three almost identical rooms. There was a fourth room, with a brick fireplace, which had been their father's study, and a fifth room, tiny, where the tutor slept. He had been a cripple, and his cane was still in the closet, along with his black cloak. When the boys grew up, my grandmother once said, he died and was buried in the garden. Another time she said he had vanished in a canoe during the annual Fourth of July picnic; he was gone, anyway, before she was born. He must have been a good tutor because her father and uncles were able to converse fluently in Latin, which they would do when they wanted to exclude the women and children from their talk. She remembered the sonorous syllables across the dinner table, their laughter, and her mother angrily hacking at the roast.

I was soothed by the colors of those third-floor rooms — maroon, brown, dark-green—by their smell of leather, and by their solitariness; each boy slept alone, in a hard single bed. One died young and one didn't marry. They owed their allegiance to the walls that housed them, to the parents downstairs, and to their independent selves. They were my ancestors, and what they knew, I could learn.

I lay on each of their beds in turn, and looked out to the river or the apple trees or the road, all of it very far away and subordinate to my bloodshot eye. I sat at their desks, opened their books, and imagined staying up here until I could speak Latin and Greek. I wished I had a tutor who would teach me everything; then I'd never have to leave the house.

Grandmother came home on Tuesday. I didn't hear the car and when she walked in I was taking a nap on the fifth stair, which as yet had no cup half full of moldy tea or dried-up egg on it. I was wearing a baby-blue nightgown, old and short, with puffed sleeves and a torn ruffle dangling from the hem.

"Stella!" I woke up and looked at her. She was dressed in her black suit with black pumps and a black patent-leather purse held in black-gloved hands.

"Oh, hi."

"What is this?" Her eyes swept over the hall, stairs, and into the other rooms. Her face was powdery and pale, and her jaw seemed swollen. "It's a pigsty," she answered herself.

"I'll clean it up," I said weakly, blinking at her.

"I called yesterday. I called several times."

"I didn't hear it ring," I said truthfully, then remembered that I'd unplugged it. "I guess I unplugged it."

"You unplugged the telephone. I suppose you didn't want to be disturbed? You had your friend over here?"

I felt myself flush under her gaze. I had meant to plug it back in and to call her at the hospital. "I broke up with Tobias," I said.

"Oh, too bad," she said. "Did he leave you for another man?" I gaped at her. "I've seen him in town. Not everyone is as naïve as you are." I felt humiliated. How dare she see him? How dare she know?

"It's a pigsty," she repeated, in a quieter voice. Her whole face was trembling, the color coming and going in waves.

"I'm sorry," I said. "I'm sorry, I'm sorry, I'm sorry. I did mean to call you, to clean up. I'm *sorry*." I started to cry and couldn't stop.

My grandmother bent and started collecting the dirty dishes, piling them up precariously. She carried them into the kitchen, and timidly I followed. She ran the water so hot it was almost boiling, and she washed all my dishes of the last week.

When the house was spotlessly clean, and Grandmother not even winded, she took me out for an early dinner. I thought it strange—we never went out—but of course she didn't want to mess up the kitchen. We ate at a place on Route 1 with red carpeting and a round salad bar. Grandmother remarked on the food but nothing else. The fox-faced waitress called me "honey." When we left, the silence continued, and the car slid smoothly onto the highway.

I wished she would talk to me. I wasn't afraid that she would scold me anymore but that she would not. I was beginning to imagine that this coldness might not go away. I read permanent disapproval in every twitch of her hands on the steering wheel, in the martial corners of her shoulders, and the sheen of her papery skin. She could be so severe. I had always known it, but I thought I was exempt for life—or at least for youth. Was that over already? I felt very young and unprotected.

As I slumped by the door, gazing at her through my tangle of hair, she said, "You know, I can understand why a woman would choose a man to love out of instinct, or curiosity or because she never learned different—I did it myself. But why a man would choose another man over a woman is beyond me." She smiled and patted my knee and I broke into a grin, tears falling down my cheeks.

Agnes's coffin was laid out in the living room. Her body looked so tiny, her hair curled as she had never worn it around a face where the flesh lay in packets over the bones like bags of dry cement. She had died the day after Grandmother drove back from Boston.

I felt a great pity for the corpse. It didn't resemble Agnes, yet the body was such an intricate structure. There was so much detail. I reached in and stroked her arm, just above the wrist. There was no dance of blood under the skin, but the skin was dense and tough. It shared the room with me as the furniture did, as a complex object with its own beauty. But I knew her lilac dress with the muted stripe would last longer.

Several women came to pay their respects. They were Agnes's and Grandmother's old schoolmates: Jenny Taylor, nurse at the high school; Dida Smith who, with her husband, ran Smith's Market; Laura Chester, aunt of one of my old boyfriends; Betty Fargus in a deep magenta hat. Grandmother received them politely at the door, but her attitude was that it was Agnes they had come to see. Agnes could entertain them. They were escorted to their hostess in the living room, and Grandmother withdrew.

If Agnes had not chosen to live with Grandmother, she would have been like these women, I thought. Married to a local man, helping to run his business, or raising kids, or working as a waitress or a clerk. She would have met them at church and sat in their houses on crisis days, and perhaps ordinary days too. If she were married, she would have had grudges against her husband; if she stayed single, she might have grown flinty with loneliness. But not like Laura Chester, surely, who was thin and prim with her beige hair and her white purse held in front of her in all its gleaming squareness. Nor like Jenny Taylor, solid, practical and loud, or Dida Smith with her lanky shyness and skewed smile, who chain smoked at the cash register and didn't notice if her ash fell in your grocery bag.

Agnes was not like any of them. I had always imagined her charmed by my grandmother, caged in a way by a love that never gave her quite enough. But perhaps it had been her free and informed choice. She, too, was an unusual woman.

I got up and joined Grandmother in the kitchen, in time to see her stuff a dozen roses in the disposal.

"Why are you doing that?" I asked.

"I don't want them here."

"You like roses."

"Not roses sent by Mr. Tarpin Boxley."

"Who's he?"

"Agnes's nephew. Horrible boy. Used to hang around your mother, wheedling her into going to town with him where he made her sick on raspberry candy. Mr. Boxley's a lawyer now."

"Is he coming here?"

"None of them will come here."

"Why not?"

"All they wanted, besides my money, was for Agnes to go look after their children when they went on vacation. All her brothers with their kids and then Tarpin with his kids. Agnes was never fond of children and told them so. They thought she preferred mine. But you know Agnes never took care of your mother or you. I did that. She had entire freedom here. They resented that."

"She made me warm milk and honey."

"That was just to put you to sleep. She preferred you asleep until you were about twelve."

There was a tap at the kitchen door. It was Jenny Taylor. She said, "Excuse me, Lally, but I wanted to ask you when the funeral's going to be?"

"There isn't going to be one."

"No service at all?"

"None." My grandmother smiled. "This is it, Jenny." I had been startled too, but Grandmother said Agnes had insisted. She wasn't going to give Father Dugan the satisfaction. She no longer believed in Catholicism. She didn't believe in anything; she was going with an open mind.

"Well, you are going to bury her, aren't you?" asked Jenny with asperity. "You don't intend to keep her here in your living room?"

I was half afraid Grandmother would say yes, and unveil some plan to have Agnes stuffed like an owl. "She'll be buried," she said.

"Where?"

"South of Bobby—east of Miranda," said my grandmother gaily.

"Miranda?" I asked. Bobby was her husband, buried in the cemetery where I'd met Tobias.

"My baby sister, who died at birth. You've seen her grave." Once, perhaps, when I was eight, and taken to the graveyard as a Christmas treat. It had been Grandmother's response to Agnes's notion to take me to church.

"Well, Lally, I think we'll be going now."

"Fine. I'm glad you came."

Jenny nodded stiffly. "Good-bye, Stella. See you in school next week?" Her sharp eyes looked me up and down. The last time we'd spoken I'd asked her for a Tampax because my period started in the middle of Math. She'd given me a lecture about "penetrating yourself," and a Kotex pad.

"Yeah," I said as she withdrew.

Grandmother made camomile tea and we sat by the coffin. She stared for a long time at Agnes, her eyes making a minute inspection. "This is how they arranged her at the funeral home," she said. "But it doesn't seem right, does it?"

"I don't know. How could it be right?"

"We'll see."

Grandmother went upstairs and came down again with a fistful of makeup cases. She sat down beside the body and opened a lipstick. One of her own colors—scarlet. She exaggerated Agnes's mouth subtly, making me notice what I never had before, that Agnes had almost perfect Clara Bow lips. Then she smoothed green eye shadow on the translucent lids, and drew rays of gold and blue extending from the eyes, as in pictures of Cleopatra. There began to be a look like a smile about the face. Grandmother rubbed dark makeup over the waxy skin and accented it with rouge, not the pink of youth but the red of assertive middle age.

The dead face soaked up the color easily. The cancer was gone now. It had left more slowly than life, wishing to display itself to all potential victims, but Grandmother had chased it off. Agnes's flesh rested profoundly in its beauty, dazzling me. It looked like her now. It looked like her as I never saw her in life, but as I think Grandmother must have seen her.

The rest of the year passed in a daze. I had been in love and lost; Agnes was dead; my parents still missing, not even knowing what had happened; what more could happen? I lay in bed on weekends until noon, thinking about Tobias. In my dreams and then in my fantasies, I was a boy, a beautiful boy, one out of a story: Tom Sawyer, innocent to the last of what the gentleman wanted; Peter Pan, prowling Tobias's darkened bedroom in the middle of the night, brushing against him as if accidentally, waking him, whispering an apology with touch-me charm, then tumbling away out the window. A dark-eyed Arabian whore, who made love with exquisite skill, caressed my darling to sleep, then stole the wallet containing, for some reason, all Tobias's savings.

In March I seduced my biology teacher, Mr. Cross, when he picked me up hitchhiking. I wasn't entirely serious when I put my hand on his thigh. I wanted to see what he would do. What he did was drive me to his apartment and fuck me insanely for hours, telling me how often he thought about the girls in his classes. Not even me particularly. All the girls. Our affair lasted two weeks, until, as he so charmingly put it, he realized that my ass wasn't worth his ass.

Then there was nobody. Even Grandmother had retreated. She had embarked on a campaign of extensive reading and was always shut up in her room. I thought she had read everything already, but apparently not. She read history, anthropology, South American fiction. I exerted myself to get all A's that year, and I waited for college, for deliverance.

liked my college roommate immediately. Janey was sitting on her bed in the dorm room at the University of New Hampshire, eating blueberry yogurt, her lips purple, and a few purple flecks in her curly chestnut hair. There was an empty bag of pretzels and a can of Fresca on the floor beside her. She jumped up to greet me and offered to help me unpack. I let her help, and she told me everything about herself in one rush, so I could decide, she said, if I wanted her as a roommate. "You were trying to find out if you wanted me as a roommate," I accused her later.

"That, too."

Janey, like me, was an only child. Her father was dead and she detested her mother. "She's got these little beady eyes and an upper lip like a snipe. I've never seen a snipe, but you know what I mean." she flopped back on her bed, laughing. Janey had a laugh like nobody, deep and gurgling. I've seen strangers come up to her on account of that laugh, fumbling for something to say. According to her mood, Janey would either talk to them with stunning warmth, or turn such darkened, suspicious eyes on them that they'd visibly shrink and hurry away. Then she'd laugh again, warmly, invitingly. "Mother eats nothing but oysters, crudités, and Perrier, wears nothing but white natural fibers, and does nothing but go to spas to have her cellulite massaged." Janey had gone to boarding school since she was ten and spent her vacations in expensive hotels, being felt up by Puerto Rican busboys and aging Italian waiters. "Once one of them got too amorous and tried to follow me into my room. He had a passkey so I had to put a chair under the doorknob. He kept calling, 'Beautiful lady, let me in. Beautiful lady!' My mother was in the next room, wearing her mud mask. I almost died."

"Did she get mad at you?"

"Oh, sure. My mother thinks I'm disgusting. Seeing me is sort of like having her period. That's why she sent me here. I got into Berkeley but she didn't think I deserved California. She knows I love it there."

"I'm glad you're here."

"Me too. I need a companion in misfortune."

"Don't say that. We're going to have fun."

"Oh, I always have fun."

In January we moved out of the dorm into our own apartment. It was a typical student place with thin walls, smelly carpets, a sheet of amber-and-blue plastic molded to look like stained glass separating the living room from the kitchenette. "Home sweet home," said Janey, and meant it. The ugliness didn't matter to her; she was so glad to be in our own place where we bought the food and paid the bills and locked the door at night. I felt some of that, especially in the evening when I cooked dinner and she sat at the table drinking cheap wine and gossiping about the people in the English department.

I liked listening to Janey, I liked eating with her, and cleaning up together afterward, but even with our Van Gogh reproductions on the walls, and our purple candles, the apartment was not my home. I felt unprotected in such a flimsy little cubicle, more so than in the dorm, which was an old building, and which, anyway, had seemed utterly unreal to me — all those girls in nightgowns. This was real, and noisy. The first time Janey had a lover, we found a note under the door the next morning: oil your bedsprings. She thought it was funny but I was upset. I used to sit by the window, watching cars roll in and out of the parking lot, and wonder how so many people could live like this, how it could all continue year after year. What would happen if one morning we all woke up and walked silently back to the forest?

But such a drastic step was not really what I needed. I remembered how as a child I used to think the wood of our house was alive, that the walls had roots under the ground and the creakings and shiftings were sap pushing its way up through hidden branches, feeding the hungry mouths of sunless blossoms. I imagined those blossoms white as milk—thin as one layer of skin and sectioned like a heart—held in place between the coursing walls.

I took Janey home one weekend so she would understand why I was discontent. Grandmother served us a leg of lamb and a bottle of Chambertin; afterward, in the library, she read aloud the poems of Russell Edson, which made Janey laugh her gurgling laugh, while I tiptoed around the room, touching the crimson drapes, the oak bookshelves, the leather and cloth and paper bindings. There was a thin film of dust on everything.

"This apartment's okay when you're feeling good," I said the Monday we returned to school, "but what about when you're depressed? Or lonely?" I could feel both states creeping up on me. "It would be an awful place to be unhappy in, don't you think?"

"We won't be unhappy," said Janey. "We won't be lonely. This is a university, Stella. There are *thousands* of men out there."

She found one. His name was Aaron and he was a skinny, dry math major with knobby knees and a brain he carried carefully, keeping his head erect, like an African woman. The first time I met him he said that math and science were the only real knowledge there was; all the rest was babble. Janey liked arguing with him; she admired his logic and his assurance, perversely present in such an ugly little body. Aaron never doubted either his brilliance or his fatal charm.

My spirits depressed rapidly. Janey said it was simply a matter of meeting more people and she dragged me to university events where we drank bitter coffee and talked to limp boys we had met in our classes, while the attractive ones, surrounded protectively by their sidekicks, sauntered in, exchanged a few greetings, and left. But even those superior boys—and they were boys—didn't hold much appeal for me. More than good looks, I wanted someone I could talk to. That's what I wanted at first, anyway. By the end of the semester I would have settled for someone I couldn't talk to, a steady lover I wouldn't have to listen to either.

I relied on Janey for emotional support. I remember one weekend at my grandmother's house when we got up at dawn on Sunday morning, took LSD, and went out into the orchard. It drizzled all day with patches of sun, the light changing constantly. A new planet grew around us, moist and greeny-gray. Janey and I sat by the river and spoke now and then. Our conversation was elliptical and strange but there were no misunderstandings. From the solitude of our visions we ascended to the high intelligence LSD sometimes brings, and we were enchanted to find our sympathy still there, as strong and sure as it was when we talked of college life.

At the end of the day, drinking wine on the porch with Grand-mother, talking of life and literature, we all agreed with each other so much, I said, "We're the three sisters in the Greek myth, who share one eye between them." Instantly we were not, we peered at each other from distant universes, each face a little scary in its depth: Janey, at nineteen, with her almond eyes, Grandmother with her sunken eyes dimmed to the color of autumn leaves under water. Grandmother made tea. I poured it, and we ate lemon cake. We leaned back into the warm night, in silence, and I felt civilization surround us like the constant, drizzling rain.

There were not many such weekends. I didn't want to be going home all the time. Grandmother was dating now, occasionally, myste-riously. She went into Boston and she had men to dinner. I couldn't understand it—why now?—but in another way, I understood com-pletely. I wanted to leave her alone. I just didn't want to be alone.

My sophomore year was worse. Nothing had changed; that was what was so awful. A few friends, a few interesting courses, an apartment I still didn't like. I was nineteen, things were supposed to happen to me. At my age my mother was married and had a child.

My friends were all busy, and if not content, at least engaged in what they were doing. Janey was studying literature, reading with passion things I had read at fourteen. Aaron was infatuated with computers and higher math, my friend Sonia practiced piano all day. I did my homework, cleaned the apartment, and sometimes got laid. There was an art professor who stopped by a few times that fall until his wife returned from the lesbian commune in West Virginia she had gone to out of feminist curiosity. Apparently her body was not as curious as her mind. School wasn't hard and I had a lot of free time. I spent too much of it wandering around the frozen streets of Durham, a boring little town, and taking long naps in the afternoons. I would wake up when it got dark and be immediately angry that the day was over, that light and warmth had been taken away from me again. In a rage I would turn on every light in the apartment, and that rage would only very slowly subside. What was the point? Who was there to be angry with?

Then, late at night, when all the apartments surrounding ours were quiet, I would take out my grandmother's old copy of *The Joy Of Cooking* and make chocolate truffles, or a chocolate soufflé. The truffles had to sit twelve hours—they weren't much fun—but if I made the soufflé, I would wake Janey up to eat it with me. She didn't mind reviving for the proper occasion. I would sit across from her explaining exactly how much chocolate you can safely add to a recipe, and what brands to use, and she would listen groggily, eating, as if what I was saying was very complicated, something she could never remember, but which she would listen to anyway, to please me. "This is great," she said. "You're a great cook."

"I think the next time I'll put in a little Kahlúa." I stayed up after she had gone to bed again, listing, in my head, all the interesting variations on the recipe that I could think of. I felt silly, clinging to this childhood craft when everyone around me was preparing for a career. I didn't think of cooking as a career; I thought perhaps I'd be a foreign correspondent, roaming the world, or an astrophysicist. That would impress Grandmother. I took physics and newswriting, and did well in both, though I would forever redden at the memory of walking in the police station, asking the fat cops sitting around for news, and being told, after a long pause while they looked me over, that I was the tenth person from my class to bother them that day.

But I wasn't really concerned with a career. I knew I could always get a job. I had done so the last two summers, working as a waitress. Until there was something I wanted to do, how could I miss not doing it?

What I missed was love. It hurt me to see couples touching each other. I thought there ought to be laws against such violence inflicted on poor, lonely students. I was glad then that I thought Aaron such a puny specimen of manhood, that my jealously of Janey stayed abstract. She was all I had, she and Grandmother. Yet I couldn't help thinking that the love of women was not enough, not enough to even keep me alive, that I was like one of those magical beings that fade away when they're not believed in.

I remember making that comparison to myself in one of my notebooks, then drily laughing. What did I mean, magical, I was inert, what did I mean, fade away, I was only too solidly here. It was an effort to drag my body to classes, to bathe it and feed it. I felt savage. I didn't know exactly what that meant, but I felt it—savage. Something solitary poised to spring. I read *Ariel* that year in a women's literature course and was surprised that other people found Plath's images bizarre. I thought they were simply honest. I wasn't mad or suicidal, but I was close enough to know the landscape.

Being without a lover was enough to drive anyone insane, I thought, you don't even need an absent father. Well, maybe you did. I didn't know too many women with nice, near-at-hand daddies. Janey, far ahead of me in analyzing these things, said you had to hate men a little in order to love them at all. She said you needed a cynical mind to appreciate the charm of their atavistic brutality. I had a few objections to this theory, but I thought she had a point.

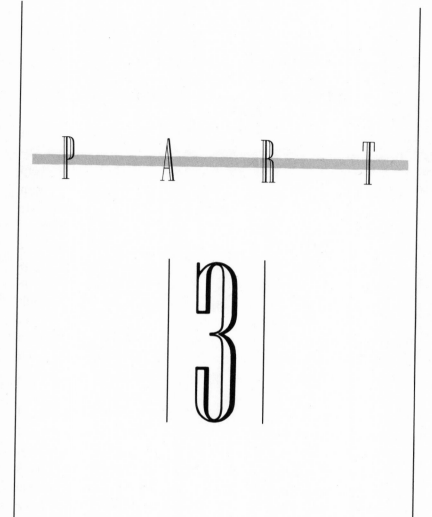

PART

3

eo had not been wrong. I loved California from the first moment. All the talk about West Coast laid-back culture hadn't prepared me for the gardens of Berkeley, full of purple irises and spiky cacti, for Victorian houses with turrets, for eucalyptus trees, for the blue bay and the bald green hills. I spent the first week walking around in a daze, stunned with color and foreignness. Northern California is where the earth opens up; you can always feel that exhilarating exposure in the air.

I answered an ad in the *Eastbay Express* and moved in with a woman my age named Callie. She lived in a white frame house on Ellsworth Street with a fence, a gate, and a garden. My bedroom window looked out on a lemon tree and five pink rosebushes. I could see into the garden next door, which also had a lemon tree, where our neighbor practiced yoga. He sat cross-legged on a slender branch, wearing white shorts and surrounded by his half dozen cats. He raised and lowered his plantlike arms meditatively.

I got along well with Callie. She was quiet and eager to please and when I said I liked to cook, she offered to do all the cleaning. One day soon after I moved in she took me to the Berkeley Bowl food market where she worked as a cashier. As she explained that the fish, meat, and coffee counters were run separately, I stared in astonishment at the bushels of fruits and vegetables in the center of the store. There were a dozen varieties of everything, fresher than I'd ever seen vegetables, even when I picked them myself in New Hampshire. There were so many things I couldn't name: tropical fruits, splendid leafy greens, flowerlike fungi. And all of it was being tenderly watered by a slim Japanese man. The seductiveness of the combination of California vegetables and Oriental respect were irresistible.

I bought some of everything—or almost everything—then took it home and laid it out on the kitchen table. My tender young beans, plump peaches, massive celery, my otherworldly broccoli. All of it without a blemish, all of it seeming in some magical way to be still connected to the root.

That night I made a vegetable soup that caused me to understand for the first time the popularity of such metaphors as "cosmic soup" or "melting pot." Any process of importance must happen this way: all the different creatures nudging each other in a softly boiling broth. Letting go their flavors. Supping on their neighbors' juices and finding themselves there.

Callie and I ate soup for a week. But still at the end there were vegetables, and even these miraculous ones rotted. I should've cooked them all and handed out soup on the streets. Instead I got a job in a restaurant.

It was not a hard job to get. I lied about my previous experience, which was easy since I said it was all in New York. Most Californians don't care to communicate with that corrupt city, and Mrs. Quinlan was no exception. She lectured me for a while on the difference between East and West Coast cooking, but when I described my reaction to the Berkeley Bowl market, she was satisfied.

The theme of Mrs. Quinlan's Restaurant was the egg, "Age-old symbol of fecundity and wholeness," as she put it. Everything on the menu was made out of these aborted fetuses, as we called them in the kitchen, since Mrs. Quinlan insisted that her symbols be fertilized. Omelets, soufflés, quiches, custard pies, frittata, waffles, broccoli with hollandaise, poached eggs with hollandaise—it was enough to make you sick. I saw more than one customer quietly leave after reading the menu, dropping his yolk-yellow napkin to the floor.

There were three cooks in the kitchen, about two too many for the business we did, and we got slap-happy early in the day, hiding eggs in each other's purses and pockets, around the kitchen, and in the bathrooms, like drunken parents on Easter morning. Mrs. Quinlan was bemused when she found eggs stuffed in unused rolls of toilet paper, or nestling in the straws of a broom. Perhaps she thought the clever things got there by themselves; they were, after all, full of Life. She didn't dare ask Jocasta, the half-Mexican boss-cook, or Renee, the sour, sarcastic niece of Mrs. Quinlan's second husband, and since I was new, she probably thought I wouldn't know. In any case, she tucked the found egg absentmindedly in her jacket pocket where it might stay for days. The egglady, even her husband called her that.

I learned enough about restaurant cooking to look for another job after three months. I wanted a place where I could do what I wanted. I knew it was a lot to ask, at that point, but I was determined. I was good, I was amazingly good.

When I walked into The Vineyard, owned and operated by George Mainwaring, I knew I had found the right place. It was a pretty restaurant, small, with a fireplace, brick walls, and green curtains. But that was not what attracted me. George was standing in the middle of the dining room, gesturing in despair with his long, incredibly muscular arms and shouting at Leo, who was scratching his chest and smoking a Winston. Judy was half-hidden behind Leo, kissing the back of his neck. Ramon was setting the tables and humming to himself.

"How in fuck am I going to find a cook when you didn't even put the fucking ad in the paper? What is wrong with you?"

"I'm a waiter, not a secretary," said Leo, arching his neck a little in response to Judy's nuzzling. He had a long pale face, long, straight brown hair, and rubbery, intelligent-looking lips. I couldn't see much of Judy but that her hair was dark and curly and she wore moccasins.

"You're a shmuck! Judy, why'd you marry this asshole?"

"She wanted a BMW," said Leo. "Her father promised her one if we got married."

"Didn't give it to me either, the bastard. Said the wedding cost too much." She poked her face around Leo's and rested her chin on his shoulder. It was a sharp-featured, good-humored, blue-eyed face.

"I gave you a deal, honeybunch," said George. "Nobody else

woulda touched that catering job with a ten-foot hotdog. Half the people on a low-sodium diet, the other half kosher; several diabetics, your mother vegetarian and your father's family all reformed alcoholics, 'No wine sauce, please.' I mean, come on. That wasn't a reception. It was a fucking hospital."

"You have company, George."

He swung around and looked at me. His face was vivid and handsome, with a big nose, square chin, and green eyes. "Yeah?"

"I'm the new cook. I saw the ad in the paper."

"There wasn't an ad in the paper."

"That's funny. I could've sworn. It must have been Chez Panisse." I turned to go.

"Awright, awright, so you heard about the job, I suppose you know these jokers here?"

"No. My name is Stella James." I stepped forward and held out my hand. Leo grinned and took it between both of his. His hands were warm and slightly damp, like buttered toast.

"Leo Karfman. Pleased to know you." He let go and I shook Judy's fine-fingered hand.

"Judy Epping-Karfman. How do you do, Stella?"

"How do you do?" I smiled at her and she winked.

George folded his arms over his chest and watched this business impatiently. When I looked back at him, he barked, "Where have you worked? What can you do? Tell me why I should hire you right off the street."

I answered his questions while Leo and Judy kissed in one corner and Ramon ran the vacuum cleaner around our feet. I got carried away describing dishes I'd like to try. George listened carefully, and when I had finished, he said, "Okay, Blondie, I'll give you a try."

The menu at The Vineyard was simple — soups, salads, grilled meat and fish, a few specials. With George's help prepping in the afternoon and an assistant named Allison in the evenings, I managed to run the kitchen smoothly. As soon as the first customer arrived, I fell into a rhythm of work where the whole kitchen — except for Ramon's dishwasher — felt like an extension of my body. The more orders in front of me, the happier I felt. I became good friends with Leo and Judy, got along with the other waiters, and listened to the sexual problems of Seth, our dessert chef, who worked out of his mother's kitchen. The only person I didn't like was Allison, who was slow and sulky, but that only made it the more fun to order her around.

George and I were friends and then lovers. He worked beside me in the afternoons, keeping up a constant line of talk: jokes, complaints, insults, and the like. He was a good cook, mainly because he could tell, by holding and smelling it, just what a particular piece of fish or meat would taste like. We got good stuff, but there were always variations, and George taught me how to spot them. He'd hold a scallop up to the light, or pull back the skin on a chicken breast, and as he lectured I felt absurdly professional, like a young doctor in a laboratory.

Then he'd start in on a dirty story about my old boss, the egglady, or one of the Japanese women at the Berkeley Bowl. He was working his way around to me. What raw beast did my flesh remind him of? I wondered. He liked to watch me stirring sauces, adding a pinch of this and a pinch of that, as Grandmother had done. George felt inadequate when it came to seasoning; he said it took a woman's touch. I scooped fingerfuls for him to taste, smearing buttery herb-flecked sauce across his lips. He told me to watch out, his mouth was an erogenous zone. I waited for him to get the idea.

When he did, one afternoon as I had just arrived at work, he swooped down on me with winy lips, tongue primed for a theft. I kissed him back and he seemed surprised; he paused, drew back, and looked at me with his wide, brilliantly green eyes bulging, and slightly bloodshot.

I laughed. He grabbed me under the butt and heaved, slapping me against his body like a hamburger on a griddle. That pretty much set a tone.

George was married and had three children. I never saw his family except, later on, his daughter Lisa. It was another life I couldn't quite picture; he seemed so entirely at home in his restaurant. He arrived loudly every day before noon, as Ramon, who slept in a cubicle off the kitchen, told me with a pantomime of his sound sleep interrupted by George's bellowing. He stayed long after the last customer had left, drinking with whoever would drink with him. When he got very drunk he would sometimes hug and kiss me in front of the waiters, who ignored him; only Ramon would watch us closely and say to George that it was very bad to kiss me, though he giggled as he said it.

In front of the customers he was never drunk. He was suave. People took to him immediately, the women flirting, the men asking whether he'd played football in college. He hated the question. He hadn't gone to college, for one thing. He had played football in high school, forced into it, he said, by the coach and his mother. He had loathed the physical contact with other boys and was repelled by cheerleaders. He wanted, he said, the pale, intellectual girls who walked home alone from the library on Saturday afternoons.

He was proud that he never exercised at all, and he claimed that wine and sex were responsible for his good health. It was no secret to me how he kept fit—rushing from market to market, often too impatient with Berkeley traffic to use his car, staggering under loads of food; and then on Tuesdays, when the restaurant was closed, tramping through land for sale in Sonoma, dreaming of his own vineyard.

And, of course, sex. We were almost violent with each other. He would wrestle me to the floor, pretending I had to be subdued, and I would defend myself with nails and elbows and teeth, glad for the chance to try my speed and wit against his bulk. I liked the fact that I could tire myself out fighting him and he was still there, unhurt. Usually laughing. I loved it when he gathered me up in his arms, complaining about how skinny I was, how I weighed nothing; I felt like I was floating on a raft in the middle of the sea, and then this big, red face bends down for a kiss.

I never saw George outside The Vineyard. On my nights off I stayed home and read or picked up men. This latter practice came as a bit of a shock to my roommate, Callie, but she adjusted. I gave her a lock for her door and promised her that I was very selective. She still didn't like it, but she liked me, and I only brought them to our house rarely.

The men were different in California, or I was. I no longer had the sharp sense of the unknown, of the adventure, when I went cruising. It was like lunching with old friends who have new lives: the physical interesting—how have they changed—yet in the end, little to remember. Perhaps I've run out of strangers, I thought. It would have made me sad, if I could've felt sad in Berkeley. Instead I enjoyed the advantages of such a life, and became even more loyal to it, defending it with conviction to Callie as the only way a woman can be free with men—by learning them so thoroughly that when she does fall in love, as Callie longed to do, she does it wisely and well. And when she doesn't fall in love, I added to myself, doesn't miss it.

I felt like my real life was at the restaurant, cooking. I had discovered the pleasure of work, which had eluded me all through school. Writing papers on Yeats had been no problem, passing calculus had been a relief, but this was exciting. I couldn't get over the beauty of red peppers. I tenderly handled a salmon steak, thinking of the leaping body. I wanted to try ginger in everything.

Although The Vineyard was popular, it was never quite popular enough. There were mysterious gaps in attendance, and rarely enough money in the bank to ride them out. This meant George was always looking for backers or arguing with the ones he had, pleading with the IRS or owing on the salaries. But there was nowhere I would have rather worked. It was nice, of course, to be on intimate terms with the boss, and I appreciated the latitude he gave me. But more important was the enthusiasm we shared about food. George's was perhaps a little greater for his astounding wine list, which took a good half hour to read, but he knew what it meant to me to pile the counters high with mushrooms, artichokes, pearl onions, yellow beans, Japanese eggplants, and plum tomatoes, to know that I could use it all, transform it, taste it. He was willing to eat my mistakes with me. I did it as a penance but he took positive pleasure in gorging himself on oversalted soup or shrimp crying under a sauce of mustard and sour chardonnay.

When I had a success he did even better: he persuaded everyone to try it, even one couple who had finished their dessert course. Why not a bowl of saffron-scented seafood chowder after chocolate mousse? He chided them for arriving too early, before the specials were quite done. He reminded them how long it was until breakfast. And the little bow-legged woman and her buck-toothed husband ate large servings of soup, said it was the best they had ever tasted, came into the kitchen to tell me so, and went out hand in hand, charmed by the originality of what they had done.

was spooning red pepper butter over fillets of salmon, arranging green noodles on the plates when I looked up to find a camera lens in my face, the shutter clicking. Another picture was taken and then another. This side, that side, up close, back again. It was like being swarmed by insects. "All right, already," I said to the guy behind the counter, slight, blond, in a black jacket and running shoes. "What is this?" He clicked a few more, circling around me until I began to feel alarmed, then put down his camera.

I was startled by the face beneath. Inward and yet irrepressible, as if he had a secret with himself, something to do with pleasure that set him apart, yet he couldn't help letting whole pieces of it escape. He leaned against the counter and looked at me out of bright brown eyes. His face was narrow and pointed, he was probably a few years older than I, and he had the nose of a Renaissance prince.

"I wanted to catch you unawares. The cook in her kitchen. I'm doing kitchens now. A middle-aged woman in the room she's spent most of her life in. A guy and an open refrigerator. All the dogs lined up waiting to be fed. Mostly home kitchens but I thought I'd try this, too. You're younger than I expected; it makes a nice effect with all this stuff." He waved an arm at the accumulated technology. "Your boss, what's his name, George, gave me permission to take your picture."

"He had no right to do that."

"He seemed to think he did." I could easily imagine that. George laughed at my distaste for extra people in the kitchen. He teased me about being an "artiste" when he brought people back to watch the process.

"What are you going to do with the pictures?" I asked. His gaze was so intent it gave me a shivery feeling.

"Depends." His tone was abrupt — another artiste, I thought. I wasn't offended by the abruptness; on the contrary. I glanced at the camera hanging from its strap around his neck and imagined my pictures traveling like ghosts through the black plastic to burrow into his flesh.

"You want to taste what I'm making?"

"Okay."

I held out a finger dipped in the spicy red butter and he sucked it clean. "Hey, that's good. Can I have some more?" I held out another fingerful. "Thanks. I don't usually need to be fed by hand. My name's Frank Mardano." I told him my name and we shook hands, which made me feel slightly absurd after the finger sucking. "You don't mind me back here?"

"You're staying?"

"I'd like to watch you."

"Okay."

"I won't disturb you." He did, of course. His eyes were on every move I made and I began to feel self-conscious. I forgot how long it took to cook a chicken breast, I couldn't manage the vegetables. Yet it was a pleasurable self-consciousness. I wanted to slow down and enjoy my mistakes. But I had to get the dinners out. To deflect his attention from my body, I began to talk. I told him about my grandmother's kitchen. It was suddenly so clear to me how all of a piece my life was. How could I be anything but a cook, growing up there? Those years came to mind so vividly, not as homesickness but rather as something I would possess forever. I felt so grateful to Frank; it was the quality of his attention that brought this forward. It was his smell, which I could just catch — woodsy and herbal, the sharp herbs of September. Perhaps I fell in love with his smell most of all.

"Tomatoes were called love apples when they were first introduced into England," I said, chopping a few to sauté. "Virgins weren't allowed to eat them. Isn't that a great idea? On your wedding night eating a feast of delicacies never before sampled?"

He didn't answer but just smiled at me as if to say: Wedding night? Feast? Delicacies? As if to make me aware of how warm and sweet his mouth looked, the bloom on his skin. My self-consciousness returned and I plunged back into my childhood. Frank listened with his head tilted at a dreamy angle as if I were reading him a story. I told more, things I barely remembered: my mother and I picking mushrooms in the woods and carrying them in a basket to Grandmother who wisely threw them away.

"Were they poisonous?"

"Who knows? My mother liked taking risks. She used to light candles in her bedroom and go to sleep with them still burning. She taught me how to run my finger fast through a flame."

"A dangerous lady."

"She was beautiful."

"So are you," he said in another shift of tone. Now he was ardent— but only for a moment. He let it go and glanced at me sidelong.

I hesitated. "And you are, too."

We kept talking. George came into the kitchen once and was clearly surprised to see Frank still with me. Frank said nothing to him and I said nothing. He shot us both a look and went back out front. I could hear his voice rise up in growly argument, and Judy and Leo went back and forth in giggles. We all laughed at George when he got surly; it seemed to be the response he wanted.

At eleven I turned off the grill and the ovens, put the food away, and wiped off the knives. It had been a slow night, for which I felt grateful. "Can I drive you home?" Frank asked.

"You'd better." I went out front to say good-night.

"Have a glass of wine, Goldilocks," said George, reaching out a massive arm.

"No, thanks." My tone alerting him, he glanced over to see Frank waiting in the kitchen doorway. Maybe we should have gone out the back, I thought. George turned his head away sharply; Leo raised an eyebrow at me and grinned. I shrugged. George knew I slept with other men. We often joked about it. I said good-night and left, although not before noticing that George was gnawing on his wedding ring.

"You know," I said as I climbed in Frank's black Chevy, "you seem to me like the kind of guy who'd ride a bike."

"Nah, you got me all wrong. I grew up in New York where they don't have bikes. At least, I had one once but it was stolen the next day. I rode subways."

"Did you ride between the cars?"

"Oh, yeah, everybody did that. We jumped down on the tracks on a dare. Jumped turnstiles—I tell you, it's a luxury to have a car. I feel like a king."

I laughed at the combination of sincerity and self-mockery in his tone. I could see he felt like a king—or rather like a New York boy made good, leaning back and driving with two fingers, his left elbow slouched out the window. Under his black jacket he wore a white button-down shirt and a thin black leather tie knotted loosely. I already felt proprietary toward these garments. I wanted to lay my cheek against the cool leather of his tie, slip my tongue between the buttons of his shirt—and I also liked the flirtiness of the distance between us. I felt what I had never felt before—not a desire that the evening turn out any particular way but a wish to play it and replay it, to put my head in his lap and then not to, to go down to a waterfront bar and drink, to go home, to go to his house, to drive all night.

He seemed to know how I felt for he drove more slowly. He put his left hand on the wheel and reached out for mine with his right. I held his fingers, cool, slender, and dry, and gazed in a kind of trance out the window at the neighborly streets of south-central Berkeley where the houses are all different colors and styles, where the family dogs stroll the sidewalks unleashed, and the plum trees drop their yellow fruit, which makes such a thick, sweet jam. "Do you go up to the hills much?" Frank asked.

"No, I don't have a car."

"I go up there all the time. What would Berkeley be without the hills?" He was suddenly enthusiastic. "There are even cows up there."

I laughed. "I've seen plenty of cows in my life. I grew up in New Hampshire, you know."

"Yeah, well, I never saw any cows. Once we went on a field trip to New Jersey and we passed some horses, and I said, like, 'Hey, look at the cows.' Nobody ever let me forget that."

"It does seem kind of stupid," I teased. "I mean, even from pictures, you should have been able to tell the difference."

"Yeah, and I knew what horses looked like. I'd seen them in Central Park. But I was just so anxious to see cows. I really missed the whole country bit. Woods, fields—I used to read books about it. We never even had a yard because my father thought it was too much trouble. Four fucking feet square. He covered it with cement. Asshole."

We had arrived at my house and I invited him in. He was abstracted—he followed as if he had been here a hundred times—as I led him into the hall and living room. Callie was on the couch reading a Wonder Woman comic. I'm not even sure Frank saw her as she scurried off.

I sat down. He wandered around the room for a minute, lifting his camera up and pointing it here and there. I imagined that this was his real face—a black shiny snout and a glass lens. I'd still like him. "Do you take pictures professionally?"

"You mean do I get paid? I've sold stuff, I've been in a couple of shows. It doesn't matter. Some idiot thinks he owns the piece, puts it up on the wall . . . so what? Once it's done, you know, it's history. Not interesting. You must know that."

"My work gets very uninteresting after a few hours," I said drily. He laughed and put an arm around me, bending over my chair to do it.

"Can I have something to drink?" he said into my ear. His breath was like a spirit, like a genie climbing into my brain.

"Yes," I said, prolonging the word as much as I could. "Would you like some wine?"

"No, nothing alcoholic. Do you have any lemonade?"

"I can make it."

"I'll help you." We went in the kitchen and as I started to turn on the light, he put a hand on my wrist. "We don't need any more light. There's a moon." I paused and looked out the window. The moon was rising between the branches of the lemon tree.

"You see that tree?" I asked. "In the afternoons it's full of little black girls. There's about three of them who come regularly and steal lemons. They're shameless. My roommate Callie tries to scare them off, but she's not very frightening."

"I think I've seen those girls."

"They laugh and chatter, look in the windows at us, and pick our roses when they leave."

"And turn into blackbirds around the corner," he said.

I took a pitcher down from the shelf and handed him four lemons and a knife. "A cook who works in the dark, trusting to the touch and smell of things," he mused.

"I can see. Can't you see?" The moon shone through the flimsy white curtains. The lemons lay in pools of shadow on the gleaming Formica. "The lemons are so bright."

"They're weirdly bright. They look like they're about to hatch." he said.

"No, a lemon is not an egg. A lemon thinks in drops. It's medicinal, though it tends toward sorcery. It has its erotic side too, and enjoys being squeezed into the hair of young girls who wish to be blond."

"You never needed to do that."

"No."

"Your hair is beautiful. So long." He gathered it in both hands and let it sift through his fingers while I stood still, unable to move with the pleasure. It was a special kind of pleasure, dizzying and more than sensual; it made me feel as a puppet must when the hand goes up. To be touched where you come alive, to be touched so that memory seems to awaken. I leaned my head back slowly and he cupped it in his hands; I wanted to fall backward, that childhood game of trust.

I said, "There's a fairy tale about long hair that I love. Whenever the princess's hair is cut, it grows back twice as fast. Soon it's miles and miles long. But they have to keep cutting it, no matter how fast it grows."

"How does it end?"

"Oh, I forget. Something about a fairy stepping in and making it all right. Her hair is just down to her feet and she gets married."

"You sound disappointed," he said.

"Well, she could put her head on the windowsill, couldn't she? With a pillow under it, and let her hair float out on the wind."

There was a silence after I said that, a disinclination to hurry toward bed yet a wish to acknowledge that it was there. Frank lifted up his hand, sticky with lemon, and I put mine against it, fingertip to fingertip. We smiled at each other as our hands stuck together then pulled them apart with a squelch.

"Shall we go into the living room?" I said.

"No, I like your kitchen better."

It was a nice kitchen. Callie had painted it yellow and I had bought a small but rugged oak table at a yard sale. There were lots of windows and an old-fashioned upstanding sink with a basin big enough to bathe a small child. Grandmother had sent me a few of our copper pots and I had gathered flowered pitchers, blue and white cannisters, a used Waring blender, waffle iron, and ice-cream maker. In the half dark even the Formica and linoleum looked good; they gave the place a shine.

We sat down at the table with our glasses of lemonade. Frank's face was in shadow. All I could see was the white gleam of his shirt and a shock of yellow hair, but I already knew his features. I imagined I was a cook in a big wealthy house, that I spent my days in this room and welcomed my lover here at night. I would save food for him, fruits and meat. We would have to whisper so the mistress wouldn't hear. And we wouldn't listen to them in the rest of the house, we wouldn't care.

Of course I didn't really know him. Hardly at all. The thought made me uneasy, as if my activities of the last year could exert an influence and keep him a stranger. Whether he felt the same uneasiness, or whether it was the comfort of the shadows, I don't know, but he began to talk.

"My mother was a lousy cook. I think she was afraid of the kitchen. My father was always buying appliances she didn't want to use. He'd get angry at the food and refuse to eat it. She'd scrape it all in the garbage. He'd take us out for ice cream. About half the time—no, probably less—on the way home from getting ice cream, there'd be a thing called 'The Test.' He'd drive somewhere out of the way, then reach back and open the car door, make my sister Marva and me get out in a strange neighborhood. Then he'd drive off. . . . We'd be alone. Any way we got home was fine with him, as long as we didn't panic. That was the key point, that was what we were tested on. I always believed he was hidden somewhere, watching, aware of every tear on our faces. Once Marva almost got raped. We never told him, we just assumed it was part of 'The Test,' which we passed that time by sheer luck and running like hell."

"Didn't your mother try to stop this?"

"She was afraid of him. I think she was even afraid of us." He gave me a crooked smile across the little table; if I had been any closer, I would have stroked his cheek.

"And then one day, in 1965, there occurred the Great New York Blackout. Marva and I were coming back from somewhere with our parents, both of them. We were in the subway station when it happened. We grabbed hands immediately. I could hear my mother scream and my father curse. He started shouting for matches. I always carried matches. Marva and I just tiptoed away. We found the stairs and climbed. On the street I lit the matches, and there were other people out there lighting matches — it was like being at some kind of wonderful ceremony. Little yellow flames and car headlights. That was all. Houses, buildings, the school blacked out, people calling back and forth. There wasn't any looting where we were, just people trying to get home or else enjoying the whole thing. We found a trio of old drunks, one of whom had a candle. God knows where he got it. We lit the candle and sat down in a doorway with them. They offered us some of their brandy and we got tipsy — soon we were singing all our school songs. I was hoping my parents would never get out of the subway. The wish terrified me — but all these people were around, attracted by our little party, and everybody was joking, like the whole thing was an excuse to have fun. I couldn't remember why I was always so afraid in strange neighborhoods.

"Marva met a guy that night, a rookie cop, whom she dated secretly for two years. He took us home around midnight. My mother was in bed and my father was furious. He wasn't sure we'd left them on purpose but he was very suspicious. He grilled us for two hours. He knew I'd had matches.

"The next day Marva explained something to me. She was fifteen then and reading psychology. She said our parents were crazy, and it was certain we'd turn out crazy, too, if we didn't resist them on all fronts. Any guilt we felt would destroy us. She was wonderfully convincing, and she was proof that growing up did actually happen, that someday I would be free.

"I spent the next four years like a prisoner preparing for parole. Seriously. I thought that way. I made contacts on the outside—hung out with older kids—learned as much as I could about survival, and when the time came to run away, I wasn't surprised at how easy it was. Marva had painted the dangers of living with my parents so vividly, nothing else seemed dangerous or difficult at all."

"What did she do?"

"She lived with them until she graduated high school. When she left for college, I left, too. I went to the East Village. I spent a couple of years there, panhandling and selling dope until I was sick of the whole scene, which had totally deteriorated. It wasn't like the sixties anymore. I moved uptown, got a job as a busboy, then as a locksmith's apprentice. That was great. I liked the old man, the father of my best friend Angelo, who was making too much money in drugs to go into the business himself. Angelo, Sr., used to send me around to all the young women newly arrived from the Midwest. I'd spend an hour or so installing their police locks and window bars, then they'd offer me a beer, and by the time I left, I usually had a date."

"With grown-up women?"

"You have to understand, I was a very cool kid. Still pissed off from my shitty childhood, I felt tough because I lived on my own. I didn't consider anything worth pursuing. I planned to spend my life watching other people, simply observe, live day to day. I didn't need anybody, just a place to sleep, something to eat . . . I was quite serious."

He smiled at me as if this were all long gone in the past. I laughed. He laughed, too. "Yeah, they found me fascinating because I was so sincere—sincerely indifferent to the world, but willing to talk about that indifference all night. And in some ways it was true. I didn't know what I wanted yet, and I wasn't afraid of anything. My family had been the only people who really made an impression on me, and Marva was in Maine, and I never saw my parents.. . . . So I got laid whenever I wanted by a lot of different women. In many ways the perfect life for a kid that age. I thought I'd live that way forever."

"What happened?"

"I got hit by a car."

"Oh, no!" I stared at him, as if he might suddenly turn bloody or lame before my eyes. I had been so involved in his story, it was hard to remember that it was done with, that we were sitting talking in my living room.

"Broke both my legs. I was in the hospital for a month. My mother found out and came to see me. She spent the whole hour she was there complaining about how I'd deserted her, and her arthritis, and my father's other women. . . . Anyway, the point is, I sued the guy who hit me — Angelo got me this really macho lawyer — and I won fifty thousand dollars. He made me into a really sad case, a little runaway on my crutches. I was eighteen but I looked younger. So, after I gave the lawyer his cut, I had thirty-odd left. I didn't know what to do with it. I knew I didn't want to blow it. I didn't want to spend it at all, yet. So I was talking to some guys at a bar, guys in business suits, you know, and asking them how I should invest it. Most of them told me the stock market, but that didn't appeal to me then. One guy said I should put it in gold, which had just been offered to ordinary investors. This was in 'seventy-five. So I thought about it for a while; then I bought it, and a wooden pirate's chest to keep it in."

"You didn't keep that much gold in your apartment?"

"At the foot of my bed. It was this pirate's chest I got from a theater supply store with a skull and crossbones painted on it that shone in the dark." He grinned.

"Weren't you afraid of it being stolen?"

"Not really. My place was pretty secure. Angelo's father barricaded it for me. Sure it was a risk, but the pleasure of having it, you can't imagine: waking up sometimes in the middle of the night and getting out of bed just to look at that skull glaring at me in the dark. I loved it."

"You never showed it to anyone?"

"Sometimes to women. I swore them to secrecy. It wasn't neces-sary. They didn't believe it was real gold. They thought I was playing with them."

"Weren't you?"

He leaned back, rocking in his chair. "I don't know. I wanted to hide it but I also wanted everyone to know. I wanted to fling gold coins into the crowd, and I also couldn't part with it. I kept working. But the longer I owned it and the more shit jobs I had, the less it seemed like fairy gold and more like real wealth."

"Of course . . . so then it went up to a thousand and you sold it?"

"It never went up to a thousand. I sold it a year ago, fifteen months ago, for eight-fifty. And that's how I got to be a rich man." He smiled at me and I understood why people like to be around successful gamblers. Maybe I was confusing my sensations, but I thought I could see the luckiness around him, the presence of a doting fortune.

"So now you don't have gold anymore."

"No, now I have stocks and bonds."

"A real capitalist pig."

"It's better than working for one."

"I guess so. How does it feel to have all that money?"

"Like somebody up there is saying, 'Don't sweat it, Jack.' He laughed. "If I still had my gold, I'd make you a necklace to match your hair."

I pictured a necklace made of gold coins. It would be heavy, like a collar. I could feel the cold, round weight on my throat. But he had no gold anymore, all he had was money, which I didn't need. He started to smile at me, one of those deliberately sexy smiles that work all the better for their deliberation, and I felt suddenly cornered by the table between us. The distance, his gaze. I stood up.

"Let's go upstairs."

He looked startled, then followed. I walked fast and he didn't catch up until the landing. He turned me around and pulled me into an embrace. I buried my face in his neck. I felt his heart beat while his penis struggled up and against me. I love that moment: it's alive. We stood like that, hugging fiercely, then followed each other into my room. The window was open and wind blew in, showering us with fragrance. I thought how ironic it was that a flower's sex smell seems so innocent to us. I imagined some higher being collecting bouquets of genitalia as we might collect bougainvillea. It didn't seem bizarre.

I undressed and sat down on the bed. Frank knelt before me with his face between my thighs. I bent over, my hair spilling down his back, my face against his spine, and I felt curiously alone on that cool expanse. Then my hands went around to his nipples and belly and penis and he was all warmly there.

I lay back suddenly. He raised his head, looked at me, then in one swift leap lay beside me, his leg over mine. His breath was in my mouth as he said, "I want to fuck you."

"Nobody's stopping you," I replied, leaning my head back away from his so he had to follow, his mouth closing over mine. The clash of our tongues, the slow, sweet feed. His cock slid like a boat into water.

As we fucked, he took turns kissing and talking. He said, "Your face looks like you've been fucking for a hundred years." He said, "I'm going to fuck you for a hundred years." I wrapped my legs around him and stared up into his face, which shone with sweat, lips parted for his laboring breath, and I knew I must surround him with passion, charm, tenderness, with everything I had. He was a feast.

woke up in a blaze of sunlight. The window was still open and I could hear laughter from the street; a fly buzzed somewhere in the room. I was unreasonably happy . . . Frank was here. I turned to look at him, remembering every separate glory of his body, but the bed was empty. In that instant, the night shrank to a candle flame, blue around the wick, burning tentatively against the stronger sun. Usually I didn't mind this feeling, it was what I expected. A sexual adventure was a superior dream, a bedtime story for adults where all the longing and violence of the day resolved itself. In the morning I sneaked out of the strange house, or if I brought a man here, quickly got rid of him. The ones I brought here were the ones I *could* get rid of easily, the cold ones, which, now that I thought of it, must have given Callie a strange idea of my tastes.

I got out of bed and went to the bathroom, anticipating his shout from below. I washed my face, combed my hair, and rubbed Givenchy behind my ears. Flower's sex odor . . . yes, I could smell the resemblance to ours. I tied my blue bathrobe and looked at myself. The face in the mirror was watchful, smooth as cream, dominated by wide, glowing eyes. I walked slowly downstairs, picturing Frank drinking coffee, and allowed myself a little anger. I expected him to understand the necessity of being there when I woke up. I expected him to understand everything.

He was not in the kitchen. Callie's teacup with its mess of wet peppermint leaves stood on the counter. There was nothing else. I filled the kettle, put it on the stove, ground coffee. The noise whined through the house. He might have left hours ago.

Callie's cat, Esteban, walked in the kitchen. I scooped him up, burying my face in his orange fur. He laid two claws on either side of my neck and dug in, meowing disapproval. "You macho grouch," I said, throwing him to the floor. He rolled on his back with a satisfied sneer on his bleary face: Esteban liked the rough stuff. I accommadated him with a sullen kick, then let him bite my foot, his front paw holding it firmly while his back legs tried to push it away.

"Enough," I said, freeing my scratched and bleeding foot. The pain throbbed pleasantly, gift to my self-pity, while I made coffee and poured myself a cup. It was so quiet in here. He probably had an appointment, I thought, but why didn't he leave a note? Some people don't like notes. Was that possible? I didn't like telephones, never had, but surely no one was made uncomfortable by notes, ink, paper, words. He was simply cruel. He liked to do it, to make a strange woman fall in love with him. It was only what I deserved, wasn't it? I didn't think so. I had never employed such promising glances, such pauses, such tricks. I was honest—mostly—but nonetheless, he wasn't coming back.

What a thief. If I was really one too, no one would ever love me. Now that I remembered how to fall in love, it would happen over and over, and no one would ever return it.

When I had finished my second cup of coffee, Frank walked in carrying a bakery box tied with string, a brown paper bag, and two pink carnations. He was shorter than I remembered, and more concentrated, his body so vivid I could almost see it through his clothes. His face was high-cheekboned, arrowhead-shaped, and bearing lovingly down on me.

"Good morning," he said. "I'd hoped to get back before you woke up, but I forgot the bakery doesn't open until ten." He put his armload down on the table and opened the box. A strawberry tart, a kiwi tart, and two croissants reposed within. He shook a wedge of brie out of the bag.

"I thought you disappeared," I said mournfully, as he came near enough to smell and touch.

"Why would I do that?" He kissed me on the mouth.

"I don't know. These look great, where did you get them?"

"At the French bakery on College. Where are the plates?"

"In the cupboard by the sink. Do you want coffee?"

"Yes, please."

I set the table, poured the coffee, and put the carnations in water. He sat down and I sat in his lap. Frank cut me a slice of brie and I sank my teeth into the ripe cheese. "You've got the day off," he said. "What shall we do with it?"

"How do you know it's my day off?"

"I ran into George."

"My God, where?"

"At the bakery. Apparently his pastry chef is out."

"Seth, yeah. His ex-wife is always dropping the kids on him unexpectedly."

"No, this time he has to go to the gynecologist."

"Seth?"

"His girlfriend has an infection, and she insists he go with her. Her gynecologist is in Sacramento."

"That sounds like an excuse George would accept. You talked about me?" I picked up the kiwi tart and bit into it.

"He told me you liked kiwi."

"You told him—"

"He knew. He was rather smooth about the whole thing, but with a kind of underground smirk."

"Underground only because it's so early in the morning."

"You're having an affair with him?"

"Sort of."

"It's not serious?"

". . . No. I only see him at work, I've never brought him here." This felt like a betrayal, yet it was the truth. I had never thought of George as "serious." Frank hugged me a little tighter. "You make a good chair," I said. "I wish there were more like you in the stores."

"Isn't one enough?"

"Oh, I'd like to have six around a dinner table. Chair men. Naked of course. Then I'd invite all my girlfriends to dine."

"Want to try it? Naked?"

"Okay, but let me get some more coffee." I stood up and crossed to the stove, pouring an unnecessary cup of coffee as Frank took off his pants. I watched him. I liked especially the careful lifting of his elasticized Jockey shorts down and over the head of his penis.

"Shall I take off my shirt?" he asked.

"No, but in the future I want you to wear one of those T-shirts that look like a tuxedo."

"Come here."

I went. He pulled up my bathrobe and I didn't wait, I impaled myself, thinking of jungle gyms and bicycles, of white stallions and the old, gray branches of apple trees. I sipped my coffee. "All I need now is the newspaper," I said.

"Or the morning post. You should be looking over your invitations to the opera and the duchess's ball." He thrust, and I put down my coffee hastily. Then, leaning forward with my hands on my knees, I was fucked over the remains of my breakfast. My hair swept up all the crumbs, and when Frank came he kicked the table leg, which knocked the carnations wetly into our laps. "I don't think this is such a good idea for a dinner party," he said.

"Let's go upstairs."

We did. It was about eleven and the sun was bright on my unmade bed. I finally took off my bathrobe and Frank took off his shirt. I loved his hairless chest, like an Indian's, and his round freckled shoulders. His nipples were as brown as his eyes, if not quite so pretty. Nothing was so pretty as his eyes—bright brown, perfectly oval, full of undiminished optimism. I felt tender, so tender. I knew a thousand caresses. I stroked him with legs and feet and breasts. I lifted the hair off his forehead and kissed the pale skin. I kissed his lips. I kissed him until he lay quietly, his heart beating fast, his penis beating slowly against my crotch. Then I stopped.

"Your turn," I said, looking into his brown eyes. His hands, resting lightly on my hips, began to squeeze, moving up and down and back and forth, finding more flesh than I knew I had. When he pushed my legs open with his, my thighs seemed to flow away from the source, rippling over the sheets. To the east, to the west.

His entrance centered me. I flung my legs over his and listened in delight to his captured, hoarse breathing. My lover, my darling.

"I'm going downstairs," I whispered. He was asleep and didn't answer. "I'll be back in a minute, in two minutes."

Callie was in the kitchen, washing our breakfast dishes. She had hung Frank's jacket in the closet. "Oh, Stella—!" she said. She was impressed because I hadn't gotten rid of him yet.

"Oh, Callie," I replied, smiling at her affectionately. "There's some Soave left, isn't there?"

"Yes, half a bottle."

I took it out of the refrigerator and poured it into two brimming glasses. "Well, tell me what you think. He's cute, isn't he?" I put the wine bottle in the trash.

"Yes, very cute. I just saw him for a second, but I think he looks like you."

"No."

"Yes, he's blond, not much bigger than you, and he smiles like you."

"Well, the way I feel right now, I guess that's a real compliment."

"Oh, that's so wonderful, Stella!" She beamed as if I'd announced our wedding. "I'm so happy for you."

"Thanks." I took the glasses of wine and some oranges upstairs. Frank opened his eyes when I walked in the room. "She thinks you look like me," I said.

"What a compliment."

"That's what I said."

We drank the wine and I got drunk, as I always did when I drank in the morning.

"So, what shall we do?" he said when the wine was gone.

"Stay here."

"No, I'm restless." As soon as he said it, he jumped out of bed and started pacing the room. He had moves like a boy on a basketball court, I thought, though according to what he'd told me he was more likely to have sunk stones through the windows of abandoned buildings. ("Of course that was just an excuse, the rock throwing," he'd said. "You have to do it. What I liked was getting inside those weird empty places. Prowling from room to room, not knowing when the floor would break through. What a rush.")

"What do you want to do?" I asked.

"Let's go up to Tilden Park and take pictures of you."

"Oh, I don't want to do that."

"You'll like it, come on."

Tilden Park covers five thousand acres on top of the Berkeley hills, and a good proportion of that is eucalyptus forest. There's something about eucalyptus—the silvery-gray leaves, the papery bark with its enlarged grain, as if you're staring at it closely—that reminds me of the way eastern trees look when you're on LSD. The association was so strong I always got a high just going up there. That and the wildness, the wine in my blood, and the winter-morning cough-drop smell combined with a blue California day, made me as giddy as the jazzed-up mad photographer beside me. I took my clothes off and he snapped pictures: One hand emerging from behind a tree. A leg on a log. Standing upright, while he shot from the ground. From the back, running, a tiny figure among the trees.

I felt more self-conscious than I ever do during sex. Usually I don't feel naked when I am; after dropping the last stitch, I feel clothed again, like Achilles. But Frank's camera made me feel shy. He noticed of course.

"Talk, Stella. Tell me something. Tell me about college, I never went. Did you live in a coed dorm? Did you learn anything useful?"

How peculiar, I thought, to be sitting bare-ass on a boulder, describing my college days—that post-Tobias blur of loneliness and depression. The nights I stayed up until three making chocolate truffles and marzipan that Janey would stuff in her pockets on her way to class the next day.

As I spoke, Frank was all around me, each shutter click like a soft punch, or a lover's spank, giving me a jumpy, slightly perverse pleasure. My memory of college was so sensual because I had been so unhappy; my thwarted desires had seeped out to color every day. Rosy classrooms, golden solitudes—the fierce ache of my belief in love. I had no detachment. Only my nights out in New York provided that. They somehow transformed the longing. It didn't burn in me but merely had residence, and each night was a postponement as well as a story in itself. Each postponement added to the delicious expectancy; each story distracted me from the tension of that.

I didn't tell Frank about my nights in New York, only what he had asked for, my college days. Finally he put his camera down and sat beside me.

"You're lucky you have a lover who can record your beauty," he said. "It would be a crime not to have pictures taken at every stage of your life. And, as you'll see, I take very good pictures. You'll be satisfied."

"I'm sure I will be," I said, although I didn't care what the pictures looked like. I lay my head on his shoulder and felt the warmth rising up through his shirt. Photography was a nervousness in his blood; I had to let it subside. I leaned into him.

"You're relaxed now," he said. "Naked up here, where anyone could come, and you're as calm as if at the first sound of a stranger you would turn back into a tree. He'd be searching and searching for that beautiful woman he glimpsed while you would stand unnoticed, shaking your long, leafy tresses." His arm tightened around me. "Don't turn back into a tree."

"Join me then. Take your clothes off. I can't stand all these clothes on you."

Naked he was as white as a peeled almond. I fed on his flesh, which remained magically undiminished. We tumbled into the slippery eucalyptus leaves and made love to the distant accompaniment of children's laughter. Frank was tireless, thrusting and thrusting, until I was almost jealous of his ability to go inside. But why be jealous? He couldn't get very far, though he would keep trying. As we lay side by side—his eyelashes on my cheek, his breath running down my neck—I knew we would never be close enough. We would never be one; and in that case, where should intimacy stop?

We drove down the hill and had a late lunch at a café on College

Avenue. As we waited for the food to come, I felt, for the first time, part of a couple. It was a curiously smug feeling. Teo had always been coupled to his booze, Tobias was never mine, but Frank, still bouncing with energy in the seat across from me, talking about the pictures he had taken, had attached himself. I felt his fingerprints whispering all over my body.

eorge was there when I arrived at The Vineyard.

"So, you showed up," he said.

"Why not?"

"Might have decided to stay in bed all day." He was leaning against the counter, looking very handsome in a red shirt. His hair had been newly cut, and even his eyebrows looked cleaned and pressed.

"Frank said he met you at the bakery. So I presume you're referring to my night with him?"

"You presume correctly. One night?"

"Two."

"True love?"

"Maybe."

He looked at me thoughtfully for a moment, then said briskly, "Let's get to work. What's for dinner?"

"I don't know. What did you buy?"

"You don't know, you don't know. You know what there is for sale," he said unfairly. "Haven't you got any ideas?"

"Yes, of course."

"Well?"

"Cauliflower soup," I said off the top of my head. "With red pepper and vermouth. Grilled tuna with tomato and onions. Vermicelli con vermicelli. Worms, you know."

"Yes? You think cauliflower is a spring vegetable? This is April, Stella. People want the green shit. I didn't buy any tuna."

"Why not?"

"Because it's shitty and overpriced, why the fuck do you think? Vermicelli con vermicelli," he muttered disgustedly.

"I think we ought to change our emphasis, George, and serve only revolting food but in an original manner. That'll be the real test for those who call cooking an art. After all, look what we put up with in literature and painting."

"Look what I put up with from you."

After that we worked in silence, but not uncompanionably. I was relieved that he had not tried to touch me, that he had known right away Frank was not like my one-night stands. For that kind of understanding, I was willing to put up with a little abuse. Or more than a little; I thought I knew how disappointed he was.

When everything was done, George went out to the dining room to start on the wine. I put lids on all my pots, covered the salad with a towel, and joined him. He poured me a glass of wine, picked up my braid, and held it loosely in his fist.

"Well, Blondie, I can't say I like the fellow, but I've been asking around."

"What?"

"About Frank. Hell, you're a friend of mine. I just wanted to see."

"What did you find out? His credit rating?"

"I don't just associate with businessmen," he said in an injured tone. "Most of my friends are artists and writers."

"Okay, okay."

"That boy of yours seems to be all right. A lot of people like him. It seems he's done some good deeds. Coaxed Mary Henderson's son out of joining the Moonies and her daughter out of joining the army. Coaxed them out of Berkeley, too, which is a damn good thing, considering their parents. Anyway, he's a real Samaritan. A little strange—"

"So?" I was surprised and yet not surprised by these "good deeds." It wasn't inconsistent, yet I had an idea he wouldn't talk about it.

"But sincere. And of course he's rich."

"Not that rich."

"He doesn't have to work for a living. He's rich."

"Okay." I conceded the point as if it were a flaw. "So you approve? You'll give me away at the wedding?"

He looked at me ironically. "I've come to that, have I? Father figure for the little girl?" I blushed, for it was not completely untrue. George finished his glass of wine and said mournfully, "Do you think Judy likes me?"

"Judy's married."

"So am I."

"But your wife doesn't work here." Sometimes I wondered whether George's wife even existed. She never called. "I don't think Leo would care for it."

"He needs the job."

"Don't tell her I said so, but Judy thinks you're a reactionary old sexist pig."

"I know, but Leo's going bald." We laughed. "He's coming to pick you up tonight, I suppose?"

"Yes," I replied, and felt a surge of giddy joy. It was really happening to me.

I made cold cucumber soup and gazpacho, chilled artichokes and cold salmon with pesto. Contrary to what is said, there are seasons in California, and not just the warm/dry and cool/wet. There are mini seasons, lasting an hour or a week and coming in no particular order. One day of fall, three of summer, a week of spring, a morning of summer—everything but winter. They were authentic enough to at first confuse, and then exhilarate. Now it was summer, and had been for a week or two. The restaurant was packed.

My soup was gobbled up with cries of delight. George poured cold white wine himself, beaming at the amount they drank and all the naked backs. People lingered over cantaloupe mousse and iced espresso. Boys with loud radios walked by outside and nobody minded. A drunk man stumbled into the kitchen looking for the bathroom and a wisp of my hair caught fire from his cigarette: a minor blaze. I clapped it out with a curse, and a few singed hairs curled acridly around my face. George brought me a glass of wine to soothe me but I didn't need soothing and poured the wine into the soup. One woman loudly praised the result, and her neighbor complained because her soup hadn't had wine in it. George brought her a second bowl and she smiled with the greed, he said, of rich people getting something free. George could always spot a rich person, even when he looked normal and left a proper tip.

When I got off work, Frank was waiting under the streetlight outside. He was wearing old white corduroy jeans, moccasins without socks, and a UC Berkeley T-shirt. "Hi, Gorgeous," I said, "what's your price?"

"Police officer," he said. "You'll have to come with me, miss." He took both my wrists in his hands.

"Just what I had in mind. You're sure cute for a cop. Where's your pistol?"

"Don't get fresh."

"Kiss me." He did so as we were crossing the street, his arms wrapped tightly around me. We walked home like that and ran upstairs to bed.

We spent most of the next month there. It was bliss coming together after any small time apart. We explored, halting at every junction to kiss, suck, bite, probe, and penetrate. Such variations were possible, variations that blurred the images of male and female; and there were times when I saw Frank's body as a newly created thing, without association. I pressed the springy flesh of his hip and the sharp bone, I slid my fingers up his buttock, gaining the round hill, and down into the gathered heat, the purse-mouth that I pried open. In the same spirit I tasted the sour wax of his ears, and pulled the dead skin off the bottoms of his feet. I felt only sensual then, without enough mentality for the opposition of gender. All was texture, color, odor, pleasure. And life, rather than femininity, flowed through my veins. This was not true, I think, of Frank. He was more sexual than I; he was never rid of it. He touched my body with purpose, no matter how slack and sleepy our flesh. And his purpose became mine soon enough.

We stayed awake late every night and woke up early. Frank brought breakfast to my room: a pot of French-roast coffee, brewed very strong, toast, honey, oranges or grapes or melon. I had some of the blue-and-white china from Grandmother's house, and a few silver spoons, so the tray was always pretty.

I felt so languorous sitting up in bed, aching from sex, eating toast spread with honey. Frank would gaze, perhaps reach out a hand to unbutton my nightgown, and I would enjoy being looked at—feel a pride as if I had fashioned this body myself. I'd tell him my dreams, if I'd had any, and he'd listen so carefully, I felt all the nights of my past reaching toward the nights of our future like a tapestry being woven from two ends.

He didn't only listen of course. As I drank more coffee, spread another piece of toast with the good Greek honey, Frank would tell me stories from his time as a locksmith. Pale Violet from Milwaukee who hadn't talked to a soul since she arrived in New York, except for her elderly employer. She said she was too shy to make friends so she put personal ads in the newspapers, asking for a lover. When the letters came, she read them and reread them, but never replied. She had a shoebox full, Frank said, which she showed to him. Then there was Stevie on the twelfth floor who wanted window bars because of demons, and Caroline who called on behalf of her roommate who was chained to the bed.

He told me about Dorothy, his first love.

"I met her in England. This was when I was about twenty-one and had a couple of thousand left that I hadn't bought gold with. I was planning to go around the world, but I never made it past London. Dorothy was an American, older than me, studying acting. Beautiful woman. I fell in love immediately. It was a shock; I had no idea I was capable of falling in love. That sounds so funny now; some idiot I was. But I didn't resist. I followed that woman around. She took me mainly to cathedrals. She was mad about cathedrals. We'd go there when there was no one else around and stand silently in the middle, eyes closed. Listening to the stone, she said. Then she'd embrace me and when I got her back to bed, she'd be crazy. It overwhelmed me but I loved it. I loved her."

I listened to this with more than a little jealousy, but it also reassured me. Any man who had not been so in love was hardly worth considering. "What happened?"

"She grew tired of me. She wanted more of a challenge." He gave me a crooked smile. "She ran off with a married Portuguese painter and his five children."

"Poor Frank!"

"I was heartbroken. I had never thought of the possibility. And I had the wife to deal with, who didn't even speak English. She came to our room . . . she kept slapping her breasts and I couldn't figure out what she meant by it. Woe is me? That she missed her children? She finally left—took out after them, I guess. I started thinking things like, We should've had children. I kinda liked the idea of having five little replicas of myself running around."

"I've never wanted children because of love," I said. "It seems like they'd only get in the way."

"There's so much you can do for them, so much more than for adults. Adults are sort of grimy." I raised an eyebrow. "Oh, not you. You're beautiful."

"I'm not beautiful."

"Of course you are."

"Nobody ever thought so before."

"Tell me about those idiots who didn't think so."

So I told him about Tobias, the whole story, every detail, and he was laughing with me, and saying, "Poor Stella." And watching, his face very close to mine. He had a way of tilting his narrow head so his big Italian nose seemed to weigh down his face or anchor it, and then his gaze would lock on mine and I felt as if he were lowering himself inside my very soul. It wasn't a conscious empathy so much as a talent he indulged in for his own pleasure, though of course empathy came with it. It was stranger than anything I could do because it wasn't tied to the ritual of sex, which is by nature self-limiting. Frank's interest was open-ended; it was almost frightening. It was frightening, yet still seductive. How could I bear such intimacy, day after day? How could I live without it?

When I stopped talking, I opened the window. The wind breathed over us, billowing in paisley shapes, warm and forcible. We lay side by side and, as I kissed him, all the love poetry Tobias had ever read me surged through my head until I felt grand. I felt great-hearted and

timeless, able to love forever. Frank kissed me back and his ardor was
an astonishment; yet also no surprise at all.

I cooked beautifully that summer. Cold mushroom soup with chopped
hardboiled egg yolks and tarragon, duck braised in port, chicken
with almonds and green grapes, a simple, perfectly baked eggplant
with an incredibly low amount of oil. When George commented on my
performance, I replied dreamily, "It's all flesh." He roared with
laughter. I smiled benignly. It was all right with me if my condition
amused him. I was glad he wasn't angry at me for breaking off. I often
vividly recalled our bouts—the sharp, uncluttered energy of them.
High jinks. Now I was too languorous for that. The Vineyard was my
refuge from passion; it was where I stored up precious hours of being
without. If I moved like a somnambulist in the kitchen it was for this
reason. I was in love, but I still needed solitude, and this was the only
place I could get it.

After several weeks, I suggested we give a dinner party. I hadn't met any of his friends yet, not even his roommate Rodney. Rodney was a psychiatrist who'd gone blind two years ago; a few months after his blindness struck, his wife Clara moved out and turned lesbian. "She's an artist," said Frank, "a wild woman. You'd like her." Although Frank had been more of a friend of Clara's than of Rodney's, he'd moved in to help out, and now he and Rodney were very close. Or so he said. Whenever I called there, I heard loud jazz playing and Frank would sound distracted.

"I'd like to meet Rodney," I said.

"Okay. Shall we invite Clara, too?" We were having this conversation in the bath, our legs around each other's waists, and Frank grinned at me as his penis floated in the water between us.

"Won't they mind?" I asked, filling a shampoo cap with hot water and pouring it over his penis. It thickened slightly, an engorgement of blood like a small crowd drifting to the scene of some minor altercation.

"No. They're friends. Clara discusses with Rodney her sexual peculiarities."

"Will we ever do that?"

"Don't we already?" He looked quizzical. I smiled and sank underwater. Sound ceased. Currents of cold nosed by. I felt like the

Goddess before the idea of creation has arisen. Frank's toe nudged my thigh: here was another body, my first desire. I surfaced and reached forward to take a kiss.

"We'll have to have Callie, too," I said.

"And Clara's lover Annie."

"You're determined to make this a strange evening, aren't you?"

"They like getting together. It's no big deal. Sometimes I think they'll end up married again. Anyway, you wanted to meet my friends."

I did indeed. If we could have friends together, I thought, the mellow sweetness of our love would not be diminished while its occasional frightening intensity would be. I imagined this blind psychiatrist as being fatherly and wise, a man who depended on Frank for so many physical offices, and repaid with counsel, a counsel I could share. Should Frank and I live together? Was I suited for it? I couldn't imagine anything better, in the short term, yet there was something monotonous about life in California.

"I think I'll make chicken," I said.

The dinner party was on Thursday. I picked flowers in the afternoon, stealing one or two from every garden on the block. Callie helped me; it's the only kind of theft she doesn't consider wrong. As we arranged them in vases she said, "I hope there won't be any trouble tonight."

"What do you mean?"

"This man who's coming . . . and his ex-wife . . . and her lover . . ."

"Well, Rodney's blind, you know," I said cheerfully. "Maybe he won't notice Annie."

"Stella!"

"Don't worry. If Frank says it's all right, it's all right. They're his friends."

"Yes, but people sometimes—"

"People sometimes act civilized about these things," I said loftily.

"Poor man," she said. Callie was the kind of person who, when she saw a cripple in a bookstore, followed his wheelchair around until he let her reach a book down from a high shelf.

"It'll be fine," I said. "Don't jinx my party."

"Oh, I didn't mean—"

"It's okay," I said.

When Frank arrived, we went upstairs to dress. "What are you going to wear?" I asked. Frank's wardrobe consisted of fifteen pairs of running shoes, several T shirts, a few skinny ties, a dozen thrift-store jackets, and one pair of blue jeans. And a pair of shorts to do the laundry in.

"I brought over my black linen jacket and a black tie."

"Can you explain to me why you wear ties with T shirts?"

"Yes, do you want to me to?"

"Never mind." I watched him dress as I rubbed body lotion over myself. He knotted the tie loosely around his neck; it looked like something he thought he might need later: a leash or a whip. Or a tourniquet. He combed his hair, which made no difference to how it looked, and put on his jacket. It was too big for him so he rolled up the sleeves. "You're so cute," I said.

"I know, I can't help it."

"What do you want me to wear?"

"Something sexy."

"How about this?" I pulled out an Indian cotton dress with a pattern of red-and-orange batik flowers.

"Perfect. Don't wear a bra with it."

"Really? It's so thin."

"I like to see your breasts lapping against the cloth."

"My breasts don't lap." I put on the dress.

"Yes, they do. Like waves."

"Oh, like waves . . ."

I looked at myself in the mirror. The dress was low-cut and clung to my hips, then belled out slightly below the knee. It was so long my feet were hidden when I stood still. I looked like a mermaid balancing on her tail.

We went down to the living room. I admired the thoroughness with which he had cleaned it, and he admired the bunch of flowers I had placed on the coffee table. There were purple irises, pink roses, white roses, and marigolds, as well as small purple and yellow wildflowers I didn't know the names of. The beauty of the flowers stood out in the shabby room. The couch especially was worn, its blue faded to a grayish color. I had an inspiration and took down my shawl from the shelf in the closet. It was cream-colored Chinese silk with delicate, bright flowers embroidered on it, and a long, drippy fringe. I laid it over the back of the couch, covering the worst spots. "There."

"It's beautiful," said Frank. "Where did you get it?"

"It was my great-grandmother's. I brought it here as a memento. It's not mine."

"Your grandmother let you take it? It looks very valuable."

"I guess it is. It's old. It's not hers anyway."

"Whose is it then?"

"My great-grandmother, Isabelle, left all her belongings to the house."

"You can't leave things to a house."

"She did. Nobody has disputed it."

"Who did she leave the house to? Was it hers?"

"Yes, her husband died first. She left it to my grandmother, of course."

"So then the shawl is hers also."

I was annoyed. "No. Maybe legally. But Grandmother understands the distinction. The things belong to the house."

"How could you bring it here then?"

"The house doesn't mind."

"Oh, I see," he said.

"Actually I always thought of this shawl as my mother's. She used to wear it. Maybe that's why I brought it with me . . . I remember how she used to stand, her arms crooked, up at the elbows, to hold the shawl, which had fallen off her shoulders. When I got close to her and smelled her perfume, I used to think it was the smell of the flowers."

I stood in a daze of sensuous memory. My mother was in my skin, her body twisting slightly with a movement, like silk fringe sliding across an arm. The wallpaper sea-green, faded—

"Let me see it around you," he said, reaching for the shawl.

"*No!*" I said, trying to hold back the flight of memory, my mother shrinking to a pinpoint.

"Why not?" he asked, hurt. I felt guilty and then angry. The moment was gone, and with it that exquisite presence. Why couldn't he tell, instantly, when to be quiet?

"Just leave it there," I said. "I don't want to wear it, I want it on the couch. Let's go in the kitchen, I have to start the food."

Rodney was the first of our guests to arrive. Frank introduced us and I took the hand held out to me. It was soft and busy, the fingers feeling mine for clues I wasn't sure I wanted to give.

"I'm very pleased to meet you," he said, and his voice was self-assured and mellifluous—sexy, if you liked that kind of thing.

I didn't.

He was very tall, with a narrow, aristocratic face and silver hair, although he was only in his early thirties. He wore a well-cut tweed suit and a silk tie. The expensive clothes annoyed me. I liked being the fanciest one at my own parties.

"Come into the living room," I said, taking his arm. The scratchy wool of his sleeve was unpleasant, and so was the firmness with which he held on to me. We walked slowly in, Frank on the other side giving Rodney a running description of furniture size and placement. He told him the colors of everything as well. When Rodney was settled in his chair, I went back to the kitchen to get the wine. I could hear Frank describe what I was wearing.

Callie came downstairs in a blue cotton dress with a sash and a quilted bodice. Frank introduced her to Rodney and she immediately started to talk to him about cancer, as she did with any M.D. she chanced to meet. As far as I knew, Callie had no personal experience with cancer, but she was deeply offended by its existence. She asked Rodney what he thought about the theory that certain personalities might be more prone to it.

"Certainly I think that's true. People think diseases of the mind have no importance, that they can be safely ignored. Men and women who wouldn't dream of missing a routine dental checkup blithely assume that their emotional problems are normal. Or at least, if nobody knows, it's tolerable. Of course it's not. Everybody *does* know, and even if they don't the body does. People with emotional problems don't think about the extent of the damage."

"Which just makes it worse, doesn't it?" asked Callie.

"Yes. Nobody can be helped before they admit the problem."

"I mean, it makes the cancer worse. To have negative emotions and not admit it, to pretend you're okay when you're rotting inside."

"Jesus," said Frank, "you sound like a preacher!"

"Well, maybe I do. People think being healthy is only fun things. Like jogging."

"Jogging isn't fun," said Frank. "It's just an excuse to wear running shoes." He looked down fondly at the pair he was wearing: black and silver.

"They think having a good attitude about things is just morality, when really it's dangerous not to."

"Curing attitudes is exactly what I try to do," Rodney said. "In a manner of speaking. Attitudes toward the self, primarily. It's not so hard, not for those willing to work at it."

"It's very difficult for those with a bad attitude, however," I said.

"That kind of bad attitude, yes."

"That kind gets punished with cancer."

He smiled at me. "It's not I who am doing the punishing."

Well, I thought, that's debatable. Who knows when we're causing each other's cancers? A shrink like Rodney could do a lot of damage. I glanced at Frank. This was his best friend.

Callie was talking about a new Norman Cousins–type cure she had read about. She was leaning forward in excitement, her face strawberry pink over the biblike front panel of her dress. I wondered how much of her mood Rodney heard in her voice. Probably all of it. No doubt he knew the exact state of her body's arousal.

He was not impressed by the cure she was describing; it didn't require a doctor, for one thing. "But think of a world without cancer," she said passionately.

"There'd still be poverty, famine, and war," I said.

"Not to mention clitoridectomies, forced sterilization, and marital rape," said someone from the doorway.

"Hello, Clara," said Rodney.

"Hello, Rodney." She smiled and strode into the room. "The door was unlocked, so I walked in." She was tall, lanky and amber-eyed, dressed in suede pants, cowboy boots, and a low-cut, coffee-colored silk shirt. Her honey-blond hair fell straight to her shoulders. "Hello Frank and Stella and Callie."

"Hello," we said and Callie blushed. Clara's gaze was very direct.

"Annie's parking the car; she'll be here in a minute." Frank poured her a glass of wine, which she accepted, still standing. "Stella, you have great hair."

"Thanks."

"There's so much of it."

"There's too much of it. Sometimes my head feels pregnant."

"I often feel that way." She smiled at me and tilted her head sideways. "Bluebirds, I think."

"What?"

"If your head were pregnant. Bluebirds would fly out—at the psychological moment—and alight on the tips of your toes."

"You're an artist," said Callie politely.

"Yes?"

"Do you paint realistically?"

"I make masks. Out of real materials. Rodney's going to give me his eyes." Callie blanched.

"What's this?" asked Frank.

"I'm going to find him some beautiful glass ones and he'll give me his, which I'll put on a mask. For him of course." Callie reached out a hand toward Rodney, then jerked it back, the fingers fluttering.

"Why should I want glass eyes? I'm fond of my own. It pleases me that I don't know what they look like now."

"They look like marble Easter eggs without the gloss. Something's sputtering in the kitchen."

"Oh!" I got up and went hastily out. The chicken needed to be turned down; I also basted it and added a little more wine. Looking at the yellowy, rosy breasts lying side by side in the pan, drops of fat and flecks of basil clinging to the flesh, I felt sorry for the chicken. It was so pretty, it would taste wonderful, but who would get the credit? Me. Nobody had respect for chickens, for their minutely organized flesh.

Clara asked from the door, "Can I help?" her tone making it clear that she didn't want to help especially, but wanted to be in here with me.

"Come on in. I was just feeling sorry for the dinner."

"Because it will get eaten by us?"

"Yeah."

"We don't have to eat it. We can just admire it on the table for a while, then go out for pizza."

"That wouldn't do the chickens much good."

"Oh, you're thinking about them. I thought you were worried that your masterpiece would be consumed."

"No. Just that we ought to be more like the Indians—thank the animals for their flesh."

She stood next to me, peering down at the baking dish. "Shall I do it?"

"Sure."

"Thank you little chickens, for your rosy breasts. Of all delights, the very best. The one that prepares us for all the rest."

"Thanks," I said. "I think they appreciated that."

"Anytime . . . so you're in love with Frank?"

"Yes."

"Madly?"

"Yes," I said, more cautiously. "Why?"

"He's a good man to be in love with. He's solid."

"I know."

"He's very much in love with you."

"He's talked, has he?" I said with mock anger.

"The man can't keep off the subject. He hasn't told me any secrets. I know, you don't like him talking. You want him to smile mysteriously when his friends ask him why he's never home anymore, why he looks so exhausted by joy when they do see him?"

"Does he?" I couldn't help but be pleased, although I didn't like to think about other people speculating about us. Especially tonight, when I felt so much on show.

"I've never seen any man so much in love. Except of course the ones who've been in love with me." She fluttered her eyelashes. "I always thought my lovers must not be the same as other people's— such gluey emotion."

"Does Frank's seem gluey to you?"

"No. It seems rather sweet. Although I'm not really in favor of love right now. I prefer independence."

"I intend to have both."

She looked at me; I was very aware of how extraordinarily beautiful she was. Her eyes were tawny, almost golden, very close to the color of her hair. She wore gold hoop earrings with rubies dangling from them, a wedding band—on the wrong finger—a pearl ring and a topaz ring, and a necklace that matched her earrings.

"Hello?" someone called.

"It's Annie," said Clara and I followed her out to where a small, black-haired person stood, the front door held open in one hand. Clara had left it ajar.

"Come on in," I said. "I'm Stella."

She hesitated for a moment on the threshold, then shut the door. "Annie McKinney," she said, holding out her hand. I shook it, feeling Clara, behind me, flirting with her lover. Frank had come out to join me by now and he said hello, smiling down at Annie with a warmth that seemed to embarrass her. I could tell she liked him but didn't think she should. It made for an awkward moment.

When we went in the living room it got worse. Annie clearly did not want to meet Rodney. I was annoyed, thinking that she shouldn't have come if she felt like this, but soon my anger was directed, instead, at Rodney. He fired off questions about what she did, where she had grown up, how old she was. "Since I can't see you," he said, explaining this last request.

Annie threw an outraged and sullen look at Clara, before she answered that she was twenty-nine. Rodney would have kept it up if Frank hadn't deflected him. He picked his camera off the table and started snapping pictures. Clara immediately began posing, stretching her leonine body along the couch; Annie faced the camera stubbornly, chin up and shoulders straight; Callie scrambled to get out of the picture; and Rodney sighed.

"He's always doing this. He talks my patients into having their pictures taken with me. I don't think it's a good idea."

"It's a great idea," said Frank from behind the camera. "Their faces are wonderful. They look at you as if you were their dead god.

They can't quite believe you don't see them."

"I do see them," said Rodney. "I see them much more clearly than anyone else ever has."

"But you don't like them, do you?" asked Clara. "It's beyond me how a person can listen to all that misery every day and then come home and make jokes."

"You would rather I get emotionally involved? Never forget about them, fall in love with them?" His tone was growing angry.

Clara smiled, silkily. "What's wrong with love? Frank? Tell us what's wrong with love."

"There's nothing wrong with love. I've always thought shrinks should love their patients more. That's what they're missing, isn't it? They already know what's the matter with them but they need to be loved before they can face this knowledge."

"But how can psychiatrists love so many people?" I asked.

He shrugged. "It's their thing. The real ones can do it. Of course some of them, like Rodney, don't know they can."

"Frank is an amateur psychologist," said Rodney with a prim little smile that made me realize he was punning on the word *amateur* and not expecting us to get the joke. "He has no idea of the dangers of inappropriate love."

"I've never run across any."

I had to wonder about that. "No woman you can't stand chasing you?"

"First of all, that's usually not love. It's something else. But if it is love, why should I mind? I might feel sorry for her but not too sorry. It's good for people to be in love."

"You're a romantic," said Rodney, as if to say, You're an idiot. Frank smiled slightly and took another couple of pictures. Callie asked Rodney how long therapy took.

"I don't know. Nobody's finished yet."

Clara let out a peal of laughter. "Someday Rodney's going to write the definitive treatise on the human mind, did you know that? Once he's managed to cure somebody. How it works and how to make it work. Without love, of course. I'm sure he's making observations right now."

Annie scowled and gulped her wine. Rodney was smiling faintly, and Callie was leaning rigidly forward, elbows on her knees and hands clasped tightly on her wineglass. She was looking at Clara with such dislike; I thought I'd better get her off to the kitchen.

I stood up, saying, "Callie, would you come help me for a second?" And we left the room.

"I was just in time to keep you from insulting her, wasn't I?"

"I wouldn't have to her face," Callie replied. "I'm sorry, but I think she's vain."

"She's definitely vain." I put water on to boil. "But I like her. She's interesting."

"She may be a good artist, but I wouldn't want to be in love with her."

"Nobody's asking you to." I took the baking dish out of the oven and tipped the juices into a saucepan.

"It must have been very hard on Rodney."

"Well, he's here, isn't he? He couldn't dislike her too much."

"He came because Frank's his good friend. She broke up with him because he couldn't see how beautiful she was anymore."

"You like Rodney, don't you?" I asked, with that special meaning of the word *like*. It was more polite than saying she wanted to fuck him, although that lopsided smile on her face when I mentioned his name was her badge of lust.

I was complimented in a chorus on the chicken. Frank poured the third bottle of wine and opened another: down to the cheap stuff. Annie relaxed with the food and wine and told us stories of the woman's bar where she bartended. I could easily imagine her there, small and swaggering, precise with the drinks. Her father had owned a bar, she said, she had learned her trade young. The Beaujolais seemed to creep up her face as she talked, until her skin was as red as the red shirt she wore. Her black hair was short, combed back straight from her forehead and shaped to her skull, shiny with oil as a duck's feathers. Her features, blunt and small, were crowded in her face, giving her a vulnerable look, as if she had once been so lonely, her eyes, nose, and mouth had had to creep together for comfort. She held forth, wineglass in hand, on the number and intensity of fistfights, catfights, screaming fights, and sudden unconsciousness during her tenure. I was very glad I had not let Callie insult Clara.

Then I told a few stories about The Vineyard. Nothing so dramatic happened there, I said, just the occasional crash from a drunk in the bathroom, a couple who had eaten their whole meal with their fingers . . . I paused, embarrassed: Rodney was eating with his hands. He ate delicately, more delicately than the rest of us, picking up morsels of chicken, swabbing them in sauce, wiping his fingers between each bite, yet I still felt awkward. Clara caught my eye and winked, then shook her head and smiled dreamily; he doesn't care, he's out of it. Rodney *was* out of it. He had switched off his attention to us while he ate. I wondered if it was hard to listen blind or if he had always been that way, used to listening in fifty-minute chunks. I smiled back at Clara. I understood her glee at being able to communicate like this. It was only what people always did — send private messages in public — but done so openly it was bizarre, as if there were no common table we sat around.

When we all finished eating, Annie and I cleared the table. I put water on for coffee, ground the beans, and she said, "Rodney gives me the creeps. I feel like he's being blind for his own purposes."

"He's doing his best," I said ambiguously, taking the ice cream out of the freezer. "Can you get some plates and cups out of the cupboard?"

"I know he couldn't fake it. But I just don't trust him," she replied, taking the dishes out. "What does a guy like Frank see in Rodney?"

"I don't know. Frank likes to take care of the house." I spooned out the ice cream and arranged everything on a tray.

"Frank's just too nice to people. You have to be careful of that."

"Make him stay home and be nice only to me?"

"Why not? I mean, not stay home, he should work. But you don't need guys like Rodney hanging around. I try to keep Clara away from Rodney. I'm not jealous, I know she doesn't sleep with him, but he brings out the worst in her. When she comes home after seeing him, she's always kind of cynical and nasty."

"Why did you come then?"

"She wanted to. And I guess I wanted to see for myself what he was like. Don't think I'm not enjoying myself. I am. I like you a lot, you and Frank, you're good people."

"Thanks, Annie," I said, surprised at the warmth in her voice.

I carried the tray into the living room and Annie brought the coffee pot. "The Empress of Ice Cream," said Frank, getting up and taking the tray from me.

"What kind is it?" asked Clara.

"Ginger."

"Oh, great."

"Stella makes the best ice cream," said Callie.

"The first time I had home-made ice cream," said Frank, "I was eight years old. My cousin Josie made it. She was sixteen or seventeen and very sexy. Curvy and freckled all over. I followed her around like a puppy. The ice cream she made was strawberry, and we picked the strawberries together out in her parents' garden."

"Where?" I asked.

"Long Island. It was June and she was wearing short shorts and a purple T-shirt. She picked most of the berries herself while I crouched close enough to smell her and watch her breasts jiggling and her sharp teeth biting into the little ripe berries."

"Oh, my," said Clara, "this is getting steamy."

Frank smiled, sipping his coffee. "After an hour or so we had enough. She was pink and sweaty and she asked me to hose her off before we went inside. I aimed the hose at one part after another while she stood there, arms and legs open, eyes shut, hair streaming down behind." He paused to take a bite. "When she was wet, you know, her clothes clung to her body."

"Yeah, we know," said Annie, and we all laughed.

"We were alone in the house. I mashed the strawberries, getting the juice all over myself, while she stirred cream and eggs and sugar. Then I poured the berries in. Josie tasted it, her fingers dripping pink goo all over her chin and down her neck.

"We cranked that ice cream for what seemed like hours. Josie's arm went round and round and I got dizzy watching her breasts go round and round too. Then it was done and we ate it, and Josie ate so much, she took her shirt off to let her stomach expand. She said."

"Oh, this is really a story," said Rodney.

"She saw my interest, of course, and decided I needed to learn about girls. So she let me feel her up. I was in heaven, you can imagine, strawberry ice cream and tits, in one afternoon."

"Which did you prefer?" I asked.

"It's hard to say. I was still a little boy with a sweet tooth, and the tits, once I held them in my hands, confused me. What was I supposed to do with them? They must have made an impression on me because I can't eat ice cream without thinking of them. I think of the different flavors as being different colors of women." We laughed.

"What about pistachio?" asked Annie.

"Martian schoolgirls," he replied promptly.

"Does he react this way to everything you make?" asked Clara. I smiled and looked around the table. Everyone was charmed by the story. I ought to have felt flattered, this rapture for the female . . . and I did. But there was something that bothered me, some blurring of the line between lust and sentimentality.

"Does anyone want any more ice cream?" I asked.

"Of course."

"How could we resist?"

I served out the second helpings and Frank put his hand on my thigh. I removed it and sipped my coffee. I was glad they were finishing off the ice cream; homemade didn't keep at all well, turning dry and crystalline in the freezer.

Annie and Clara ate with exaggerated pleasure, rolling the ice cream around on their tongues, licking their spoons, and smiling at each other. They reminded me of little girls at a birthday party, best friends unable to neglect their private and exclusive bond for even a moment—the world was too funny. Rodney was eating with his spoon by now, and presently he dropped a lump of ice cream from the tilted utensil. Callie, ever vigilant, dove for it and caught it in her napkin before it hit his thigh. Rodney's spoon was still waving in the air, as if he thought the ice cream might have arced upward for awhile. We all stopped eating to watch.

"I caught it," said Callie in a small voice. She held it melting in the white napkin in her hand, her face a vivid blush, then dropped the napkin, with a little spring of her hand, back in her lap.

"Thank you," said Rodney, bending his blind gaze on her. I thought for a moment he was looking for his ice cream. "That must have been quick. I'm glad I have you beside me." He said this with such rank possessiveness, I was startled. Could he really be interested in Callie?

Clara was trying to contain her laughter. Frank gave her a stern glance. Callie was still blushing and she picked up her napkin to cover her mouth, dabbing falsely at her lips. Of course the napkin made it all that much funnier and soon Clara and Annie were giggling helplessly.

"I think we'll have to send the children from the table," I said.

"Why don't we all go into the living room and have some brandy?" Frank suggested.

"Have you any cigars?" asked Clara with lovely composure, looking about seven. She caught Annie's eye and they began laughing again, mouthing to each other the word *cigar*.

Callie was helping Rodney up from the table. He had paid no attention to Clara and Callie was struggling not to. Her face had a dutiful, besotted look about it.

"We're going to the bathroom," Clara announced, holding Annie's arm firmly. Annie, drunk and disheveled, looked like an airplane pickup expecting to get fucked in close quarters. But as they went upstairs, Clara dropped her arm and they adopted that hurried gait of women for whom the bathroom is a source of emotional relief.

When Frank put his arm around me and whispered, "Shall we go up next?" I smiled absently.

Callie was asking Rodney how he coped with the advent of his blindness. "It was very difficult at first," he said. "Memorizing the layout of the rooms, judging distances, and so on. It took concentration. I would often forget, just for a moment—long enough to crash into something."

"How awful," she said.

"I still miss my old habits, more than anything else."

"More than beauty?" I asked.

"Of course I wish I could still see women's faces and bodies. Yet other things have compensated. Voices, conversations . . . Clara and Annie, for example," he said, showing off, "are talking about how much they like Stella . . . how I give Annie the creeps." He smiled. "And now Clara is confiding that I always gave her the creeps, too."

Frank and Rodney laughed. I felt alarmed. Had he heard all the conversations in the kitchen as well? What had I said? I determined never to spend a night at their house and was very grateful for the instinct that had kept me away before.

"I don't see how he lived with her," Callie whispered to me as the men went into the other room.

"Don't bother whispering, he can hear everything you say," I said irritably. Why did I live with such a jerk?

"Not everything," said Rodney, turning his large face toward Callie, who was looking a little frightened.

"More than enough," I replied, feeling outrage that this should happen in my house.

"More than enough what?" asked Clara. She and Annie stood at the door, clean and shiny, their hair combed and sobriety restored.

"Rodney has super hearing now," I said. "He was relating your conversation in the bathroom."

"Oh, shit," said Annie. Clara smiled silkily and tiptoed over to Rodney.

"I can hear you coming," he warned. She picked a rose out of the vase on the coffee table and dripped water down his neck.

"Don't," said Callie. He swung an arm, Clara danced out of reach and brushed the flower across his face. He sat still then, sporting a little smile, and she pricked him once with the rose's thorn, then dropped it in his lap.

She flung herself into a chair and said to me, "It loses its charm, like bear baiting."

"I should hope so," said Rodney. He lifted the rose out of his lap, where it left a wet stain, and held it out for someone to take. Callie got up out of her chair, walked over, and took the rose, which she put back with the other flowers in the vase.

I felt like suggesting that they all go home. All of them, even Callie, who lived here—even Frank. I thought with longing of solitude, then of my grandmother's house. What would she do if she were me? Go upstairs to read, no doubt. Leaving her guests to wonder if they were supposed to leave. If they were allowed to leave. I had seen her do this when she entertained—so rarely—seen the bewildered guests go in the library to say good-bye as she lifted a benignly malicious face from her astronomy book, perhaps detaining one or two to look at a particularly nice illustration. I remember her sharp fingernail tapping the glossy pages while one of her wine-fuddled second cousins creased her lips and eyebrows trying to think of what to say. And then, at some later time, her insistence on courtesy and hospitality.

"Are you getting tired, honey?" asked Frank. I was annoyed that he brought me back to this company, all of whom were looking at me except Rodney. This was probably a normal dinner party to Frank, I thought. Most of his friends were undoubtedly even weirder.

"No," I said.

"But you want us to go," said Clara. She didn't wait for a reply but got up and Annie followed suit. "It was a wonderful dinner and I'm glad I met you. You'll have to come over and see my studio."

"I'd like to," I said. "I'm glad I met you. And you, too."

"Me, too," said Annie and they laughed. I felt friendly toward them again, and wanted to say more, but my melancholy was carrying me off. I felt suddenly drunk as well. They said good-byes to the others who were all standing around—Rodney putting his coat on, Callie helping him—then left, their voices starting up loudly once the door shut behind them.

"I'm going to walk Rodney home," Frank said to me. "He gets confused sometimes when he drinks."

"He seems pretty alert to me," I muttered, then replied, "Okay, and why don't you sleep over there? I'm tired, I just want to go to bed alone."

He looked surprised. "Okay. You're all right? I'm sorry if everything was too—"

"No, I'm fine. I'm just tired."

"You sure you don't want to me to come back? You want me to call?"

"No. I'll call you tomorrow. I just feel like being alone."

"Okay, I'll see you tomorrow."

He kissed me and I kissed him back. I said good-bye to Rodney and went back in the living room and curled up on my great-grandmother's shawl. On the table there was half a glass of brandy, which I drank, remembering Teo's complicated explanation of how certain peaks of drunkenness could be gotten over by drinking more; the higher level of intoxication being a calmer place, a plateau.

Callie shut the door behind the men and peeked timidly into the living room at me. "I didn't think having those two together would be such a good idea," she said.

"I remember. Go to bed, I'll do the dishes in the morning."

"The food was very good, you know."

"It stank."

"Oh, Stella, it did not! How can you say that?"

"Forget it."

"It was delicious."

"I know. Go to bed."

"I'll go if I want to. You're not my mother."

I got up, wrapped the shawl around myself, and walked out the door. "Stella!" she called after me, "come on, don't be such a baby."

"I'm going for a walk," I shouted back. "I'm not mad and I'm not a baby." I stooped down to take off my high-heeled shoes, then ran down the dark sidewalk, in the opposite direction from that which Frank had taken. It felt wonderful to be alone. Why had I ever wanted anyone near me?

I wasn't angry anymore, though I thought Callie was a jerk and Rodney a toad; I was just glad to be free of them all, and I started laughing in a girlish conspiracy with myself. The night air was bracingly cold, although I was not entirely braced; I had too much wine in me for that. But as I slowed to a walk, breathing hard, the cold did force me to consider where I was going. I didn't want to be at my house with Callie; I didn't want to be at Frank's house with him; I didn't want to be at anyone else's house. It was too late for Moe's or the Mediterranean, which left the bars. That began to seem like a very good idea. I stopped and put my shoes on. I was at the corner of Shattuck and Bancroft, which made the Bancroft Lounge the closest place. It's not the sort of bar that attracts people like me, but then I wasn't looking for people like me. What I was looking for I didn't think about; I just walked into the barroom, sat on a stool, and ordered a brandy.

There were two men alone at the bar, one tall and well-dressed, with soft hands, the other drunk, blue eyes rolling like marbles under his square forehead. He was young and nice looking, the drunk one, with a sweet, sensuous mouth. He had tight beige curls and was wearing a tie with I LOVE NY on it. I smiled at him. "This is California," I said softly.

"You wanna know where I come from? Columbus, Ohio. Whenever I leave Columbus, Ohio, I'm always drunk. So what's the difference? It's dark in here. You wanna drink?"

"I have one."

"Oh, I guess you do. Okay, you wanna talk to me then?" I laughed. "You wanna talk to me," he said. "Good. My name is Neil Poster. I've been in this bar since one P.M. I was with these guys . . ." He waved an arm.

"They left you here?"

"Well, I didn't want to go with them, for goshsakes. They were ugly critters." He leaned closer. "Polyester suits, you know. Just like me. From Columbus, Ohio."

"Well, you're in Berkeley now, don't fret. You don't ever have to go back."

"You wanna know what it's like there?"

"Yes. Tell me." He told me about his job, which seemed to consist of traveling, trying to stay sober for appointments, and filling out forms; his doctor who gave him Valium for his drinking, which he fed to his girlfriend to relax her enough for sex, and his mother who called him at seven thirty every morning to wake him up for work. "Stay here and start a new life," I suggested.

"Oh, no, I couldn't."

"Why not?"

"It would be the same. That's the kind of guy I am. I'll always have this kind of job, and a girlfriend like Nancy."

"You could get away from your mother."

"But you need a mother." He finished his drink, pouring the last drop on his tongue, and glanced beseechingly around for another. The bartender set it down, Bacardi on the rocks, and Neil brought it to his lips almost furtively, like a herbivore gliding to the water hole.

"You should at least try to see some of Berkeley while the sun is out."

"I'll try."

He smiled at me sweetly, his blue eyes beaming a lifetime of good intentions. He was really very good looking, with a solid, Germanic bone structure and clear, dewy skin. We sat in silence for a while. The tall man at the bar was watching me, waiting, I thought, for Neil to get too drunk to talk. Then he would saunter over. I knew how he would be: smooth and snide, buying drinks, his padded fingers doling out the dollar bills like tickets. Neil was humming to himself as he drank, his shoulders swaying. I thought I'd better get him home before he slid to the floor in oblivion, waking up, no doubt, in Columbus, Ohio.

"Let's go," I said.

"To your place?" he asked, putting an arm around me.

"No, yours. Where are you staying?"

"I don't remember. Around here, not too far."

The bar watched with mild interest as I led him out the door. I imagined they were wondering what I was doing with such a drunk. Since Teo, I had not been attracted to the type — you never knew when you'd be alone again. But tonight I didn't mind that; I even enjoyed the uncertainty. I wanted to be both by myself and with someone.

Neil's arm around me was surprisingly firm. I thought of the alcohol struggling with his body. Which would be stronger?

"This way," he said, turning the corner.

"The Berkeley Motel?"

"Something like that," he agreed.

As we walked he told me about summer nights in Columbus, his first beer, euphoria, hitchhiking all night in the rain; then, with no transition, it was years later, he was drunk and lost in his own neighborhood. He fell and broke his leg and his mother refused to visit him in the hospital. He laughed and hugged me tighter, and for a moment I felt like an old girlfriend, someone from grade school listening to this tale of adult woe.

It took him a while to find his door key. I stood with one hip against the side of the building as a car drifted by, catching us briefly in its lights, then with a swivel of tires, presenting me with its long, crimson flank and a woman's dangling arm. I had always felt some guilt for picking up men, though not much. Those who might disapprove were so far from my own life. Even Callie was far, in the sense that I could not take her opinions seriously. But Frank was not far, although I was pretending tonight he was.

Neil turned a dreamy, drunken face to me, a face of gentle triumph. The door was open. We went inside. The room was small, with a large television set and cheap carpeting. I helped Neil take the suitcase off the bed; then he laid a white handkerchief down and poured a half-full can of cashews on the handkerchief. When I sat down to one side of it, he opened warm Cokes for us and lay down across the picnic from me.

"What are you doing here?" he asked suddenly.

"I like strange men."

"Seriously?"

"What do you think, I'm spying for your girlfriend?"

"Nope. She doesn't operate outside Ohio."

"Don't you like picking up strange women?"

"Never done it before. It's scary."

"Oh, come on. What do you have to be afraid of?"

He ate a cashew. Then he smiled at me. "I guess not of you."

"I'm the one should be worried. I've got a boyfriend here."

"He's jealous?"

"I don't know. I guess so. What if he doesn't want to see me anymore?" I already knew I would tell Frank eventually.

"I thought I asked you that already? What are you doing here? But never mind. Don't leave."

"I'm not leaving. We haven't talked about this sort of thing. I want to feel free."

"Nobody's free."

"That's easy for you to say. You come from Ohio."

"You're not a California girl, are you?"

"No, I was born in New England." I drank my Coke. "I know I'm not free in any absolute sense, but still—"

"You love your boyfriend?"

"Yes. But I'm fond of you as well."

At the moment Neil was the more real to me. To leave now would be like waking up from an erotic dream, that great sadness of learning the man you were loving doesn't exist. After I broke up with Tobias, I had a lot of such dreams. I would be at a party and would wander off from the main action into an empty room or out on the beach. Then he was there suddenly, a man I called Tobias, although he didn't always look like him. I would walk with him, or sit with him, and sometimes we spoke. All the time I was waiting to be touched. The waiting was exquisitely felt, my body was so prepared, but it was the preparedness of an image; I had no center or boundary, there was no *place* where the sensation gathered. All of a sudden memories of waking life would arise, and I would become restless, wanting to act. I couldn't quite move but I yearned forward. I made whatever passes for a pass in such dreams. The man beside me would begin to bleach away. The figure was still there but the erotic association was gone. I knew he had never been Tobias but I wanted to love him anyway, and it was too late. The love-stuff, the dream matter I had made my dream emotion out of had dissipated. There hadn't even been enough for a kiss.

"You don't even know me," said Neil.

"Sure I do. You come from Ohio, you like to drink, you hate your job, you're nice—"

"Isn't your boyfriend nice? He must be nicer than me. Do you want me to shut up? I don't know why I'm talking about this."

"It's okay . . . he's nice, too, he's very nice, but I just like this, going out in the dark. I feel—I feel like this has no relation to regular sex, in a relationship. It's a thing of its own."

"A thing of its own," he said. We laughed. "Well, okay, Stella, I don't understand, but I guess it's your business. Your boyfriend won't go looking for you at that bar, will he?"

"No. Don't worry. Oh, I don't know what to do . . . I used to be very jealous but I don't think I am anymore. I can imagine him in bed with other people and I don't mind. But I don't think he'll feel that way. Can men be cured of jealousy?"

"Men will do anything for love."

"That's a comforting thought."

"On the other hand, jealousy inspires a lot of action, too. I don't know what I'd do with a girl like you. Probably run away."

"That's not much of a solution," I said, rolling across the cashews toward him.

"You're getting in the food," he said, bemused, as he put his arms around me.

"I had to do something. You're sobering up too fast."

"What do you mean?"

"I liked you drunk. In another world."

"Okay." He reached down and pulled a fifth of Bacardi from the drawer of the night table. I drank with him, though not as much, and we kissed and dribbled rum on each other and giggled. He was a lot of fun to be close to. When his eyes got bleary, I undressed him, running my hands over his thick, muscled torso. He lay as if dead drunk, but when I was done, he had a hard-on. I undressed, feeling squishy with alcohol and late-night lust, and lay down happily on top of him. His body smelled like Ohio, like rum, like a prescience of me. Why am I here? I thought as he entered me, I'm here because I have to be. This is the path that's all lighted up.

16

It was almost dawn. I got dressed quietly, looking at his bunched-up body with detached curiosity. You're a good fuck, I thought, do you know that? Somebody ought to tell you. Then maybe you'd pick up girls more often, have a little more adventure while you're traveling. I considered leaving a note to that effect, but decided it wasn't very good manners. I looked at him closely, memorizing the sturdy nose, the bulge of his shut eyes, the bow mouth, the pale, springy curls, the hefty penis, handsome even in repose.

It was so sad; what was so sad? I didn't regret fucking him, I wasn't sorry I'd never see him again, I pitied his life, but not that much. What was so sad?

I could hear Teo's voice in my head again. "Alcohol is a depressant, that's why you feel depressed the next day. It has nothing to do with your real emotions." I wondered about that; even if it was true, this was my real emotion. Yet even as I thought that, the sadness evaporated. I was out the door, in the chilly motel parking lot. Nobody else was around and all the windows were dark. I had to walk slowly, because of my high heels, and I was cold, but I felt fine. I wrapped my great-grandmother's shawl tightly around myself, the creamy fringe dripping over my wrists, and made my way home past houses where cats mewed on doorsteps to be let in, and houses where dogs barked at me, past trucks with men sitting up high, drinking coffee, past a wandering old woman talking into her fingers.

When I got home, I took off my shoes and walked barefoot through the green and gray dawn garden. There was a small wooden bench on the porch, something of the landlord's that I had carried out there, which had been stolen and brought back again. I sat on it and imagined myself at my grandmother's house, a task made easier by the smell of the shawl I half covered my face with.

In Grandmother's house I had my hiding places, but I had not discovered them. The hollow between the two most distant apple trees, the twisty natural path that made a rough circle around the pine glade within the larger woods—I felt welcomed there. My affair with Tobias especially pleased the house, I thought, which had seen so many virgins and married women. The week I spent mourning him, trailing teacups and bread crusts from kitchen to library and up the stairs, gave those rooms a thrill of vicarious sorrow, of self-pity and thwarted teenage lust. Even now when I talked to Grandmother on the phone, I always asked what room she was in as I described my California adventures. I'd gotten into the habit of telling her more than I would in person, when her ironic eyes, growing lighter every year, commented too severely on my erotic life. Over the phone that personal element lessened; I was speaking for the record. And I was sure the lonely third-floor rooms understood my passion for strangers, and would understand why Frank hadn't been able to secure all my desire.

Yet as I thought of him I was flooded with affection. I remembered how everyone last night, scornful or jealous of each other, had liked him—even Annie, who didn't like men, and Callie, whom he didn't like. I imagined going through life surrounded by the goodwill he attracted.

Then I went inside. Callie had done the dishes and cleaned up; everything was in order. She was sitting with her teacup at the table.

"Hel-lo," she said. "You went over to Frank's?"

"No, I went to the Bancroft Lounge. Met a man." I poured coffee beans into the grinder.

"Stella, you didn't! Stella!" she shouted over the noise of the grinder.

"What?" I said, sulky, tipping the coffee into the filter.

"You didn't?"

"Yes, I did. Why not? I've done it before."

"I thought you were serious about Frank." She put down her cup and watched me anxiously.

I turned the flame on under the kettle and peeled a banana. "I am."

"Well?"

"Well what? I can be serious about him and still like to fuck other guys."

"I don't see how."

"That's your problem. Look, Callie, it's the way I am."

"Are you going to tell him?"

I shrugged. "I don't know. I guess not right off, like 'Guess what I did last night?'"

"You'll lie then?"

"Perhaps. Maybe I'll tell him, sooner or later."

"Sooner or later he'll find out and what if that's it then? What if he breaks up with you?" Callie was close to tears. I poured boiling water over the coffee and swallowed the last of the banana.

"I don't know. I don't want to hurt him. Maybe he won't mind. It's so stupid—faithfulness. It has nothing to do with me."

"It does now," she said. "Stella, he's such a good man. It would kill him, really."

"Oh for Christ's sake, don't be so melodramatic. He's not a Victorian husband, you know. He's fucked around as much as I have." Well, maybe almost as much.

"Yes, but he's not doing it now, is he?"

"How should I know? Maybe he and Rodney picked up a lady and got into a threesome last night. Frank describing what she looked like every step of the way." It was an interesting idea.

"You know he didn't."

I pulled a bowl of leftover tunafish out of the refrigerator. The mayonnaise had separated out and was clinging to the rim in little globules. I stirred it back in again with my finger, my finger that had last been noticed patting Neil's balls good-bye.

"Stella, I know we don't agree about this. I've never seen the appeal in going to bed with strange men. That's your business, I guess. But you have to think about what's at risk. Most people don't agree with you, you know. Most people are possessive and jealous.

And jealousy isn't much fun. Nobody wants to feel it for long."

"I know, what am I going to do?"

She looked anxious again. "Is it like an addiction? Do you think you need a psychiatrist?"

"If it's an addiction, a shrink won't help. But it's a thought. Maybe I'll go to Rodney."

"Stella!"

"I know, Callie. Believe me, I'm taking it seriously. I know that you're right that it's going to cause problems. I just don't know what to do about it. I *like* it."

"I guess you'll have to talk to him then," she said resignedly. "Can I have the rest of that tunafish?"

"I guess so. There isn't much left." I went upstairs with a cup of coffee and an oatmeal cookie. I didn't want to talk to him about it.

I called. He answered on the first ring. "Hi, honey," I said.

"Hi, darling. It's good to hear your voice."

"What're you doing?" I leaned back and nestled the receiver between my ear and the pillow.

"Nothing much. Rodney has a hangover and I'm ministering to his needs. Bloody Marys and black coffee."

"I didn't know he was that drunk."

"He wasn't. We had a few on the way home."

"Oh. Alka-Seltzer ice-cream sodas are good. I used to make them for Teo. When am I going to see you?"

I heard him shouting to Rodney; then he said, "I think your suggestion made him throw up. What are you doing now?"

"Nothing. Wanna come over?"

"I was hoping you'd ask."

He arrived wearing a sky-blue nylon jacket and a pale pink shirt with two daisies in the buttonhole.

"You look like a young lamb gamboling among the flowers," I said. He took off his jacket with a surprised look.

"Did you ever read the Archie comics? Archie always used to call Veronica 'Lambchop.' I could never figure that out. Why he'd call his girlfriend after something for dinner."

"You understand it now, don't you?" I asked as he hugged me from behind, his chin resting in the crook of my shoulder.

"No, not really . . . I still see the chop sitting on a plate with those little panties on."

"There you have it."

"I'd never be satisfied with such a meager portion of you. I want it all."

I pulled away. "You can try. Where are we going for lunch?"

"I'll take you anywhere you want to go."

"Where do you want to go?"

"You decide."

"I don't want to decide."

"Well then, let's go to Tilden Park and have a picnic. Bread and cheese and wine."

"Okay." I had us out of the house in four minutes flat.

We found a spot in the woods in a grove of eucalyptus trees. Frank took off his jacket and his shirt and lay on his back, his torso faunlike in the dappled light.

"We should have a goatskin for the wine," I said, "then I could squirt it into your mouth."

"You've got beasts on the brain," he said. "Lambs, goats, what else?"

"Lions and tigers and bears."

"No swine?"

"Not yet. Can I take off my shirt too?"

"Beasts and breasts," he murmured. "Your beastly breasts." I leaned over him. "You breasty beast."

"You can be Adam," I said, "and I'll be one of the animals you've named."

"You can't fool me. I know you're really God in disguise."

"It's agonizing. I keep trying to make everything perfect. I don't understand what keeps going wrong. I should have finished college, I guess."

"You should have everything perfect, Godhoney. What do you need?"

"You."

"Well, that's no problem."

Later we talked about the party the night before. Frank was apologetic about Rodney and Clara's behavior but didn't seem to take it too seriously. I couldn't either, anymore. All those tangled emotions—jealousy, possessiveness, one-up-manship—what did they have to do with me? A lot, of course. But up in the hills in the sunlight with my darling, I couldn't believe we really had a problem. Our loving was so sympathetic, our lust so generous; we lay naked in the warm breezes, peeling papery bark from the eucalyptus to drape ourselves in should company come. By the time I had to go to work I felt as drenched in him as I ever had. I felt limp and glowing, as if after heavy exercise—although our sex had been gentle—and when he kissed me good-bye in front of the house, his kiss lingered and lingered until I was surprised to see he was a block away.

George was in an expansive mood and came into the kitchen to help me cook. He was full of optimism; the summer had finally started, people were ready for a good time. He tied an apron around his waist and peeled prawns for me, eating every third one raw, washed down by a disgusting drink he had invented: beer in which cloves of garlic had marinated. He was planning to serve it during garlic week, Berkeley's answer to such inventions as Grandparents Day. Chez Panisse was serving garlic ice cream and George did not want to be outdone.

"George," I asked, "did Eva ever know you were fucking me?"

He stared at me in amazement, the tail of a prawn dangling from his teeth. He bit it in two, dipped the end in curry powder, ate that, and said, "Of course not. I wouldn't tell that woman anything."

"I know, but did she suspect?"

"Why should she? I always went home at night, as I remember. You never let me darken your maidenly door."

"I assumed you wanted to be discreet."

"Did you?" He laughed, poking another prawn into the curry so a jet of it spurted out onto the counter.

"Don't be such a slob, I don't want curry in everything. And don't blame me if you didn't get what you didn't ask for."

"I'm not blaming you. I just understand you. You wanted to be fucking the boss, or else you wanted to be fucking the food provider, maybe it was a fertility rite to bless your cooking."

"Maybe. But what about the past? Did she suspect your other affairs? You did have other affairs?"

"When it got shitty between us, I started with other women. I'm no fool, I'm not going to tie my prick to the bedpost."

"And she knew?"

"She knew. She screamed for a while, but it was in her best interest. She didn't want to fuck me anymore."

"George, I don't understand why you're still married."

"You think I want my children brought up solely by someone who hates to fuck?"

His face was red and I regretted bringing up the subject. Everyone at the restaurant knew George had an unhappy marriage but we'd never actually talked about it. I had assumed that his putdowns of his wife were partly for show. Nobody could hate the person he lived with that much. It was scary.

"What's all this about anyway?" he asked. "We're not fucking anymore so you're surely not worried about Eva. And Frank knows. He doesn't seem to hate me for it." He looked at me keenly. "You've been with somebody else, haven't you?" He laughed and pinched me. "Can't quit, can you?"

"I guess not."

"Franky boy know?"

"No." But everyone else does, I thought, anxiously.

"You going to tell him?"

"What do you think I should do?"

"Deny everything."

"There's nothing to deny, yet."

"Good. Keep it that way. Never tell a man you're sleeping around. It's not safe."

"Oh, come on."

"Jealousy is a dangerous thing. Not only in men, mind you. Did I ever tell you about my grandfather?"

"No."

"Fooled around with another woman. Took her right home with him. His wife showed up—she was supposed to be at her sister's—and caught the two in bed." He paused.

"And?"

"Picked up the poker and poked out his eye."

"Oh, gross! Really?"

"He was my one-eyed granddad. She was a little-bitty woman, not even five feet high. Always chuckled when she told the story. 'Cured that wandering eye!' she said."

"Oh, George, I don't believe you."

"S'true. I've been afraid of women all my life because of her."

"Ha."

"Look at you with that knife. Gives me the chills."

"I'm not your jealous wife. . . . I don't approve of jealousy."

"I don't approve of a lot of things. I haven't noticed the world paying attention."

"Well, I'm not talking about the world."

"Okay, you think you and Frank can do things different from other people. Maybe so, but it won't be easy. Like I said, he doesn't seem to hate me, but I'm not his favorite person either. And you and I aren't even in the present tense."

"I know. Do you think I'm crazy?" I asked mournfully.

"Hell, no. You just shouldn't have fallen in love with him. You were doing fine before that."

"I like being in love," I said softly.

He was silent for a minute. "Just don't have any kids. That's when the nightmare really starts." I put my arms around him in sympathy. "And don't start making up to me. Let's get some work done around here."

George hung around the kitchen all evening, sampling every dish I cooked, even rooting through the salad for radishes, which drove Allison wild. Salad was the only thing she was unequivocally in charge of, mainly because on the days she was missing—due to George's cost-cutting and her own ennui, her simpering—"I don't really need a job, I live on practically nothing"—any idiot, even

Ramon, could handle making it. George speared calimari rounds out of the frying pan with a skewer and tipped them into his mouth like a giant invading the ring-toss game at the playground. He took food off the plates I'd put out for the waiters, and only their keen eyes kept us from serving half portions to the customers.

Around ten o'clock George returned from one of his forays into the dining room to tell me, "There's this incredibly beautiful woman out there. She looks like a cross between Lauren Bacall and Marilyn Monroe. She asked for you. *And she's eating with her fingers.*"

"Does she have a short, dark-haired woman with her?"

"Yes."

"That's Clara," I said, taking off my apron. "Here, take over, I wanna go out and say hi. Don't bother coming out. She's a rabid lesbian."

I stood in the doorway, looking over the room. Clara and Annie were in the far corner, sharing a table with two plates of sautéed squid and a bottle of champagne. Clara saw me and waved a few buttery fingers at me. She was looking gorgeous in a white tube top and narrow white skirt, her bare neck and arms adorned with a half a dozen silver necklaces and twice as many bracelets. Her hair was up in a knot, with white ribbons woven through it, and her mouth was as wet with butter as her fingers.

I went over to her table, which was being watched by practically everyone in the room. Clara picked up a ring of squid, let it dangle from her index finger, dripping its sauce onto the plate, then slid it between her lips with a little sucking sound. Annie was blushing. She ate with a fork.

"Stella! So, he told you we were here." Clara beamed at me.

"You could have announced yourself more discreetly," I said, smiling.

"Sit down, have some champagne with us."

I sat down and Annie poured me a glass. "What are you celebrating?"

"The full moon. The female glory in the sky. The light of lunatics, mistress of tides and wolves, goddess of blood, restorer of lost virginity."

"I wouldn't want my virginity back," I said. "I prefer the wisdom of experience."

"It's a spiritual virginity I'm speaking of," Clara said. "Which men have sought to destroy by making so much of the other kind. Artemis, you know, liked to fuck as well as the next woman. But she was a virgin because she was the huntress and never the prey. No one could violate her."

"You speak of her in the past tense," I said.

Clara smiled. "I have not yet achieved the vision to see her striding across the sky with her bow and quiver," she said, and threw back her head and laughed. "But the moon is full, you must admit."

"It's beautiful," I agreed.

"It makes you want to drink champagne," said Annie, pouring herself the last glass.

"And eat squid," said Clara.

"Why squid?"

"It comes from the sea, it's white and has rings like the ring of muscle at the entrance of the vagina." Annie looked slightly disgusted as she pushed her squid around on her plate. Some people don't like to think of eating what they love.

"But a whole squid looks more like a man," I objected. "Long tentacles, round sack of guts."

"Men cut up become women," Clara replied. "They return to the original state. Any sex-change doctor could tell you that."

"I'm losing my appetite," said Annie. "How about another bottle of champagne?"

"No, we can't get drunk yet. We have a long night ahead."

"What are you doing?" I said.

"We're going to a full moon festival. A group of lesbian werewolvesses meets every month at Diana and Cynthia's house on Euclid Avenue. They're a pair of rich, middle-aged sapphites, as they call themselves, with plenty of objets d'artemis about the house, and lots of wine, cocaine, and young hangers-on. It's not so bad actually. There are a few full-fledged witches to add tone to the thing."

"What do you do?"

"It's a secret ritual, but it involves drunkenness and lewd dancing."

"And wishes," said Annie. "Each woman asks the Moon Goddess for one wish to come true. She says it aloud for the group to hear."

"So Cynthia can't wish for Diana to die and leave her the Exxon stock."

"The wishes aren't supposed to be impossible but more like what each woman wants to achieve that month."

"It works for Annie," said Clara, "but not for me yet."

"You asked to become pregnant," said Annie accusingly.

"You want a child?"

"She doesn't fuck men," said Annie.

"I want a little me," said Clara. "Doesn't everyone? So why should I fuck a man and mix up the genes? I trust in the Goddess. I'm sure 'virgin' births happen all the time. Men just never believe women who say so. They don't believe anything we say if it offends their sense of their own importance."

Annie said, "You just don't want to ask for anything possible because you're afraid you'd get it and then you'd have to believe."

"What did you get, Annie?" I asked.

"She asked for her true love," said Clara, fondly. "And then met me."

"She came in late," said Annie, "just as I finished asking. I had never seen her before, but I knew. Pretty amazing, isn't it?"

"I don't know," I said. "It's rather nice to be someone's wish-come-true."

"Oh, she's used to that," said Annie.

"The month before Annie asked for a car, and Cynthia gave her a sixty-nine Chevy in exchange for bartending at her daughter's wedding."

"It's a good car," said Annie, "and a night of bartending isn't worth that much."

"Yes, but she wanted a lesbian bartender to piss off her ex-husband and nobody wanted to do it, because of the creeps who were going to be there."

"It was okay," said Annie. "I poured stiff drinks and got them all shit-faced. One of the uncles threw up on the wedding cake."

"A job well done. Do other people's wishes come true?"

"Most of the time," said Annie, earnestly. "Sometimes they ask for really asshole things that shouldn't come true. The Goddess knows better what's good for them." Clara smiled at me and licked the inside of her tulip glass. "I guess there's no proof it works. I just feel like it does. Shit, we need somebody on our side."

"And we have a good time," said Clara. "We all dress in white and silver, as you can see, Holly and Jean play their flutes, we drink out of silver goblets . . . What else?"

"Everybody takes off their clothes," said Annie.

"In the light of the moon we recite the invocation, which was written by the poets among us. We call down the moon."

"I get all whirly, like a crazy drunk," said Annie. "But it's more than being drunk. I can feel her power, sort of enveloping me. Inside. Like water in a sponge." She looked surprised at the image and hesitated. "Some people don't really get into it, it's just a party to them, but it's so much greater than that. Shit, I used to hate the Virgin Mary. My mother would take me to church. Confession. I didn't tell that fucker anything but he still made me do ten Hail Marys. When I was a teenager I thought about raping her. In my fantasy the statue had come to life. It was littler than me, I could've held her down easy."

"Unless the Holy Ghost came to her rescue," Clara commented.

"Yeah, I don't know. Maybe I just felt rejected because she only liked good girls."

"And Annie is a very bad girl," said Clara with a pornographic smile.

"This Virgin is different. She's tough."

"Come with us," said Clara. "I'm sure Diana will lend you a silver tunic. Though she'd probably ask to buy your hair."

"It's not for sale."

"Not even to buy your lover a little trinket: a little, shall we say, token of your esteem?" Annie giggled and Clara continued. She put on an oily, self-conscious, southern-accented voice. "You're young, you're *so* young, it'll grow back — like the moon, my dear, while mine, oh mine, mine has gone forever." Her voice died away as she lifted mournful, merry eyes to me. "What would you wish for, Stella?"

"Oh, I don't know."

"Are you happy with your true love?"

"Yes."

"You don't sound sure."

"I wouldn't mind going to a thing like you're going to, but I'd feel uncomfortable with just lesbian women. You know? I'd like one for hetero women."

"Hetero women are too uptight," said Annie. "Excuse me, I mean most of them."

"I know. Why?"

"It's child-raising that does it," said Clara. "Oh, I know children are beautiful. They look cute in little overalls and smell like milk and green grass and, face it, there's no other way to keep the race going, and new minds and all that, but—"

"Yes?"

"But they're death, all the same, to the parents. That's really why I don't want a child. Responsibility is such a trip, you can't escape it, it swallows you up. Like the women who want baby after baby until they're forty-five."

"Well, I don't want children myself," said Annie, "but it must be nice to feel that way about somebody."

"Hungry," said Clara. "Mothers, fathers, especially now, are hungry. Having a child upsets the chemical equilibrium of the brain, and forever after the hapless parent is searching for something. She doesn't know what it is; she thinks the child has it."

"She's very big on chemicals in the brain this week, ever since she read about endo-something that joggers get."

"Endorphins," said Clara. "Think about it."

"About what?"

"About coming with us sometime. We could make you an honorary lesbian. Do you masturbate?"

"Sure."

"Well, you've made love to a woman then. No problem. What do you want, Stella, to dance by the light of the moon while naked men converge on you, bearing gifts?"

"Sure," I said again.

"Annie will have a word with the Goddess for you. I presume you want this in addition to your true love, not instead of?"

She smiled at me, the stretchy cotton top molded to her breasts, her bare shoulders catching glints of candlelight. I imagined them naked under the moon: Clara, Annie, other women with deep bosoms or flat bosoms, powerful or spindly legs, the contrast pleasing to the Goddess hungry for the sight of her children as they were hungry to be looked upon.

"Yes," I said. They left with many good-byes and a generous tip left under the champagne bottle. I went back to the kitchen where George was finishing off a mocha fudge hazelnut pie. "My friends are going to a full moon ceremony," I said. "Pagans, witches, you know."

"I always wanted to be a warlock when I was a boy," said George. "You?"

"Yes, when I was twelve and thirteen. I didn't think they existed anymore but I still wanted to be one."

"Well, you are in your own way," I said.

"I used to think so. I really fucking used to think so. It's amazing, isn't it, how people have the nerve to do things like get married, have kids, start businesses."

"I don't."

"With you it's not lack of nerve, but lack of feeling."

"George!" I was surprised.

"It's true. You have a healthy kind of selfishness I admire. Stick with it, don't let them tempt you with guilt, compromise . . ." He said this very earnestly as he pawed the last crumbs from the pie tin and licked his fingers.

"Well." I was uncomfortable. Guilt and compromise are the very fabric of the world. Virgin dances under the full moon, or their counterpart—one-night stands—had only the strength I put into them. They lived on pure imagination. "Guilt I can do without, but compromise is something I ought to learn—don't you think?"

"No. Yes. I don't know. Of course you have to learn it. You want too much not to have to pay for it eventually. But you don't have to pay full price. Scout the bargains."

"This doesn't jibe with the advice you were giving me earlier, does it? You seemed to think it was hopeless then."

"Oh, are we still talking about you fucking around on Frank? I was merely being profound. I don't know. What the fuck do I know? You should be asking your girlfriends for advice."

"Callie thinks I'm a slut and Clara's going to ask the Goddess to intercede on my behalf." I suddenly felt like crying. All this was nonsense; I just wanted to be loved. I would simply explain it to Frank. How could he be jealous when he knew how much I loved him? He would understand me; that was the point of all this. To become like one, to suffer that union. The test of love is not faithfulness but knowledge.

"You go on home, Blondie, I'll finish up here."

"Thanks."

"Stella?"

"Yes?"

"Good luck."

I sat down with Frank at the kitchen table and told him. He listened carefully, his eyes wandering over my face and hair and the wall behind me. I started out with my experiences in New York, then here before I met him, and finally Neil. I explained how it had begun, why it continued, the sensations of mind and body and even soul that accompanied my adventures; they are adventures, I said. Quests into the dark—or, as with Neil, something kindly and restorative: female magic to enable me to keep loving you. I didn't say that last bit, but whatever I did say came out wrong. My voice was thin, nervous with lies that I didn't wish to tell but that were told, not lies of fact but of interpretation. I started talking about freedom, though I had long ago realized that this wasn't freedom, if anything was.

Then we sat without speaking. Already his body looked different to me, his posture and the lines of his face subtly askew, like the alphabet read in a dream. That difference upset me terribly. Frank hunched his shoulders suddenly and I saw his misery, a hundred times worse than my own. I was powerless to move or say anything. His face completed its rearrangement and looked at me; I squirmed: he was smaller, tighter, uglier.

"I'm sorry, I can't deal with it," he said.

"Why not?" I asked, despairing.

"It humiliates me. Not what you do but how I feel. Jealous.

"I might even agree with you in theory," he went on, "but I can't stand feeling jealous."

"The jealousy will go away," I said faintly.

"No."

"You're angry at me?"

"Of course."

"Don't be."

"I love you," he said, and I started to cry. He was suddenly furious. "Don't start that! You say you can't change. How do you expect me to? You knew I would feel this way about it. You didn't even wait to discuss it."

"It's not a thing you discuss beforehand."

"Oh, no? You're discussing it now pretty easily."

"You think this is easy?"

"No." He was silent for a minute; his gaze shifted away. "So you decided to test me," he said softly, "see what I would do?"

"No!" I was angry at his assumption that everything related to him. "I didn't exactly plan it."

"So, why then," he said, not making it a question. He looked down at the table, his hands interlaced. I realized suddenly how much he wasn't saying and it drove me wild. If only he would tell me everything, I thought. I had tried to tell him. Yet I had the sensation of a drama being acted out in which we could speak our lines, no more.

"I know what it feels like to be jealous," I said. "But I refuse to give in to it anymore. It's not a natural barrier like the speed of light. It's subject to change."

He didn't answer but sat with his face averted, his lips drawn close together. Why did he look so still, like an animal in hiding? Jealousy should be a shriek or a curse. No, I didn't want that. I wanted sweet reason; how had I hurt him specifically? I knew how jealousy felt but why can't it be overcome? Since he was feeling it, it seemed up to him to defend it. He said nothing, I said nothing. I got angrier.

"Jealousy is such a petty emotion, can't you see that? It's powerful because it's become so sanctified. It's a righteous feeling, unless your suspicions are wrong and then you're an asshole. Everyone knows there's something pathetic about jealousy but they won't admit it, except for the cases of paranoid jealousy."

"Maybe all emotions are petty," he said, his eyes narrowed and very distant from me.

"Oh, please," I said, "I'm not one of your New York girls listening to the locksmith's apprentice."

There was another silence. "Perhaps we should break up."

"I don't want to!" I wailed.

"Yeah, neither do I." He reached over the table and took my hand. I clung to his. "Stella, I know what you're saying but I'm still angry, and I'm still jealous, and I don't want to start hating you."

"You can't hate me, you love me. I won't let you hate me."

"Listen," he said, kneading my hand, bending the fingers as if he would break them, "I'm going to go home now. I have to be alone. I'll come over in the morning."

"Where are you going?"

"I'm going home," he said patiently.

"You'll come back?"

"Yes." He got up. He looked so apart from me, as if we had never met, as if I had fallen in love all by myself, with a face in the crowd.

"It's too soon to break up," I said.

"How long do you want it to take?"

He left and I crawled upstairs, feeling a certain scorn for his unwillingness to bear pain. I didn't think it might really be unbearable, because once he spoke of leaving me, I began to suspect that he didn't love me after all, that he never had, that it wouldn't, in fact, be too hard for him to live without me. He had a formula for what a woman should be. I wasn't it, therefore he would break up with me.

But I would make it hard. I had all night to think of my strategy. I undressed, put on my lavender nightgown, turned out the light, and sat cross-legged in the middle of the bed. I had no ideas in mind. It was more like prayer.

I willed myself to blaze with seductiveness, to become irresistible. I would ensnare him, like La Belle Dame Sans Merci. It would not be so awful. He would enjoy our voluptuous pleasures, until he was worn out, of course, and then he would palely loiter. Rage and fear foamed through my body, my temperature rose a degree or two. I felt dizzy. Everything in the room was in motion; lust was woven in the stitches of the curtains that bellied out with wind. The darkness pressed in like a horde of horny demons. Was it possible? Had I attracted the Devil himself? Or simply madness? There was a streak of that in me; nothing to worry about, but still.

The truth was I couldn't remember how I managed to be happy before I met Frank. Everything I used to do was fine, I still did those things. But how could they have been enough? I tried to picture my entire life, from before my parents left until now. The result was dry and faded. I couldn't recall any vivid sensation. My mother, my father, my grandmother, Tobias — all were practically weightless, together of less importance than one night in Frank's company. They had no power, only I had power — a very little, because he loved me. Because he said he loved me.

I sat in bed in the dark thinking about him. About all the things he had ever said and ever done. Then I just looked at him in my mind — an image that I could see around and inside him. All I knew about him was there, in that portrait. I saw two things especially. One was that he had flaws. He attracted people for his ability to listen, for the attention he paid, but he revealed very little. All the stories he told me didn't quite add up. His closeness with his sister, the awful parents, his restless youth. What had that to do with the pictures he took, all of which startled me with gorgeousness? He photographed me as something lush and wild; he photographed everything the same way. His world was sensuous, beautiful, emotional, and yet I felt, looking at the pictures, as if there was a bit of flattery going on. As if all that beauty was a diversion.

Yet he did see that way. And I loved him for it, for the sweet, intimate mood he sank into when just the sound of his voice was enough to enchant me. To enchant me and excite me, to provide a sort of rapture in which there is no danger. Or was there danger? There was danger I might lose him. He was so easily hurt. He was humiliated by jealousy, he said. My jealousy of Tobias had been so childish, so full of pure self-pity, I had never felt humiliated by it. I had felt humiliated by him, but not by jealousy. I understood it would be different now: I would not take the emotion so lightly. I would vanquish it. That's what I believed. I would feel stronger doing so. Obviously Frank felt differently; what he said was he couldn't, but he also meant that if he did, it would depress or degrade him. He got no pleasure in competition, even with himself. Was that a flaw? Perhaps.

The second thing I saw was that I loved him irrevocably. And I knew that he loved me, no matter how I offended his jealousy. A moment ago my past had seemed dried out and lifeless; now it rushed back in, filling me with a sense of my own indescribable being. I had known this being before Frank, but he gave it a depth and certainty I could never find on my own. He loved me for the right reasons, for the qualities I wished to have loved.

The trouble with thinking things out like this, to the impasse, is that it becomes clear the only thing to do is give in. Somebody has to, and one only has control over oneself. As soon as I thought this, I felt iron gates clang down around me; I looked out through the bars at the rosy air, at the lips and eyes of strangers, men of no account, men whose teeth and bones held no extraordinary secrets, who spent one day after another in the same way, moving toward death, but who were so accessible. They could be gone right up to, led away and kissed. Men with no idea of treasure until the unexpected event restores it to them, and through them back to me.

After all, I had had that, and perhaps would again. For now, I could do without. What I had wanted most of all was for Frank to understand, and not in the way he said he understood. Yet if that wasn't going to happen, it wasn't. I still wanted him. More than that, I couldn't bear to give him up.

Frank came back at five o'clock in the morning. I woke up at the sound of his footsteps on the stairs, and I turned on the light. I was afraid of an intruder, although I knew it was him.

He didn't say anything but stood looking down at me and undressed. The room was gray with dawn and the lamp's glow at my bedside cast a weird light. I wondered if the demons of last night were still around, waiting to grant me power for a price. I opened the bedclothes with a wide sweep of my arm.

He climbed in. He took off my nightgown and threw it over the side. The pain in his eyes was not matched by his cock, which had no subtlety of expression. He was very stiff. He laid cold hands on my hips and parted my legs.

Once in, he started to cry. I was disappointed that the tough sex was over. I felt a certain ferocity I wouldn't have minded expressing.

"Darling," he said, between sobs, hugging me tightly, his legs long and bony on top of mine.

"It's all right," I said soothingly. "It's all right."

"No, it isn't."

"I won't sleep with anyone else, I promise. I've decided. It's all right." Irrevocable words, I thought, to which his cock responded by kicking wildly.

"You're sure?" he asked, looking down into my face. His eyes had been pouched and bloodshot, but already they were clearing up. Ready to stare me down, I thought, now that I've done it to myself.

"That was the past. It's all right."

"I love you," he said.

"I love you, too." Code words, uttered like an actress, although it was the truth.

"I need you so much. I just couldn't stand it, sharing you or giving you up, I couldn't bear it." He thrust vigorously.

"Everything's okay, sweetheart." I closed my eyes and let it all go but what I had—Frank, his body inside me, his breath on my neck. I felt anger, pity, lust. I thought, It's so much easier for the one who gets his way, and I let it go. I held him gently and opened my mouth to his kiss.

here followed a few weeks when we were always doing things. We went to North Beach to hear jazz, we had a picnic on Mount Tamalpais, we went to the art museum and had dinner at Ernie's, The Blue Fox, La Pergola, and the Mandarin. I realized Frank was trying to make up for the loss of my strangers by making my life more fun. I did have fun. I enjoyed going out as a couple, meeting Frank's friends.

But I missed our days of innocence. Especially those times before and after sex, hours when Frank held a glass of wine to my lips, or opened the window so the rose scent blew in, warm midnight, then shut it again at dawn, leaning over where he thought I slept until he felt my kiss on his unprotected rib. The texture of that rib, of the slidy flesh, and the harder yet still fragile bone. My own lips' spongy, parting.

It had been fading on its own, that happiness, I knew. Other selves surfacing, other desires at work. I should be glad the first nights had sealed it off so neatly. Our falling in love was for seduction purposes only, like a perfume that mingles with enduring sweat. We couldn't live like that. Nobody could. Nobody I knew.

So we had fun. We went out drinking with Clara and Annie, and Clara took off her shirt in Larry Blake's and swilled beer barebreasted for quite some time before they kicked us out. We had brunch with Callie and Rodney, who had started dating and talked about life after death, with everyone but me agreeing that existence without a body would be worth nothing at all. We took a stack of comic books to Leo, who was recovering from having his tonsils out, and stayed at his house all afternoon reading them, listening to old Beach Boys records and eating chocolate ice cream.

We had sex. That was the least changed of all. My nostalgia vanished when I had arms around me and could wrap my own arms tightly. His body was so beloved by me; the more familiar it became, the more secrets I had with it, not least the one I had read in a text of metaphysics, that each cell had its own rudimentary soul. I whispered to those souls, coaxing them from submissive sleep. I dared them to be great.

Well, perhaps sex did change. We spent less time kissing and more time fucking. Our fucking was friendly. It was a fine family entertainment of parts and personality. His cockhead positioned itself between my labia, rubbed up and down ceremonially, letting us admire its breadth and color, then advanced; my hips traced a slow orbit, showing off their female circularity and particular skill, my vaginal muscles sucked in. We found our orgasms, one, two, three, half a dozen. We had fun. And afterward Frank fell asleep instantly, as if coming had drained all the blood from his brain. I lay awake with a terrible feeling of having the meaning of life on the tip of my tongue and knowing it would never come any closer. How had I progressed from the usual postcoital sadness to this worse urgency? It seemed the sadness had always been just this—the flavor of meaning, divorced from any possible context—which the brain interpreted correctly as a recipe for sorrow. I imagined that this sensation was an evolutionary holdover, a tip as to how our minds developed. Once there was an ape with a mutant taste to his orgasm, to which he became addicted. He pushed desire past previous limits, he respected no hierarchy and sired many young. He was perhaps not the strongest nor the fastest but only the most frenzied: one of us.

I very much minded Frank going to sleep so easily, yet when he was awake I began to demand more solitude. On my nights off I told Frank to go out without me, tendering my apologies to Rodney or Clara.

I'd stay home, drink tea, and brood. To his credit, he never thought I intended to break my word and slip out for a tryst with a stranger. He respected my need to be alone. He didn't take it as an insult. He'd give me a lingering kiss good-bye, then leave cheerfully, saying he envied my quiet night, and after a brief, fierce joy at his absence, I'd start to feel sulky. I'd think about him enjoying himself and wish I'd gone, too.

Sometimes in these moods I'd call my old college roommate, Janey. She was at Columbia, starting her Ph.D. and recovering from a third abortion. She claimed it helped to be pregnant at exam time — she was suffused with psychological well-being and would sail through, imagining herself washing diapers, barefoot and happy, never having to read criticism again. The savage depressions the abortions brought on, her despair at her unquenchable fertility, her rage at the inadequacy of birth-control methods — all this I knew, but she rarely talked about.

What she talked about was her determination to do well in school, and I admired this, although each day away from the university made me the more glad to be past all that. She listened to my problems and reminded me they had once been worse. She gave me news of Teo who was now attempting A.A., and her voice with its laughter like an underground river dispelled the gloom that settled over me when I thought the past was slipping away.

By the time Frank returned, I would wholeheartedly miss him. I would remind him that he had forgotten to pick up milk or coffee; I'd insist that he should not go out again but instead kiss me. Then, in the morning, I'd complain again. I took pleasure in seducing and complaining at the same time, with my fretful tone and my hungry-cat-like affections.

Frank took it well. He thought I was still angry that he had won, which I was. What else I felt about the nature of experience, the loss of our first love, and the tease of sex, I didn't mention, since it seemed so sad. Actually I did mention it, but he forgot.

It was the beginning of July. I went in to work to find George in a towering rage. He was pacing the floor of the dining room, holding a

wine bottle by the neck and swigging it, his hand jerking it up with a motion suspiciously similar to the gesture meaning, "up yours."
"What's the matter?" I asked.

"The IR-fucking-S."

"What do they want?"

"What do you think they want? A night on the town and a wet kiss? Moneymoneymoney."

"George, I'm aware of that. I meant, how much and when?"

"Eight thousand in ten days. Shit! I could have half of that, no problem, though of course nobody would get paid. Who cares. You're all so loyal, right? But the whole fucking amount. I told them if they close me I'm not likely to find the money under a fucking stone. This is where it comes from, *comprende*, this is the fucking goose. They sit there like clones — I think they make those creeps in their laboratories. They say they can't do anything. No . . . they can close me down but they can't do anything. The guy says, 'Maybe you can find an outside source of funds.' Yeah? Like robbing a bank? Shaking down my mother?"

"You have a mother?"

"I have a mother. She lives in Florida."

"Well, can you borrow money? From her or anybody?"

"Shit no. How do you think I've kept this place going so far? The fucking thing is, we're almost beginning to make it. One more summer! We're established, we've learned what works, you're a better cook than Sandy—"

"Thanks, George."

"Will you quit with the thanks? I'm talking. I knew when it started it would take a couple of years. So, I didn't know how much it would cost—is that a crime? We take a dive all spring, so where do they think I've put the—if you can call them that—'profits'?"

"Do you really think they'll close you down?"

"Yeah, they come and put a fucking seal on the door."

"Oh, I saw that. A florist in New York. I noticed it because all the flowers in the window were dead."

He gave me a look. "Shall we put some produce in our window so the world can watch it rot?"

"Can't you put another mortgage on your house or something?"

"Eva wouldn't allow it."

"She wants you to lose the restaurant?"

"Sure. She thinks I should get a regular job. 'Food management.' At one of those places where the food goes out sealed in little cardboard boxes."

"Could you get that kind of a job?" I asked curiously. I couldn't imagine a company hiring George.

He shrugged. "I used to do that kind of shit."

"You never told me!"

"And I'm not going to now. I pay myself a salary, Eva hasn't suffered from this venture yet. So she can keep her mouth shut. But the house is off limits; it's in her name too . . . This is strictly solo torture, Blondie."

"No, it isn't. I'm on your side. We all are."

"Think Ramon would lend me his life savings?"

"Oh, come on. Surely sympathy counts for something. I mean, we would lose our jobs."

"Yeah, I know. I'm sorry. Well, at least you have a rich boyfriend. Do you think he'd give me the money?"

"You can ask him."

"No, thanks." He took a swig from the bottle. "Want some wine?"

"No. Want to help me cook?"

"Do you think it'll take my mind off my troubles?" he asked sarcastically.

"It might."

"Sure, Blondie. I love to see you fingerfuck filet."

"Just for that, you can do it." So George skewered the meat and inserted slivers of garlic, while I marinated scallops, cut up vegetables, and rubbed chicken breasts with ginger root.

By the time Allison arrived at five we were laughing. We told her of the possible shutdown and our solution: we would run an illegal restaurant where the food was served in the dark by blind waiters— fixed menu, of course—with no one allowed to speak above a whisper. We predicted it would cause a sensation among those for whom chocolate binges weren't sin enough.

We had a good night, taking in over a thousand dollars, and George seemed reassured. Of course the problem had always been that we

didn't have good nights consistently, that we weren't quite fashionable, and not quite homey either. But he decided, opening a bottle of
Zinfandel, that our luck would hold from now on; I suspected he had
thought of something to do, something that he didn't want to tell me
about yet.

When I got home I called Grandmother to wish her a happy birthday.
She was sixty-seven. "Thanks for the champagne," she said.

"Oh, it got there? I was afraid it wouldn't. They didn't arrest you at
the post office, did they?"

"No, your crime went undetected."

"Well, have you tasted it yet?"

"Yes, I had a bottle earlier. It was very good, made a wonderful
celebration." I wanted to ask her who she'd been celebrating with but
was afraid she'd say nobody. Champagne was not, perhaps, the right
present for someone who lived alone.

"What have you been doing?"

"Planning my trip."

"What trip? Are you coming out to visit me?" I'd invited her several
times but she always found excuses.

"No, not out there yet. I don't have a yen for California."

"But I'm here."

"I was hoping you'd come visit me before I left. I'll be gone quite a
long time."

"Where are you going?"

"India, Malaysia, Africa." Her dry voice strung the names out
lengthily, in a way that seemed to me almost old-fashioned, as if there
was something exotic she knew about that I could never find, that I'd
been born too late for.

"All at once?"

"Well, time seems to be running out for the world. If I want to see
lions and tigers and elephants I have to hurry."

"I didn't know you wanted to see them so badly," I said slowly,
wondering at the keen envy I felt. I didn't want to see lions and tigers,
particularly.

"I always took them for granted. When I was a girl, people shot them for fun. My father did. He went out with Baron Blixen in the twenties. My mother sent him off to recover after my little sister was stillborn. I don't think he managed to shoot anything. But the point is, now that they're disappearing so fast, I feel a great compulsion to see them."

"But how long . . .?"

"Perhaps a year. Perhaps longer. I'm getting bored here. And Ernest—you know Ernest?"

"Your beau."

"Yes. Well, he's taking a similar trip. Our paths will crisscross."

"Why don't you go together?"

"No, I don't think so. I'd get tired of him. We'll meet now and then."

"Do be careful. When are you leaving?"

"At the end of August. Would you like to come visit before then?"

"I don't know if I can. Well, I might be able to . . . The Vineyard might be extinct by then."

"Why is that?"

"George doesn't have the money for the IRS."

"Those repulsive people. Why don't they dun Ronald Reagan instead? I'm sure he owes more money than poor George."

"I'm sure. But Nancy gave her pajamas to a San Francisco museum and took a tax deduction."

"I hope she washed them first."

"But if George manages to get the money, and somehow I have faith in him, I really should stay here. Summer is our busiest season, you know."

"Yes, of course. Well, I'll send you a ticket if you decide you want to come."

"What if I send you a ticket to come here?"

She laughed. "Perhaps . . . we'll see." I suspected she wanted to be able to say that she'd been around the world and back, but had not yet found time for California. She had a bit of eastern prejudice in her. Or more than a bit. But I thought I could maybe persuade her—the Schramsburg had been a first step. I knew she had never drunk California wine before, at least not on purpose.

"Grandmother, who's going to take care of the house while you're gone? You can't just leave it empty."

"Of course not. Tobias is here."

"Tobias . . . what do you mean?"

"Your old friend Tobias. Didn't I tell you? He's been living here a while."

"Why? Since when? No, you didn't tell me, as you very well know."

"I was sure I'd told you. Maybe I forgot to mail the letter." There was an undercurrent of amusement in her voice — lately she'd taken to pretending to be absentminded, old ladyish. It was a joke that could be irritating, especially when I'd start to believe her, thinking that, after all, I hadn't seen her in so long. Always at that moment her slyness and sharpness would come back, like a buzz saw shredding my worry into ribbons. "Well, you see, he was giving a poetry reading at the library about three months ago. I went to it out of curiosity. I was surprised at how good he is, really, Stella, you never told me — "

"Go on."

"Anyway, we got to talking and he mentioned he had no place to live. So I offered him a room."

"Just like that?"

"It's worked out quite well. He doesn't bother me and I do need someone to help out."

"You should have asked me first."

"Why?"

"When I visit! It'll be very awkward, to say the least. Didn't you think about my feelings at all?"

"You've gotten over him by now, haven't you? He's no longer an object of desire, I can assure you."

"Of course I've gotten over him . . . what do you mean?"

"Well, he might be still attractive, to some tastes, I suppose, but he's so utterly queer. No danger to young girls anymore."

"I don't think I want to see him. It would depress me."

"No, I doubt it, he's a different man . . . he's very good about doing errands and he washed the windows last week."

"I can't believe that."

"He cleaned out the basement and painted the living room. Not very well, but then he is a poet. He does enough; I have no complaints."

"Lucky you. Still, Grandmother—"

"My dear, he's a charming man. And he's very fond of you. Of course he was in the wrong but you were too innocent for your own good. Some men aren't meant to love women."

"Thanks a lot. I mean, that's my past you're resurrecting."

"You did the same to me. I never expected to raise another child."

"Oh, shit!" She's been waiting to use that line for years, I thought. She laughed. "You see, you can't argue with me."

"That's not a fair argument."

"Of course not."

"Well, I hope the bastard steals your silver spoons."

"Don't hope that. I'm leaving them all to you."

"I just can't believe it," I said to Frank the next day.

"Well, she's got a point, you know. She does need someone."

"Someone, yeah."

"How many people would she get along with? Who wouldn't bore her?"

"I don't know, but still . . . Tobias. It's just not fair. He's a slime to take advantage of her."

"I think your grandmother's being very generous."

"You would. Aren't you even jealous?"

"What for?"

"Well if I go home to visit, I'll be there in the house with him."

He laughed. "He's gay, Stella. I'm not worried." He reached a hand out and lazily caressed my hair, pulling it over my ears, then pushing it back again. I twisted away.

"He liked me well enough before."

"People change. Don't they?"

"Some people." There was a pause.

"You know, a lot of gay men check out women in their youth. When they get older they know what they want."

"You're so wise. Street smarts, I guess."

"I could say something about you and street smarts."

"Go ahead."

He shook his head with an infuriating smile. "You still want this guy?"

"No." I wasn't sure. I suspected I wouldn't, if I saw him again. Yet I was, in a way, glad he was there. In my house. Secured. I thought of the fantasies I used to have: Tobias in my power. "Christ, you're no good. You're jealous when I don't want you to be, and not when I do want you to be."

"I thought you disapproved of jealousy altogether?"

"Why should I bother disapproving? I have no choice."

"You always have a choice." His tone was so serious it scared me.

"I'm jealous of your past. I often imagine that Dorothy didn't leave you; that I never had a chance."

"Even if she'd stayed, once I met you I wouldn't have loved her anymore."

"How do you know?"

"I know." He looked at me steadily.

"You have magic eyes, you know."

"Yeah, all my girlfriends tell me that."

"Shut up." I took his hands and held them against my cheeks. I looked down his arms to the crook of his elbows. "You know how in dreams, or rather right before you fall asleep, you imagine you're sliding down an endless hill? Or at least I do. You look like that hill. I'd like to slide down your arms forever."

"Come on."

"Kiss me."

"Kiss *me*."

We stayed like that for a moment, at arm's length, then both bent forward. As our lips met I remembered the taste of wine when I was a little girl. Sweet, fruity. Profoundly adult.

At The Vineyard, George was cleaving chickens. I was surprised; he usually had the butcher do it. I watched from the doorway of the kitchen for a moment. He raised the cleaver, swung it down with vicious force, the bird halved and the blade stuck in the wood; he wrenched it loose, raised it again. Breast split from thigh, blade struck again. "What's wrong now?" I asked. He had been cheerful the last few days, working hard to raise the tax money. "The IRS?"

He turned and smiled at me sourly. There was a bruise over his left eye. "Nope."

"What then?"

"You wanna know?" He raised the cleaver again, positioned a little bird.

"I asked."

"Eva wants a divorce." He swung the cleaver. I wondered fleetingly what her head would look like split open. I had never met her, so I could hardly speculate.

"Why?"

"Because I'm using Lisa's college fund for the business."

"Oh. Is it your money? How old is Lisa, anyway?"

"She's sixteen. It's my money. I earned most of it, and the rest came from my father's estate. It was supposed to be for her college, but I'll replace it. Anyway, we gotta eat. I can't go bankrupt so she can go to a fancy college."

"I don't see how a divorce would solve your financial problem."

He laughed shortly. "It's my attitude. She can't take it anymore, this is the last straw, etcetera."

"What does she expect you to do?"

"Go out of business, say sorry to everybody who lent me money, forget what I put into it, and get a job."

"Selling cardboard food?"

"Yep. But I refused."

"Well, maybe it won't be so bad. You don't like her anyway."

"I hate her guts! But I haven't left. What gives *her* the right to leave? I've suffered more than she has and my sons both have that smarmy little mouth of hers. It's disgusting."

"I get an idea why she wants to leave you."

He glared at me. "We happen to have children together. I don't know why I was such an asshole as to marry her, but I was, and she did, and we have three kids. Christ! She never makes the slightest effort to see my point of view on anything, or rather, she listens then shunts it aside. I'm just an adjunct to her ambitions — fancy schools, new cars, the 'right' friends. If any of the kids gets in a bit of trouble, she hushes it up so the neighbors won't know. She's got the soul of a . . . cockroach. I feel so sorry for my poor kids, growing up alone with that bitch."

"But, George, you can still see the kids if you get divorced."

"I run a restaurant, remember? I work at night. They only see me on weekend mornings as it is. I can't very well have visiting hours between eight and eleven A.M."

"Sure you could."

"Fat chance. She'd move to Connecticut or something, I know. She's pissed off because I'm not making enough money, because I'm not there to take her to her stupid parties. She's never even set foot in this place. I tell you, Stella, she's treated me like a beast for the last ten years. Worse than a beast. She's got three goddamn bloodhounds she lets sleep in the bed with her. They slink around, hairy and smelly, with those ugly eyes. And they really are bloodhounds. I found one chewing on one of her used Tampax once. I guess he got it out of the trash but, who knows, maybe she gave it to him. I called her to see what the monster is slurping on the rug and she comes in with a little smile on her face, like she knew all along, it was a special treat for him. When I get in the bed, on the side covered with dog hairs and old dog farts, she's got a pile of books like a wall between us. She reads at night and never takes the books out. I'm constantly rolling over on some illustrated history of Africa or whatever. She even keeps the fucking *Oxford English Dictionary* in bed. *And* the magnifying glass. I guess the dogs like to read it. She pretends that she's more intellectual than me but as far as I can tell it's been the same books for the last five years. She speaks to me over her glasses, with her nose all pinched up, in this husky, creaking voice like a haunted house. Questions me about money. Or if I think the dogs are looking sick. Never about the kids. They're *her* property. My advice is not sought or heeded. If one of the kids comes in the room and asks us something, like whether they can go to a party or not, Eva ignores anything I try to say. She fixes her beady eyes on the kids and they obey her. Lisa, my eldest, listens to me, but the boys don't. The boys and their mother have a pact that I don't exist. I'm sure they fix it up when I'm not there. 'Let's get rid of Daddy.' I knew she's wanted me to be the one to move out; she's been working on that for years so she could play the deserted mother."

"How did you get the bruise?"

"She threw Carl's lunchbox at me."

"Did you hit her?"

"No. I called her a diseased cunt." He looked a little ashamed. "I'm disgusting, I know, but she's worse. She said, 'You've had your fun,' as if this place was a kid's game, and now I had to go back to Mommy and learn about the real world. What I know about the real world is you have to fight the fucking thing! The more shit you eat the more they'll make you eat. She's a great teacher of that, for sure. Where's the benefit of spending my days in misery, copping out on all my backers so Lisa can go to some shit-ass college that will teach her how to get ahead in banking. That's all they teach these days anyway. What the fuck, I'll give her a job here."

"Here?"

"Sure. She can start learning the business this summer, take over when I retire."

"George, you're only forty, and anyway, she might not like it here."

"So she'll work her way through college. Anyway, I'll help her, even if I go bankrupt and have to work in a Chinese butchery, cutting up chickens."

"You'd probably terrify them. Butchery, indeed."

He severed a few legs and surveyed his handiwork. "They do it with kung fu, anyway. Have you ever seen that in a Chinese restaurant — you order Peking Duck and the waiter comes with the whole duck and whacks off pieces of breast with his bare hands?"

"No. Are you sure this is a real ultimatum? Maybe Eva will give in when she realizes you won't. If the money's yours . . ."

"I don't know what the fuck her idea is. But I don't think we'll make up this time. We haven't yelled at each other in front of the kids like this in ten years. She thinks I'm a sinking ship is the whole story. I can't make the business pay, so I'm a washout, as well as being personally disgusting to her. She'd put up with my disgustingness if I had more money, but as it is . . . she's in a hurry to get out. She's getting older and uglier every minute."

"You must have loved her once. You married her."

"I guess so. I don't like to think about it. It gives me the shudders. I can't stand that it's my own fucking, goddamned, stupid, shit-headed fault for not seeing what she was. I let her in, I let her do it."

"That sounds like a tag line for a vampire movie."

"Damn fucking right."

"George. Listen, I hate to say it, but Eva's right. You should get a divorce. You're crazy to live this way."

"Well, it's happening."

"Have you moved out?"

"Not until she gets a court order."

"What's the point of staying? Just to annoy her?"

"No, I need to talk to the kids, before it's all set up that they stay with their mother."

"I thought you said they couldn't live with you. Your hours."

"Well, it's possible Lisa could. She's sixteen, she could stay alone at night. Or she could come here and help out. You've met her."

"Yes. What does she think?"

"She was very upset. Asked me if we couldn't make up. I would for her . . . Eva thinks Lisa is too attached to me but she also thinks she's too attached to her boyfriend. She just can't understand a woman who actually loves men. Dogs maybe, but not men."

"It would be fair then—for you to take Lisa and Eva to take the boys."

"Yeah." He put the cleaver down. The small mountain of chicken parts began to look like dinner instead of murder. "Lisa's sixteen, so it's really up to her. The courts generally let a child of that age choose. She's such a sympathetic girl, she understands more than the others."

George went on talking about his family for a long time. I cooked and listened, trying to put together a picture of Eva from what he said. All I could get was a witch. Was George married to one? For all his violent talk, he was a sweet man; I couldn't imagine him hating without good reason. Marriage itself might be enough of a reason, I thought. Eighteen years with the wrong woman, both too stubborn to leave.

George got very drunk that night. Leo had to take over in the dining room, which thrilled him—he'd always wanted to be suave— and Allison and I took turns pouring brandy and agreeing that Eva was a vicious bitch. At one point Lisa called and George told her repeatedly that he loved her. When he hung up he turned to us wonderingly.

"She said I was drunk. What does that have to do with it?"

The next day he was in command of himself again. Wearing a dark blue shirt and white pants, he looked almost nautical. "She'll come round," he said to me.

"Eva?" I was startled.

"No, Lisa. She'll live with me. She as much as said so. At her age, little brothers are a pain. She'll work here part time, what do you think?"

"She can't be a waitress. She isn't old enough to serve liquor."

"She could work in the kitchen with you."

"I don't need any more help. Not with Allison." That wasn't strictly true, but I didn't want Lisa. Not here.

"We'll work something out. Maybe I'll fire you, what the hell, I should have fired you when you stopped fucking me."

"You want this rolling pin up your ass?"

"Sure. Shall I take off my pants or will you do it for me? I mean, you break my heart and I let you keep on working, as if nothing is wrong."

"What are you talking about?" He was sitting on a stool beside me, drinking red wine. He smiled, shrugged. "George, I knew you were sorry when we stopped, but . . ."

"You weren't too worried about it because I'm so tough."

"Well, you were then," I said irritably. I didn't want to talk about this at all.

"Hell, Blondie, it'll take more than that bitch—"

"And don't call me Blondie. It sounds stupid."

"You mean you think it makes you sound stupid, or me sound stupid?"

"You mostly."

"I figured. It's part of my appeal for you."

"I haven't seen that appeal working overtime," I said, and then regretted it. The fact is I felt very much appealed to. He didn't say anything for a minute, then threw his glass out the open door where it smashed on a rock. He gave me a kiss on the top of my head and sauntered out.

I looked at the pile of boiled lobsters in front of me and wished I could unboil them. I needed something alive to talk to. What a jerk I am, I thought. Of course I had always known George liked me more than a little; I liked him more than a little. It was true I hadn't worried about him because he was tough. I had wanted him to be that way. For him to be fond of me was one thing, for him to be in love quite another.

I cracked the lobster shells efficiently and extracted the soft red-and-white meat. Then I sautéed the shells in butter. This was not how you were supposed to do it. The lobsters should be killed with a knife and then sautéed raw, so the shells don't lose any of their flavor to boiling water. I tried it that way once but couldn't find the right spot to stab them. They refused to die. I kept trying, expecting them to succumb momentarily, until I was surrounded by the writhing green crustaceans, many of whom managed to crawl to the edge of the high counter, there to fall off and sort of slither around my feet, broken, with white foam frothing from their wounds. George had rescued me then and taken over the cooking.

Okay, it was true, I thought. I had not paid enough attention to my breakup with George. It had all happened so smoothly; I hadn't even thought about why it happened so smoothly. From my perspective, our relationship hadn't seemed to have changed that much. It felt natural to do without the sex. Our intimacy had already been established. The point was, I had hurt George and not paid attention. I wasn't sure whether it mattered that he obviously had not wanted me to pay attention. He was fond of his toughness, too, and he had quite a lot of it, if not so much as we pretended.

I stood by the stove, pushing the lobster shells around in the pan, and felt purely guilty. I was heavy and sealed up and the thought of Frank being in love with me, and George being in love with me, made me squirm. It was too much. I would be punished.

By the time George came back, everyone was around and we weren't able to talk. During the evening he shouted orders more obnoxiously than usual—Big Boss time, as Judy called it—and Ramon shook his head with peasant knowingness as he gathered George's empty bottles to throw out. I made a beautiful dish with the lobsters and cream and cognac, and it occurred to me how useless this skill really was. A boiled lobster was enough for anybody. The rest just gave you a stomach ache, especially if you'd been drinking wine all night.

"The old man was certainly drunk tonight," Frank remarked as we walked home.

"He's been drinking a lot lately."

"Is he still in love with his wife, do you think?"

"No. He hates her with a passion."

" 'With a passion.' "

"I guess, though after so many years—"

"Of course. It's rough."

We walked in silence for a few minutes. So I hadn't told him. I had thought I might. He was my best friend, after all. I thought of the kiss

George gave me after breaking the wine glass. I could think of it as a way of sealing the secret in.

Late, after Frank had gone to sleep, I went downstairs, poured a glass of wine, and called The Vineyard. George answered on the seventh ring and said, before I could say a word, "For Christ's sake, bitch, leave me alone." I hung up. It had been a stupid idea anyway.

The next few days at work George came in late, avoiding being alone with me. I cooked like a demon, making more and more elaborate dishes. It got to the point where I didn't want to make separate things at all; I wanted to throw everything in one pot. Sausage and chicken and shrimp and scallops and lamb; mushrooms, green beans, white wine, and okra; red peppers and yellow peppers and onion and garlic and rice. Then I began to season it. Then I added tomatoes. Then I asked Leo to taste it and he said no, it wasn't kosher.

"Well, there's nothing else to eat tonight. I've used all the ingredients in this." That wasn't quite true. There were steaks and trout.

"George will be pissed off," said Leo, spearing a shrimp from the caldron and dunking it in Chinese mustard.

"Wanna bet he won't say anything?"

"Nope. You have unfair sources of information." Judy came in the kitchen, tasted my creation, and dubbed it Gluttony Goulash. She thought it would be a good meal for a woman pregnant with twins. George didn't notice it at all, not even when several plates of it were cleared off the tables barely touched.

He seemed to be in a good mood though. He told everyone about his impending bachelorhood and soon half the female diners were flirting with him, Judy said. It's good for business, I replied. She laughed, and I realized I was jealous. I had shrunk from the prospect of talking to him about his broken heart, but that would have been better than being neglected.

"I just can't stand all this drama," I said to Judy, who nodded, although she didn't know what had happened between us. "Why can't he just calm down?"

"Oh, my god," she said, peering through the kitchen door. "Mrs. Attley is kissing him good-bye."

"She's always drunk when she leaves here."

"Now he's got his arms around Mr. Attley."

"Let me see." I crowded beside her in the doorway and watched George escort the doddering old couple to the door. "Some dress she's wearing," I said. George gave them a gorgeous smile and strode with that late-evening gait of his back into the room. "He looks like he just jumped off a fucking horse," I said.

"Or a fucking something." She giggled and we went back into the kitchen. I told her a few anecdotes about George in bed—or rather on the table—and she told me a few things about Leo. We agreed that we were not surprised by each other's stories. "You can tell," she said.

"I can't," said Allison, who had heard the tail end of our conversation when we stopped whispering.

"You must lead a life of surprises then," said Judy. "How fun for you."

"I don't," said Allison, and we didn't answer. She could go on like this all night: I can't, I don't, I haven't, I won't. She never explained any further but waited, her square face stony, for someone to come along and excavate her.

Lisa came in, clearly with an eye to working there, or at least hanging out. She watched everything closely, was very admiring of me, and convinced George to let us make fresh coffee more often. George didn't approve of coffee; he thought a good cognac was what people needed after dinner. But he yielded to his daughter, obviously charmed to be doing so, and the waiters all agreed Lisa would be a great advantage for their side. I said nothing, not sure anymore what my side was.

Lisa was very pretty, with soft eyes, long hair, and long bones, and a way of taking George's glass out of his hands and setting it a little distance away. He seemed used to this, his hand pushing hers aside and reaching out for the glass without interrupting his conversation. She would sigh and say, "Daddy," in a pleading, only slightly exasperated voice, and he would pat her shoulder, only slightly annoyed.

I had never thought of George as drinking too much, since the alcohol seemed to intensify his personality, rather than dismantle it. Perhaps it was simply one more instance of not wanting to see any weakness in him. Yet, even realizing that he might be overdoing it, I thought Lisa ought to leave him alone. It was not her place to tell him what to do.

Then she asked me if I would teach her how to cook. "My mother is a lousy cook," she said with a smile.

"Your father's pretty good."

"I couldn't learn from him. He's too impatient."

"I'm pretty impatient myself. I don't know how to teach, I've never done it."

"How did you learn?"

"Just by doing it," I lied. "I've always loved the magic of combining different foods and coming up with something unlike any of the ingredients. A dish is a kind of symphony of flavors."

"Yes, I know what you mean. I've always loved food, too. So you just started out by yourself?"

"Yes. I feel like I always knew how to do it. It's something inborn, I think. Even now, I don't use recipes. Ingredients differ so much, you know." I caught a glimpse of Leo, grinning at me from the kitchen door, and I blushed. Fuck it, I thought, I'm not paid to teach.

"Can I watch you from now on?" she asked.

"Well, I'm just about finished. The kitchen closes in fifteen minutes."

"I mean whenever I come in."

"I guess. George'll probably have things for you to do."

"He said I could do whatever I wanted."

"That's nice of him."

"He's okay," she said. "I don't think I'd want to work for him though, if he wasn't my father."

Frank picked me up at eleven, as usual. I was silent all the way home, thinking of Lisa being in the kitchen with me from now on. So even if George started talking to me again, he couldn't really talk to me. Not privately. I had realized in the past few days how much I enjoyed George's companionship, how much I had come to depend on it. He was my only solid friend, besides Frank, and he was older; I respected him. It was a lot to lose.

Frank asked me what was wrong. I said, "George's kid wants me to teach her how to cook. I don't want to."

"Why not? Don't you like her?"

"No. Oh, she's okay. I just don't want to teach her. It's a big favor to ask. She shouldn't just assume I'll do it."

"She didn't assume, did she? She asked you."

"It's awkward saying no. I mean, her father's the boss."

"I'm sure George will let you decide for yourself whether you want to teach her how to cook. He may be her father but he's also your friend."

"Yeah, but he'd be hurt if he thought I didn't like her. He thinks she's the greatest sixteen-year-old in the world."

"What do you have against her?"

"Nothing. Stupid things. I don't want to talk about it anymore."

"Okay," he replied.

was making lettuce soup. Young heads of Boston lettuce, light chicken stock, cream, Chablis, a bit of cardamom, and white pepper. The soup was a beautiful pale green color, like the blood of a frail boy, heir to an extinct throne, who lies on a couch all day, offering his veins to a dieting vampire. I turned on the tape player. George had brought it over from his house the other day; he claimed he needed Frank Sinatra at a time like this.

I listened to "Strangers in the Night" as I stuffed the trout with shrimp, "Come Fly With Me" as I trussed the Cornish game hens, "That's My Baby" as I pounded the veal, and "I'm Getting Married in the Morning," which I danced to until George came in and laughed at me.

"Shut up," I said. "Taste this." I gave him a spoonful of soup. I was so pleased to see him in early; he must have forgiven me his confession.

"Not bad. Listen, guess what? It's all set, Lisa's going to live with me as soon as school starts. I've even found an apartment."

"I thought you were going to stay at the house as long as you could."

"Fuck that. I don't need the aggravation. Eva was furious but there's nothing she can do. I admit it's not all me. Lisa knows she can get away with more at my place. Great. I want her to be independent."

"The IRS called."

"Don't worry," he said expansively, slurping another mouthful of soup. "I've got the money now. And don't worry about Lisa—she's so smart she can get a scholarship if she needs to."

Smart, and two inches taller than me. That's one thing I liked about Allison, she was little. When I ordered her around, it seemed only natural. I wondered what George would say if I told him that as chef I ought to have power to hire—or at least approve—my subordinates. I decided not to chance it. Lisa could grind the coffee and keep George's wineglass filled.

"You were right, baby, I should have gotten this divorce a long time ago. I feel fantastic."

"What a change."

"My head's clearing, I tell you. She had me under a spell." He turned up the volume on the music. "May I have this dance?" He looked so happy I couldn't resist and went into his arms.

I'd forgotten what it felt like there. He was so much bigger than Frank. He swept me along, practically crowing with good humor. I began to feel nostalgic—for the old days with George, for Teo, for music. Frank and I never listened to music.

"The summer wind / came blowing in / across the sea / lingered there / to touch your hair . . ." George sang along as I laughed, pressed up against his chest. "I lost you to / the summer wind."

I looked up at him and he kissed me. It was a light kiss, not meant to express more than regret, but the song went on about autumn and winter and loneliness and I don't know what I was thinking exactly— something like "Get it while you can," Sinatra seguing into Janis Joplin. I kissed him back passionately. He hesitated a second, then his hand clutched my ass, each finger pressing separately into the flesh. As his tongue poked into all the corners of my mouth, his hard-on was born in an instant. I felt so comfortable in that manically horny embrace. I leaned away from him and pulled up my shirt. He made fond little kissing noises at my breasts, the way you do to a baby, and unzipped his pants. I laughed.

"I can't believe this," I said.

He smiled hugely and slid his pants off, then started on mine. I looked down at him appreciatively. I'd missed those hairy thighs. "You haven't changed," I said.

"Nope." He stuck his hand between my legs. "You neither."

I let him revel in that familiar ground for a while, then pulled away. I had changed. I walked halfway across the room, my jeans inching down my legs, then turned and gave him a slow striptease, summoning up an eroticism I'd never shown with him before. We'd always been rough and casual with each other. When I was naked, I stood stock still, feeling the sex build in my flesh, like a secondary webbing of muscle, then, with all my strength, threw my desire out at him.

He caught it. I could see it take hold. His stance changed, became more assured and more excited. He unbuttoned his shirt and laid it on the back of a chair. His naked body seemed massive; I tiptoed forward. I pulled the bobby pins out of my hair and shook it free, shaking my breasts too, and seeing myself with his eyes. And seeing him seeing me; and seeing him—all the views converging as I thought with a dreamy gravity, This is wrong, I promised not to. George turned the music even higher.

He put his hands out and lifted me up. He slid me onto his cock easily, we both knew the way. With my arms around his neck and his hands still holding me, with his feet braced and his back against the wall, with the music drowning the cries I loosed with abandon, we went at it. We fucked through "My Way," "The Lady Is a Tramp," and "Blue Heaven." I felt lustlike power, something that drove me forward until it seemed I would have to climb inside his body; it was so impossible to satisfy, I grew away from it at the same time I was farthest inside. I watched it play out to a gorgeous orgasm, shocking me with pleasure, and I felt serenely responsible, the way you must when something isn't really under your control but is yours anyway.

Then George came and I slowly slid off him, to my knees, and dried off his cock with my hair.

"Jesus," he said in amazement, "you're going all out today. There's nobody better, I tell you. Why so sweet?"

"No reason," I replied, pleased with the effect. I got to my feet and felt immediately sad. I started to put my clothes on. I got as far as my shirt when George pulled me down to his lap. "I've missed you," he said. The tape had run out and it was very quiet.

"I know."

"More than I thought I would. This kitchen will never be the same. Are you really serious about this guy?"

"You know I am."

"He's not your type."

"Yes, he is."

"He's too inhibited for you. He's jealous. He tries to control you."

"I'm jealous, too, in other ways. George, don't talk about him. It has nothing to do with me and you, really."

"Except that it keeps us from being able to fuck. I won't even mention what else, because I know it's my fault it never went any further." No, it was my fault. I hadn't wanted it to.

"Yeah," I said. I felt comfortable on his lap, comfortable and affectionate, but still terribly sad. It had to do with the moment of strongest desire when I felt switched on to another, vaster self, one endlessly hungry and alone, who didn't know yet that she was alone. I rarely felt it with Frank, his love was a dome over me, keeping me woman-sized. But I couldn't say I didn't want to feel it again. It was there, and I had a weird belief it would be waiting for me when I died.

He said, "I guess I know you've made up your mind. But what happens next? Are you going to keep this a secret?"

"Yes."

"Good. I won't ask if you want me again. If you do you can let me know. Give me another kiss before I get dressed." I put my arms around him and kissed him longingly. If only, I thought, not even knowing what.

"You're sweet," I said, and he laughed.

"Yep."

"I mean it. I mean—"

"Okay, Blondie, I know you're fond of me. Now get your ass up."

I went over to the sink, thinking I'd wash my hair before starting work. George put his pants on and went into the dining room. "What the fuck? What in fucking hell are you doing here?"

I ran out. I already knew. Frank was sitting at one of the tables, looking at me with an expression both hot and cold, both defiant and yielding to a passionate misery.

"Sorry I eavesdropped," he said. "I couldn't resist. Don't always get a chance to hear such . . . goings on."

George was turning scarlet but I felt only very faint, as if I had nothing but my lettuce soup in my veins. My extinct throne. The line dying out.

"Get out," growled George. He looked at me in apology and I touched his arm.

"Just a minute," I said, as Frank got up. "Wait for me." He waited, looking at the ceiling, while I put my pants and shoes on. We went out the door, me first, not speaking, and we walked two feet apart down Telegraph Avenue.

"So you came with me," he said.

"Of course. I'm sorry, y' know."

"Yes, but *you* know George was right. I am too jealous for you. I can't handle it, Stella. Maybe I wish I could. And I can't tie you up — though maybe I should — so what the fuck can I do? Why do you have to be like this?"

"You make it sound like I'm some kind of monster."

"No. Just a woman who doesn't want what I want."

I was too defeated to argue with him. I still didn't believe it couldn't be straightened out, somehow. Yet I was also terribly ashamed, especially about him hearing me tell George I would deceive him. That was the worst of it, I thought, but I knew he wouldn't mention it. He understood all too well why I would lie, and what could I do? I could promise to change, and I could probably stick to it, for a while anyway, but I knew he wouldn't believe me.

"Listen," he said. "I don't want to hurt you, but I have to break up with you."

"No, you don't," I said.

"Stella, Stella." He was shaking his head as if he were humoring me. "Don't be unreasonable."

"I'm not unreasonable." I watched his face. "Okay, I am unreasonable. But I just know it's wrong — for you as well as for me. You won't be happy."

"As I recall, I got along before." He spoke coolly but walked defensively, his whole right side ready for my attack. I considered it — elbowing him into the gutter and jumping up and down on him. He gave me a twisted little smile, then stopped. "I'll go on ahead, I think. Good-bye."

"Wait a minute. You can't go off like this. So fast. Let's have a drink or something."

"I don't want a drink."

"A cup of coffee?"

"No, thanks."

"A hamburger?"

"Stop crying. You'll be fine. George is in love with you."

"Fuck George! That's not the same. You know it's not the same!"

"I know," he said quietly. "But it's too much the same. Good-bye, Stella."

"Kiss me." I didn't give him a chance to refuse but put my arms around him. He kissed me, at first stiffly, but then with passion. I closed my eyes and summoned all the sexual power I had left, but it wasn't much; I called on the female magic of the universe. It was too slow arriving. He pulled away. "Good-bye," I said, and walked off.

When we were a block apart I began to sob. I wept all the way home where, with shaking hand, I could barely fit the key in the lock. It took me a few minutes of struggling with the door. Then I slammed it behind me and screamed until my throat was raw.

I sat down at the kitchen table. I sat there for three hours, watching the daylight fade and coming to believe he might possibly mean what he said. Perhaps it was over. My love.

I went back to The Vineyard around eleven. I entered through the back door and Judy was there with an arm around my shoulders, urging me to a chair. "Sit down, sit down, you look awful. George told us what happened. That's really bad luck. Is he very angry?"

"It's over," I said, surprised that George had told her.

"Oh, not really? What a bastard . . . Yes, he is! Men are just too possessive. I'm surprised they can part with their own shit in the morning."

"That's about what I feel like."

"No, Stella, you're just a passionate woman. George is a hunk, I don't blame you. Frank is a hunk of course, too. Did you bang your head against the wall?"

"Against the table."

She nodded and poured me a glass of wine. Ramon was smiling and shaking his head at me from the dishwasher, and Leo, as he passed in and out of the kitchen, gave me sorry-kid-what-can-I-do? smirks, rolling his knobby shoulders in sympathy. Only Allison paid no attention to me, cooking stolidly and slowly through the orders that were piling up.

"Where's George?" I asked. "How come he isn't back here? Allison can't do it all herself."

"He just went out for more ice. It *is* crowded tonight. I've been helping her."

"Who's in the dining room?"

"Just Leo and Simon."

"Well, you get out there. I can work."

"Are you sure? George said if you came back—"

"I'll handle George," I said. Ramon giggled. "Shit, give me a break. Are they eating my soup?"

"You've got such a thing about soup," said Allison in her whiny voice.

"They love it," said Judy. "They're thinking of nominating it for a Nobel Prize."

"My poor soup," I said mournfully. "Sometimes I wish I could keep it."

"Oh, my god, now she's having a career crisis," said Leo, patting my shoulder. "How you doin', honey?"

"Surviving. I'm not having a career crisis. I want to cook."

"Move aside, folks, the lady wants to cook. Yeah, she's really going to cook tonight. We've got the press waiting out here, ABC, NBC, Calvin Trillin . . ."

"Judy, take your husband away, he's cluttering up my kitchen."

"Sure thing, Big Boss Lady."

"Stop it!"

"What's going on in here?" George was in the doorway, hefting a bag of ice. He looked very happy to see me.

"They're teasing me."

"Anybody who teases Stella gets fired." Allison rolled her eyes; I stuck out my tongue at her. George came up behind me and rubbed my back. "You okay?" The others moved away.

"Yes . . . no . . . We broke up."

"I'm really sorry, Stella, I shouldn't have—"

"Don't apologize, it wasn't your fault. Why'd you tell everybody?"

"I don't know. I think I felt guilty."

"You shouldn't. I don't regret your end of it. It was fun."

"Yes, you do, sweetheart. You wish it were still last night and your fairy godmother was standing at your bedside, warning you." I thought of Grandmother, coming in a dream to say, Beware.

"It would've happened sooner or later. Can we have some music?"

"There's people out there, Stella."

"Well, people listen to music."

"Not in my restaurant they don't. Background music is crap."

"Turn it on low."

"Okay, okay. What do you want to hear?"

"Summer Wind." He gave me a peculiar look, but he played it. I listened, asked to hear it again, drank another glass of wine, and rolled a few duck breasts around in foaming butter.

I got very drunk. George invited me to spend the night at his new apartment but I declined. I thought Frank might have reconsidered. Maybe he had gotten drunk, too, and found the solution magically at hand: we would just love each other more until jealousy withered away.

Leo said to me, when he drove me home, that my mistake had been not waiting longer before sleeping around. "When Judy first did it, I was crazy, I wanted to kill her, but I didn't even think of leaving because she'd become family by then."

"You didn't fuck me for three months," said Judy from the back seat.

"But we're still together," he said triumphantly.

"Do you still have lovers?" I asked her; she'd never mentioned any.

"Sure she does," said Leo. "I have to share the fucking Sunday paper with them, and not one of them knows how to make coffee."

"Bullshit," came Judy's sleepy voice from behind. We were at my house then, and I didn't ask which part of what he said was bullshit.

Frank wasn't there. He had been and had taken his things. I got into bed and pulled the covers up to my neck. I was furious. He said he fucking loved me, he claimed to understand me. What did he expect? My faults weren't any worse than his. I wasn't cruel to him, I didn't neglect him; I adored him and amused him and inspired him. I knew what our love was worth, and it had been of my making as much as his. He had wanted trust and he got it, I had believed he'd never abandon me. It was unforgivable. There was no way my fuck with George—a fuck: that innocent, sweaty thing—could be equal to the crime of leaving me, for which he would surely suffer in Hell.

I woke up with a hangover that was a series of shivers—the shiver of my tongue tasting my mouth, the shiver of my brain remembering, the shiver of my hands brushing the hair that grew painfully out of my skull. I put my clothes on, slowly and carefully buttoning them with that old childhood achievement that comes back whenever life is especially crushing. Downstairs I opened a beer but put it down after one swallow. I had enough trouble without that.

I went to work early. George was there, waiting for me. I said I had a hangover and he made me a banana milkshake, pressed cold towels to my brow, and took my clothes off. "But it took so long to get them on," I said piteously.

"Your shirt was on inside out anyway."

"So that's why it was so hard to button." He put his mouth on my hot skin, drawing out the pain of the hangover. It felt as if his lips were sinking into my flesh, probing each cell for its wrongness and righting it. The medicine of the kiss healed me; then the kiss grew stronger, bringing me the exquisite sensual joy of the queen of the roses sucked by a bee. As his mouth moved on, the pain returned, but I soon found I could direct my attention only to where his mouth was. The rest of my body did not exist. My mind barely existed; it was a cup to hold my pleasure, with feeble threads of memory latticing out into the gloom.

Then he lay me on the table and thrust his penis inside. I felt an immediate rush of humanity, although not my own particular humanity. It was like one of those drug states when you realize We Are. We Are One. It Is All Real. I was timidly grateful to the universe for this revelation.

Afterward he wiped me clean and gave me a glass of wine. I sat quietly and drank, still diapered with the dishtowel. I was for the moment becalmed; I couldn't imagine feeling anything strongly.

"Are you okay?" he asked. "You seem kind of listless."

"I'm fine."

"You didn't come; do you want to?"

"No, I feel good. Restored."

"Cured your hangover, did I? It's nice to know I have a function in life."

"You comforted me."

"Okay." He worked in silence for a while, cleaning squid. I drank, noticing how the wine affected my diminishing sense of universality: it imitated it, badly, yet there was a reassurance in its tinny glow. This was something I could cling to.

"You want me to call him and say it was only the one occasion?" he asked finally.

"No, he knows that. He heard our conversation, remember?"

"What did we say? Shit, that pisses me off, to skulk like that."

"You asked me if I was going to tell him and I said no. He couldn't help it. You know, it was a shock."

"Shit, Blondie, you should get angry. It would do you good."

"I've tried. I can't sustain it very long. I just get depressed again."

"Drink some more wine," he said anxiously.

"I am drinking. Don't worry, I'll get drunk a lot from now on. Maybe I'll turn into an alcoholic."

"I doubt it. It gets you through bad times is all. The days pass easier."

"And the depression doesn't wait on the other side?"

"I wouldn't know. I haven't come out the other side yet."

I sighed. "I wish I knew if it were for real. If he really means not to come back. I know he thinks he does."

"You ought to think about whether you want him back."

"Not much to think about there. Except that I'm always thinking about it."

There was a silence before he said, "Why don't you get off your ass and help me?"

"I thought you were going to let me sit here all day."

"Not a chance, Blondie. Not a chance."

I sighed, finished my wine, and slid off the stool to help him with the squid. That night we made black fettucine out of the ink. It was beautiful, glossy and dark. We called it Vampire Pasta, sauced it with lip-shaped slices of red pepper, olive oil, and anchovies, and served it with a free glass of zinfandel. It was a bit much for most of our customers, who preferred the cold squid salad with snowpeas. So George and I finished it off at midnight, feeding each other noodle by black noodle, pretending to be high government officials feasting on the entrails of lesser demons.

The next three weeks passed like one long day. I don't mean I didn't sleep—I did, I even passed out a few times. But sleep didn't seem to mark an end or a beginning. I mostly lived at The Vineyard. George brought in the rest of his tapes and we listened to Otis Redding and Ray Charles, to "You Don't Miss Your Water (Till Your Well Runs Dry)," to "Lonely Avenue," and "Mr. Pitiful." I turned the volume up very high, until the air was so dense with music we had to swim through it. And I played with George. We liked to wrestle—we always had—but now he let me win. When I had him on his back, I stripped him, and ran my hands over that broad chest and solid shoulders. I measured how many hand-breadths each part of him was, how many finger-lengths, and calculated his proportions. I was glad even of the age marked on his flesh; it meant he had been a man longer. It still wasn't enough but it helped. I'd been having dreams of giants, acres of flesh I laboriously climbed, one moment in a mountain glade, the next dangling from a pair of meaty fingers. I would wake up with the kind of sideways shift in consciousness peculiar to drunken sleep, and my twitchy, sensitive, hungover body felt insatiable, daydreaming armies of colossi. George took the burden of this. He let me fondle him as I chose.

Then he would kiss me slowly, sucking on my lips and tongue and nipples until I urged him to get on with it. I would give him a kick to hurry him up. He would tell me shut my fucking mouth, and I would laugh. I would keep laughing until he fucked me, when I would frequently start crying. Neither of us mentioned my tears. He'd continue, furiously, while I lay limp and languid, jolted by sex into more and more vales of elaborate emotion, like flipping very fast through a book of embroidery samples. I didn't have time to express them, even if I'd wanted to. I lay as if dead while George worked hard, and if I came, it was something else, appearing from an unexpected quarter and setting off its small, hot explosion. Then George would come with a lot of noise—he got louder every day—and I would gasp weakly, like a fish.

Gradually the music would revive me. I would want to dance. George was agreeable, holding out his arms. I would lay my cheek on his shoulder, looking at his reddened, sweaty neck, the pads of flesh on either side of his spine, the brown moles with whiskery hair sprouting, and the small girdle of fat at his waist; and I knew I would love his body no matter how old, fat, hairy, and mole-covered he became. It seemed he was doing a great thing by being George, that he could've chosen to be someone else, but hadn't.

We danced clumsily. I wanted to be held like a child against his chest and he would try, gripping me with a hand under my ass and staggering to the music. Inevitably he would get horny again, prodding me inquiringly. I would yield, not out of desire but simply wanting to do it again. It was almost as good as beating my head against the wall.

Sooner or later, of course, we got to work. George had told Allison not to come in till six—and Lisa not to come in at all—but it was not only the privacy to fuck we wanted. (We always quit that by four.) It was good for me to have to work hard, with not nearly enough time to do everything. George understood this, because he was the same way. We had shrimp-cleaning contests and veal-pounding contests, and once I managed to slice a dozen cucumbers faster than George, who was using the Cuisinart. Afterward my hands trembled so with exhaustion that when I tipped the wine bottle over the stewpot, I poured in ripples—and kept pouring because I was too tired to lift it up again.

I didn't think about Frank very often at The Vineyard, I made sure of that, but I was afflicted with a terrible itching that I knew was my body missing him. George said it was from drinking too much and would scratch me with a long meat fork, standing well away in case, he said, bugs started breaking out of my skin. He gave me red stripes from shoulders to wrists, adding ache to the itch. When it got bad I would clutch my arms, fingernails digging into my sore flesh. Then I would hear in my mind the words "Poor Stella, poor Stella," like a far-off fairy voice in the woods calling, a voice with no sympathy at all.

At home it was different. At home I always thought of Frank. There was my bedroom, of course, with all its associations, and there was Callie, who was dating Rodney steadily and saw Frank every day. I didn't allow myself to ask about him directly; the one time I had, she had said he was "resolute"—not a word I wanted to hear. I told her of my misery, hoping of course that it would get back to him. She suggested I see a psychiatrist.

"George would probably fire me if he knew I was spending my salary that way," I said facetiously.

"That might not be a bad idea," she replied, her apple-cheeked face staring intently into mine. She had acquired a new way of looking at people since she met Rodney, as if she were taking extra for him. I thought it impolite. "How do you think Frank feels about you still working there?"

"If he wants me to know how he feels, he can call me up and tell me. George is my best friend."

"Maybe you should marry him then," she said nastily, "now that he's getting a divorce." Callie had never liked George.

"No, thanks," I said. "I'd never marry a divorced man. Who wants to be second?" She looked stricken, and I smiled as I left the room. Actually I meant what I said, although not in the way she took it.

Eva called up George at The Vineyard every night now, screaming about how miserable she would make his life if he didn't give her what she wanted: the house, the car, and two thousand dollars a month. He conceded the first two, but said he couldn't afford more than four hundred a month. Well, you better find a way to afford it, she said, I know enough about you to ruin you in this town. He threatened to skip altogether. She'd hiss that he'd never see his kids again. He bellowed that he doubted she would either, once they turned twenty-one.

"How that woman holds a job is beyond me," he said to me. "She goes hysterical when she doesn't get her way. You can see her face freeze up, and then it starts to crack. I should've yelled at her years ago. She can't take it. I was always too nice. That's what she wanted, nice: 'Let's discuss this in a reasonable tone of voice,' while she puffed her smoke at me across the table like a goddamn communist negotiator. Hear how her voice quivers when she screams?" I heard.

Once she got started, he would set the phone down on the counter to rave at the broccoli while he fixed himself a fortifying drink. "She's not up to it — she'll have a heart attack one of these days." He went on, listing all the possible grotesque ways she could die. His favorite was her dogs rearing up in righteous disgust to rip her throat out. I learned more about her life and sins than I could bear to know.

"She's grown into the thing she hated most when she was twenty. If anyone had told her the future back then, she would have thought it a nightmare."

"So would you."

"I would've strangled her on the honeymoon. Now we have kids and I can't."

"What a pity. Now you don't get to go to jail."

"I'm already in jail, Blondie, believe it. Do you realize she's gonna be around my neck for the rest of my life? We'll have grandchildren together." He cracked his knuckles ferociously.

"A few weeks ago you didn't even want a divorce."

"A few weeks ago I was an asshole."

It upset me to hear him talk like this. It seemed as if he were preparing for a lifetime of hate, a kind of antimarriage rather than a divorce. I knew it wasn't his fault he was tied to Eva, and I didn't expect him to start feeling benevolent toward her. But it wore me out. I wasn't as strong as he was. I started to hate her, too, and not really because of the things she did, but just because his feeling was contagious. It was violent, it swept us all up. Even the waiters started in on it, referring to obnoxious customers as Evas and making nasty faces when they answered her phone calls. I was glad I didn't want to marry George, or live with him. I preferred to make my own enemies.

Finally I took an evening off. I'd worked more than two weeks straight and I thought I'd just keep on until something happened, but what happened was I got tired. All I wanted to do was lie in bed and read *The Dawn Treader* by C. S. Lewis, which was one of my favorite books from childhood.

When Callie left for Rodney's house, stealing almost guiltily out the door in her new dress, I shut my bedroom door and climbed in bed. I opened the slim volume, surprised at how short the novel was. It had seemed endless once.

I had gotten to the part where Eustace turns into a dragon when the phone rang. It surprised me. I was so sure of my utter solitude: at home, upstairs, in bed, under the covers, in the story. I considered not answering it. It might be for Callie. It might be George, checking up on me.

"Hello?"

"Is that you?"

"Frank?" I dropped the book and curled around the telephone, the covers slipping off my naked body. My hair poured over the night table, a lock of it falling in my glass of ice water, where it darkened.

"No, um, this is Robert. Is Shona there? Can I speak to her please?"

"You've got a wrong number," I snapped.

"Are you sure? You don't know where she is? I have to talk to her." He sounded as if Shona were in the habit of pretending to be someone else when he called.

"There's no Shona living here. I live here."

"Okay. Sorry." He hung up. I didn't. The line stayed open for a minute, then another; if he tried to reach Shona again, he wouldn't be able to, he was connected to me. How was it possible for his voice to be so similar to Frank's while mine resembled that of the woman he was calling? Why hadn't he noticed how strange this was? I shouldn't have told him it was a wrong number.

The connection clicked off. Now he could get through if he found the right number. Shona. I pictured her as having warm, wavy brown hair with a silver streak through it. She was tall and bosomy and stood close to you when she talked; she smelled like apricots; she had big doe eyes and perfect teeth; she wore clinging knit dresses. Robert called her every night and sometimes in the morning. She was never alone for more than an hour; then she would drink a glass of amaretto and lie on a divan, slices of cucumber on her eyelids.

I got out of bed and paced around the room. Here I was surrounded by inanimate objects—furniture, clothes, books, blankets, window shades—and what was the point of it all? This room was so ugly and so messy. Rotting fruit, dirty underwear, sweaters draped like flayed-off skins, coffee cups and dust. It would be more honest to lie in a cell. I welcomed the thought of chains around my legs, their friendly clank, their anchoring.

I suddenly thought of the pictures Frank had taken of me in Tilden Park. I wondered if he looked at those pictures now. If he held them up close to his face, yearning toward my flesh. I had no pictures of him.

It occurred to me that perhaps I didn't believe anymore that Frank would come back. I'd thought of him gradually inclining my way as the days went past and he missed me, but he might have already gone through the worst. If he was really resolute, he could have suffered all at once and now be on the mend. That was a ghastly thought: each hour carrying him further away.

Inevitably I would meet someone else. I felt a surge of panic. For a second it seemed real, this alternate future, married to another man. He wore a pale blue suit, he had very pale skin, he looked like David Bowie after he took off his human disguise in *The Man Who Fell to Earth.*

One thing at a time, I thought. No future just yet. Here and now, Berkeley, where I have many friends. Or at least some friends. I could call them. I could call Callie or George. I could even call Frank.

There was just so much of myself in this room. And myself was about as welcome as a drug slipped in my drink by a toad-faced seducer. It shot me impulses: I wanted to gnash my teeth and bite my flesh, I wanted to roll my face in the dust. I knew this feeling. I'd gone through it in college, and I still had the wit to know it would pass. I could remember how I felt an hour ago, when my situation was just as unhappy but I was sane. The danger would come later, if this madness had time to infiltrate memory. Then I'd kill myself, fuck it. I wouldn't go through it again.

The first time I was interested: how grotesque everything is. So this is desolation. If anyone knew how I felt— But now I was aware of how many people feel this way; it's why they have mental hospitals. I could just imagine Grandmother visiting me in the loony bin, smuggling vitamins to swallow with my Thorazine.

Tomorrow I'd stay at The Vineyard until I passed out. There was only tonight to get through. I could cut my hair and stuff a pillow for Frank with the remains. Or I could put on a record—Chopin—and as the piano was played by the invisible fingers of Arthur Rubenstein, masturbate, whispering endearments to myself as they advised in women's magazines. *Ma petite*, you are as soft as velvet, as sweet as a rose.

I got dressed and went out. I thought I'd go to the Med for an espresso and perhaps buy a pack of cigarettes. Since high school I smoked occasionally, when I was disgusted with the world. I remembered Cathy telling me about her pure, white lungs and took pleasure in darkening mine to a sooty depression-gray.

I walked for a while. It was a chilly night with a sharp wind blowing in irregular gusts, interrupting my thoughts, which, left to themselves, would have been miserable but featureless. Walking could bring me a sort of low-grade peace. Instead I was faced with this irritating wind and with couples going by who paused to kiss and fondle as if I weren't there at all. (Red shirt and loose breasts, a young girl's laugh; penetrating eyes of a much older Arab man, open collar, gold watch turned inward on his hairy wrist. I wished them both to Iran and hurried past.)

I wondered what Frank was doing right now. I knew he had dinner with Callie and Rodney almost every night. Callie went over there to cook. I think she considered it kinder not to have Rodney at our house, not to flaunt her happiness, as it were. But I wasn't jealous of her happiness. I was jealous of her seeing Frank so often, of her feeding him dinner with recipes she stole from me. Every night another book was missing from my shelf. Julia Child, Madhur Jaffrey—the girl was ambitious. The way to a man's heart . . . Especially a blind man. She had even gained a few pounds, there was such an orgy of eating going on over there.

I imagined Frank at the table, pale and hollow-eyed, being urged to take another serving. "I made it myself. It's good for you." He came back every night to eat with them. Somehow Callie always managed to mention this. Of course Rodney would have things to say about me. How he had always suspected. How there are certain psychological verities one ignores at one's peril: the clear and present danger of castration, of giant cunts devouring mankind. Callie with earplugs in, so she would have no advantage over his blindness, serving soup. Rodney growing as fat as Buddha, Frank wasting away.

Actually, I had no idea what Rodney thought of me. Probably he didn't care one way or another, just worried about his friend, instructed Callie to prepare fine dishes for the suffering man, and gently hinted that life was still worthwhile. Frank grateful for this, asking for it. *Comfort me with curry, for I am sick of love.*

But was he sick of it? Or was he just lying low, preparing for his next big romance? Dorothy, me. Unfaithful women. But he wouldn't give up, he'd find the perfect one yet. Callie told me his sister was visiting last week, on her way to a teacher's conference. Marva, whom Frank had been so sure I'd like, whom I did not get a chance to meet. Callie was very impressed by her. A career, three kids, and so nice, so interested in everything.

What advice would she have given her baby brother? Forget that woman, you deserve better? Get her pregnant and she won't have time to fuck around? Get a job?

I reached the Med and looked inside. It was almost empty, as it often was in summer, and the man behind the counter gave me a bold stare. Fuck you, I thought, don't look at me. I'm the observer around here. I walked on, thinking again about buying cigarettes. It seemed too much trouble. I could blacken my lungs with sheer willpower.

I walked faster. Soon I would get to campus and have to decide which way to go. It annoyed me that I couldn't just keep walking straight ahead forever. The monotonous rhythm of my steps was the only cheer I had; it was little enough.

I reached Bancroft and turned right, up the hill. Frank wasn't meeting another woman, I knew. No one was touching that smooth torso in its white shirt, no one hearing his voice, or reading his thoughts — which I had imagined I could do when we lay next to each other. Or rather, we were so close, it seemed I would be able to, had I only tried. I had just never needed to try. He told me whatever I asked, promptly relating dreams, memories, opinions, hunger, thirst, desire. That trustfulness, which was my only way in, seemed boundless then. And why not? I wouldn't take back my love, or lose curiosity.

Now I wished I had learned to really read his mind, secretly, from a distance. It would be an immoral act, no doubt about it, yet I wouldn't resist the temptation. I would be like the bird in the fairy tale who flies in by night to sample the fruit in the prince's garden.

When I reached College Avenue, I turned right again. I was very tired by now, and I thought I could sleep. My loneliness had dissipated; what I felt was grief. It wasn't very good company, but it would do.

Then I ran into Clara. She was standing by herself in the middle of the sidewalk laughing. Her amber eyes beamed at me, and she put her soft, white hand on my shoulder. Her hair was all in curls tonight. "Stella! What are you doing out on a night like this?"

"Walking off my sorrows."

"Poor honey! Hasn't he wised up yet?"

"No." She took my arm and I caught the odor of her perfume: exotic, spicy, with a suggestion of debauch. She was wearing a crimson silk sweater and white pants, with gold bangles around her wrists, and a gold chain around her neck. Her hair was tangled and her lipstick smeared.

"I'm a mess, aren't I? Making out in bars, you know." She rubbed her lips. "Is that better?"

"Yes. Where are you going?"

"I was just going to ask you that question. I have no idea. I was dropped here by a very boring woman. I told her I lived in that house." She waved at a large, stately, white Victorian. "She's coming back in fifteen minutes, so I have to get out of here. Want to come home with me?"

"I'm tired."

"I'll make you some tea."

"All right."

It was so pleasant to be with someone, to be held by the arm and talked to. She told me about the friends she'd been dancing with in the women's bar in Oakland, who was flirting with whom, who was jealous, and the fact that I didn't know any of them made it more enjoyable, like reading about the divorces of TV stars whose shows I never watch.

The front door of her apartment led into the kitchen where she made me a drink instead of tea. It seemed the right thing at the moment: rum, lime juice, sugar, brandy. Her studio occupied the rest of the apartment except for a loft bed in one corner.

It was a startling sight. The walls were covered with masks of every description—dogs, devils, monkeys, sorceresses, old men, puffy-eyed babies, rats. They were made out of papier-mâché and painted in vivid colors, intensely expressionistic. It was like a mad scientist's illustration of the theory of evolution: the animals lose to humanity, which continues to struggle; gradually the struggle fails; the animals return, purified by their long eclipse, more bestial than ever.

"They're fantastic," I said.

"A bit overpowering at first, I know." She sipped her drink. "Annie hates it here. She feels like she's being watched."

"I can understand that." Of course I was being watched, but I didn't mind. The masks weren't much concerned with me anyway; they were roaring and screaming at each other across the room.

"They're my darlings," she said, stroking a wild-eyed green dog on its snout. "The only trouble is they lose their life after a while. Then I have to make more. These—you see?—are dead; I made them last year."

"They look alive to me."

"But not to me. I should get rid of them. This one is my baby now." She lifted down a monkey mask with bared white teeth and wide, fanatic eyes. A creature hungering for the ultimate weapon—a big brain.

"Looking at that, I understand totemism. I'd rather be descended from a bear or a wolf myself."

She laughed. "Something nobler, yeah. But this *is* what we were descended from. Monkeys. The only animal that likes to jerk off in front of an audience at the zoo . . . I did make one beautiful monkey. She had the most mysterious, soulful eyes. I gave her to Frank."

"When did you give it to him?"

"Recently. I could tell he was lonely. So now she hangs above his bed. I whispered your name in her ear so that while he's sleeping she can whisper it into his."

"It doesn't seem to be working yet," I said.

"Perhaps you should try it yourself."

"What do you mean?"

"Sneak into his bedroom at night. Wake him up slowly with kisses. I did that once with someone who wanted to break up with me. He was charmed." She used the word in its old meaning.

"I don't think I could do that. Anyway, I want him to miss me."

"He misses you, but he's very stubborn. He's got his eye on the future. He wants to make sure he's chosen the right woman for ever and ever."

"I know. How can I convince him?"

"Are you sure you want to? He's awfully in love." She was stroking her savage monkey along the rims of his eyeholes.

"So am I."

"That kind of love restrains you, you know, even if he finally agrees you can play with other people."

"I don't think it will restrain me. I don't want other men so much anymore, at least not in the same way. I feel like I've found out most of what I wanted to know. In emotional moments, of course—I mean, I'm not ready to swear fidelity."

"But you'll do it, only for love, not for adventure? You see, he's already restrained you. Anyone can learn to be comforted with a hug instead of a fuck, if there's reason to, but to give up the excitement of the unknown . . ." She slitted her eyes and smiled at me.

I thought about whether I'd given up the excitement. It was true that sex seemed to be more connected now to my personal life, less a venture into the wilderness, but it was not yet something a hug could replace. It satisfied me in quite another way than simply knowing I was cared for, or even desired. But she was right in one sense; I could imagine now doing without it. Not giving it up for Frank, but for myself. Vaguely I assumed that someday I would lead a more "advanced" sort of life.

"Where's Annie tonight?" I asked.

"She went to Yosemite. She's angry at me. I don't think we'll be together much longer."

"Are you sorry?"

"Oh, a little bit. Not too much. I was getting tired of her; she was so jealous, always wanting to spend every night with me."

"Poor Annie."

"I told her not to fall in love with me."

"Clara! You know you try to make everyone fall in love with you."

"Only up to a point. When it looks like it's really serious, I warn them."

"I can't imagine your warning works very often."

"It worked with Frank. But then I don't think he was really in love with me."

"When was this?"

"Right before you came on the scene. I intended to have a little affair with him. But I had to tell him that's all it would be, and then he didn't want to go to bed anymore."

I laughed. I had made no promises to him our first night. But how many times can one refuse? He was not an unyielding man, not with me.

Clara smiled. "Actually, I think he would've given in, but then he met you, and it was all over. He's very cute. I just don't like men for long at a time. A few nights, then I'm tired of it."

"I can't imagine getting tired of it."

"Have you ever had a woman?"

"No."

"Have you ever wanted to?"

"I've thought about it."

"Women are really much more satisfying. Their beauty and softness, the curves of their body, their taste. And of course their minds are more subtle. They know how to be gentle and fierce at the same time; they're more passionate, and more interesting to talk to. Not to mention that they usually know how to make love better."

"I know what a woman is."

She handed me the rum bottle. I drank. If she was going to seduce me, I thought, I'd rather be a little drunk. Either that or leave now, and I didn't want to leave. I disliked the idea of sleeping alone.

She put on some music—Brazilian—then we looked at the rest of her masks and at some erotic figurines she had made. They didn't arouse me so much as make me feel affection for the tremendous bawdy energy of human beings. Men with balls so big they had to support them with both hands, grinning in foolish pride. A fat woman sucking on her own breast. A dog ridden by a naked girl, both laughing.

Then she put her arm around me and kissed my cheek. I got another breath of her perfume, subsumed now in the smell of her body, which was also spicy and exotic, but much more profoundly so. She paused a moment, then kissed my mouth. Her lipstick had mostly worn off; only a faint taste of it remained. I liked the taste, it reminded me that these were a woman's lips, which I was kissing now with passion, imagining myself for a second as a man. Then our tongues met and I felt a shock at the snaky, wriggling feel of hers. Subtle, yes. Skillful. Almost too much so.

Clara stepped back and smiled at me, pushing her hair out of her face. "Nice kiss," she said.

"Not bad," I replied. We both laughed and she took a hit from the rum bottle.

"Shall we continue?"

I thought about it. The situation had momentum, I was curious, I was horny and lonely. "No."

"Oh, too bad. You're so sexy tonight."

"I don't think I'd be turned on."

"I bet I could turn you on." She stuck out her pointed tongue at me and crooked her little finger.

"So could a carrot."

She burst out laughing. "Did you ever use a carrot?"

"Once, when I was a teenager."

"I could strap on my dildo. Wear a man-mask. Swagger. No?"

"No." I sat down on her couch and poured myself a glass of rum. She didn't appear to be at all offended. "Why did you stop liking men? I asked. "Was it because of Rodney?"

"Frank told you I left Rodney when he went blind?"

"Yes."

"And you think I'm an awful person?"

"Not necessarily."

"I just couldn't deal with it. I got so angry at him. I found myself making faces at him all the time he was talking. I couldn't stop. I'd walk around nude, and he wouldn't notice."

"That was hardly his fault."

"Yes, but you see I realized he had never seen me. Not really. Men can't see women. It's not their fault, it's the nature of things. That's why sex gets so outrageous, like dressing for the mirror when you're not planning to go anywhere. Since they can't see us, we flaunt ourselves, we dare them to figure us out. And they do the same." She had sat down across from me and was swinging her bare feet in circles. She was wearing blue glitter toenail polish.

"But isn't that what makes it exciting—the attempt?" Frank can see me, I thought. Not in the same way a woman could; there was more opposition as well as more intimacy in his gaze. He had more to lose was what it came down to. And so did I.

"That's the general opinion. But once I realized that nothing was going to happen—there would be no denouement where all is revealed—I lost interest. I still like my adventures, but I don't expect them to last. The mystery of sex is like the mystery of God: What if you decide there isn't one?"

"But you can't deny sex exists," I said.

"Fucking exists. I don't deny that."

"Not sexual attraction, desire, love?"

"I feel them, but, as I said, not for long. I accept them as emotions, sensations, not as something to devote my life to."

"Not even with women?"

"It's easier with women, less complicated. But I don't fall in love with them either."

"It never occurred to me that love might not 'exist.' I just don't think in those terms. Even when I imagined I'd never fall in love again, I still believed it was out there."

It was out there. I found it whenever I pleased. Those nights didn't last—yet my love for Frank was built out of the same stuff as my passion for strangers. The difference was our connection was not only one of the soul—which the body follows in all matters—but of the mind. Our minds were where we knew each other. Souls can't know; they can only recognize. How I loved that recognition, how I craved it; yet Clara was right, there would be no denouement. Not as far as we can tell, anyway. But does it matter?

"I know you think it's out there," she said. "That's the first thing I noticed about you. That's why you're so sexy."

"Well, if you're attracted, maybe you should try it again yourself. Let go."

"I have. Completely. This is what's left."

She smiled at me with her red mouth, whose color was picked up by her crimson sweater, whose curve was echoed in her cheek, her brow, her curls. I felt so like her in so many ways, yet I'd never be content with her life. Lovers and art and beauty and merriment: it would only make me lonely. Why did I have to be so recklessly in favor of my freedom, which was essentially solitude, yet so lonely?

"I have an idea," she said.

"What?"

"Let's have a slumber party."

"I've never been to a slumber party."

"I used to have them all the time. Seven or eight girls, sometimes the whole class. We'd sleep downstairs in the living room with all the furniture pushed against the wall. The floor was covered with sleeping bags and pillows and we'd stay awake all night. Or at least we meant to. We'd tell secrets. It's better to tell secrets in the dark."

"Can we have some food?"

"Of course. Lots of food. Lots of rum."

"And tea."

"Let's go make it and take it upstairs."

"Up the ladder, you mean?"

"Yeah. If you can climb it after all these drinks, you win a gold star."

We filled a tray with grapes, cherries, cheese, M&Ms, nuts, tea, limes, and the rum bottle. Clara climbed the ladder nimbly, I handed the tray up and followed her. The mattress was tucked into a corner, taking up ninety percent of the floor space, and there was a ledge that ran around two sides of the wall. On the ledge were cigarettes, marijuana, a red dildo, and a leather whip. She put the whip, the dildo, and the dope away in a small, carved wooden chest at the foot of the mattress.

"This is a slumber party, my goodness, not an orgy," she said.

"Do you really use the whip?"

"None of your business . . . no, not really. It's fun to crack it through the air though. Gives some people a scare."

"I bet."

She lit the candles and turned off the overhead light. Immediately our shadows dominated the little room: they were long and witchlike as we lifted grapes, cherries, and candy to our lips. I felt like I was out in the woods, around a campfire, and the stories we told were meant to shore up bravery. We laughed a lot.

Clara said that we were only eleven years old and so couldn't talk about sex anymore, except as eleven-year-olds would and we went on about it for a long time after that. I wished she was my sister.

Finally we slept. I woke up in the middle of the night to find her arm around me, and her face next to mine, smiling as if she were just about to speak. Then I passed out and stayed that way until noon.

When I got home the phone was ringing. It was Grandmother; she had some bad news for me. Her voice was cool. She paused for me to collect myself, then told me my parents were dead. They had been killed the day before in a car accident. For a weird second I thought she had known where they were all along, and had not bothered to tell me; then she said she'd been notified when her address was found among my mother's things by the owner of the Hello Motel on the outskirts of Memphis, where my parents had been living for the past six months.

She said she would like me to come home as soon as possible; she said a lot more to which I barely listened. *They didn't come back, they didn't take me with them, I want to go, oh, I want to go, too,* a sobbing voice in my head poured out. *It was so long ago, eighteen years, how could I have let so much time pass, taking me away from the one moment when I should have cried hard enough to change everything.* That moment was when I was most alive. Yet not enough so. Most in love, wasn't I, yet not surprised. Nor angry. Not angry enough. A little pathetic girl in the bushes but it was *me and my mommy and daddy lay dying, they died, they are dead. Why didn't they get away? Why didn't they go somewhere safe? If they had stayed home I would've nursed them into old age, wouldn't I. I would have sat faithfully at their bedside. I would've closed their eyelids and carried them to the*

*river. I would've let them go downstream at the new moon, let the
current and the rocks bash them.*

I said what I needed to and hung up the phone. My face was
drenched in tears, it felt old and swollen, yet so young also, younger
than a child, young as an idiot. I stood up, swaying a little, and
walked to see whether I could, and ran my hands down my body to
make sure I was a woman and not some shapeless protoplasm imagining that I was a woman. *It's just the chaos of time, just the past, only the
past,* I said, murmuring aloud as if the child in me could be comforted
by the adulthood of my actual voice. I quieted myself, but not for long.
Yes, they had gone away; no, they had not taken me; yes, it was a long
time ago. But right now they were dead in Tennessee, rear-ended by a
drunk at a stop sign, their bodies tossed forward against the windshield, blood, triangles of glass in their hair, on their eyelids,
embedded in cheek and lip. I remembered my mother in a sleeveless
blue dress spinning around and around obsessively until she tottered
to the couch and crumpled, saying, "I'm so bored." My father
practicing in his room, then, when my mother left the house, playing
his horn down the stairs and into the kitchen where Agnes was
making one of her potions. He sat on a stool and played for her while
the roots boiled. Grandmother brushing my mother's hair when she
was sick with the flu, her head drooping like a wilted flower as she
complained about fever and bad dreams, her flannel nightgown
sliding off her shoulders and up her thighs. My father in the dining
room one day grabbing her from behind and not letting her go,
pinching her as she threatened to scream, squeezing breasts and
belly with hands I had never noticed before were so much stronger
than those of a woman.

These two people were dead; I needn't look for them any longer. Yet
when did I ever look for them? I never did, not once. I thought my life
was secretly looking for them, steering me here and there . . . I
followed my impulses to New York, to California, I was doing my part
. . . but had I ever thought of my mother, my real flesh and blood, my
middle-aged mother in the streets of Berkeley? Sometimes perhaps at
my house, on a blazingly sunny morning as I lounged on the porch
steps, I fashioned her out of memory and sat her on the grass. I gave
her nothing to say and made her leave when it was time for me to go to

work. Yet I thought Berkeley the perfect place for a magical reunion. The gardens were lush, the seasons awry, the natives friendly and credulous. Where else could they appear but here? Why go to Tennessee? Runaways should run west, toward the Pacific, like the pioneers, like Frank . . .

I left the house. I ran down the steps into the beautiful noon, the flowers in their beds damp from a morning watering, deep and delicate, purple and pale rose. I went quickly through the gate and turned right; that was the way to Frank's house. The familiar blocks sped me along. There were no disturbing apparitions like last night's lovers. I passed only a little black girl, skipping rope, who gave me a sly smile—the smile of a lemon thief, a hooky player.

I thought of the nights of lovemaking with Frank, those long nights in the beginning, and then of the lovemaking between my parents. I remembered their privacy, their delight, yet I couldn't imagine it— not as something real, subject to death. Their faces, ageless when I knew them in the way of those you can't believe have ever been children, were now old, worn, torn, wounded, soon burned up. Grandmother was having them cremated very early tomorrow morning. I had thought of objecting but I didn't want to see the damage. Nor even their coffins. Let them hide. They were so good at it.

I reached Frank's house and knocked on the door. I knew he was home, he had to let me in. I knocked faster, one fist after another, while my breath rose and sank alarmingly; the terror was back, it rippled out of the wood of the door, like something gathering its forces for attack.

He opened the door. At the sight of me his face turned inward, hidden, like a river otter diving underwater. He was pale and heart-breakingly handsome: the way the blond hair fell over his forehead, the firm set of his shoulders. Then his face changed again, a faint color came into his cheeks, and he stepped forward. "What's wrong?" he asked, taking my arm.

I was shivering. I broke free and walked ahead of him deeper and deeper into the house, into its farthest reaches, where I sank down on the black leather couch. He kneeled beside me and took my hands.

"What is it?"

"My parents are dead. My grandmother called me. They died in Memphis, Tennessee, in a car crash." The words sounded false to my ears, full of outrageous self-pity, as if they had died years ago and I was only now conveniently remembering it. I looked up at Frank beseechingly and was shocked out of my own misery by how miserable he looked; such stark sympathy for me shining out of his face, and more than sympathy.

"Oh, darling," he said, taking me in his arms. *In his arms.* Every pain eased there. I could almost say, Never mind.

"I felt so lonely," I said.

"Of course you did."

"Not now. But—a minute ago. An hour ago. Yesterday. When I was a little girl. I always thought I would find them someday."

"I know."

"I thought it didn't matter how long it took. That they were always somehow the same. Now I'll never know what they were really like."

"I know, honey, it's not fair." I was silent a minute, listening to the tenderness in his voice. He still loved me. Of course he did. How could that ever change? How could anything ever change?

"I miss them just the way they were. They *were* the same. I miss them."

"I know."

"You don't know how they were. My father played the saxophone."

"You told me."

"I thought men sounded like that. Like lions roaring. They do."

"Do I?"

"Yes. I love you."

"Really? Stella. Do you really?"

"Yes."

His face shone with a fierce gladness. "I'm so happy you came to me." Yes, I had come and he had let me in. I had thought I was waiting for him to come to me, but it wasn't so; I'd been waiting to come to him. For a moment, that seemed to be all; everything was done. There was a silence between us as he held me—what you would have imagined, had you been in the next room, was a kiss. But it was quieter than that.

Then I began to cry. It wasn't very painful and the sound was homely to me, like the rain on Saturday mornings that make you stay in and color by the fire, filling page after page with whatever the flames make you think of.

Frank held me gently, stroking my hair the way he does, as if it has feeling. After a while I was empty of tears, and I lifted my mouth up to his, pressing my salty lips against his sweet, full, so long unkissed ones. What a pleasure! If I were to live my life over, I thought, I'd live it as a virgin, fed on one long kiss a year, though they'd have to tie me down between times.

When he put his hand on my breast I was suddenly visited with an image of my grandmother's house with nobody in it, all the shutters open and drooping down, the house sagging toward the river, which flowed faster and grayer; everything was a dense, dark gray. I tried to will the lights to come on, and they did. They glowed dimly in the gloom, but the light dried out, it lost its bounce; finally it hung like the shutters, limp and leathery, from the windows.

"What is it?" Frank asked, his hand sliding up my throat.

"Nothing."

"Tell me. I want you to tell me everything now."

" 'Everything now'?"

"From now on. You didn't before."

"I don't remember keeping any secrets."

"You had secrets. Your parents were a secret, you kept everything of theirs in a little drawer."

"But I showed it all to you!"

"You wouldn't let me touch your mother's shawl, the night of the dinner party. You had to keep one thing inviolate, didn't you?"

His tone was reproachful and expectant. I felt drawn in to a warmth I could barely imagine and I said, in token resistance, "She was my mother."

In her yellow sandals, in her yellow dress.

"But I am your lover. I don't care anymore if you fuck other men because only I will be your lover. Your true lover, whom you love most of all, and are completely honest with. Unless you don't want me." His eyes glowed with an implacable expression, and I believed him. He wouldn't care. He had found another way to bind me.

"I want you. You can have my mother's shawl. You can have her dead body if you wish." I said it recklessly but I meant it. What had she done to deserve my loyalty? Frank might be asking a lot but somehow this jealousy made sense to me. What I felt for them had been inviolate—and so sweet—but in my cowardice (I hadn't really wanted to look for them) slowly turning rotten. "I adore you, do you know that? Forever and ever."

He was so happy. He was confident as I had never seen him before. I hadn't noticed it missing but now he radiated a certainty that was very different from his earlier boyish trust.

"Tell me what you were thinking about," he said with his new confidence and I felt buoyed up; I didn't resent the use he made of my grief but was rather pleased by it, that it should be of use. That the path lay forward. I told him what I had imagined, and in the telling the horror faded. It didn't leave me but it dispersed, and its strange gloom was a kind of steel in the texture of my thought. I felt made of something very tough; and possessed of something infinitely tender.

"I didn't tell you everything yet."

"Tell me."

"I have a brother."

"Stella! Your parents had another child?"

"His name is Oliver. He's six years old."

"Was he hurt in the accident?"

"I didn't think to ask. But no, he couldn't have been. Grandmother would've said. She's down there now, picking him up."

"But that's fantastic! A little brother . . . I wonder if he looks anything like you?"

"No, it's been too many years since I was born."

"I don't think that makes any difference," he said with a fond, considering smile.

"Everything makes a difference."

"Aren't you excited about meeting him?"

"I feel this tremendous potential jealousy. You know, it doesn't quite exist yet."

"He didn't have any more time with them than you did."

"I was five when they left," I replied promptly.

"Honey—"

"I know. I know. But still—"

"What did you tell me? Jealousy is a petty emotion?"

"But I don't know how to be a sister," I said plaintively.

"You know more than my sister did when she was four years old and they brought a baby home."

"Oh, God, am I going to have to compete against your sister? You know you think she's perfect."

"It's your parents you'll be competing against. Oliver's never had a sibling before either."

"He'll like me. My parents probably neglected him. They were probably on their way out of the state when they died, and he would've had to grow up as a servant in the motel, cleaning toilets. Now he'll grow up as I did, with Grandmother."

"When are we leaving?"

"What?"

"To go to your grandmother's house. Tonight or in the morning?"

"You're coming?"

"That's what this is all about, isn't it? We're together."

"In the morning, I guess. I'm so tired."

"I can't wait to see the house where you grew up. Your bedroom, the kitchen—the fields . . ."

"Well, you will. There's nothing to do there but just be there. Although the company will be a little peculiar. She's got Agnes in her bedroom, in a tin box. She was planning to bury the ashes but she said she couldn't part with them. I wonder where she'll put my parents? On the living-room mantel maybe, in twin urns with 'They tried to get away,' inscribed on the bottom."

I started to laugh and Frank was holding me and shushing me for a long time before I realized he thought I was hysterical. I don't know, maybe I was; I just couldn't stop thinking of the way they looked sneaking out the garden gate, my mother plucking the lilac, her yellow sandals, and then a scene from some movie, an old man with a stick poking among the ashes for a wedding ring or a gold filling . . .

I was laughing and then I was crying and when I quit crying I felt frail. Frank put me to bed on the couch with a bowl of strawberries beside me in case I felt hungry, and he called the airlines to make our reservation. We got a flight leaving Oakland at 10 A.M.

We arrived in Boston at six the next evening. I was tired but
full of a strange lightheartedness, which I had noticed as
soon as I woke up that morning. At first I attributed it to my
reunion with Frank and rewarded him with lots of kisses
and declarations of love. But as we drove to the Oakland
airport through a fog so dense our surroundings were almost anonymous, white tendrils floating in the windows, I realized it was not
Frank who was affecting me but the death of my parents. I felt free.
They couldn't come back now, stepping through the garden gate, still
so young, come back for their little girl, to lead her a gypsy life on the
cold roads.

Instead I was flying home to Grandmother, whom I missed ardently
all of a sudden. On the plane I told Frank stories about her, everything I could remember, and it was such a pleasure to watch him
listen, to know she was taking shape in his mind, that I was somehow
increasing her.

They were waiting in the baggage claim area. I saw Oliver at once;
unlike the other children in the room he wasn't trying to climb on the
suitcase carousel, or even looking at it, but was standing, neat and
poised, by the door, wearing a blue-and-white seersucker suit. His
hair was dark with reddish glints in it, and his face was an exact

amalgam of my parents'. My mother's deep-set eyes and round pink cheeks, my father's beaky nose and firm chin. It was very strange, like looking at a puzzle that's been put together wrong.

Then my grandmother saw us and came over. I hugged her for a long time wordlessly. She looked much older, her skin chalky and forlorn, and she had a faint medicinal smell about her. Her body felt strong and sinewy though, and when I stepped back and looked at her again I saw that her eyes, though bloodshot and faded in color, were undefeated. I introduced her to Frank and she introduced me to Oliver.

"I've heard a lot about you," she said.

"I'm very sorry about your daughter," he began, and as he went on, talking very naturally about his sorrow and mine, I saw her respond to his charm and was relieved. What if she hadn't liked him?

"How old are you?" asked Oliver.

"Twenty-three," I said.

"I'm six. My birthday is November twentieth."

"Mine is October twentieth."

"Really? That's cool."

"We have the same nose too."

"No," said Grandmother, "Oliver's juts more. And he has Madelyn's eyes." She spoke in a flat voice and I was suddenly glad that it had not occurred to me as a child that I was, or could be, in any way a replacement for my mother.

"Mom wore Nile Green eyeshadow," said Oliver. "I have it in my suitcase."

"Well, I'll get our suitcases," said Frank. "I see them."

"We got in from Memphis this morning," said Grandmother. "I've spent the day showing Oliver the city." I had forgotten her pride in Boston, a pride based, as far as I could tell, its one-way streets, lack of parking, and restaurants that closed by nine. She liked the challenge.

"And buying me this suit." My brother looked down at himself in satisfaction. A funeral suit, I thought, though there would be no funeral.

"Yes. You're looking well, Stella. California must agree with you."

"Oh, it's okay." I could feel Oliver's narrow, shining eyes on me though he was pretending to watch Frank bring the suitcases. I hadn't expected him to be so self-possessed. When our parents left *me* I'd had a high fever for days. Agnes had brought me cup after cup of gentian tea. "I really feel disoriented, you know? In space and time."

"Yes. We have a lot to talk about."

"You can talk in front of me," said Oliver to Grandmother. "People usually do."

"We are not 'people.' We are your sister and your grandmother, and of course we will talk in front of you. We will also talk when you're in bed, as I'm sure 'people' have done before." He smiled at her, as if she were a wonderfully funny old creature whom he'd had the luck to find.

"Are we ready to go, kid?" Frank asked Oliver when he returned.

"We're ready," said my brother, proudly, looking around at us.

"Yes," said Grandmother. "The car is just outside."

"She doesn't get tickets," said Oliver. "We parked wherever we wanted today and no policeman gave her a ticket."

"This car is too old to bother with," I said. "When they give you a ticket, you know, it only costs as much as tickets cost when you bought your car. And tickets were so cheap in those days that it just isn't worth it to write one up."

"You're like Daddy," Oliver said as we got in the car. "He told me that when you saw a car driving with its lights on during the day it was because it was a blind person driving it."

"That's true," I said, thrilled by this coincidence—was it a coincidence?—of jokes.

"And he said that cars with chauffeurs are for dead people."

There was a silence. Grandmother and Frank were in the front seat, Oliver and I in back. I wondered where the ashes were. In the trunk? Had Oliver seen them put there?

"Mommy and Daddy don't need a chauffeur because their bodies got burned up. I'm glad. Now they can go into other bodies to be born. Mom wants to be a boy and Daddy wants to be an eagle."

"When did they tell you this?" I asked.

"I don't know. Mom read her tarot cards for herself and said she couldn't see any future, which didn't surprise her, and she hoped next time she would be born as a boy. Daddy said he'd be an eagle and carry her off."

"What did she say to that?"

"I can't remember. I'm tired."

"Oh . . . you must be. You want to lie down with your head in my lap?"

"Okay." He rearranged himself and fell asleep instantly. His head was heavier than I would've imagined, and very warm. I watched him breathe, I watched his eyeball move under the lid, and I gazed into the pink recesses of his ear. My brother, one of the several million or more possible combinations of Gabe and Madelyn . . . out of so much possibility, how could I predict anything about him? His father's mother was a religious fanatic, his mother's father was fond of sports and children and war, until he got his head blown off. His parents liked to run away from home.

He might inherit all of this, or none. He might have plucked his genes from obscure ancestors who left no diaries, who died before their children knew them. The revelation of his personality would be slow indeed; I remembered how my own came as a surprise to me, year after year, until I was seventeen or eighteen.

I was passionately interested. I wanted to lift the top of his head off right now and look inside. I imagined his brain as a labyrinth imprisoning the future, which I would defeat by my novel approach from above. Yet surely my personality had come as a surprise only to me. Grandmother must have seen things I hadn't seen myself. It must all be present right from the beginning. His mouth, I noticed, was mine. It was the one I inherited from my grandfather, which my mother had handed down to us, although not allowed it herself. It was a good mouth; I was fond of it. Oliver was using it now to snore with — a high, songlike rattle.

Grandmother said, "Don't be deceived by Oliver's manner. It took me two hours to persuade him to leave the motel with me. I don't think he's sure his parents are dead. It wasn't until I showed him the picture of Maddy in my wallet that he agreed to go with me. And he insisted I leave my address with Mrs. Chisholm, just in case."

"How was he to know? You could have been any stranger come to kidnap him," said Frank sympathetically. "Had they been living there long?"

"Just six months. He's used to being alone, I think, used to moving. Maddy told Mrs. Chisholm they'd moved a dozen times in the last few years. She was working as a waitress in the restaurant and reading tarot cards for a few dollars."

"Did she say anything to Mrs. Chisholm about us?"

"No. They were both very vague about their past, I gather. Just that they'd traveled in the South, doing the same kind of work, Maddy waitressing, Gabe playing his saxophone, bartending . . . she thinks he worked as a newspaper reporter for a few years, but she doesn't know where or when. There were no clues of any kind among their things."

"Their things! Where are they?"

"I had them sent to the house. There wasn't anything but clothes, a few cups and plates, a hotplate, a frying pan, paperbacks . . . there might have been more in the car—your mother's purse—but nothing was recoverable. The car burned after they were thrown clear."

"Did you talk to anyone else there? Friends?"

"I talked to the other waitress and to the musicians Gabe was playing with. I didn't have time for more; I wanted to get Oliver back. They were all very upset. Your father was respected as a player, or so they said. He was starting to be ambitious; he wanted to make a record someday. I think Maddy was very unhappy, although that little waitress didn't come right out and say so. Apparently she had quite a stream of customers for her tarot. Her readings were always sad, the girl said. But people came anyway."

I could imagine it only too easily. Those soft, cool fingers of hers turning the cards, her lips poised to speak and then not speaking, as if the words were just lingering inside, then, when she finally did say something, her eyes wandering. With my mother you were always aware that she was thinking, and that her thought was private. This was so palpable that it was an enticement, like a woman wearing a revealing dress she has no intention of ever taking off. That her readings were sad must have immeasurably helped. My delicate mother could be trusted to see the sorrow in life; I imagined her clients walking off in an unusually sensitive mood, yet glad of their own robustness, and doubting that things were as grim as pretty Maddy-the-horn-player's-wife had said.

"What about Daddy's saxophone?"

"I have it for you."

"Oh." I had been sure she would say it was lost, or forgotten, or had been burned with the car. What would I do with it? I had no musical talent. I could hang it on the wall, like the sword of a Confederate ancestor. It would serve as a good focal point for late-night meditations on mortality. Better hurry up if you want to leave any record. Remember to keep in trim for the heavenly choir. Perhaps I would give it to Oliver. Once Gabe was on the wall, his jokes would not have to be retold. And my brother would grow up in the country, as I did, with Grandmother, whose love was so much stronger than that of our parents. He would not even imagine their return and would be happier for it. Instead he could look forward to my visits, which would, I decided, be often and long. Somehow I would work it out with George.

When we got to the house, Grandmother turned in the driveway and stopped the car, instead of going around back as she usually did. I guessed she wanted to show the place off to Frank and Oliver and I felt like a spectator myself. I hadn't been here in the summer for a few years and had forgotten the light, lacy, almost sea-green of the willows and locust. The apple and lilac had long since gone but there were white peonies and flame-colored roses by the front door. The lawn between Crandall Road and the house was wilder than ever, nearly knee high, and studded with daisies. The stone dogs that used to stand by the front door were far out in the grass and were smiling faintly, as if our appearance could only slightly delay their escape.

"Where are they going?" I asked, pointing to show what I meant.

"I don't know. We found them that way one morning. I think some boys were trying to steal them but they were too heavy."

"Or too fierce."

"Yes," she said, getting out of the car. I woke up my brother and we climbed out, Oliver drowsy at first, then excited as he looked around him.

"Do you have horses and cows here?" he asked Grandmother.

"No."

"Can we get some?"

"No."

"Can I explore by myself?"

"Yes." He ran off, the tall grass already brushing the cuffs of his suit pants with its green stain. As he reached the beginning of the apple orchard, I felt suddenly envious that he was still young enough to climb those trees. I remembered summer afternoons lying on one of the branches, blissfully aware of my smallness and agility, of potential I never wanted to touch. Grandmother took my hand and held it for a moment, her fingers so dry they were almost glassy.

"This is a beautiful place," said Frank, looking out over the woods and fields. I knew what he was thinking. This was the real thing. Country.

"July is the best time," said Grandmother. "I used to like autumn the best—when you were a child, Stella."

"I remember."

"Then early spring. I looked forward all winter to the first week in May. Now I feel happiest in summer. Even the mosquitoes don't bother me. They light on my skin, then fly away."

"They know who they're dealing with."

"You know you've lived in a place too long when the insects start respecting you," she said. She made no move to go in the house and we stood there with her, breathing in the warm July air. I could hear the drone of a lawn mower far down the hill; it was seven thirty and as bright as day.

"When was this house built?" Frank asked.

"Eighteen fifty. My great-grandfather built it when he got married. He was one of seven children and planned on having that many himself. There was a bedroom for each of them: four boys and three girls. The boys' rooms were at the top of the house, the girls' on the second floor with the parents. Only one boy was born, who kept the third floor to himself, and one girl who slept in her mother's bed after my great-grandfather fell off the roof. There haven't been any large families since."

"That's probably helped to keep the property from being divided," said Frank, with something close to possessiveness.

"I suppose so. It's sad though, isn't it?"

"Would you have had more children?" I asked.

"Oh, yes, if Bobby hadn't died in the war." I imagined her surrounded by sons, tall and strong and fiercely loyal, visiting en masse at holidays.

Grandmother walked suddenly to the front door without another word to us. It opened just as she reached it and Tobias came out. My blood slammed against my veins as I recognized him, leaving me weak. Then, as he finished greeting Grandmother and started down the steps, the weakness vanished. He was just a man I used to know. His hair had thinned, his skin had a yellowish cast to it, and he moved with a kind of slither. He was wearing black pants that stopped short of his ankles, mustard-green socks, and a brown T-shirt I remembered. He had a length of clothesline around his waist for a belt.

"Stella," he said, "it's such a pleasure to see you again."

"Hi, TB," I said, which is something I started calling him in my mind after we broke up. He had affected me like a disease then; now he looked as if he had one.

"Is it that bad?" he asked, lifting an arm and peering at it. "I have degenerated, I know. I have nightmares. Last night I dreamt that there was a horrible growth on my neck, quite painful, and when I went to the mirror, determined to rip it off, I saw that it was a tiny figure of Christ on the cross, pushing its way out through my skin. That unmistakable shape. Finally it emerged and clung there, like a kind of leech."

"Gross," I said cheerfully.

"It was frightening. What did he want with me?"

"God knows. Maybe it's time you repented your sins."

"I've been trying." He looked as if he wanted to say more, but smiled instead at Frank, who'd been watching him with fascination. "And this is your friend?"

"Yep. Frank, Tobias; Tobias, Frank."

"This is interesting," said Frank, shaking his hand. "I've heard so much about you."

Tobias smirked. "I'm glad."

"I wouldn't have recognized you from Stella's description, though." They both laughed uproariously and I felt a little put out. I couldn't help it if he used to be gorgeous. Then Tobias composed himself.

"I'd like to offer you my condolences, Stella, on the death of your parents."

"Thanks."

"I hope you don't mind my being here?" he continued, while giving Frank conspiratorial sidelong glances.

"It's not my house. No, shit, I don't mind. It's nice to see you. I guess you must have been some help to Grandmother." He was surely not as strange as he looked to me, I thought; the void in my feelings where love had been must be distorting my perception. I had an image of him creeping off into the weeds, a few years from now, his skeleton folding up like a collapsible chair.

"She's quite remarkable. I'm writing a long poem about the creation of the Universe and she's given me a lot of ideas."

"Yes. Have you met her boyfriend?"

"Corky? That's what I call him. A real gentleman. Carries a walking stick, you know. Says 'ahem' a lot."

"Where did she meet him?" asked Frank.

"Oh, he's an old classmate of her husband's. She saw an announcement of his wife's death in the paper and went to the funeral."

"She never used to like men," I said. "It's strange."

"She was married," said Frank.

"Yeah, but I always assumed it was social pressure or something. Why didn't she remarry, or at least date when she was younger? She couldn't really like men, or she would have."

"It's an acquired taste," said Tobias. I gave him a look. "Perhaps she just likes old men," he said brightly. "When they're harmless. Toothless tigers, just wanting their port and cigars, please. Ready to pop off into the grave at any moment," he said mournfully.

"Arnold Popper," I said.

"What?"

"Arnold Popper. I told you about him, the first day we met, and you asked me how he popped off."

"I don't remember. Who was he?"

"Oh, just a guy who was buried in the cemetery."

"I do remember the cemetery, and seeing you sitting there with a book, the picture of depraved innocence."

"I envy you," said Frank.

"Oh, she was lovely."

"You never told me so."

"I was afraid to. You were so intense." Frank put his arm around me and gave me a hug. Tobias looked at us, then stepped back, smiling. He was still beautiful, if you can imagine a laughable beauty. One that would excite derision on the streets, and giggling in the bedroom—a prelude not without its erotic effect.

Oliver appeared from around the other side of the house. From a distance he looked so much like my father—the shape of his head, the way he walked with careful, humorous attention to the bushes, the grass, the clouds—but my father never had such a shining glance as the one Oliver bestowed on Tobias as I introduced them. It was the look of an elf prince deciding whether this dragon should be slain or stupefied.

"I live here with your grandmother," Tobias said to him.

"Are you her boyfriend?"

"No."

"Are you the butler?"

"Do I look like a butler to you?"

"Yes. You look like a crazy butler."

"I'm a poet."

"I know. She told me. But you could be a butler, too. There ought to be one here," he added thoughtfully.

"I agree," I said. "Surely, TB, you can show the young master to his room?" Oliver laughed in delight at being called 'young master' and again he looked like my father, my father seized by spirits and played with until he went silly, then led back home again by a good fairy who smoothed away the worst of it and granted him youth to forget, but couldn't do anything about those eyes . . .

"Which room?" asked Tobias.

"I don't know; ask Grandmother."

"My grandmother," said Oliver. "Here," he said to me, producing a yellow rosebud out of his pocket. He gave it to me casually, our fingers touching, and I felt absurdly moved by the sweetness in him. I sniffed the rosebud and put it in my buttonhole, and he smiled at me, then put his hands in his pockets, where I could see he had other things hidden. More flowers? Stones? Berries? Dead frogs? Birds' eggs? He had barely had time to traverse the yard, much less the woods, much less explore, yet I felt he had seen the important things, he had scouted the land and found it good. He wouldn't sneak out of the house at night and hitchhike to the Hello Motel.

Frank and I watched them go inside; then I showed him the property. "This was my favorite apple tree, the one I would lie on all the time. I wanted to build a treehouse but Grandmother said the wood wasn't strong enough, I should use the oak tree. But I didn't like the oak tree. Here's the garden. It looks very subtle after Berkeley gardens, doesn't it?"

"Oh, God, yes," he said. "It's got so much more dignity." He spoke with such force I felt a twinge of pity for my blowsy Berkeley garden. The lemon tree. The little black girls. "Everything's more beautiful here. You can see the age of the place—like those woods, been here for hundreds of years."

"Actually not. Those woods are young—see how thin the trees are? Like so many woods in New England, they were pasture lands a century ago."

"I guess I don't know much about it. But there is a feeling here . . ."

He was looking around him in what appeared to me a trance of aesthetic bliss, and I led him gently inside. His enthusiasm touched me and made me feel grateful; Grandmother had, after all, given me so much.

Tobias and Oliver were in the kitchen making dinner, Oliver peeling potatoes, Tobias tearing up lettuce leaves for a salad. I turned my eyes away from the bottled dressing on the counter. They were drinking Coke out of Grandmother's sherry glasses as they worked. Frank admired the old oak table with its many drawers and hooks for hanging utensils and the big country sink, standing by itself in the corner. I showed him the cabinet where Agnes's medicines were kept:

oil of roses for headache, peony seeds for nightmares, wormwood wine for diarrhea. "There used to be so much more," I said. "Tea, ointments, syrups, and jellies."

"You must have looked forward to being sick."

"Not really. Agnes would monitor me so closely it was tiresome. She wasn't sure of all her remedies, you see. She suspected *Culpepper's Herbal*—circa 1650—might be the least bit out-of-date. She would read parts of it aloud scornfully—I remember one bit about how smelling basil causes scorpions to breed in the brain—and then comment that what could you expect, it was written by a man, they'll believe anything."

"She was experimenting on you, was she?" asked Tobias.

"I guess so."

"How come you don't use any of her remedies now?" asked Frank.

"I don't know. I suppose I never thought they'd work in California."

"You'll have to tell me all about California," said Tobias.

"You ought to go see it for yourself."

"No, I'd rather imagine it. I don't think I'll ever leave here."

"This house?"

"Yes. It has a wonderfully peculiar sort of atmosphere, don't you think?"

"Yes."

"I feel related to you now, Stella. I'd like to be your uncle, if I may."

"Indulging in a little retrospective perversion, Tobias?" I wasn't sure how to take his news. I was resentful, of course, but also glad that he saw the magic of the house. I'd always been afraid, when I loved him, that he wouldn't. That was the main reason I had never brought him home.

"There was always that, wasn't there? Your youth."

"Your corruption."

"Perhaps Oliver would allow me to be his uncle then." He addressed Oliver. "Your sister doesn't trust me, but I assure you I am harmless."

"I know," said Oliver matter-of-factly. "But do you have any money?" Frank laughed out loud and I smirked. Tobias looked only slightly discomposed.

"Some. Having money is not important in an uncle, Oliver. It's the willingness to spend it that counts. What monies you want almost any adult could supply. But they won't, you know. They're naturally stingy where children are concerned. They resent their pleasure."

"While you," I said, "have found a way to feed on it."

"Taking pleasure in the pleasure of others, Stella, is a virtue."

"A dubious one, in your case." Frank was watching us with folded arms, smiling, and Oliver was still methodically peeling.

"You can be my uncle for a dollar a week," he said when he had finished with the last potato.

"Done," said Tobias.

"I intend to charge a bit more," I said.

"Well, I don't know if I need you, now that I'm related to Oliver."

"Oh, yes, you do."

"Let me know your price then."

"I'll think about it."

I showed Frank the rest of the house. He saw reflections of me everywhere: in the living room where I had entertained the women after Agnes's death, in the dining room, on the third floor where my ancestors lived in their various solitudes. It was flattering, but I thought he was missing something. This house wasn't so much me as it was my grandmother, her long life lived between its walls. Here was her childhood, her marriage, motherhood, many deaths, and ordinary days. Here she worked in the kitchen, read through the long winter; from here she imagined distant galaxies.

We ended up in my bedroom. There was not much to see, since most of my stuff was in California. We looked out at the view—green fields, woods, stone walls, and a gray cat sniffing peonies—then lay down and kissed until Oliver came to collect us for dinner.

Dinner was not too bad. Tobias had cooked a roast beef and Grandmother opened a bottle of burgundy. She questioned Frank about his family and he told the truth, that he disliked his father and never went home. This seemed to please her. She really didn't think any family but ours merited loyalty. Tobias quizzed Oliver on the books he had read and Oliver told him a few—*The Wizard of Oz*, the *I Ching*—then started making up titles. I remember *Dead Dog Days* and *Car Wars*.

Afterward Frank, Tobias, and I put Oliver to bed. He was sleeping in Agnes's room. He undressed in front of us, not in the least embarrassed, put on his blue pajamas, and crawled under the covers, pulling them up to his chin. The room still smelled of sweet herbs from the sachets Agnes had made and left everywhere. I had found one under the pillow when I first came in; it was in the shape of a heart, bleeding crimson drops of blood. I slipped it in the bedside drawer before Oliver could see.

Frank and I sat down on either side of the bed, and Tobias hovered in the background, like the fawning priest of a medieval household.

"Sing me a song," said Oliver.

"I'll try." I sang "Summertime," which was the only thing I knew that remotely resembled a lullaby. He listened attentively, his gray, shining eyes fixed on mine. By the time I had finished tears were running down his cheeks, which Frank wiped away. Oliver closed his eyes.

"I want to be alone now," he said in a distant voice.

"Are you sure, kid?" asked Frank. He sounded so fatherly it startled me.

"I want to think about my mommy and daddy." Frank got up and switched off the bedside lamp. I couldn't move. I wanted to think about my mommy and daddy too; I wanted to stay with him. He was so close to them, it was almost as if they were in the room, whispering in his ears.

Frank put his hands on my shoulders and slowly I got up. "Goodnight, Oliver," I said. He replied in a voice even more faraway. We left the room. Tobias climbed the stairs to his own bedroom—to pray, he said—while Frank and I went back down to join Grandmother.

She was just finishing the dishes as we came in. "You should have left them," I said as she hung up the dish towels to dry.

"I'm perfectly capable of washing dishes. Is Oliver asleep?"

"No. He's thinking about them. He wanted to be alone."

"Yes, I'm not surprised. How Madelyn ever managed to have such self-reliant children, I'll never know."

"You think I'm self-reliant?"

"Aren't you?"

"I don't know." I smiled at Frank. "I don't think so."

"So you two are quite sure about each other?"

"Yes," I said.

She looked at Frank. "Oh, yes," he said, "I love her very much."

"I'm glad you do. She is precious to me." She put a hand on each of our shoulders. She looked like an old, grand actress, her ranginess softened by the black silk, her hair waving profusely around her face. "I'd like to talk to you both, then."

"Yes, you said so before. Of course, Grandmother." I was surprised by this leading up. She never did it.

She sat down at the kitchen table and we sat flanking her. I'm not sure what I expected; some fact about my parents, I suppose. "Stella, you know I planned this trip around the world."

"Yes."

"Well, I intend to go. I've been here too many years. I'm attached to this place — it's more real than other places — but it occurs to me that I have not seen so many other places. I have certainly not seen India or Tibet or China. Perhaps it's just the restlessness of old age, but I want to wander." I knew what this meant, of course, and it terrified me. "What I'm asking you," she continued, "is to rear Oliver. You're not that young anymore, you can do it. It will be good for him, better than being brought up by an old lady."

"You're not an old lady." How could I possibly be better for him than she was? "Of course, Grandmother, I'll do it — but I don't know how."

She laughed. "Have you forgotten everything about your own childhood?"

"Of course not."

"Then that's how to do it — unless you decide to do it differently."

"I'll help you, Stella," said Frank. "You'll make a wonderful mother."

"Sister," I corrected. "When are you going?" I asked Grandmother.

"In a week. I'll leave you some money for Oliver."

"No, thanks. I can get a job."

"I thought you already had a job?"

"I'm staying here," I said. "Oliver is going to grow up here. You can go wherever you want, and come back whenever you want, but we'll be here." I hadn't thought about this until I spoke, but I knew at once it was right. In Berkeley I couldn't raise a child, I would resent him, everything would be wrong. Here, as Grandmother had said, I would remember what to do. She looked wonderfully pleased.

"Is that all right with you?" she asked Frank. "What about your work?"

"It's fine with me. I can work anywhere." He gripped my hands across the table.

Grandmother smiled and said, "Would you like to see my itinerary? I'm going to begin in Paris. I look forward to the paintings. I've always been so fond of Gauguin."

We followed her into the library and sat up late that night, leafing through the atlas and drinking brandy. My terror remained but became increasingly thrilling. What the hell, I thought drunkenly, I could always run away.

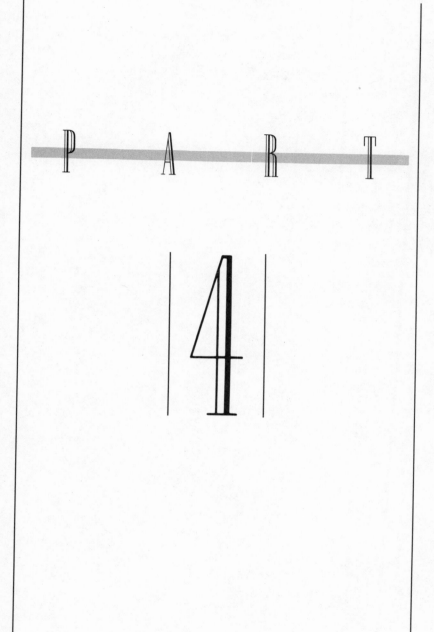

PART

4

We've been living here a year now, the four of us; it's summer again. I cook lunch in a restaurant in Boston, a place with none of the charm of The Vineyard but where I make wonderful food quietly and am well paid. Frank and Tobias stay home, taking care of Oliver. Tobias is working on his Creation poem and making forays into religion, while Frank takes endless pictures. He's set up a darkroom on the third floor in one of the old boy's rooms and it's weird to look up at it from the outside and see the windows blacked out. Grandmother writes us long letters, full of descriptions of beautiful scenery and horrible social practices, but makes no mention of coming home. Her gentleman friend has been back six months and every so often calls plaintively from Cambridge to ask when she'll return. I assure him that he'll know as soon as I do.

I get up early in the morning, when Frank is still asleep. At first he tried to get up with me, but when he realized I simply got up even earlier, he desisted. I like to see him lying on his back, the sheet neatly tucked under his arms, his face mobile with dreams, as I get dressed. I never thought, when I lived here before, I'd have a lover in this bed; lovers were for the outside world. What a luxury it is.

I walk downstairs and through the house while the dawn light falls forgivingly on the worn carpets, joyously on the old, mellow wood. The solid boards under my feet reassure me; when Grandmother left,

I was afraid everything would deteriorate, but I take care of things and they take care in return.

In the kitchen I make tea. (I drink out of a mug Oliver gave me for my birthday; it has a ceramic frog glued to the bottom. I think of him every time the head of the frog rising from my tea startles me—which is more often than you'd think, considering that I use this mug every morning.) I take a lot of honey in my tea, and the hot sweetness tunes me to the pitch of the summer morning, with its flowers opening and spiders climbing, birdsong, and tiny, transparent wings crowding the air. My mood lifts and sparkles. I talk to the flies buzzing in through the open door. We have to get the screen fixed, I tell them. Frank will do it. Oliver will watch him, I will thank him, and Tobias will probably break it again, throwing a baseball with admirable strength and pathetic aim. Everything that leaves his hands, leaves it crooked. The flies buzz in reply, they land on my honey-covered spoon. Sometimes I feel such sadness that I don't still love Tobias; the more peculiar he becomes, the more I wonder what it would have been like to continue it. Of course he doesn't desire women anymore; he won't tell me when that changed, he just smiles mysteriously.

I take my second cup of tea out to the porch and sit with my feet dangling in the grass. It's already so warm. The lacy look of the fields in summer reminds me of my mother's Mexican skirts, the ones she used to twirl when she danced. She never had one this shade of green though; it wouldn't have suited her. It suits me, I think. Perhaps I'll make a dress of leaves and woven wildflowers—something to amaze Frank, who already thinks of me as a force of nature, who's becoming increasingly enchanted here.

After a while, Oliver joins me. Though he has just awoken, his eyes are bright with attention. He's ready to go swimming. I put down my cup and we walk the few steps to the river.

Oliver slaps his feet on the stone steps and slides in, his shorts left on the bank. He looks up at me a minute, then disappears. What he likes is to sink, to feel the water close over his head, and his body tumble down, then to save himself with a great leap when it gets painful. I watch where he went under the smooth, placid river, and wonder if he will really come up again. I've told him that when I was a child I believed there was a serpent in the river covered with green-and-gold scales who could carry me off through miles of underground streams to a cave where I would be either eaten or adored, I wasn't sure which. He replied that there isn't a serpent, he would know if there was, but there are other things. What things? Things.

He doesn't come up for a long time and I think about saving him from drowning. I would like to. Then he shoots up out of the water, hair streaming behind, and our eyes meet. He laughs and falls back, floating idly downstream. I undress and follow him in. The water envelopes me. I go under and my hair swirls around me in greenish tendrils, I feel the serpent's tail languidly stroke me as I go by. Oliver is far ahead, his shoulders wriggling, arms still, feet kicking at odd moments. I taught him how to swim but he prefers to do it his way, to invent a means to stay up and move forward without resorting to the dull rhythm of breaststroke or crawl. Sometimes his legs climb the sky while his head sinks down and I wonder if those thrusting toes have learned how to suck the air up. Then they waver and are still; he's posing on his hands; he lurches forward through the muck, feet waving hello.

We never go very far. Neither Oliver nor I like to leave our part of the river, and he even objects when people paddle by in canoes. But this doesn't happen at six thirty in the morning. We're alone and we swim around and around, our naked bodies brushing against the reeds and the roots. He asks me questions. Why did our parents leave me behind? Did I prefer our grandmother? I tell him the truth as far as I know it; but the truth has changed since I met him, since I learned something about our parents' life. I can't think of them as romantic adventurers anymore, yet I can't not think of them that way either. I simply describe what I remember, I repeat the conversation in the garden that day in June. It occurs to me that this is history, now that I'm telling it to someone to whom it matters for its own sake, and that frightens me a little. Perhaps I only imagined it. But I don't think so; and Oliver doesn't think so.

He feels sorry for me. He explains that our mother often left things behind and would miss them terribly, but never agreed to go back. There was always something—a motel clerk who didn't like her, an ugly dog, cockroaches—that she couldn't face, and she'd just live without it. He tells me he would've liked having me along but he doesn't say he was lonely, he never says anything like that. He asks for more stories of my childhood, of Grandmother and Agnes. I tell him everything I can remember. He wants to be sure that I really lived here—for years; that I am really his sister; that we own this land and this house and this part of the river; that when my grandmother comes back she will not send us away.

I confide in him my suspicion that she will never come back, although her letters are full of disapproval of foreign life. I say perhaps I am destined to be abandoned by my family, as one by one they succumb to a wanderlust stronger than my own. Oliver likes the word *wanderlust*; he asks if it can mean what you feel about your own property if you like to wander around it. His feet are tracing circles in the grass, clean, brown feet that would fit snugly into my hands. Yes, I say, why not? First you walk one way, then another. By the time I grow up, he says, I'll walk every way around there is. You can't miss even one, I say. Not even one, he agrees. I imagine him out in the fields at night, walking; spending whole afternoons in the woods treading each fallen leaf; creeping so close to the house he can't be seen from the windows. Such devotion doesn't seem strange to me; it's what I did all those years.

By the time we get back to the house, Frank's up. I make breakfast, pancakes with fruit and yogurt, or an omelet, and Frank drinks his necessary three cups of black coffee. Oliver drinks peppermint tea. They talk, getting louder as the meal progresses, and I barely listen; at that time of day I think about work, what to cook for all the hungry city mouths. It surprises me sometimes that it's so different from cooking at home. At home I make mistakes.

Frank likes to tell tall tales at breakfast. Oliver doesn't know quite whether to believe that Frank once had an apartment in New York where everything was made out of gold; he doubts it, but in support of the story are the checks that come, every month or so, when obviously Frank does nothing to earn them. But doubt or not, he listens eagerly, waiting for the good parts: how the gold toilet was sold to an Arab, who wore it on his head, how during the famous blackout of '65, Frank and Marva were carried away by bandits into the subway tunnels, where they lived for months, holding up trains with pistols and making their fortune.

I leave them to their laughter and the dishes, and go to work. There's always a fear when I leave that something will prevent me from coming back: that I will return and find the house abandoned. Yet I enjoy my days in Boston, I wouldn't want to stay home.

I make artful salads and arrange them on the plates like paintings, as my boss has instructed me. He wants the first course to look like a flowering almond tree. I'm disappointed; I'd hoped he had a real painting in mind—*The Garden of Earthly Delights* perhaps—that would have been a challenge. White mushroom slices make the blossoms, the parslied dressing the leaves, I make red birds out of peppers, and it occurs to me as the waiter takes the plate away how the customers must love this: proof of the cook's devotion to each individual serving, proof of the cook's service.

I usually get home about six or seven. Once I turn off the highway the interest of the day fades to mere experience. Now I begin to live, the evening is the best time. There is a stretch of empty meadow climbing the hill to our house. I drive Agnes's twelve-year-old Cadillac and the low-slung beast glides silkily up as the sounds of the neighborhood disappear. I admire our white fence, which Frank and Oliver have recently painted, and the new plantings by the garage: marigolds and sunflowers.

I park the car, take off my shoes, and walk around the house. Frank is sitting on the grass with a pitcher of lemonade, somewhat warm, which I drink thirstily. Oliver is down by the river, launching a homemade boat. Frank takes my feet in his lap. It's so hot I feel sleepy. The sun has slackened since noon but only so much that it seems to have found its stride, a pace it could keep up forever.

Oliver flings himself at our feet. He wants to know if I have brought him anything from Boston. I tell him there's a wedge of strawberry shortcake in the car and he's content; as long as there's something, he doesn't care what it is. I ask him what he learned today, and he replies at length, showing off. Oliver can add, subtract, multiply, divide, and do fractions. Tobias constructs elaborate word problems for him, prose poems really, which Oliver often repeats to me. I refuse to compete; I concentrate on the details. "So the blue monkey mask came to life, did she? Clara must be thinking of us."

After the mathematics lesson, Tobias and Oliver read a few chapters of *The Jungle Book,* and Oliver wrote a synopsis of what didn't happen and a poem to Shere Khan, whom he feels sorry for. Then Tobias went to take a nap, or whatever he does to replenish himself, and Frank and Oliver had lunch and went for their daily walk. This is the high point of the day — of Frank's day, at any rate; they set out as if on a journey, with Oliver's hand in Frank's. I used to watch them, last summer before I got my job, and was certain that Frank's attentiveness to Oliver and to the countryside would wane, that it was, in part, a seduction meant for me. But it was not. At times I'm jealous.

They are learning to identify the trees and plants they come across, and they bring home whatever flowers, leaves, stones, or toads catch their fancy. They also climb trees, ford the river, hack their way through brambles, and of course take pictures. They come home with studies of lichen that remind me of the surface of a soup as it starts to boil. Frank shows me what he calls "portraits of neighborhoods" — places in the forest where the trees grow tall, where the rocks are smooth and the air crisp, places where the air is rotten and the trees pale and stunted, where the round-limbed birches breathe a female serenity into the air. He is eager to see if I will recognize these places, so eager it makes me laugh. Yes, I recognize it, I say, but that branch was not always fallen, nor the wasps always nesting there. Frank talks with such enthusiasm about the value of walking in, observing, and remembering the woods, and I agree with everything he says; and I know that Oliver goes back there some nights to fulfill his task of wandering our property alone.

Tobias and Frank are very serious about Oliver's education. Tobias has devised a reading list that includes practically every book ever written for or about children, such as *My Childhood* by Gorky, in which all the women and children are beaten by the men, some of them to death. It's a story of survival, he says, and of course he's right; yet I crossed it off the list for this year.

Frank teaches Oliver history. He does it anecdotally with tales of bizarre characters, strange practices, and sudden change. Oliver likes to learn about when things were invented and why, and what people used before; he's also fascinated by kings and slaves, harems, human sacrifice, and outlaws. As yet he has little sense of the chronology of events and only a vague one of geography. That will come later, Frank assures me, but right now it disorients me to hear them talk of gladiators and pioneers and Queen Guinevere as if they were all still living somewhere nearby, in the forest perhaps. Tobias has suggested that we never teach Oliver chronology, that he is closer to reality as he is, and that I would understand this if I stayed home and listened.

But I don't think we'll have much choice. There's the question of the school board and whether they'll allow our private education. Tobias has written a proposal, which they are considering, to exempt Oliver from school next year; last year we simply lied and said he wasn't six yet. I doubt we'll be approved. There's a thing called socialization — what Tobias calls the great choice of whether to bully or be bullied — that we're likely to be found deficient in. I don't think it will hurt Oliver to go to school. He's bound to get sick of us sooner or later.

Tobias and Frank, of course, feel differently. They have so many ideas, they outdo each other. Tobias read me a chapter of Ouspensky on the fourth dimension and asked me how old I thought Oliver would have to be to understand it. Since I couldn't understand it myself, I said I had no idea. Probably thirteen, Tobias mused, in six years.

They both like to sit at the kitchen table with him and paint; he explains patiently that he doesn't know how to draw properly, his cows are always malformed, but he will learn. They talk about defying the school board, or of starting a school here, but neither is practicable. More likely Oliver will simply have to go to school twice, and to make him endure that, they will need all the fascination at their command — a considerable amount.

When Oliver has done telling what he has learned, it is time for dinner. On these hot nights we eat in the living room, which is the coolest room in the house. Our meal is simple: fresh bread, which Frank and Oliver make, cheese and salad. Oliver likes to toss the salad, and his hands among the vegetables are as quick and deft as if he were making pastry.

Tobias comes to the table in his monk's robes, signaling his entrance into his religious phase. The robes, which he stole a long time ago, are too big for him and he's dyed them purple. I pointed out to him that the color of royalty is hardly suitable for a lowly petitioner of God and he replied that the original earth tone dulled his spirit—his spirit, which he insists is Neptunian: poet and magus. He hasn't given up his old occult beliefs but merely added Christianity, which appeals to him primarily because of the possibility of mental sin. It's so much easier and more convenient to commit, and it provides him material for the abasement and repentance that is his way of exposing himself to the supernatural. Looking at him in his purple hood, his face shadowed, waxy, triangular, a sick gold in color, his eyes swimming in a perpetual film of tears that occasionally leak out and slide down his cheeks, I think that if there were a God, and he wanted Tobias, he could have him. This fickleness and drama would be wiped out if the deity announced himself. But so far he hasn't—and Tobias is left to toy with his ideas, taking them apart and recombining them like the broken corpses of virgins.

This religious fit only comes on him once in a while, about once a month, and when it's over, the tears dried and the robes in the laundry bleeding purple over everything, he holes up in his room for a week or more, working ferociously on his poem. Then he's the Tobias of old, with no time for us unless we're willing to listen to a dozen lines read over and over.

The poem is wonderful, I think, although he hasn't read me the beginning and it has no end. There is nothing in it but stars, light, planets, space, and fire, but it is full of emotion and provokes the most profound sense of time, of time everlasting, of eternity alive. When I listen to it, I begin to understand the raptures of the mystics, and I wonder why Tobias, when he can write like this, wants more. He says he is not content with beauty, he needs to find something personal in the universe. Just one shred of personality would be enough, one irreducible atom of selfishness.

I don't understand, really. People are here, billions of them, all the personality anyone could want. Does it matter where we come from or why? No destruction will erase our having lived on the Earth.

Frank is more sympathetic. He is even less religious than I am, but probably for that reason views religion uncritically, and seems concerned that Tobias find just the right one. He talks about the need to create new gods to deal with the peculiarities of the twentieth-century Western psyche and gets excited at the possibilities; I tell him to watch it, only the faithful are allowed to find God—the rest find bullshit.

He agrees—and continues to observe Tobias, paying much more attention to him than I do. Frank was the first to notice that Tobias was in love with Oliver. Of course once he mentioned it, it seemed obvious. Tobias's eyes are always on my brother, and when he reads to him his voice is like that of a great orator, strolling with ease through a thousand shades of emotion.

It is my revenge, certainly, for Oliver will never return this love, and Tobias will never touch him uninvited. I don't think he lusts after him anyway. He loves him romantically, though his store of romance is so dry. It makes him nervous. His hands hover a lot when Oliver is in the room, the fingers curling into claws, but claws held tenderly, poignantly.

Tobias borrows, every week, a dollar from Frank to give to Oliver as an allowance. He has no money of his own. The ceremony of handing over the dollar is always drawn out; he looks through all his pockets while my brother waits; he unfolds the bill, inspects it, then lets it go, watching as Oliver puts it away in his own pocket. This is the money for which Oliver calls Tobias Uncle, although I don't think Tobias likes being called Uncle anymore.

Oliver knows he has power, though he doesn't understand what it is based on. It exhilarates him. Often he ignores Tobias, not answering when he is spoken to. Then Tobias withdraws, shaping his love into an ever-subtler design. Soon he will be a genuine Master Teacher, devoting himself, his life, to the pupil who will surpass him—but I imagine things. Tobias is a poet, a very fine one, and what Oliver is I can only guess.

Tobias does not have it too bad. He has a lover, a nineteen-year-old youth who visits him at night. Tony is big and black-haired with a strong, open face and blue eyes that refuse to look at me. He is shy, I suppose, or jealous. There would be no reason for Tobias to have told him of our affair, which doesn't mean he didn't do so.

I told Tobias his lover couldn't come through the house anymore because to get to Tobias's room on the third floor he had to pass Oliver's and Oliver always sleeps with his door open. What would he think, I said, waking in the middle of the night, seeing this big stranger plodding by, and gone by morning? He wouldn't think anything, of course, as Tobias well knows. But this is my equivalent of Oliver's dollar a week, and Tobias did not protest.

I suggested a ladder to his window. How could he resist it? To lie in bed at night waiting for the dark head to appear above the windowsill, for the awkward clambering of pale limbs inside. I picture Tobias in his old green dressing gown, which is unfastened and lies at his side like two leaves, his slender body lit only by the moon, listening to what is coming in from outside. Tony, his unnatural love—yet more natural to him than I was. The duplicate of his own flesh, of his own desires; I wish I knew how that attraction worked, I feel like I should know . . . but of course Tony is not a duplicate at all; there is no duplicate of Tobias, nor of me.

So the ladder is up and leans against the house day and night. Oliver loves it. He climbs up and down with spurious messages and genuine gifts—birds' nests, stones, cookies—which Tobias accepts. I've seen Oliver up there fifteen times in one afternoon, amazed and excited by the reception awarded his offerings. "Here," said Frank, "give him this," and handed Oliver a Jehovah's Witness pamphlet with the good parts marked in purple. It was accepted. "Try this," I said, and handed him, in succession, an empty beer can, a pair of broken sunglasses, and a plastic cup full of deer turds. When Oliver finally went off on his bicycle, these items came down on our heads.

After dinner, we go back outside. The sun is setting behind the hills across the street. In the woods we see slivers of rosy light, and the grass we sit on has its own light, green blades of it hidden inside vegetable envelopes. Frank puts his arm around me, Tobias sits a little way off, and Oliver lies down in front of us. This is our cinema, which we attend with naïve expectations, and which does not disappoint us. Frank has explained to Oliver that the sun sets a little to the south every day and we check to make sure this rule still holds good. I want to know why the colors differ from evening to evening. Frank says atmospheric conditions; Tobias says angelic whim; Oliver gives me a deep smile and says nothing. He will find out.

Tobias begins to recite Shakespeare, "Shall I compare thee to a summer's day? / Thou art more lovely and more temperate / Rough winds do shake the darling buds of May / And summer's lease hath all too short a date . . ." Oliver asks what *temperate* means. Tobias, explaining, doesn't content himself with Shakespeare's meanings but ranges far afield — temperance societies, Temperance in the tarot, and so on. Oliver listens although he's also chewing on a stalk of grass, and scratching a mosquito bite, and keeping an eye on the sunset. Tobias's conversation is a kind of river for him, in which he fishes for sport. He pays more attention to Frank and me.

We are his parents, as far as that is possible; Frank is also the outsider, and I that mysterious thing, a sister. But it is as parents that we spend most evenings. As we watch him do somersaults and stand on his head, we marvel at the smooth, brown limbs, the hollow at the small of his back, the soft down on the nape of his neck. All this is bigger than it was last year. His feet change size every few months. We feel faint with new emotion, and wonder how people stand it, who actually bear a child. This humanity in our veins is like the blood of a stronger tribe, introduced without warning.

Then the sunset is over and Frank takes Oliver up for his bath. I do the dishes, listening to the laughter from upstairs. Tobias joins me. He sits at the table, tilts his golden head, and asks me who I'm seeing in Boston. I invent experiences that he knows are invented, yet as I supply the asked-for details, they become real to us both, and we share an erotic moment. Alphonse the hairy-chested waiter, Raoul the lawyer with underworld connections. "His skin is dark and his eyes are blue."

"And his hair?"

"His hair is black and he sweeps it off his face with an imperious gesture."

"Imperious?"

"Violently imperious."

Tobias leans forward and strokes my knee. "If only you were a man."

"If only you were," I reply, and head upstairs. He follows.

Oliver lies, damp and pink, well tucked in, his curly hair spread out on the pillow. Frank is wet all down his front and he has a towel folded over his arm. Tobias pats Oliver goodnight and Oliver smiles sleepily. I lay my cheek against his rounded one and kiss his brow. "Goodnight, sweetie." Only at night am I allowed to call him that.

Frank kisses him firmly on the mouth and says, "Sleep well," in a voice no one could disobey. He is the last one out and he turns off the light and props the door ajar. Tobias bids us good-night. I watch his ass as he walks upstairs, twitching mournfully. "Tony'll come," Frank says, reading my thought.

"He doesn't love Tony." I turn and kiss him fiercely, then break away and go into the bathroom. Frank goes back downstairs to check the doors and the lights.

Clean and naked I pad through the dark corridor, through our room, and into bed. The sky is a bright, royal blue, untouched yet by stars. We go to bed early here, before we're too tired to enjoy it. As Frank climbs the stairs, all the familiar boards creak. He opens the bedroom door and the hall light crowds in. He shuts it and I hear the chink of his belt and his money. Then silence as he finishes undressing, though I strain to hear the cloth fall. His body looms beside me and I open the sheets. A sudden wind rattles leaves against my window to cover the sound of our escaping breath as we cling and join, holding on as if we'll never again divide.